Cat in a Neon Nightmare

A MIDNIGHT LOUIE MYSTERY

Carole Nelson Douglas

A TOM DOHERTY ASSOCIATES BOOK
NEW YORK

CAT IN A NEON NIGHTMARE

Edited by Claire Eddy

A Forge Book
Published by Tom Doherty Associates, LLC
175 Fifth Avenue
New York, NY 10010

www.tor.com

ISBN 0-765-34592-7
EAN 978-0765-34592-9

First edition: May 2003
First mass market edition: August 2004

Printed in the United States of America

0 9 8 7 6 5 4 3 2 1

PRAISE FOR CAROLE NELSON DOUGLAS

"Midnight Louie defies critical comment. To some cat fanciers, he is as tasty as a fresh bowl of Fancy Feast." —*Booklist*

"Move over, Miss Marple, Midnight Louie's back in town." —CATS Magazine

"You never know what madness and mayhem you'll find in Douglas's mysteries, but you can be sure it will be wild, witty and utterly irresistible." —*The San Francisco Chronicle*

Cat in a Midnight Choir
"For the right sort of cat fancier, the idea of a hard-boiled feline remains enticing." —*Booklist*

"The inimitable Carole Nelson Douglas strikes again! A strong, fun story made even more appealing by Midnight Louie and company. For people just starting this series, Ms. Douglas also does a fine job of explaining the connections between all the characters." —*Romantic Times* (4½ stars)

Cat in a Leopard Spot
"Fans of debonair anthropomorphic feline Midnight Louie will be delighted." —*Publishers Weekly*

Cat in a Kiwi Con
"A keen observer of human foibles, Ms. Douglas deftly fans the flames of our curiosity in this elegantly choreographed tale in which nothing is as it appears and mystery is the name of her most excellent game." —*Romantic Times* (4½ stars)

Cat in a Jeweled Jumpsuit
"Cat-crazy readers with a thing for both Elvis and Vegas will enjoy Douglas's blend of goofball coziness and Midnight Louie's mock noir slinkings and sleuthings." —*Dallas Morning News*

"[Douglas] introduces a thoroughly fictional Elvis Presley and inhabits him with enough real emotion to make you wish you had known the original." —*Tampa Tribune-Times*

Cat in an Indigo Mood
"Feline PI Midnight Louie prowls the alleys of Las Vegas, solving crimes and romancing runaways like a furry Sam Spade. This time out, his quick-thinking daughter, Midnight Louise, lends a paw as the always engaging Louie stalks a serial killer." —*People*

By Carole Nelson Douglas from Tom Doherty Associates

MYSTERY

MIDNIGHT LOUIE MYSTERIES:

Catnap
Pussyfoot
Cat on a Blue Monday
Cat in a Crimson Haze
Cat in a Diamond Dazzle
Cat with an Emerald Eye
Cat in a Flamingo Fedora
Cat in a Golden Garland
Cat on a Hyacinth Hunt
Cat in an Indigo Mood
Cat in a Jeweled Jumpsuit
Cat in a Kiwi Con
Cat in a Leopard Spot
Cat in a Midnight Choir
Cat in a Neon Nightmare
Cat in an Orange Twist
Midnight Louie's Pet Detectives (editor of anthology)

IRENE ADLER ADVENTURES:

Good Night, Mr. Holmes
The Adventuress (*Good Morning, Irene*)†
A Soul of Steel (*Irene at Large*)†
Another Scandal in Bohemia (*Irene's Last Waltz*)†
Chapel Noir
Castle Rouge

Marilyn: Shades of Blonde (editor of anthology)

HISTORICAL ROMANCE

*Amberleigh** *Lady Rogue**
Fair Wind, Fiery Star

SCIENCE FICTION

*Probe** *Counterprobe**

FANTASY

TALISWOMAN:

Cup of Clay *Seed upon the Wind*

SWORD AND CIRCLET:

Six of Swords *Heir of Rengarth*
Exiles of the Rynth *Seven of Swords*
Keepers of Edanvant

*also mystery
†reissue

For Panache and Longfellow, our first alley boys,
and for the original and real Midnight Louie,
stray cat extraordinaire,
nine lives were not enough

Contents

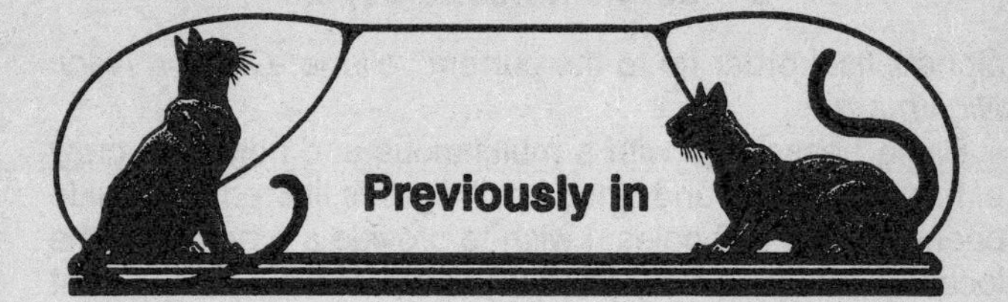

Midnight Louie's Lives and Times . . .

Heavens to Mehitabel, folks! After the turn of events last time out, so many of my human associates have their fat in the fire that I am not sure even an ace feline PI is chef enough to extract all their skins from the conflagration in one piece.

As a serial killer–finder in a multivolume mystery series (not to mention a primo mouthpiece), it behooves me to update my readers old and new on past crimes and present tensions.

None can deny that the Las Vegas crime scene is a pretty busy place, and I have been treading these mean neon streets for fifteen books now. When I call myself an "alpha-cat," some think I am merely asserting my natural feline male dominance, but no. I merely reference the fact that since I debuted in *Catnap* and *Pussyfoot,* I then commenced to a title sequence that is as sweet and simple as B to Z.

That is when I begin my alphabet, with the B in *Cat on a Blue Monday*. From then on, the color word in the title is in alphabetical order up to the current volume, *Cat in a Neon Nightmare.*

Since I associate with a multifarious and nefarious crew of human beings, and since Las Vegas is littered with guide books as well as bodies, I wish to provide a rundown of the local landmarks on my particular map of the world. A cast of characters, so to speak:

To wit, my lovely roommate and high-heel devotee, freelance PR ace MISS TEMPLE BARR, who has reunited with her only love . . .

. . . the once missing-in-action magician MR. MAX KINSELLA, who has good reason for invisibility: after his cousin SEAN died in a bomb attack during a post-high-school jaunt to Ireland, he went into undercover counterterrorism work with his mentor, GANDOLPH THE GREAT, but Gandolph was murdered the previous Halloween while unmasking phony psychics at a séance.

Meanwhile Mr. Max is sought by another dame, Las Vegas homicide LIEUTENANT C. R. MOLINA, mother of preteen MARIAH . . .

. . . and the good friend of Miss Temple's recent good friend, MR. MATT DEVINE, a radio talk-show shrink who not long ago was a Roman Catholic priest and has tracked down his abusive stepfather, MR. CLIFF EFFINGER. . . .

Speaking of unhappy pasts, Lieutenant Carmen Molina is not thrilled that her former flame, MR. RAFI NADIR, the unsuspecting father of Mariah, is in Las Vegas taking on shady muscle jobs after blowing his career on the LAPD . . .

. . . or that Mr. Max Kinsella is hunting Rafi himself because the lieutenant blackmailed him into tailing her ex. While so engaged, Mr. Max's attempted rescue of a pathetic young stripper soon found him joining Mr. Rafi Nadir on Molina's prime suspect list, although both are off the hook now, on that case at least.

In the meantime, quite literally, Mr. Matt has drawn a stalker, the local girl that young Max and his cousin Sean boyishly competed for in that long-ago Ireland . . .

. . . one MISS KATHLEEN O'CONNOR, for years an IRA operative who seduced rich men for guns and roses for the cause. She is deservedly christened by Miss Temple as Kitty the Cutter . . . and—finding Mr. Max impossible to trace—has settled for harassing with tooth and claw the nearest innocent bystander, Mr. Matt Devine . . .

. . . while he tries to recover from the crush he developed on Miss Temple, his neighbor at the Circle Ritz condominiums, while Mr. Max was missing in action, by not very boldly seeking new women, all of whom are now in danger from said Kitty the Cutter.

In fact, on the advice of counsel, i.e., AMBROSIA, Mr. Matt's talk-show producer, and none other then the aforesaid Lt. Molina, he has tried to disarm Miss Kitty's pathological interest in his sexual state by losing his virginity with a call girl least likely to be the object of K the Cutter's retaliation. Except that hours after their assignation at the Goliath Hotel, said call girl turns up deader than an ice-cold deck of Bicycle playing cards.

All this human sex and violence makes me glad I have a simpler social life, revolving around a quest for union with . . .

. . . THE DIVINE YVETTE, a shaded silver Persian beauty I filmed some cat food commercials with before being wrongfully named in a paternity suit by her air-head actress mistress, MISS SAVANNAH ASHLEIGH. . . .

And just trying to get along with my unacknowledged daughter . . .

. . . MISS MIDNIGHT LOUISE, who has insinuated herself into my cases until I was forced to set up a shop with her as Midnight, Inc. Investigations, and who has also nosed herself into my long-running duel with . . .

. . . the evil Siamese assassin HYACINTH, first met as the onstage assistant to the mysterious lady magician . . .

. . . SHANGRI-LA, who made off with Miss Temple's semi-engagement ring from Mr. Max during an onstage trick and who has not been seen since except in sinister glimpses . . .

. . . just like THE SYNTH, an ancient cabal of magicians that may take contemporary credit for the ambiguous death of Mr. Max's mentor in magic, Gandolph the Great, and GG's former lady assistant, MISS GLORIA FUENTES, as well as the more recent death of the CLOAKED CONJUROR'S assistant, not to mention a professor of the metaphysical killed in cultlike surroundings among such strange and forgotten zodiac symbols as Ophiuchus, PROF. JEFFERSON MANGEL.

Well, there you have it, the usual human stew, all mixed up and at odds with each other and within themselves. Obviously, it is up to me to solve all their mysteries and nail a few crooks along the way. Like Las Vegas, the City that Never Sleeps, Midnight Louie, private eye, also has a sobriquet: the Kitty that Never Sleeps.

With this crew, who could?

Fallen Woman

She looked like a fashion model photographed by Helmut Newton for some slick, slightly sick ad in a fashion magazine.

Or like a butterfly pinned on a mosaic of fire opal.

Or like just another dead woman in the City that Never Sleeps—West Coast edition.

Lieutenant C. R. Molina gazed down at the gossamer straps attached to the extreme curve of a high-heeled, paper-thin sole dangling from the dead woman's bare big toe on one foot. Gucci or St. Laurent, probably. Talk about an upscale toe-tag. Grizzly Bahr would get a kick out of hearing that when he got the body.

Medical examiners got a kick out of things most people would consider grotesque.

"How are we gonna get the body off that?" came a disgusted male voice from behind her.

Alfonso had joined her in gazing at a victim ten feet below who was seemingly suspended on the intricate galaxy of neon that formed a ceiling for the hotel's vast gaming area.

The chatter, chimes, and clinks of Las Vegas games of chance drifted upward in the vast central atrium above the false neon ceiling, like sound effects from a faceless computer universe.

"There must be a clear Lexan ceiling above the neon," Molina guessed. "That's the only thing strong enough to resist extreme impact. Otherwise she'd have crashed right through the neon tubing down to the casino floor."

"Bullet-proof plastic. That's a security application."

"That's what the hotel needed. One kid on an upper floor dropping a BB could fatally bean a customer."

"Makes sense," Alfonso conceded. "I'll check to make sure."

"Any idea how far she fell, or how long she's been there?"

Alfonso shook his head like a doleful basset hound. He was one of those sloppy cops: fifty or sixty pounds overweight, baggy suit, mussed hair, puffy face, sleepy eyes set in a bezel of perpetually bruised skin. The package made him a very successful homicide detective. As with Peter Falk's Colombo, everybody always underestimated Alfonso.

Not Molina, who devoutly wished that someone other than the crack team of Alfonso and Barrett had been "up" for this case. Abie, they were called, as in *Abie's Irish Rose.* A.B.

"We'll have to treat it like a wilderness retrieval," she said. "Lower some techs down to record the scene, then bring the body up in a litter and go over it on solid ground."

Alfonso nodded and winced at the same time. "Depending on how far she fell, that could be like loading liquid shit into a beach pail."

Molina only winced internally. Cops and coroners had dirty jobs and found harsh words to describe them. Normally, the distancing techniques of pros at scenes of crime and dissolution didn't bother her, but normally she didn't feel personally responsible for the dead body under discussion.

What was the subject's name? Probably a lavish phony, but they'd soon pry the Plain Jane moniker from beneath the façade. They almost always did, and the corpse almost always proved to be someone's not-so-darling little girl all grown up wrong. This one looked like a solid-gold success, even after the rough hands of death. She had been a *Vanity Fair* woman: long, elegant, impossibly thin and impossibly busty—Molina would bet on implants—dressed to kill. Or to be killed.

"The staff know her?" she asked Alfonso, although she suspected the answer.

"Too well," he said, acting the usual morose when he wasn't being downright lugubrious. "One of the hotel's top call girls. High-rollers all the way. Or at least fat money rolls."

Molina looked up, past the building's gaudy neon-rimmed ribs to the soaring true ceiling maybe twenty floors above. "So she was a penthouse suite sweetie."

He nodded. "I hate these cases: JFP. Jumped, fell, or pushed. Damn hard to prove, any which way but dead."

"Yeah." Molina's nerves unclenched a little. Bad as the situation was, Alfonso was right: damn hard to prove what she privately called an ASH: accident, suicide, or homicide. "So you haven't pinned her to a room number yet?" she asked.

"Barrett's still on it, questioning staff. Trouble is, the lady was such a regular that they didn't even bother to notice which rooms, which night."

"She looks like she could have made money enough doing something legit," Molina mused. She was no fashion maven, but she recognized the expensive flair that clothed the twisted body. Why not model? Or act? Why hook?

Who could answer why women who could ride in limos on their looks so often ankled over to the shady side of the street? They might have thought the money was better, but breaking out in legitimate modeling paid off massively for the few dozen who made it. Maybe an underlying self-hatred? Lately Molina was getting a bit too comfy with that feeling, but she wasn't about to turn tricks to deal with it.

Alfonso nodded, still gazing soulfully above them with his hound-dog eyes. "That Barrett! You'd think he was in the cast of *Rescue 51.*"

Just then, as if summoned, Alfonso's partner, thin and bony, leaned over the sixth-floor balustrade, directing a tech team that was descending from a wire stretched across the atrium's architectural chasm.

"Randolph Mantooth, where are you?" Molina muttered, watching their herky-jerky progress.

"Your kid watch those old reruns too?" Alfonso asked.

"Religiously."

"Kids today! Growing up on yesterday."

She nodded, too intent on observing the shaky operation to comment. She had no time to watch TV, or reruns of long-cold TV shows. Being twelve-year-old Mariah's mother kept her current, but not much.

"Just how old is the Goliath?" she asked suddenly. "You'd think they'd know not to design interior atriums in a town where people lose their shirts and their self-respect every day and night. This is no place for Hyatt-style hotels enamored of atriums."

Alfonso nodded, smiling fondly. He was a native. He loved every manifestation of the city's phenomenal entertainment explosion along the Strip, like a research scientist enamored of cancer growth.

"Yeah," he said, "they didn't worry as much about divers in the old days. Maybe what, gosh, twenty years ago? The exterior balcony doors at this hotel didn't used to be sealed shut, but they are now."

"So this was the only way to fall," Molina said. "Inside straight, so to speak. Over the internal atrium edge. Or to be pushed. Who spotted her?"

"Some ma and pa tourist couple on fourteen, waiting for

an elevator and ambling to the edge to be brave and look over. Took her for part of the design at first."

Molina had to agree. Well-dressed supine women always looked decorative, or sexy, or decadent. Or dead. The functions seemed interchangeable. She'd seen a lot of dead and never had found it decorative or sexy or even glamourously decadent. So shoot her.

They were shooting the woman below now. From every angle, videotape and still camera. She was a featured player on Dead TV and soon she'd be a star on Grizzly Bahr's stainless-steel autopsy table while he droned the dreary statistics of her internal organs and external injuries into a microphone for an audience of one. Himself.

"Mine eyes dazzle," Alfonso murmured, his hangdog countenance even droopier as they both blinked at the flashes illuminating the dead woman like heat lightning.

"Huh?" Molina stared at him as if he were a stranger.

He jerked her a weak grin. " 'She died young.' That's the rest of the line. Webster. Elizabethan playwright. Grim guy."

"Webster? I thought he was the dictionary guy. Elizabethan? You?"

"You can't help what sticks in your head in this job," he said, shrugging. "There are a lot of pretty women in Las Vegas who die, and we gotta be there. 'Pretty Woman.' Roy Orbison. Greatest singer since Elvis."

Elvis.

That was another subject Molina couldn't stand, not since becoming involved with the Circle Ritz gang.

Who would think that ditsy, sixty-plus landlady Electra Lark could have assembled so many usual suspects under the fifties-vintage roof of the round condo-cum-apartment building she called the Circle Ritz? Not only former resident magician Max Kinsella, Mr. Now-you-see-him, Now-you-don't, was possibly involved in a murder, or three, but now, as of last night, so was Matt Devine, Mr. Altar-Boy Straight Arrow. Not to mention the object of their joint affections, Miss Temple Barr, who confused being a public relations freelancer with imitations of Nancy Drew! Molina just wished TEMPLE BARR, P.R., as her business card read, would decide which of the two apparently shady Circle Ritz men was on her personal Most Wanted list.

And now Molina herself was involved with the whole crew both professionally, and, on unhappy occasion, personally.

Involved. The word chilled her as many much harsher ones couldn't. Speaking of which, there was a nasty task she couldn't put off any longer.

She took a last long look at the dead woman. This was as good as this Jane Doe would ever look before she was dissected like a frog princess, unless someone sprung for a casket funeral and they sutured and shined her up to surface beauty again, but Molina doubted anyone would bother.

Molina's eyes dazzled all right, but in Las Vegas that was just part of the eternal illusion for suckers to sop up and she wasn't buying anything on face value.

The woman lying on the neon net below, though, had indeed died young, and Molina was horribly, terribly afraid that it was her fault.

Adam's Apple

Matt Devine dreamed of falling.

It wasn't pleasant.

He woke up with a jerk, already sitting up. He was groggy, sandy-mouthed from rich food and too much wine and talk, and had to wonder where he'd been for the first time in his life.

Remembering made him cradle his aching head in his hands.

Vassar. An Eastern Protestant madonna. A call girl. Did that mean she was like a dog? You called and she came? Yes. That's how demeaning the whole thing was. Buzz for a body. Pay for a person.

He wondered if he was still a little drunk.

Not that he'd been drunk last night . . . just high? High on anxiety.

He'd tried to forestall one woman with another and had ended up feeling both had cheated him somehow.

Trying to embrace the occasion of sin had become not . . . sin, just self-disgust.

The phone rang.

It was an hour of the morning when he was used to sleeping deep and hard, thanks to his night job. But he'd had the previous night off, so to speak, and had only hit head to pillow in the early morning hours. What time was it? Who could be calling him now? Didn't matter. Drift away. Forget the night. Forget yesterday.

The ringing drilled into his consciousness. Wouldn't stop.

He fumbled for the phone on his makeshift nightstand, giving his sluggish self mental marching orders. Lift the receiver, substitute a nagging human voice for the intermittent ring of the phone.

Wait. Wake up, even if you don't want to. If that's not the phone, then it's the . . . doorbell?

Now he distinguished the mellow notes of the Circle Ritz's fifties doorbell.

Someone is at his door.

No. Go away.

Come again another day.

That's the rain. Right? The rain is ringing his chimes?

He's so tired. Tired of himself and his problems. As if he were the only one in the world. . . .

Ring. Ring. Go away. Come again another day.

It won't.

He rolled off the narrow bed, surprised to find himself still clothed.

The door was many stumbling steps away. He was drunk on too little sleep, that's all.

Finally. He opened the door.

Rain, rain, go away. Especially if your name is Molina.

Carmen Molina. *Lieutenant Molina. Mother Molina, pray for us now and at the hour of our death. Amen.*

"You look like hell," she said.

She didn't capitalize it. He could always tell when people were referring to hell versus Hell. Not going there, just referring.

"Look," he said. "I normally sleep until at least noon.

Night hours, if you recall? Whatever it is, I'm in no condition to talk to you right now."

"Tough."

She brushed past him like a Las Vegas Strip Rollerblader. Rude.

Matt turned to find almost six feet of female homicide lieutenant adding no ambiance at all to his cozy fifties-vintage entry hall and adjoining kitchen. She wasn't about to move any more than his heavy metal refrigerator was.

"I'll put some coffee on," he said.

"Good idea." She had wandered into the living/dining room and was peeking into the bedroom.

He was surprised to find her being so obviously nosy, so unmannerly, but police people must come to think the world owes them a peep. Still, she'd always treated him more like a human being and less like some seedy suspect before.

He put a saucepan to boil on the stove top and pulled two mugs out of the cupboard, checking to see if dust or anything mobile had collected in them. Didn't often have company for breakfast, like never.

"Hot water and instant coffee? You're still living like a transient," her voice came from behind him. "Planning to leave town?"

"The world is way too full of costly, trendy, one-task gadgets."

"You've still got Rectory-itis. Father Frugal. First you reject labor-saving domestic devices as effete, then you get devout Catholic grandmothers to come in and do it all for you free."

"You make frugal sound corrupt."

"Maybe it's because I'm a cop and tend to think everything's corrupt."

He turned. He'd never seen Molina with this particular edge and it wasn't nice. "This isn't a social call."

"We've got to talk, and you're lucky I can't afford to do it at headquarters."

"You can't afford to do it here." He glanced at the unit's various walls and tugged at an earlobe.

She got the message instantly, having forgotten that Matt was possibly or even probably being bugged by his stalker, Kathleen O'Connor.

"Oh, shit!"

Matt stared. Molina had always been a lady, for a cop.

She motioned him into the hall with one finger, turning off the heat under the saucepan with the other. It was fascinating to watch a cop play hausfrau.

"You go get that book you loaned me from the car," she told him. "I'll watch the boiling water."

Her gestures shooed him out into the hall. Through the ajar door he glimpsed her conducting a rapid search of his rooms. Max Kinsella had been the last person to hunt for bugging devices. Matt found it interesting that Molina followed virtually the same path: under furniture, inside tabletop items like the phone, up in lighting fixtures, and down in wall outlets.

After about fifteen minutes she circled back to the door, did a double take, and zeroed in on something on his entry hall wall. The plastic-covered box for the door chimes.

Last was lucky. She pulled out a tiny object that instantly explained the name "bug." In another moment she had put it in one empty mug and drowned it in tepid water from the saucepan.

Matt felt as invaded as if he accidentally swallowed a dead fly from his coffee cup. It's hard to define the sense of revulsion you get from knowing that someone's been listening to you every moment. And what was to hear? He lived alone, didn't talk to himself, had only the occasional phone call or visitor. Sick.

Molina nodded him inside again and rechecked a couple sites, as if finding the one bug implied an infestation.

They mutually rejected the coffee without consulting. She walked into the living room, stood before the red sofa that was its biggest piece of furniture, and regarded it with her back to him, as if it suddenly was significant.

"Did Kinsella check the doorbell unit?"

"No," he said.

He could sense her smile even from behind. "But I didn't see everywhere he went and everything he did," he added.

"Isn't that always the case with Mr. Kinsella?" She turned, and her face was as expressionless as he'd ever seen it. "For once I'm not interested in that slimeball. He's not a suspect. You are."

"Me? What could I have done?"

"That's a very good question. You might as well sit down." She gestured to his own sofa as if she was the hostess and he was a guest, an unwanted one.

Matt sat.

Molina didn't. She began pacing back and forth the length of the long red sofa. She reminded him of a big cat in a cage. She was a tall woman, and she wasn't slight. Not fat, just there. She was wearing one of the dark pant-suits she favored, even in summer, a look-alike for a man's business suit. She never carried a purse, as if that sniffed of patent leather Mary Janes and other girly images. He knew there was at least one firearm on her plain-Jane person, and probably latex gloves, maybe a ChapStick, a nail file, and some keys, but that was about it, except for a shield and an ID tag.

Her dark hair was thick, straight, and cut chin-length, a non-style designed to affront any professional stylist. Maybe she wore some lip gloss. Maybe. Matt smothered a smile. She reminded him of a lot of nuns who'd had to give up wearing the habit and had settled on a "uniform" quite like this. It was a way of dampening sexuality, and Matt could see that a female homicide lieutenant would want to do that. It certainly made her look like she meant business, every day, every hour, in every way.

Only now it was 8 A.M. in his living room and *he* was apparently her business.

"What's this about, Carmen?" he asked. They knew each other's history. Didn't much talk about it, but they had a few things in common: growing up Catholic, serving as role models, working in "helping" professions that encouraged or enforced a code of behavior.

"Lieutenant." She articulated the word like a machine gun shooting staples.

Okay. This was official. Then he didn't have to go out of his way to be a friendly neighborhood snitch.

"Is this about Kinsella?"

"Screw Kinsella!" She didn't shout. She spoke in a low, intense tone that was much worse. Carmen, using casual language? The never-part-time mother who didn't want her preteen daughter growing up anything but a good girl? "I don't give a flying . . . fig . . . for that lowlife at the moment, count my blessings."

She had pronounced "fig" with such intense articulation that Matt thought the obscenity it stood in for at the last moment would have been less harsh.

"I'm sorry," he said, spreading his hands, the classic gesture of the poor soul who was without a clue. "Something very bad has obviously happened—"

"Where were you last night?"

"Ah, not at work. I had the night off."

"So where were you?"

So this was about him, not Max Kinsella. Matt tried to shift his mind and emotions 180 degrees.

"Don't rehearse an answer," she pushed. "Just tell me."

"Why?"

"Why? Because I'm the police!"

"If this is an official interrogation, then there might be reasons why I shouldn't 'just tell you.' Do I need a lawyer?"

"I don't know. That's what I'm trying to find out. This is off the record. You could tell me you offed Jimmy Hoffa and I wouldn't have a shred of evidence."

"Unless you were wired." Matt eyed her encompassing outfit with a certain wariness.

She paced again for a few seconds, then stopped front and center. "Look. I'm trying to help you. I tried to help you before, remember? I don't need evasions now. I need the absolute truth. Where were you last night?"

"Truth is never absolute," he began.

"Enough with the hair-splitting. You want to search me?" She stopped again, spread her arms.

"Good Lord, no." The idea was completely alarming. "I just don't understand . . . I'm still half asleep. You've completely changed. I don't get it."

"I'm not wired. Just being here is putting my career on the line. I'm trying to help you . . . yes, and me too. I need the truth. I need to know. Where were you last night?"

"Doing what you told me to do."

"Oh, God." She put a hand to her mouth. "Where were you doing it?"

"At the Goliath Hotel."

Her breath came out in a huff. And then all her tensile energy sifted away like flour into a bowl. She sat on one of his gray cube tables. "Take me through it, step by step."

"It's kind of personal."

"No, Matt. It isn't."

She nailed him with her police look, with the one personal attribute that was utterly riveting, her Blue-Hawaii-intense eyes. How did a Latina woman come by that Anglo-Saxon imprimatur? He guessed he'd never know.

"I did exactly as you said," he began, fascinated that the statement made her wince. "I burned and dodged all up and down the Strip to lose any tail. To lose Kathleen O'Connor, the bane of my existence, the woman who wants my supposed virtue."

"What do you mean 'supposed'?"

"Only that chastity isn't a much-valued commodity anywhere but in the Church, and even there nowadays it's proved to be a pretty tawdry concept, sometimes a matter more of hypocrisy than dogma."

"So you shouldn't feel so bad about having to 'lose' it to save everybody you know from a vengeful stalker."

"I shouldn't, but I do. Think Mariah."

She looked away, as if her hard-nosed act had cracked a little, maybe a lot.

"Believe me," she said, "I don't want to eavesdrop on your psycho-social-sexual-spiritual struggles. I just need to know where you went, and what you did. And when."

"I got to the Goliath about . . . before seven. It was still light. I didn't check the time. I had the night off, didn't I?"

"Boys night out," she murmured.

"I did everything you said. Took a room with cash. Changed at the last minute as if I were a superstitious gambler worried about the number. Tipped the bellman a hundred bucks for my lowly single bag." Matt decided not to mention splurging on expensive new clothes for the occasion; it made him sound like a total hick. "Asked if he knew some entertaining young ladies."

"And—?"

"Worked like a charm, Lieutenant. You sure know Las Vegas. Within ninety minutes there was this vision in my doorway. She was everything you said. Beautiful. Sophisticated. Smart. Dressed like a movie star at the Oscars. Downtrodden? Hardly. She was willing to hit the tables, but settled for dinner in the room. She ordered, knowing the hotel menu, and it was as expensive as she was."

"Good dinner?"

"Best I ever had."

The interrogation had become a bitter point/counterpoint, each side elaborately not quite acknowledging a certain collaboration.

They were in this together, Matt thought with a queasy feeling, as much as he and Vassar had ever been. A tacit accommodation.

"And—?"

"We talked."

"Oh, come on."

"We did. You were right. She was a total professional. Proud of her role in the sex industry. No way was I going to 'exploit' her. Why do you need to know all this? You want to arrest the poor woman?"

"If only I could."

"Well, I'm glad she's out of your jurisdiction, then. She really was terribly bright. I'm politically incorrect enough to feel she could have had a better job, didn't have to be doing what she was doing, but she was having none of that. I was insulting her to question her profession. And myself."

"Did you explain your particular situation?"

"Yeah. She was fascinated. Liked the idea of being the one to 'minister' to such a newbie. Acted like a shrink. Freaked me out."

"So—?"

"Isn't there a name for this, Lieutenant? Prying into other people's intimate affairs?"

"Yeah. It's called 'need to know.' Trust me. I don't like this any better than you do. Cut to the chase. You ate, you talked, you took care of business, and then what?"

"I left. Left fifteen hundred-dollar bills on the marble shelf in the bathroom, fifteen feet long. The shelf, not the fifteen hundred-dollar bills. I was worried about underpaying, so I probably went overboard. Could have saved four or five hundred maybe. What do you think?"

"Don't sound so bitter. It doesn't become you. What time was it?"

"Too late? Oops. Bitter again. I don't know. I deliberately didn't wear a watch. Didn't want to know what time the cock crowed. I went out through the casino to the Strip. It was still dark, but a stiletto of light outlined the mountains in the east. It made me think of those thin tall heels she wore, and the snakeskin thongs that held them on."

"Snakeskin stilettos. Tools of the trade."

"Yeah. She was a lovely girl. Bright. Beautiful. Vassar-educated. Cultured. Victim of date rape. You see, Lieutenant, dig deep enough, even with a seasoned, fully cognizant pro, and you find a wound, maybe even if you just made it yourself."

"Was?" Molina asked.

The way she said it, the accusing, probing way she said it, made Matt catch his breath.

For the first time, he feared for something more concrete than his soul.

Cat Haven

I am lying on my back with my pins reaching for the sky, or ceiling. I am not surrendering, but airing out my underside.

I have commandeered the bottom half of the bed on a forty-five degree angle. This way I am able to stretch out to my full three feet toe-to-tail without touching a hair to anything solid except the zebra-striped comforter I recline upon.

There is no more blissful position in this world, especially when it is accompanied by the knowledge that my resident human, Miss Temple Barr, is curled up like a snail in what is left of her portion of the bed. She is so cute when she is sleeping in such a way as to accommodate yours truly. That is when I realize why I have deigned to share my life, my fortune, and my sacred self-sufficiency with her.

Poor little thing! She has had quite a stressful time lately, almost being strangled by the Stripper Killer, and her not meaning to play a decoy.

Luckily, I had realized her tonsils were imperiled and mustered a rescue party. I also managed to rescue—in the same night, mind you—my upstart supposed daughter (all the supposing is on her part), Midnight Louise, from durance vile in the Cloaked Conjuror's hidden estate behind a faux cemetery.

Is this Las Vegas, or what? You gotta love it.

While I am basking in my achievements of the damsel-saving sort I pause to wrinkle my brow. It is true that my upstart maybe-offspring took on the evil Siamese feline fatale Hyacinth all by her lonesome, thereby usurping my customary role of muscle man.

(However, since my long-term plans for the aforesaid Hyacinth may include an alliance of a romantic nature, perhaps it was best to let the little spitfire do the dirty work.)

Speaking of dirty work, I lather my chest hair into a damp curly tangle that the dames love to run their nails through.

Apparently my washing motions shake the bed, for my Miss Temple uncurls, sits up, squints at me as she does when her contact lenses are out, and says like this: "Louie! Are you getting your nice smooth ruff all messed up again? Enough already with the compulsive grooming! I know that you were at Baby Doll's and wailed 'Sweet Tail-o'-Mine' or whatever along with your Pet Shop Quartet of alley-cat buddies to alert me to the lurking presence of the Stripper Killer. Thanks, but settle down now. I need my beauty sleep."

At that she turns over and ignores me.

So much for my irresistible chest hair. Sometimes dames can be unpredictable, but what the heck, that is why we love them.

So I sit upright, pounce down to the floor, and swagger into the main room, ruffled but unreformed.

Barely do I hit the living room than I am aware of a soft scritching sound on the French doors to our unique triangular patio.

There is nothing unique about that sound: a feline footpad is out and about and I think I know who.

I amble over to the glass framed between these frilled wooden rectangles. In the lowest one on the left of this particular door is featured the jet-black kisser of my erstwhile daughter and new partner-in-crime-solving, Miss Midnight Louise.

Woe is me. I take her into the family enterprise last night and here she is at the crack of dawn making like an alarm clock. First rule of the experienced shamus: do not rise until 10 A.M. Noon is even better, but I do not want my moniker to be High Noon Louie, so I settle for ten o'clock, as in scholar. A self-employed dude cannot be too erudite in this town.

I jump up to unlatch the door and watch Miss Louise swish in. For an offspring of mine she is long in the fur, but I must say that it looks good on the female of the species. Any species. I do wish Miss Temple would let her curly red locks grow, but that does not seem to be her style.

"I am surprised you are up and about," Miss Louise notes, passing me with a half-hearted brush of greeting.

We may be partners in Midnight, Inc. Investigations, but she is as antsy about the alliance as I am.

"I am surprised that you are up already," I return politely, "given the hair-pulling match you got into with Miss Hyacinth last night."

"That! That just smoothed the rough edges off my nails," she says, sitting down to manicure the razor-sharp appendages in question.

"No curare, huh?"

"I am walking, am I not? You must not believe every public line a deadly dame will throw a private dick, Daddykins. Curare on her nails? More like Cutex. Get real."

"Cutex" means nothing to me, but I suppose it is some beauty product the ladies use on their nails. I try not to know too much about their little deceptions in the looks department. I like to be surprised.

"So why are you here?" I ask.

"Why not? We are partners now, *n'est pas*?"

I cringe. Louise is alley born and bred. She has no right to assume the adorable foreign habits of the Divine Yvette, *mon amour*.

"*C'est* yeah," I reply loftily, "but that does not mean you can take liberties and muscle in on my relationship with Miss Temple."

"Muscling in? Who sez I am muscling in? If I were, you would know it, Daddy-o." Miss Louise narrows her golden eyes. "I thought you might be interested to know the fuzz is in the building."

"The fuzz? You mean those martial arts ninjas from the Cloaked Conjuror's place? Havana Browns and Burmese, by their body types and buzz cuts. Ugly customers."

"Not that kind of fuzz! The human sort. Lieutenant Molina is chitchatting with Matt Devine one story up."

"So? It is his place. He can entertain whom he likes. And frankly, my dear, I am pleased that he is out of my Miss Temple's hair. I detest romantic triangles."

"Dream on. Your human ginger cat is a meal ticket, and that is all. Besides, she has a human panther for a partner."

I wrinkle my nose at mention of the Mystifying Max Kinsella, ex-magician but unfortunately not ex-significant other in my Miss Temple's life. He is not good enough for her, but neither is Mr. Matt. I would be, if I were about six-three and 180, instead of being a thirty-six long stretched out and eighteen going on twenty . . . pounds.

"Miss Lt. C. R. Molina is hardly going to mess with us," I point out. "She does not speak our language."

"Apparently she does not speak Matt Devine's either, from what I saw through the patio window. He looked like a grilled catfish fillet."

"You spied on them?"

"We are an investigative unit. Undercover surveillance is what we do best. Speaking of what we do, why are we so interested in the Cloaked Conjuror's hidden digs?"

"Because Mr. Max is, and I always find that trailing him leads to crime. Who do you think has been sneaking around that place as much as you and me these days?"

"It is not hard to figure," she says, sitting down to slick back her whiskers. "Mr. Max is a retired magician. He would have much in common with the Cloaked Conjuror."

"Not so!" I protest. "Mr. Max has done the Cloaked Conjuror a good turn or two only because CC is a target of those disgruntled magicians, the Synth, that Mr. Max wants to smoke out. CC is so presona non grata among the magic-making set that someone has sent death threats his way faster than a vanishing dove. That is why CC always wears a full-face mask, and his assistant may have been killed at TitaniCon because he was dressed up like CC. Mr. Max is interested in the villains CC attracts, not the man himself. He has no more time than the Synth for a so-called magician whose act betrays the secrets of magical illusions in his show nightly."

"Why would Mr. Max care? He is not a practicing magician anymore. No, I saw him lurking about after the excitement last night, visiting our pals the Big Cats."

"Osiris the leopard and Mr. Lucky the black panther? I guess that figures. Mr. Max helped us rescue them from certain death during my last big case."

"Previous case, Pop. 'Last' always sounds too final in the PI game." Miss Louise eyes me slyly through the mitt that is doing a mop-up operation on her shiny little nose. "Or . . . Mr. Max may be interested in that Lady Mandarin magician who also hides out at CC's Los Muertos spread."

"No way! Mr. Max is utterly bewitched by my Miss Temple."

"Are you sure? I watched the two of them have a little heart-to-heart out by the Big Cat compound last night. I admit that they did not seem on lovey-dovey terms, but among humans you know how the mating dance can start with a preliminary spat."

"Among us felines too, if you ever had a chance to experience such a fandango before you got the politically correct surgery."

"Who needs to know the steps to recognize the dance? This Shangri-La magician dame was giving off plenty of pheromones during their tête-a-tête."

"Love and hate are not as easy to read among humans as among our superior species. I cannot believe that Mr. Max would be seriously untrue to our Miss Temple."

"Who is to know what the male of any species may be up to?"

"And that is the way it should be. How else can we keep you nosy females guessing? So that is your report? Fuzz a floor up, more nocturnal slinking at Los Muertos. None of that is worth writing Holmes about."

Louise stops her eternal grooming—dames!—to cock an ear at the door. "Oh, good. I was hoping to observe a police interrogation firsthand and I believe I am going to get my wish."

Before I can express surprise or doubt or disdain, the doorbell rings.

At the Circle Ritz, doorbells do not just ring. They chime. In a related series of notes. Like a song. In other words, they make a production number out of it.

But like most production numbers, it does raise an audience: in this case, my Miss Temple from the depths of sleep, who robot-walks from the bedroom to the front door in her Hard Rock Café T-shirt and (cringe) Christmas bunny slippers from her mother.

"Fasten your seatbelt," Miss Louise advises me out of the side of her mouth that is not busy licking whiskers into submission. "It is going to be a bumpy ride."

Now I know what human dame she reminds me of!

Fallen Angel

Temple shoved her glasses back up on the bridge of her nose before reaching for the doorknob.

She hated being seen in glasses now that she wore contact lenses, but no way was she going to find anyone still at the door if she paused to insert the contacts.

She hesitated before turning the knob. Maybe she didn't want to see anyone. Talk about a hard day's night. It wasn't every morning she woke up with a stiff neck from being half strangled and runny eyes from being half basted with her own pepper spray. But this might be Electra, the landlady, who had heard about the showdown at Baby Doll's and was worried about her.

So she edged the door open enough to know she should never have left the soft, warm solace of her bed. Molina! At nine o'clock low in the morning . . . Temple's own personal nine o'clock low, when she needed to sleep in after getting home assaulted but safe. Thank God Max was gone already. She blinked. Max was gone, wasn't he? Oh, God, there'd be hell to pay if he wasn't.

"You can unchain the door, Miss Barr. I *am* the police," Molina pointed out.

"I'm not sure I want to see the police."

"Too bad. I want to see you. Open wide."

"I had a rough night," Temple complained on a half yawn, fumbling with the chain mechanism. "Can't this wait until later? I'll come to headquarters and make a statement or whatever."

Molina marched in the instant the chain released. "I don't want you at headquarters. I don't want a statement. The officers at the scene wrote up a pretty lurid report as it was."

"Lurid? About me?"

"No, about 'Tess the Thong Girl.' "

Temple cringed, but had to hustle to follow Molina into her living room.

The Looming Lieutenant—Temple, at five-feet-flat in bunny slippers couldn't help regarding the almost-six-foot tall homicide officer as akin to the Great Wall of China—stopped so suddenly that Temple almost rear-ended her. What a revolting thought that was!

"He replicates?" Molina demanded.

Temple peered past Molina's navy-blue personal uniform. Louie. And Louie? Omigod, she was seeing double. Maybe Molina'd make her do a drunk test. Touch her nose in a straight line, or walk on her toes, or whatever.

Trying to focus, Temple immediately noticed certain inalienable differences in the two black cat images confronting them.

"That's Louie on the left," she explained, "and the other one is smaller, longer-haired, and female, as even a blind man could see. That's Midnight Louise, from the Crystal Phoenix hotel."

"I must say the fine points of feline anatomy are lost on me," Molina answered. "They look like clones to me. I'd hate to think there was anything in any way resembling Midnight Louie in greater Las Vegas or Clark County."

"Louie is an original," Temple asserted huffily. "But

then Nicky and Van from the Crystal Phoenix hotel renamed little Caviar Midnight Louise. Don't you remember, Lieutenant? It was during the champagne celebration in the Ghost Suite after the Gridiron show. You were there."

"I must have been there earlier. No champagne for working cops."

"Oops. Maybe you weren't there right then. It seems like you always are, though."

Molina's smile was tight-lipped. "No, I missed the feline renaming ceremony." She eyed the two cats sitting side by side near the living room's single sofa. "I suppose I should take a quick look around."

Before Temple could say yea or nay—or what the heck for?—Molina was bowing and stretching all over the place while doing an intimate search of the furnishings and accessories.

After ten minutes she returned to the living room. "I figured the place would be clean, but better safe than bugged."

"*I* am bugged, Lieutenant. I am bugged that you're here, this early, upsetting my domestic routine. And my . . . cats."

Molina eyed the duo, who were returning from accompanying her every move. They settled in tandem in the exact same spot she had first seen them. Obviously she was not used to cats that behaved like paired Dobermans.

"These animals are acting like police escorts and I don't like it."

"So sit down, chill out, and don't move. I'm sure they'll stay put then. Can I get you some coffee?"

" 'May I,' " Molina corrected automatically, and then had the grace to look embarrassed.

Temple guessed that she was getting the grammatical correction reserved for the lieutenant's daughter, poor little Mariah. Well, the twelve-year-old wasn't so little anymore, she was taller than Temple! But she was still "poor" for having Molina for a mother.

Temple forgot the coffee and sat. "Is this going to be a maternal lecture or a police warning?"

"With you wearing those slippers—?" Molina's dark caterpillar eyebrows lifted as she stared at the paired bunny faces on Temple's toes.

"My mother gave these to me for Christmas, so what's it to you?"

Molina lifted her hands in tandem, presenting the palms of peace, and forestalling further banter.

"Far be it from me," she said, "to critique a mother's abysmal choice in Christmas presents. I've inadvertently committed a few of those myself. I can see that anthropomorphic slippers are off my list forever. For that I thank you. The lecture part is this: you are a civilian. You have no business playing undercover investigator at striptease clubs. You have no right to risk Midnight Louie's happy home life by risking your own life in a dark parking lot. I don't care that it came out all right and the perpetrator was captured. You could have gotten killed, and, believe it or not, Miss Barr, I would be very unhappy about that. But you know all this and will take me about as seriously as you would someone who would give you bunny slippers for Christmas."

"I *am* wearing them," Temple said uneasily.

"That's the lecture part," Molina went on. "The police part is this: you may think I'm off base keeping an eye on you and your associates, but as of last night you are now involved with not one, but two murder suspects. Some people might consider that a coincidence. I am a law enforcement professional and I consider it a weakness."

"Two? What's wrong? Is persecuting Max not enough for you now? That's why I went to Baby Doll's, you know, because you were so bound and determined to nail him as the Stripper Killer. Were you off base!"

"In this case. That doesn't change the fact that he was all over the scenes of the crimes in various guises."

"As were you!"

"Me? What gives you that idea?"

"Max. Max saw you more than you saw him. He is a magician, after all. You want to talk about me taking risks! What about a homicide lieutenant who's secretly undercover investigating her own ex . . . whatever as a murder suspect and trying to pin the rap on my current . . . whatever."

Molina's nostrils flared. Temple shut up. She'd been goaded into committing truth, but realized that the truth always came with a sting in the tail: the other person's particular truth. Molina would lash back.

"This is not about Michael Aloysius Xavier Kinsella," Molina said shortly.

Sails collapsed, Temple could only wait for Molina to paddle on. Meanwhile, she bailed brains to figure out what Molina's point really was.

"This is about Matthias Anthony Devine."

"So you've looked up everybody's birth certificates. What's *my* middle name?"

Temple had asked for it, and she got it.

"Ursula," Molina intoned promptly with a smirk. "I believe that's a saint who founded an order of nuns."

"I'm not Catholic. I'm Unitarian. Ursula is a nonsectarian name in my case. I don't know why it's in the family. An aunt got saddled with it too. So, what about Matt? You're going to accuse an ex-priest of murder?"

"It's not that unthinkable. Non-ex-priests have been accused of a lot of felonies lately."

"Right. Matt. You have really flipped."

Even as Molina sat back on the sofa, a black cat jumped up on either arm, as if to say: *I'm all ears.*

Feline muscle, or eavesdropping, did not dissuade her.

"All I can say," Molina went on with a relish Temple would have to describe as personal, "is that you sure know how to pick 'em. So I can't prove Kinsella was involved in the matter of the dead man in the Goliath Hotel ceiling over a year ago, so I couldn't prove he was the Stripper Killer, but he's guilty of something, and proving it is only a matter of time.

"Then there's nice Matt Devine. I must admit that I was rooting for you to ditch Kinsella for Matt. What's not to like? Sincere, ethical, untouched, good looking, apparently honest—"

"What do you mean, apparently?"

Molina shrugged, shifting the polyester-blend navy-blue jacket on her shoulders.

Polyester-blend, navy-blue. *Ick*, Temple thought, trying to distract herself from the ugly news that was coming. Who could believe anything that came from the lips of a P-B, N-B-wearing person? The unlipsticked lips of such a person? Whose eyebrows needed a serious shrubbery trimming.

But no matter how much she denigrated Molina's persona, Temple couldn't banish the chill, sick feeling in her stomach. Molina wouldn't be here unless she had some serious stuff on Matt. Molina wouldn't be here unless she thought she could use Temple to turn Max—or now even Matt—against his own best interests. Temple curled her toes in the bunny slippers until they dug into the walnut parquet floor and braced herself. With a cat it would be called digging in; with a short woman, it would be called maximum resistance.

"Who, where, when, or why could Matt ever be a suspect of murder?" Temple asked. *Give me your best shot.*

"A call girl, at the Goliath Hotel—your favorite and Kinsella's too for mayhem—last night, because he freaked at the idea of sexual intercourse, or he had sexual intercourse and freaked afterward. Take your pick."

Whew. Temple's toes did not uncurl, nor did her hidden fists unfurl, nor did her breath stop being held.

"That's your idea," she finally said, "of who, where, when, why. I still don't get the why. Why on earth would Matt be there with that kind of woman to do that? Never in a million years. I don't believe it."

"One answer, three little words, your own, and quite brilliant in their way. I can see why you're a public relations ace: Kitty the Cutter."

"Kitty O'Connor? The poison ivy of Ireland? Oh. She assaulted Matt once, but that was a long time ago."

"It didn't end there. She's been stalking him."

Temple said nothing. She couldn't believe it. Couldn't believe that Kitty's attacks had continued, and especially couldn't believe that Matt hadn't told her.

"My own daughter was involved."

"Mariah? That's crazy. What would she have to do with Kathleen O'Connor?"

"TitaniCon?" Molina asked, invoking the recent science fiction convention at the New Millennium hotel. "The car that chased you from the parking ramp over the pedestrian bridge and crashed into the hotel's glass doors while your party escaped down the escalator? You, Matt Divine, and my own daughter. Oh, yes, I heard about it. Matt said that every female in his company was in danger at that event, including Mariah. Kitty had claimed him for her own; either he'd cooperate, or she'd take heads."

"He didn't say anything to me."

"Amazing. Can it be that anyone in Las Vegas fails to confide in Temple Barr, amateur sleuth?"

"Sarcasm does not become you, Lieutenant. I like it better when you're just plain mean."

"I am not mean," Molina answered rather astoundingly. "I am trying to save lives, including my own daughter's. The fact is that Kathleen O'Connor elected Matt the most dangerous man in Las Vegas to know. Her price was his virtue, and he's probably the only man in Las Vegas who still has . . . had . . . any."

Temple was on a dizzying mental merry-go-round fixated on tense: has . . . had. She had no idea she cared that much. Or did she?

"So . . . to save all the women he knew, he had to find a woman he didn't know and . . . render himself undesirable to Kitty the Cutter?"

Molina nodded.

"Hence the call girl. Last night? But—?"

"But what?"

"I mean, we were all so busy last night, you and Max and I, chasing each other and trying to catch the Stripper Killer all at the same time, Matt was . . . oh, poor Matt. How'd he ever find a call girl?"

She looked to Molina for an answer, admitting her superiority in this one, sleazy instance, and met an evasive gaze, a slightly flushing face, a guilty expression.

"You? You turned him on to a call girl? And you're really Catholic!"

"This not about religion. This is about abusive stalking."

"Which is not the stalkee's fault."

"It is if he snaps under the pressure and kills the very woman who is the source of his salvation. You probably know Matt better than anyone. Could he snap? Get violent?"

"No!" Temple spoke from gut defense, before she remembered how Matt had torn his own apartment apart once, almost a year ago, when she'd first met him, when he'd been hunting his abusive stepfather. "No," she repeated more softly, more sanely. Matt had acknowledged the rage within himself. Didn't that banish it? Unless he had been forced into a corner so against his every instinct. "No." This last one sounded pretty unconvincing.

"You defended Kinsella, and look where he stands. Are you simply a sucker for flawed men? There are plenty of women like that. I see them every day."

"You work on the dark side," Temple answered. "The rest of us live in the light. Mostly. Or maybe we just like to think so. But thinking so can make it so. I will never believe the worst of my friends. I won't. You'll have to prove it to me."

"No, I won't. You don't fit at all into this equation. I have to prove it to a prosecutor."

Molina stood up.

Temple stood, too, although in her case it wasn't very impressive. "Are you saying something happened to the call girl Matt was with last night?"

"It's more something that didn't happen," Molina said.

"She didn't wake up to have a morning after."

On that information she turned on her pathetically low heels and left.

Temple was too shocked to move to show the woman out, which allowed Molina to pause and call through the ajar door, "Fasten your chain-lock. There may be a murderer in the building."

Temple still didn't move. For one thing, she didn't believe for a moment that Matt had murdered somebody. But then she'd have never believed he'd patronize a Las Vegas call girl. And what was this about Kitty the Cutter stalking him? How long had that been going on? And why did Molina really call on Temple with all this bad, if vague, news, other than to lecture and to taunt?

She must have wanted exactly what was just about to happen. Too bad. It was going to happen anyway.

Temple rushed to the kitchen door to grab the keys to her apartment, then her glance fell on her bunny-slippered feet.

"Watch the door," she instructed Louie as she skied over the slick wooden floors to her bedroom to change into proper interrogation garb. "Don't let in any sex killers," she mumbled as she fled.

Midnight Louie eyed Midnight Louise. An observer, of which there was no longer one, could well imagine the two consulting each other: Did she say "sex killers" or "sex kittens"?

Flaming Sword

Midnight Louie did not watch her half-open door while Temple changed into a capri-pants-and-top set with so many chicly beaded hems at the extremities that she felt (and rattled) like a Victorian lamp shade. . . .

He and Louise had absconded the premises by the time she came charging back from the bedroom, her feet attired in black patent leather mules instead of the soft and soulful bunny faces.

Temple's outfit had all the bells and whistles that passed for current fad except a pocket, so she dangled her unit key ring from a handy thumb and ran, not walked, up the service stairs to the floor above.

She knocked on Matt's door, rapped really, and was ready to start scratching like a rodent when the door didn't instantly fly open.

"Who is it?" he asked from inside finally, as he had never done.

"It's me!"

The announcement brought silence.

Temple's courage faded at this unhappy omen. Matt was always glad to see her. Well, almost always. Except lately he had seemed . . . distant. How could she have missed it? Dummy! He was trying to avoid the targets of Kathleen O'Connor's hate campaign.

Temple rapped again. "Compared to the women you've been hanging out with lately, I'm pretty harmless, really."

The door jerked open. Matt's face was about as stiff as the mahogany the door was made of.

"What do you know about the women I've been hanging out with lately?" he asked.

"That they're dangerous. Kitty the Cutter. Lieutenant Molina. Your friendly neighborhood call girl."

"How do you know any of that?"

"Molina told me."

"Molina?"

He had spit out the name in a way Temple found totally satisfactory. At last someone else beside her was regarding the homicide lieutenant as the Great Satan, the Enemy, She Who Is Not to Be Obeyed!

"Why in God's name," he went on, mostly asking himself, not her, "would Molina run right off to you and spill her guts and mine?"

"I think she's trying to do with you what she did with Max: use me to pressure you. But I didn't fall for that the first time and I'm hardly about to do it the second."

"Temple, just your being here is pressure."

"I'm sorry. Maybe I can help."

"Nobody can help, least of all you."

"What did I ever do to deserve that 'least'?"

His expression softened into resignation. Not acceptance, just resignation. He stood aside to let her enter. "Nothing."

Temple decided brisk professionalism was the best approach. She looked around. "I imagine Molina did a bug-search of your place too?"

"She find anything in your rooms?" Matt was suddenly alert and interested.

Temple shook her head. "Yours?"

He walked into the adjoining kitchen and handed her a mug.

"I'm not thirsty."

Matt just nodded to the cup in her hand.

It was a cream-colored pottery mug, bereft of motto or design. A standard-issue drinking vessel available in any discount store.

"Euw!" Temple had detected the dark bristly form submerged in the clear water. "Is that the kind of bug I think it is?"

"Yep. Molina found it in my doorbell chime unit."

"Most ingeniously . . . revolting." Temple peered at the high-tech pest. "It looks creepy-crawly even if it's just wires and circuits. So Kitty the Cutter really was stalking you, all this time?"

"You mean since I first . . . met her and she razored me?"

Temple nodded and put the mug down on the counter.

"No, actually." Matt's voice made a more optimistic lilt as he realized that Temple had asked a key question. "Actually . . . she left me alone after that. It's only been lately."

"Maybe after your stepfather's death early this year?"

"Well, there was that fourth nun attending his fake funeral we never found another trace of . . . yeah. You're right. Since about then."

Temple moved into the living room, sat dead center on the vintage red suede couch she had helped Matt buy from the Goodwill a few months before. She was deliberately reminding him of a time before Kitty had become a secret fixture in his life, when they had been able to go out and hang out and he didn't have to worry about someone watching.

"I can't figure out why a redhead looks so good on that scarlet sofa," he said. It wasn't a line, just a comment.

"It's got to make me look good." She grinned. "I brought it home from the pound."

His smile was almost transparent, but it was there. "You're always trying to save something."

"Yes," she said, and didn't add anything else, not easy for an energetic redhead.

He sobered again. "I'm beyond saving."

"You can't believe that. You're an ex-priest. Priests are born to save."

"Are they? Not to read the newspapers lately."

"That's not bothering you, the church scandal?"

"Of course it does, but it's strangely . . . remote. That's what these last weeks have done to me. Made me a zombie, mired me in my own stupid troubles, made me no good to anybody else."

Temple shrugged and clasped her hands over her crossed knees. "Sometimes it's more than enough just to be good to ourselves. What is Molina trying to lay on you, Matt? What's she really trying to get out of you? Why doesn't she simply send a team of detectives to arrest you if she thinks you've done something?"

"Because she wants to peel my head like an orange just to see what's in it, mainly to protect her own career."

"Did you really have an . . . appointment with a call girl last night?"

"I think the word is assignation. Or . . . deal. Yeah. I was desperate. Everybody told me that was what I should do. It began to make sense, under the circumstances."

"Everybody?"

"Ambrosia . . . her off-air name is Leticia, my boss at work. Molina."

"You told them, and not me?"

"I would have told anybody, except you."

Temple must have looked like a kicked rat, because he suddenly leaned against the grass cloth covering the living room wall as if facing a firing squad with Ronald Colman's classic-film resignation and weary gallantry.

"But Molina's undone all that. Everything I wanted to preserve at any cost. Between her and Kathleen O'Connor, they've left me nothing to protect, not even myself."

"What was seeing a call girl going to preserve and protect?"

"Not her. She's dead." Matt stared at the same parquet squares that tiled Temple's floor, as if he saw a corpse there. "Molina made that plain, although she wouldn't tell me where, when, or how—just wanted to know every move I made last night. I wouldn't tell her."

"Aha! That's why she came to rattle my cage. She knew I can't resist . . . a mystery. Listen." Temple sat forward. "If Molina thinks she can use me to get to you, just like she wanted to use me to betray Max, you've got to see that it doesn't work. It hasn't worked for more than a year. If we don't let her divide us, we can survive."

"No! Vassar is dead. She was killed because she was with me. You're with me here, now. You could be next."

"Vassar? That was the girl's name? Was she really?"

"Really what?"

"A college grad."

"Probably."

"You're saying that Kitty will kill any woman you're with, for any purpose?"

"Probably. She doesn't make any exceptions for likelihood or age, young or old. Remember Sheila and Mariah at TitaniCon? The almost-accidental injuries, the car that drove after all of us into the bank of glass doors?"

"That's right. Mariah Molina was a target at that convention too."

"So was I. Remember the aspergillum I picked up after we got off the elevator? It's a sacred object, a holy water sprinkler. Kathleen used it as a goad in my back as we descended, like a gun. Just to remind me she could get that close to me, or to Mariah, or to you."

"Mariah? That's why . . . that's why you went to Molina about this, not me! You figured she needed to know, and that she could help you."

"I figured . . . wrong."

"So why was a call girl the solution?"

"That's what Kitty wanted. My innocence."

"How could she be sure you still had any?"

"Like any personality hooked on controlling others, she knew how to sniff out any vulnerability."

Temple collapsed against the sofa's hard upholstery. "So you and your staff advisors figured a call girl would be invulnerable."

"Yeah. Were we wrong." Matt sat on the couch, at the other end. He hunched forward, laced his hands, not quite approximating prayer. "The unspoken assumption was that since Kitty coveted something so personal as my virtue, that if I 'lost' it, as the expression goes, she'd lose interest. And if the means of my 'loss,' was a stranger, a professional, it would be too impersonal to merit Kitty's rage. Plus, everybody thought, including me, that a call girl counted for so little that Kitty wouldn't regard her a suitable object of revenge. Looks like everybody was wrong."

"You can't know Kitty did it."

"No. But I did it. Somehow I did it, even if Kitty never came anywhere near Vassar. So Kitty has destroyed my innocence, one way or another. I'm responsible for a woman's death. Vassar is dead. I left her alive just hours ago, Temple, and now she's dead. Something I did led to her death. I'll never forgive myself."

Temple had heard that phrase a few times in her life. She had muttered it herself. Never with the finality, the seriousness that Matt Devine used.

"I'm sorry. I guess Kitty wins."

"It's not a game. It's a woman's life. Death. Vassar . . . she was on a threshold. She wasn't the stereotype I'd expected. She was a living, bleeding human being. She had a past and future. Now—"

"Matt, I am so sorry. I hate to see Kitty win. She's bedeviled Max's life for almost twenty years and I hate, hate, hate to see her mess you up too."

He nodded. "I've seen the guilt he carries for his cousin's death. He tries to move beyond it, but it seeps out, no matter how sophisticated or cynical he tries to appear." Matt regarded Temple with a look from the heart. "Molina has always tried to prove that Max isn't good enough for you, but a man who feels that deep a guilt, that long, has worth that a man—or a woman—who's never been tested can't guess at."

Temple found herself unable to speak for a few seconds. "Thank you. It's been kind of lonesome defending my druthers this past year."

"That's why I never—"

"Never what?" Temple held her breath, knowing that a revelation hovered.

"It doesn't matter now."

"Yes, it does! It matters that this one person has blighted Max's life, and now yours."

"Temple, I admire your heart in defending Max and would be honored to have it defending me, but I'm . . . indefensible. We're talking here and now, and a woman dead within hours. Molina only came to me privately because if I'm identified as a suspect, her role in my actions will have to come out. I told her I wouldn't say anything—"

"What did she say?"

"She said I damn well wouldn't say anything unless I was brought in for questioning and then I'd have to tell the truth. I think she's hoping to avoid an accounting. She wouldn't tell me much about Vassar's death, except that it was from a fall, and could be judged an accident. Or"—his expression grew even graver—"a suicide."

"Then it's not an obvious murder."

"Does it matter?"

"It does if there's no evidence to charge you with a crime."

"I'm charged already, in my own mind. So it wasn't Kitty O'Connor, it wasn't murder. So Vassar jumped to her death somehow? So I drove her to suicide? I was the last person she ever saw. It must have been something I said. Or did. Or didn't do."

"And you didn't tell Molina exactly what that was?"

"No. She wouldn't tell me the details of the death, and

I wouldn't tell her the details of my . . . assignation. Just how I followed her directions and got there, I thought, unfollowed. And that I was there."

Temple couldn't stifle a smile.

"What?" he asked.

"You and Molina, good Catholics both, tiptoeing around the moment of truth."

"You Unitarians would face it straight up, huh?"

"Yeah! Better than acting like two parallel lines and driving past each other. It reminds me of some crazy Puritan dance where couples don't ever touch. Whew. Molina is *so* not the right person to pursue this case."

"What case? The woman is dead. I was there. End of story."

"Matt, there is so much story you haven't told me."

"And that would make a difference?"

"I think so. And so would Max."

"Kinsella?"

"Yes. He's got to be in on this."

Matt ducked his head. "Well, he already is, in a way."

"You told *him* too! You turned to everyone but me. This . . . Ambrosia chick, Molina, Max, even Max?"

"Yes, I guess I did." He examined the parquet floor between his feet.

"Why? Haven't I proven I have a nose for news, for skullduggery? Didn't I nail the Stripper Killer? Am I so unsympathetic I don't listen to my friends' problems, so stupid that I wouldn't have a clue to how to deal with a stalker, so selfish that I don't care what happens to other people, so . . . useless I can be left out of the real adult talk like a dumb kid—?"

Matt finally looked at her, driven to her defense. "No, Temple. You're smart and tough and kind and true and nervy and beautiful and—"

Her eyes opened. Literally. There was a kind of wonder in what they saw.

"Matt. The other day. When we had an . . . encounter in my hallway. You know, with the groceries. You almost—

Then you blamed yourself for being 'selfish.' Was it because of your situation with Kitty, that you were seeing a way out of it, but just couldn't do it? That it was . . . me?"

He shook his head and shut his eyes in denial even as he said, "Yes," as if confessing a failing.

"Oh." Temple sat back. She thought for a minute. "I'm flattered. And I'm too smart and tough and nervy to let Kitty the Cutter win. So we are in this together, with whoever we can get on our side, sans Molina. Okay? Okay. This means Max and Midnight Louie, too. Louie saved my hide just last night, so that's no measly ally."

Temple had deliberately omitted from her list of admirable attributes the one that had thrilled her the most: beautiful. Really? He thought she was beautiful? Strange how something so shallow could resonate so deep.

Of course she immediately felt guilty for feeling that way.

Max was the one she'd fallen madly, manically, magically in love with, the one she had followed from Minneapolis to Las Vegas, the one she'd lived with at the Circle Ritz. When he had vanished without a word after finishing his magician's gig at the Goliath Hotel, her world stopped. Then Molina had shown up, pushing Temple for information she didn't have on Max's whereabouts, accusing him of a murder discovered at the Goliath the same night he vanished. Temple feared Max was dead too. Molina was sure Max was alive and well somewhere, and a murderer.

Max had come back months later as suddenly as he'd disappeared. It was no one's fault that Matt had come to live at the Ritz in the meantime. That Temple had begun to learn the secrets of Matt's past, begun to be a part of his present. . . .

Max was back, and his reason for vanishing was . . . her safety. Sheer gallantry. He did indeed know about the Goliath's dead man and was afraid the killers had been after him. He had fled to keep Temple safe. Turns out even Max had secrets in his past.

Max was back. He had been her only live-in lover, her only partner on the tracks of true love leading to Matrimony Junction. You didn't throw away a mutually monogamous commitment in the Age of AIDS. You hung with the one who brung you. Who stuck with you. Who didn't deserve to be cut out while he wasn't looking, only because he cared enough about you to leave you for your own good.

Still, it seemed she had been wrong somehow in becoming Matt's friend as he was trying to return to a secular, freshly sexual world from the Catholic priesthood. She had somehow been unfaithful to Max and unfair to Matt, without meaning to, without knowing it.

She clutched the one truth in the whole sordid mess that touched her to the quick. Matt had hoped she could be his salvation. Maybe she hadn't been in a position to help him disarm Miss Kitty before the fact—and she understood that they could never have been intimate without betraying who they were and the very reasons they were tempted to be intimate—but she could sure kick stalker ass now that all had been said and done.

Body Bag

People who don't work in a medical examiner's facility wonder how the staff can do it. How can they take fingerprints from the fire-eaten tips of charred hands? How can they stare headless bodies in the missing face?

Molina inhaled shallowly in the cool corridor, absorbing the sickly scent of decay with its inescapable overlay of orange, the counter-scent deemed most effective. She was reminded not of orange blossoms, the beginning, but the bitter, curled rind. The end.

As a visiting police officer, she had quickly discovered the paradox that perfectly intact bodies are far harder to cope with than the ones bloated or burned beyond recognition.

Vassar's was one of those disturbingly intact bodies. She lay naked on the stainless steel examining table in the autopsy room. As if she could wait for anything anymore.

Despite the trauma of her fatal fall, her skin was simply bruised, as if she'd been in a minor automobile accident. The color was not as pallid as Shangri-La's white stage makeup, but almost normal. She was as fresh as they ever came here. Worse, stripped of her high-fashion clothing and jewelry, she resembled an old-fashioned department-store mannequin underneath. Motionless, naked, as angular as an anvil to which exaggerated female secondary characteristics had been added: full lips abutting a cadaverous cheekbone; full breasts, a ripple of ribs.

She looked as if she could rise and leave any minute, as if her vacant, haughty model's features would animate in an instant. She would yawn or smile. Sit up. Leave. Get on with her life.

Not, Molina thought, once Grizzly Bahr had finished eviscerating her like an Egyptian mummy in the name of forensics.

"This the downed bird?" the ME's voice boomed from Molina's rear. As burly as his nickname, he couldn't avoid brushing against her as he barreled by. He stopped, arrested. "Say, there's almost an expression on her face. Makes you wonder what her last thoughts were."

Molina had noticed it too: a not-quite-expression of surprise and even perhaps a hint of distress. Only extreme trauma left post-mortem expressions on the dead, a death resisted. She'd seen that once, in a victim who had choked on a latex glove, an autistic adult. They'd never determined whether the death was accident . . . or suicide.

"You in for the duration?" Grizzly asked, his virtuoso eyebrows arched to their highest. Either he couldn't believe she really wanted to do this, or he was relishing another opportunity to gross out the civilians, which in his opinion included police officers.

"She's a real mystery," Molina said as she accepted the mouth mask and clear safety goggles he extended. "I want to be the first to know."

"*Hmmm*, may not know much even afterward." He stepped to the corpse's side as if about to ask her to join him in a macabre dance. "Pretty woman. Too skinny for my taste, but at my age I'm not the target audience anymore. The bruises all look impact-induced. Nothing in the thigh and genital area. She wasn't raped."

"She was a call girl."

"They can be raped."

"Not a veteran. Not often."

"This one irritate a client, you think?"

"I have no idea. Maybe a client irritated her."

"And it was such a shock she dove to her death?"

"You know what the multiple choice is: accident, suicide, or homicide."

"Which one would you like it to be?" Bahr's eyes were slightly blurred through the goggles, but Molina found his expression especially avid.

Grizzly Bahr could smell when a cop really burned to make a case.

"In this instance . . . accident would be nice."

Her choice startled him. Homicide lieutenants seldom rooted for an innocent death. Then he shrugged. He was a scientist. Only the evidence would count and that needed to be exhumed from the body before him.

Molina was having an unwished-for epiphany. She had stood through more than a few autopsies, and was used to the ME's droning voice as he or she confided the long, Latinate medical terminology to the confessional of a tape recorder. She was aware of Bahr's spare but invasive motions . . . the long Y incision of the trunk, the grueling revelation of the brain by sawing a literal skullcap off the top of the head.

These actions, this sequence, this ritual and its accompanying inventory of comment were familiar.

Except that now, today, for the first time it reminded her of another ceremony over another table. Altar. The mass. This is my body. This is my blood.

In a way this body and blood were communal property now, and literally community property. Their sacrifice upon the altar of science would free them from the eternal damnation of a known resting place reached by an unknown cause.

Unless of course, the autopsy was completely inconclusive.

Instruments clanged into stainless steel trays. Molina finally heard the inimitable squeaky, sucking sound of latex gloves being stretched and drawn off like alien skin.

Vassar now lay disassembled like the department store mannequin she had evoked earlier.

"No bruises or other marks consistent with the application of force from an outside source," Grizzly Bahr summed up for her ears only, the tape recorder already turned off. "The presence of semen, but no indication of force. A contraceptive implant was the only anomaly in the body. Nothing remarkable."

"Semen?" Molina was startled. "Hookers don't hook without condoms nowadays." Her second thought was chilling. That might be evidence to hang Matt Devine. Was he dumb enough to forego a condom? And even if he was, which she doubted, Vassar certainly wasn't. "How are you going to rule it?"

"Death by misadventure?" He pulled off his mask and grinned, widely. "No, that's only in the murder mysteries, isn't it? Guess your people will have to work on the definition, Lieutenant."

"Guess we will." She didn't have to add that nobody usually cared much about a call girl but her cell phone service.

Wait a minute! Where *was* her cell phone?

"Her things are upstairs?" she asked.

"Bagged and tagged. Just like the remains will soon be."

Molina glanced in passing at the table and its contents as she removed her mask and goggles. Not even a discarded mannequin anymore. Just remains.

"Any next of kin?" Grizzly had paperwork as well as bodies to process.

"Not that we know of. Yet. Maybe the clothes will be more talkative than her body parts."

"In this case, then, clothes would 'make' the woman."

Molina quirked a weary smile at his joke. She didn't expect the expensive labels from any of a dozen casino shopping malls to reveal much more than the extent of Vassar's clothing habit. But a cell phone might be a lot more "talkative."

There was no cell phone.

"Now this doesn't make sense," Molina commented aloud.

The technician in charge was a multi-earringed twenty-something whose eyes were still glued with envy on the slinky, shiny clothes Vassar had worn.

"This stuff is to die for."

Molina avoided the obvious comeback. Most coroner facility mid-level techs were high school grads so ecstatic about the rewarding pay scale that they overcame any nicety about peeling fingerprints off the dead and other unpleasant tasks.

And they lived in a world where black humor was the best defense against depression.

"If any relatives step forward to arrange a funeral," Molina said, "they'll have to find something else to bury her in, that's for sure."

"Oh, these are too cool to bury." The gloved technician pushed the soft silken folds back into their paper bags. Paper was more preservative than plastic when it came to fabrics.

Molina frowned at the iridescent snakeskin purse as it disappeared. One of those glitzy toy purses that cost a bundle but were only big enough to hold credit cards, tight curls of cash, and a decorative lipstick case.

No cell phone.

Vassar had to have carried a cell phone, or a pager.

Where was it?

Beasts of Eden

Max Kinsella stared at his own words on the computer screen with a sense of disappointment.

Temple made writing, and talking, look so easy. With her it was a flow, a part of her personality. He could sling a bit of patter himself. A professional magician had to be a silver-tongued devil to some extent. But when it came to setting word after word down on a computer screen, he found something lacking.

It wasn't as if he hadn't had a head start. Gandolph the Great's memoirs were packed with fascinating stories about debunking phony mediums. Max had taken them up after Gandolph's death last Halloween to finish what his mentor had started.

He was living in the man's house, after all, and one bedroom was crammed with the machines of his stage illusions. The ghost of Orson Welles, former owner of the manse, an amateur magician of note and a film genius, hovered over the place as well.

Why couldn't Max make something of what Gandolph had started?

Maybe he wasn't a writer.

He was probably too tired to worry about this project now, but he was also too wired to sleep. His face and body ached, not a lot, but enough that three ibuprofens didn't totally kill the pain.

Last night had been taxing, to say the least. After weeks of undercover work on both their parts, he and Molina had missed out on capturing the Stripper Killer. While they'd been duking it out *mano-a-mana* in a strip-club parking lot, Temple had been fighting for her life with the killer in another strip-club parking lot.

He'd finally allowed Molina to capture him, knowing no handcuffs would hold him, but the fact left an ugly taste at the back of his throat, like bile.

He'd never gotten into this kind of a macho contest with a woman before and his mid-thirties' mind was old enough that a touch of chivalry cramped his style with the combative lieutenant.

Then to know that she'd made him too late to save Temple anyway, that it had been her hated ex-lover, Rafi Nadir, who had been there to do it . . . the only consolation to Max's ego was that the pepper spray he'd given Temple had helped her hold off the killer until Nadir could come along and deck him.

He was an ex-cop, Nadir, and must still relish a bust, even if his shady present didn't permit him to hang around to get the credit.

Max grinned at the annoying words on the screen. His words, that wouldn't obey and look gracious. Molina would split her spleen to know that her loathed ex had chivalrously come to Temple's rescue.

The Iron Lieutenant had looked pretty spleen-split when he'd left her handcuffed to her own steering wheel. Max chuckled. Never mess with a magician.

Then he frowned. Someone had messed with Gandolph the Great. No one had been charged with his mid-séance murder at the Halloween haunted house attraction. Garry Randolph had been Max's mentor in magic and the counterterrorism life, his only family for years. Max had done nothing to avenge or solve his death except try to finish his book, and to do a mediocre job at that. Temple could help him fix the book, and she might even help him clear up Garry's death.

Max tapped his fingers on the keyboard so lightly that no letters appeared on the screen.

Several psychics and mediums had been present for Garry's death. He had been there in disguise to expose the frauds among them. Garry would say all of them. Someone more open minded, or imaginative, like Temple, would say *most* of them. She had been impressed by a couple of the psychics.

But Garry, he hadn't performed for years. His mission the last years of his life had been revealing the tricks behind the illusions. Unlike the Cloaked Conjuror, he hadn't built a mega-million Las Vegas headlining act out of it. Now the Cloaked Conjuror was facing death threats, and Max had to wonder if Garry's death had been the first act of a plot to kill renegade magicians who gave away trade secrets.

Which brought up the mysterious Synth, supposedly a band of magicians who punished magicians who told. Even Garry's former assistant, Gloria Fuentes, had been found dead a couple months ago in a church parking lot, one of a series of strangled women whose deaths might, or might not, be related.

And now CC had partnered with the strange female magician Shangri-La.

Max ran last night through his head again, but it didn't come out any less cluttered. First there was the realization that Temple was a target for the Stripper Killer, then his own compelling need to reach and protect her. Yes, he was protective of Temple, call it what you would. He was bigger, sadder, wiser. She was the last, best hope the limited life his work as a counterterrorism agent had allowed since his late teens. While he had roamed the world working onstage illusions, he had foiled offstage attempts to kill innocent civilians. It was a career choice he hadn't chosen and no one retired from.

Max was trying to be the first. Gandolph had preceded him in that attempt and Gandolph was dead.

Max wasn't dead yet. He grinned again at the screen. And he sure wasn't a writer. Where there's imperfection, there's hope.

Back to last night. He had tried not to damage Molina to the point where she could press charges, which meant he'd had to take a few blows, yet appear subdued. That was the hardest part. Max had built a life on refusing to be subdued.

When the news of the attack at Baby Doll's had come over Molina's radio, he had raced there to collect Temple after the crime scene officers let her go and whisk her home to the Circle Ritz and the frantic comfort of a man with nothing good in his life but her. Then, restless in the wee hours, he had stolen away from a sleeping Temple to seek out his own kind, the caged Big Cats, trained to perform, who had been saved from fates worse than death to join the Cloaked Conjuror's menagerie. It was the best situation for them, but they were as trapped, in a way, as he was, by what they were and what they could do. Dangerous beasts.

And then she had appeared: the most dangerous game of all. Shangri-La, whose likeness and act were a combination of Japanese Kabuki theater and Kung Fu. He could still see her flying though the air above the stage at the Opium Den like an ax, sharp and lethal, all tattered robes and tongues of sable hair, crimson nails as long as a switch blade, face hidden by dead-white makeup with a scarlet mask defining the cheekbones and eyes. And lips.

She had confronted him on his visit to the big cats, broadcasting contempt and threat. A small woman with major mojo.

He didn't know who she was or where she came from,

but he recognized personal threat when he felt it.

The Synth. She had to be an agent, or perhaps a director, of this mysterious alliance of magicians that had its roots as deeply in the past as the arcane ceremonies of the Masons.

He must find and infiltrate the Synth.

It would be the most dangerous assignment of his career, if he had already been targeted by the shadowy organization. If it existed.

Max read the section he had rewritten on Gandolph:

Garry Randolph reinvented himself twice. He led three lives. The first was as the curious and clever adolescent, enchanted by the idea that he could instill wonder in watching eyes. That was the emerging magician, the teenage prestidigitator, renamed as an inverse of an old Western film star, Scott Randolph. (He had always loved the common name, Garry, with its oddball spelling. Hadn't Garrison Keillor been a plain Gary once, and gotten famous by Easternizing his name on NPR?) Garry Randolph figured that two R's had double the mystique.

Then he progressed from a good amateur magician to a gifted professional. Somewhere in the process he began to believe in his own magic and took on a stage name that reflected that journey: Gandolph the Great. It was an ingenious reference to that most benign of fictional magicians, and a bow to Garry's sixties youth: Gandalf the Gray from The Lord of the Rings *fantasy trilogy, the one man of power strong enough to leave its use to less lethal beings than man or magician, like the hairy-footed, pint-size simple folk called hobbits.*

In an odd way Garry's life mirrored that fictional character.

At the height of his fame and career, he began undercutting his own stage illusions by debunking false mediums, and ultimately, the trickery practiced by magicians.

He ended as he had begun, better known as Garry Randolph than by any stage name. And so he had died. While disguised as a heavily veiled woman medium, in fact, at a phony séance, perhaps murdered by some charlatan's hand.

In death, as in life, his passing through was a mystery. No one has yet been charged in his death, although several persons present had motives. Was he a victim of the ancient Synth? Had he trespassed against the timeless brotherhood of magicians?

Or is this sense of conspiracy only another stage illusion, created to dazzle the ignorant and the suggestible?

There the narrative ended. Perhaps because Max had only questions and no answers. Actually, it read a lot better than he had thought it would while he was writing. But now his thoughts had ricocheted from the unsuspected difficulties of the writing game to the hidden side of the magic world.

If there was a Synth, he had to find it. Then he had to penetrate it, expose it, survive it.

And he could tell no one.

Especially not Temple. He had to do this solo, much as she wanted, needed to help him in his quest. She was grittier than he had imagined. Max's lone-wolf life had precluded real intimacy until he had met Temple at the Guthrie Theater in Minneapolis and broken all his own rules.

She was smart, creative, and otherwise adorable. He'd always understood that he needed to protect her from the dangers of his counterterrorism past. When it came to international politics, good guys made bad enemies.

He hadn't understood, until he was forced into a corner, that she was ready, willing, and able to protect him. She'd stone-walled Molina for months while he was gone. She deserved to know, but she didn't have what the espionage industry called "a need to know."

The Synth was too much an unknown, too risky, to allow Temple to know too much.

Who would even believe such a medieval entity still existed?

Only Garry Randolph, perhaps, and one fact about him was certain.

He was dead. Gone.

Hobbits with Claws

"All things come to he who waits," I tell Miss Midnight Louise.

"I am tired of trite and gender-limiting clichés," she tells me right back.

"The truth is often uncomfortable, but I do not intend to be." I settle back into the soft spot I have dented into the sofa cushion through long custom.

Miss Louise is still sitting upright on the opposite arm, twitching her tail, and she does have a long supple one to twitch.

"We should be ratcheting up the side of this crazy building right now," she tells me. "I know we could eavesdrop an earful on Mr. Matt Devine's patio."

"Eavesdropping through solid glass and wood is a taxing affair."

"Maybe for the senior set," she shoots right back.

"And it would be hard to conceal our presence. The undercover operative is most effective when he—or she—is unseen. Around Miss Temple's digs, a cat, or two, is ho-hum. Although I must admit that our double presence did cause the intimidating lieutenant a certain unease."

"It was *my* unexpected presence that unnerved her. That, and the thought that you might be multiple. What did you do to scar the poor woman's psyche?"

"That lieutenant is no 'poor woman.' Save your sympathy for someone more deserving, like the great white shark in *Jaws*."

"You are referencing stuff way too old for my generation, Pops. Since when did playing the couch potato pass for head's-up investigation?"

At this juncture I hear the key turn in our door. "Since now. Listen and learn, kit."

Sure enough, Miss Temple bustles in and throws her key on a kitchen countertop. Then she snags the portable phone on the coffee table en route to casting herself down right alongside me on the couch Miss Louise finds so hospitable to potatoes.

She hits one digit that I know leads right to a certain cell phone.

On her perch, Miss Louise lifts an airy set of eyebrow hairs.

"Come on," Miss Temple urges the phone, jiggling the sofa cushion unnecessarily as she idly caresses my ears. "Answer!"

Well, who would dare disobey my Miss Temple when she is in crisis mode? Not the phone system.

"Max!" She always sounds so glad to hear his voice. I admit to being a wee bit jealous, and stretch out so that my toes are tickling her thighs.

She returns the favor to my tummy while Louise makes audible growling noises of disgust.

Despise my methods if you must, but they are effective. I am now poised to pick up every nuance of the ensuing conversation and am getting a professional-level massage at the same time. Try *that,* Mike Hammer! I have never gone in for the hard-knocks school of private investigation. If it is that private, it should at least be pleasant.

"You will never guess who was just here," Miss Temple is continuing. "Molina!" she tells him right out before he can exercise his guesser even a little.

Miss Temple is to information dispersal what Exxon is to an oil spill.

"No, it wasn't about your set-to last night. Not at all. It seems she thinks I know another filthy rotten murderer. In fact, she's so hot on this new suspect she has forgotten all about little you."

Mr. Max does not cotton to rivals in any area, even bad ones. I can hear his basso grumble over my low-level purr.

"No, this time she is after Matt. Yeah, Matt. For murder. You know that little enterprise that apparently half of Las Vegas was aiding and abetting him in? Operation Call Girl? Well, the call girl had a big fall and now Molina's trying to figure out a way to keep Matt from being accused of her murder, as he looks like the last person to see her alive.

"No, I do *not* think he did it! But neither is he helping out Molina with lots of alibis and denials. And none of you—none!—told me about Kitty the Cutter's turning stalker and forcing Matt into a corner. We need to find and expose that psycho before she gets more people killed. Why 'we'? Because she hates you most of all and if she can do this to Matt, who she never even knew from Adam until a few months ago, think what she could cook up for you. Or me."

Then Miss Temple does something uncharacteristic. She leans back into the sofa and listens. And listens.

I can learn nothing from good listeners, only world-class talkers.

Miss Midnight Louise yawns and casts me a bored glance.

I realize that I no longer look good.

Miss Temple rises, phone still clapped to ear. She heads for her bedroom. "I will get over there as soon as I can," she is saying.

I know she will change clothes first. She has not exactly had time to concoct a wardrobe today.

Miss Louise gives her ruff a lick and a promise and leaps

down to the floor. She is even hotter to trot than my Miss Temple.

I give up my Nero Wolfe spot and reluctantly push myself upright. "It looks like we need to do some fieldwork," I admit. "My usual sources will be going in for recriminations before they get down to business."

"So we head for—?" Miss Louise is already at the French doors, gazing over her fluffed shoulder at me. She would be as cute as a cricket were it not for the expression of hunt-lust on her piquant face.

"The Goliath Hotel. We need to do some firsthand scouting on the scene of the crime."

I leap up and loosen the latch with one practiced blow from my mighty paw. The door bounces ajar and Miss Louise noses through it without mewing so much as a thank-you for my doorman service.

That is what a dude gets for being a gentleman toward the weaker sex.

The Man That Got Away

Temple gathered several admiring, and a few envious, looks as she spurted her new red Miata through the clogged Strip traffic, the wind currying her hair. All she needed was a long white scarf and she would be the Isadora Duncan of the twenty-first century, prima donna dancer and unintentional suicide.

The thought slowed her down to a decorous forty miles an hour even though her mind was still supercharged.

Little did they know that her apparently carefree spin to Max's house was a matter of life and death.

She hadn't had a minute to calm down and consider things. First she got a case of pre-breakfast bad-news indigestion from Molina, who she knew was an enemy, followed by multiple doses of kept-in-the-dark-itis from everyone she thought was a friend.

Even with her thoughts in chaos, she could see that the tenuous relationships of a number of people, all of whom she knew and some of whom she loved or liked, were teetering on the brink of a disaster engineered by a common but elusive enemy.

On the drive she had a chance for the first time to think about the victim. "A call girl." It conjured images from B movies of faceless women with cynical smiles as shallow as their cleavage was deep. Bit-part players who were there only as a fleeting sex/love interest/motivator for the weary PI or cop, for a bit of smacking around by the mob boss, for dying hard and too soon to earn little more than minimum pay until the next film.

She just couldn't picture Matt in that scene. That desperate.

But then she hadn't really seen or been told what was going on for some time.

But a call girl? Paid-for sex with a sleazy stranger? If that wasn't a mortal sin in his church, what was? It made no sense. Or . . . maybe it did. A call girl was already damned, according to strict religions. Was sex with a sinner less damning than sex with a—?

Temple decided not to mull that question while she was driving when she almost wandered into the same lane that had been staked out by a Humvee. Oops!

Sex and Matt Devine didn't make any sense, period. She'd never seen anyone who took it as seriously as he did. Kitty O'Connor had to have gotten under his skin with a lot more than a razor blade.

She squealed onto Max's street, then braked fast to avoid attracting, er, attention.

She parked four houses away, looked around, then hiked to his door, nervous and impatient and not feeling at all inconspicuous.

Max was there waiting to open it. He admitted her into the high-security inner sanctum that this former home of Orson Welles and Gandolph the Great had become.

Its interior shadows felt like an oasis from the relentless Las Vegas sunshine and blazing cynicism.

Temple leaned against the closed door behind her and breathed deep sighs of relief. Max took her hands. Their warmth made her realize how cold her fingers were.

"You've had a rough morning," he said.

"It was a rough night, then . . . Molina first thing."

"I can't imagine anything worse than waking up to Molina. I should have stayed."

"No." Temple pushed her sinking spine off the temporary brace of Max's solid-steel front door. "She would have found you. She walked right into my bedroom."

"I bet. Nosy Parker." He noticed her confusion and laughed. "British expression for a snoop. Come on. Let's try breakfast sans Molina. I haven't had much sleep since I left you either. I'm having a case of what I think is called writer's block."

Temple followed him down the house's dark halls to the kitchen. The place was a quintessential magician's residence: a maze of dim passages that opened onto strange, large, enthralling rooms.

The kitchen was one of them. State-of-the-art, filled with stainless steel food machines with a canopy of contrasting copper-pan warmth above. Like a sunset-metal sky.

Max whisked up a giant omelet in one of the copper pans and iced it with hot raspberry chipolte sauce. Goblets of cranberry juice shone like jewels as Temple and Max settled on stools at the huge island unit to eat.

Temple hooked her heels over the highest rung of her stool and ingested a tricolor of pepper strips, bland eggs, and mushrooms, all heated up by the sweet-spicy sauce.

For a moment everything ugly drew back, like reality does when you feel about to faint, or to go down the biggest dip on a roller-coaster.

"So . . . writer's block? You?" she asked. Maybe jeered a little. It wasn't often she was expert at something and he was the amateur.

Max scratched his cheekbone where the asphalt burns

from last night were hardening into scabs. Chalk up another nasty surprise to Molina.

"Molina can really get that mean?" She nodded at his face.

"Cops who don't make collars fast and hard risk losing their weapons, and their suspect." Max shrugged. "I have no complaints. I asked for it, and she did it by the book. Well, maybe she enjoyed it a bit too much, but I suspect she enjoys so little of anything that I don't mind giving her a thrill."

"Oooh. Odious idea. She seems to despise you even more now than before. Just because you got away?"

Max's shrug was slightly uneasy the second time. Temple had the oddest notion that he wasn't telling her something.

"I threw every trick in the book at her to get away in time to race to your rescue." He shook his head at the memory. "That probably didn't sit too well. She just thought I wasn't fighting fair, and anyway, she didn't believe me that you were in danger . . . until the news came over her car radio." Max chuckled. "She was not happy with it."

"What, that I was alive?"

"No, that you were alive and the uniform cops had the Stripper Killer in custody."

"My being alive didn't tick her off at all? Then what's the use?"

"She doesn't want you harmed, Temple, just out of her hair. I, on the other hand, want you in my hair, so let's stop talking about Molina."

At this welcome invitation, Temple ran her fingers through the thick dark hair at his . . . well, temple.

Max flinched and she jerked her hand away.

"Guess that's another spot that kowtowed to parking lot pavement last night," he admitted.

"That must have been some fight. I wish I'd seen it."

"No thanks. One car did come by, shining its headlights on us, but otherwise that fiasco was dark-of-night anonymous. It wasn't a shining moment for either of us."

"Speaking of shining moments, what's happening with your new writing career?"

"I was rereading my expansion of Gandolph's book. I had no idea putting one word down after another could be so frustrating. It's not saying what I want to say, it's not saying what Gandolph would want me to say. Trying to finish his book was a nice idea, but I don't think I'm up to it."

Temple, busy eating, nodded.

"Exposing fake mediums had become Gandolph's life work," Max went on. "Now that he's dead, I wanted to fashion a worthy memorial for him. But—" He spread his large bony hands that must have overwhelmed a keyboard. "The student is not worthy of his instructor. Maybe I don't care enough about exposing frauds. Maybe I feel they are us."

"Well, after this morning, I don't know that I can disagree with you."

Max had only played with the omelet of his creation. Temple watched his fork tines draw stucco-like patterns on his plate.

"You're feeling betrayed," he said.

"*Ye-es*! Everybody I know was talking to everybody else, except me. What's wrong with me that none of you trust me?"

"It's not that we don't trust you. We don't trust ourselves to do right by you."

"Molina?"

Max smiled, as she had hoped he might. Even when she had a legitimate grievance she couldn't stand to make someone she cared about glum.

"Not Molina," he said. "Molina would never insult you by treading around your feelings. It's not that we don't care about you, Temple. It's that we care too much."

"We, White Man?"

"Me." Max made a face as he carved bloody inroads of

chipolte sauce into his untouched omelet. "And probably Matt Devine."

"Great. So being an ignorant idiot becomes me. It's the way you guys love to see me."

"Being alive is the way we love to see you."

"You really think that was at stake?"

"You don't know Kitty O'Connor like I know Kitty O'Connor. And, I suppose, as Devine does now."

Temple thought about that. She swigged a bunch of cranberry juice and thought about it.

"Oh, my God."

She looked into Max's eyes, mild blue now, unabetted by the magician's panther-green contact lenses that he had used as a professional adjunct. "It's a parallel, isn't it? You, and now Matt. What . . . seventeen years apart? Did you see it the moment I called?"

"No. I had to brood about it while you were on the way over."

"Writer's block will do that to you. Make you brood."

"So you're saying, paradoxically, that in writing, a *block* is a sign of progress?"

"It's a sign of no progress. But . . . you have to not get anywhere to get somewhere."

"So where have you gotten, my darling ignorant idiot?"

"You're sorry, aren't you?"

"Yes, especially now that you've caught us out protecting you. *Mea culpa*."

She had heard the Latin phrase from Matt, the ex-priest, and knew what it meant. *My fault.*

"*Mea maxima culpa*," she retorted, having heard the ritual follow-up, also from Matt.

Max, good Irish-Catholic lad that he had been, only nodded. *Mea maxima culpa. My most grievous fault.* He got up and poured two cups from the coffeemaker, dosing them with swigs of Bailey's Irish Cream.

Then he came back and waited for her to piece out the truth that had been kept from her for her own good, the kind of truth that hurts worse than any deliberate attack.

"Matt hit on it, way back when," she began. "When he said that maybe Kitty had arranged your cousin's death. There you and Sean were in northern Ireland, back there before any hint of truce between the Protestants and the Catholics. Two naive American teenagers visiting the Auld Sod. And there was Kathleen O'Connor. God, I wish I'd seen her, Max. I know she's been lurking around now, but she must have been really gorgeous back then, teen angel symbol of the beloved country's tortuous history and noble fight for freedom from hundreds of years of British domination. And you and your cousin Sean, kicking up your heels from an American high school graduation. Drinking in pubs! Flirting with the colleens. On your own, together. Cousins and Irish-American soul brothers getting your ire up about centuries of injustice in the Auld Country. Away from your parents, the nuns and priests, and so hoping to get laid. Have I got it?"

"Amazingly well for a Protestant and a Scots/English/French lass and a grown girl."

"It was spring break, European-style. Irish Spring. And you, Max, you devil, you amateur magician who may have been a twelve-year-old geek but you were growing into your post-adolescent sexy guy, you were dueling Sean for who could drink the most and get the girl. And Kitty let you be the one."

"Stupid adolescent competition. We were like colts in a field, kicking up our heels, too young to know what any of it meant, the sex or the politics."

"You won the lady fair. While you were dallying with her, Sean consoled himself with a pint of Guinness. In a Protestant pub that had been targeted for an IRA bomb. So you lost your innocence, in every possible sense of the word. Except you didn't lose anything, Max. She spoiled it."

He nodded. "Yes, she did. Forever. You could say I did some good with my years of covert counterterrorism work later. I saved lives. I know I did. But none of them were the one life I wanted, needed, to save. I never loved. Until you. And then I couldn't be there when you needed me because of that past. Then she came again, and, indirectly, she was threatening you.

"If she knew how much Devine cared about you, you would be Sean. Dead. That is the one thing that he and I believe in common."

"You . . . believe that he cares that much about me?"

"Who could not?" Max shook his head, as if angered by an invisible gnat that never stopped flitting in front of his eyes. "Temple, I worry that you don't really know how much I care about you."

"You've got a lot on your mind—"

"No. I've always had you on my mind, first and foremost. On how to keep my damnable past from hurting you, our future. Maybe I had no right to contemplate a future."

"You more than anybody, Max. After that woman tried to taint it forever. We've got to be happy, just to piss off Kathleen O'Connor."

He laughed then. "You always do that. Turn my black Irish depression inside out. I admit I'm jealous of your neighbor. Our neighbor." He smiled at the surroundings, claiming them again. Claiming her because she'd told him to.

"And now . . . irony of ironies." Max sighed theatrically. "We've become co-conspirators, Devine and I, as Sean and I never had a chance to be. She divides and conquers, Miss Kitty O'Connor, but, like all extremists, she also unites where she doesn't intend to."

"Amen!" Temple said. "She's united us here and now. Max, I hate what she's done to you, and I hate what's she's done to me. We've got to stop her."

They sealed the vow with a cranberry juice toast.

Peeping Tomcat

I must admit that it sometimes comes in handy to have a minion.

I mean, a minor partner. Junior partner? Maybe Junior Miss partner better describes it.

Whatever you want to call it, Midnight, Inc. makes a most auspicious debut at the Goliath Hotel and Casino, as Miss Midnight Louise and I embark on our first intentional venture as a crime-fighting team.

We enter the premises by my favorite route: the hotel kitchens.

It is not only the plenteous foodstuffs that attract the seasoned senses of Midnight Louie. What pulls my chain is not calories, but confusion.

You see, I have never encountered a commercial kitchen that was not in a constant state of chaos. Where there is chaos, there is opportunity for the canny operative.

When large numbers of people are running around like fish with their heads cut off (in fact, large numbers of fish are lying around here with their heads cut off), it is easier for those of Louise's and my stripe (even though we are solid color) to tiptoe unseen through the blizzard of discarded meat wrappers, flying greens, and peevishly hurled chefs' hats.

I particularly like the chefs' hats. They are as big and puffy as giant souffles and are just the thing to duck and take cover under. The ritzier the establishment the kitchen serves, the more likelihood of errant chefs' hats.

In fact, Louise and I are inching along under two of the same when she smothers a squeak of outrage. It seems a runaway lobster has pinched her tail.

We are in a protected corner of the kitchen, crouched between a huge trash can and a stainless steel steam table. I am not averse to a little lobster now and then, but this is not a little lobster and it is in a distressingly lively condition.

It is all I can do to pry its bony claws off my partner's posterior. I consider asking it a question or two, but after studying those beady little eyes on their creepy stalks I decide that the creature's brain is as little and creepy as the rest of it, and prod Louise on. Pinching an inch really gets her moving now.

We dash under the steam table and make our way to the constantly swinging door to the dining room. Getting through this aperture is like dashing through the blades of a fan set on high. And then there are the flying feet that dominate the space for the few seconds the door is open.

"Talk about Scylla and Charybdis," I mutter.

"Friends of yours?" Miss Louise asks.

There is no use explaining a classical education to a classless street cat, so I tell her to follow me when ready and hitch a ride on a pair of thick-soled sneakers. I take it on the chin a few times, but the busy waiter mistakes my hide for some floor flotsam unworthy of glancing at, so I am soon concealed under a tray stand in the restaurant proper.

I watch the swinging door. Nothing but footwear comes through.

Is it possible that Midnight Louise does not have the

nerve her old man—I mean, her senior partner—was born with?

While one part of me is feeling smug, the other part is feeling disappointed. I hate to be torn between two emotions. In fact, I hate emotion. It is the enemy of the effective operative.

While I am dueling my own mind, something large falls past my vision to the floor. It is Midnight Louise!

"How did you get out here?" I ask. "I had my eyes on the door the whole time."

"Maybe so, Pop, but you probably had them glued to the floor. I opted for the over-the-pole route."

"Huh?"

"Why walk when you can fly? They had some sort of fluffy dessert the size of a Himalayan chocolate-point under this nice shiny stainless steel dome. I ditched the dessert and took its place. Baked Alaska, they called it. Apparently it was rare and expensive, but I cannot see why. It was mostly air. Though it *was* chilly."

Miss Midnight Louise gives a theatrical little shudder.

"And the waiter did not find you a bit heavy for one of these airy desserts?"

"Of course, and I wanted him to. All I had to do was wiggle a bit after we were safely through the door. He dropped the platter and its dome faster than you can say 'Baked Alaska,' and I was away and out of sight before you could say 'Bananas Foster.' "

"I would never say any of those obnoxious phrases. 'Bananas Foster' sounds like he should have been in partnership with Bugsy Siegel. Let us leave this high-priced dessert haven and head for the parts of the joint where we can pick up some scuttlebutt."

Louise pauses only to lick a bit of Alaska snow from her formerly jet-black whiskers. Then she joins me in a game of hide-and-seek through the restaurant and out into the vast noisy area of the Goliath casinos.

Here everybody's eye is on the cards or the dice or the spinning cherries. As long as we do not work at attracting attention, we can go as unnoticed as a pair of deuces next to the makings of a royal flush.

I sit under an unoccupied slot machine stool to gaze at the ersatz heaven above, a neon night sky that overarches the gaming area like a stained-glass ceiling.

"That is where the little doll landed," I tell Louise. "It is a false ceiling. We need to get up there and check it out."

Louise makes a face.

"You would look pretty funny if your whiskers froze in that position," I tell her.

"You mean that we will have to get 'down' there, Pop. That means taking an elevator up. We are not exactly routine riders."

"Tut tut. Nothing is routine in Las Vegas. Follow me."

I dart and dash my way around the floor until I spy an elevator. This is tough, as it is disguised as a pagan temple door, the Goliath's decorative theme being biblical. The floor is a piece of cake, though, maybe even Baked Alaska. Las Vegas hotels know better than most that bright, busy carpet designs will hide a lot of spills for a long time. Maybe the killer, if there is one, thought that a lot of neon would hide a high-class call girl's body.

Anyway, Louise and I blend into the carpet's black background fronting the Mardi Gras of carnival colors and no one so much as spots us.

I dive behind the convenient cylinder of sand meant for dousing cigarettes. It is right next to the elevator door. Louise has to make do with sheltering under a potted palm.

A few people come and go, taking the elevator. I wait. I want a crowd. Finally a knot of tourists toting Aladdin DESERT PASSAGE shopping bags ankles along and I ankle right after them through the open elevator doors. Those extended claws I hear ripping carpet behind me are Midnight Louise's dainty little shivs.

She gets with the program faster than she did on her acceleration, though, and hops into a shopping bag. The owner glares at the man beside her, as if he had brushed her precious bag.

I am not exactly shopping bag material, but I snag a bit of ribbon from a package another tourist is toting and push my head through it. The man who was glared at looks down, ready to pass on the courtesy. There I sit as tame as a toy poodle, a collar of fuchsia ribbon adding luster to the muscled dignity of my neck.

His lip pulls back as if to snarl, but he would look silly behaving so doggishly toward a pet pussycat, so he clears his throat instead.

The laden ladies debark on floor six and so do we.

Louise has wriggled out of the bag as the women were fighting their way forward to the doors, so we both dart around the corner to take cover in the refreshment bay next to the elevators, where the ice machine is gurgling as if it was terminally ill. I imagine all ice machines in Vegas must be ready to give up the ghost from overuse.

When the coast is clear (okay, there is no coast anywhere near Las Vegas; this is just an expression we hard-boiled dudes like to use), Louise and I loft to the wooden railing of the balcony overlooking the neon sky now three floors or so below us.

We would gasp if we could. Even from here we can see the CRIME SCENE DO NOT CROSS tape twined above a particularly purple patch of neon below. The lurid yellow with its black lettering does not look in the least like the jewel-tone spirit of neon lighting. No sirree, bobcat!

"*Hmmm,*" Miss Louise observes, and she is not purring. "I detect a certain reflective quality from below. I say it only *looks* like a fragile web of neon tubing. I say there's a solid surface down there. What else would they affix that crime scene tape to?"

With that she flips over the edge, digging her built-in pitons into the wooden rail-cap. Dangling, she winks. "See you down below, Pop." And the chit lets go.

I nearly swallow my canines.

And then I nearly barf them back up when I see she has made a perfect four-point landing on the wooden railing a floor below.

She repeats the maneuver and is yet another floor below me.

Well! I cannot allow a mere junior partner to out-acrobat me! Even if I outweigh her two times over.

Not for me those agile twists and turns. I shut my eyes and jump. Luckily, I land on the railing below. It is a perfect four-point landing: my set of two front shivs and my two front teeth. I am hanging by a pair of canines, so there is nothing to do but let go and repeat the trick a floor lower.

So we both get to the railing that overlooks the neon ceiling, only my teeth hurt and Louise's do not. At least I will not have to pay for braces for her. *Ouch*!

"Pretty awesome with the ivories," Louise says, sounding sincere.

I grin knowingly, not being able to talk yet.

However, I do see from this nearer perch that something indeed covers the dreadful neon sky below: call it Plexiglas, or Lucite, or just plain plastic, it is tough, so low-profile it is virtually invisible, and highly supportive. Kind of like the way I am with my Miss Temple.

I take one last leap, on faith, and do a belly flop onto a floor of see-through plastic. Louise lands beside me and rolls away from any too-solid impact.

I grit what is left of my teeth.

But she is not concerned with how we got here. She is sniffing around like a prime-time news-show bloodhound.

"Mania by Armani," she diagnoses.

"What is that? A rock group or a terrorist cadre?"

"Very expensive perfume. Very Rodeo Drive."

I am not about to descend to a name-dropping contest with the likes of Midnight Louise, who hangs out at the Crystal Phoenix and is up on the latest fashion victim trends, so I rely on my sterling sense of deduction to get back in the game.

"Costly scents only confirm that the call girl was high dollar."

Louise wrinkles her shiny black nose. She could use some powdering, but far be it from me to tell her. Right now she is wrinkling it as she squints up into the light-spangled actual ceiling high above.

"Star-gazing?" I ask.

"I am wondering who might be accustomed to hanging out up there and have seen something."

"Nobody who would talk to us," I point out.

"Maybe not." She begins to sniff the area inside the crime-scene tape, which I think is a rather silly gesture.

"It must have irritated the cops to have a body found in thin air," I say. "None of the normal procedure would quite work."

She is still sniffing and I confess I feel a certain embarrassment, as it is such a doggish occupation. I have always relied on using my noggin, as opposed to my nose. But I cannot deny that an occasional whiff has helped me figure out a modus operandi now and again.

"Leather," Miss Louise pronounces, lifting her petite nose as if to wrinkle it like an elephant's gross proboscis.

"Shoes, belt, or handbag, no doubt."

Since she is vacuuming the area I feel obliged to put my face to the transparent floor as well. Well, well. I spot some spider-web shatters in the clear Plexiglas and point them out to Louise.

She gets excited and runs around like the Maltese proboscis, Nose E. the drug- and bomb-sniffing dog I have worked with, reluctantly, before. "Good work! The shattering matches the exact position of the body. The police may not have left any convenient tape to outline the corpse's location, but we have an impression, no matter how cloudy."

I take the long view Miss Louise suggests and observe that it indeed etches a ghostlike swastika image of a human form into the transparent surface.

"Wait, Louise! Stop that disgusting sniffing and do not move. This stuff would not shatter. This looks like a glass ceiling, a thick, industrial-strength glass ceiling, but it must be extra-strength plastic. It is inset into panels and with all those flatfoots walking around up here, a weakened framework could give at any moment from a weight as dainty as a butterfly."

Louise's eyes grow as big as the twenty-four-karat-gold charger plates they use in the upscale restaurants.

"How are we going to get off of here?" she wonders quite logically.

Luckily, I have had a close encounter with a bunch of neon before. These touchy gas-filled tubes need maintenance like flowers need rain. There has got to be an access tunnel somewhere.

Besides. We are in Eye in the Sky territory. Despite the apparent transparency of the neon ceiling, surveillance cameras must be filming away somewhere.

Surveillance cameras! That is who—or what, rather—would talk to us, if we can just find command central.

First things first.

"I suggest," I tell Miss Louise, "that you crawl on your belly like a snake. Fast!"

She melts into the supine position with gratifying speed. I only remember to assume it myself after a few seconds of smirking. The fact is I have already spotted our exit, which is disguised as a mirrored lozenge on the surrounding rim of wall.

So we elbow-crawl like soldiers carrying rifles under an iron curtain to the perimeter. (That is how we talk in the army.)

I run my shivs over the mirror frame until it snaps ajar.

"Devious," Louise comments.

I cannot be sure if she is referring to the mechanism or me, but I will take the credit.

I usher her through with a gentlemanly gesture and follow fast upon my own good manners.

We are in a tunnel, but it is of ample size, at least for Miss Louise, who slithers through to the other side like a black feather boa animated by a Slinky. I have to do a little more grunt work to maneuver my masculine frame through, but we both tumble out into another world.

"Awesome!" Louise comments in the patois of her unimaginative generation.

I have seen it all before. The high-tech hardware, the Mondrian wallpaper of small TV screens showing bird's-eye views of the gaming tables below. There is a guy in a dark uniform seated before this banquet of visual eye-dropping, his head jerking slightly from scanning screen after screen so he resembles a robot.

"Ingenious," I whisper in her pink-lined little ear. "The surveillance is done from a circular perimeter, in the round, so to speak."

"Then it should have captured the woman falling from above."

"Yes. But the police have taken those tapes by now. I believe they are recorded over every-so-many hours."

"Phooey," says Louise. "You are probably right, for once in your life."

"Apparently I was right twice, or you would not be here," I point out.

It takes her a minute to realize that this is probably a compliment and maybe even a concession, although nothing one could take to the *People's Court*.

"There has got be someone else who saw something from one of the higher floors," she hisses at me, "even if the police have hogged the surveillance tapes."

"I would not call it 'hogging.' It is their job, after all."

"Listen," Miss Louise snarls as if I am the enemy when I am only an innocent, helpful dude who does not deserve snarls. "Mr. Matt was nice to me when I was new in town, as he was. He let me crash at his pad for a while. I am not about to let him swing for what has to be a frame-up."

"Uh, they do not hang people nowadays."

"Whatever! We need to figure out what floor the lady took a dive from, and find a witness who saw her go over."

I shrug. I am sure the police have moved heaven and earth and a bunch of neon to figure out the same thing. We might be better off eavesdropping on the conversations of our nearest and dearest, except that I doubt that Lieutenant

Molina will ever again obligingly stomp into the Circle Ritz and reveal much about the case, now that she has got Miss Temple's wind up.

It is no big trick for us to reach the regular-size door, tease it open, and duck out. We are the same color as most of the decor in the surveillance chamber.

After we dart down a nondescript hall or two and through a door, we are back in the hotel's public areas, no one the wiser, including us.

As we pause to catch up to our breaths, I note the obvious. "From the shape shattered into the glass, the victim did fall facedown onto the surface. That bespeaks a suicide as much as a homicide."

"You are saying that after a dalliance with Mr. Matt the lady in question would rather dive than live?"

I regard Louise's incredulous expression and realize that she is another female who has fallen under the influence of Miss Temple's favorite path not taken.

"He could have pushed her."

"Why?"

"Maybe he did not want any witnesses to his fall from grace."

"He was not the one who fell!"

"Not literally. I am merely thinking like a human. So sue me."

"I never want to see your sorry hide on the *People's Court* again."

"We did win, after all."

"After a lot of embarrassing revelations."

"I do not know what is embarrassing about being abducted by a Hollywood has-been starlet who sends me for unnecessary surgery because she erroneously believes I got her precious Persian princess, the Divine Yvette, in the family way."

"The name of the game nowadays is 'blame the victim.' Besides, it seems to me that you go out of your way even when not in court to deny paternity. Methinks thou dost protest too much."

"Do not quote Shakespeare at me, Louise. What does he know about it? He never had any kits, and may not have had any plays, to hear the scholars debate the, er, issue."

But Miss Louise is busy eyeing the elevators, already dismissing my notorious day in court. "There must be someone with an open eye on the upper levels. I am going up and will scout around."

Of course I am obligated to accompany her. And of course my superior height and strength are called upon to summon the elevator.

I bound up to press the call button, then groom the hairs between my toes, which are a continuing problem for an older guy. They grow like weeds, or Andy Rooney's eyebrows!

Luckily the car that whisks to answer our summons is empty. The hour is before dinner and after cocktails, so the people are either ensconced in the lounges or up in their rooms debating how to dine.

We get off, arbitrarily (that is to say at Miss Louise's suggestion) on floor twenty.

It is a nice round number and I waft up to the railing to gaze down on the killing field below. *Oops!* It is a lot harder balancing like a window-washer on the twentieth floor railing than the fifth. Given my druthers, I would take the fifth.

I feel a jerk on my extremity. Louise has taken a tiger by the tail under the guise of preventing a domestic accident. A domestic feline accident.

"Do not be dumb, Popster! At your age you could lose your balance and fall."

I am not interested in demeaning speculations on the part of my upstart partner. I have spotted a witness, dead ahead about 350 feet, its claws clutching the opposite railing about as desperately as mine own. And this bird speaks!

I jump down, nearly flattening my solicitous partner, and race around the soft angles that make up this central atrium.

"What?" she cries. "Have you gone nuts? What?"

I have no time to answer foolish questions; my quarry

might fly the coop, which it shows evidence of having done already.

In about four minutes of mad rush, I reach the opposite position and—*Oh say can you see!*—find my witness still there.

It is not quite a flag of red, white, and blue, but it is white and blue, with a touch of orange.

"Pretty boy," it greets me warmly.

"You getting inappropriately personal, or referring to yourself, I hope?" I ask.

"Pretty boy," it repeats.

Louise eyes the stripes of black and blue on my discovery's back. "Daddy Dimmest, this is a jailbird. You cannot trust a word he croaks out."

"Pretty boy," my new friend produces promptly after eyeing Louise.

Obviously, he has indeed been in stir too long.

Still, I am encouraged by the encounter. He is a small chap, more white than blue and easily overlooked in the Goliath's gaudy multistory atrium, which is crammed with luxurious greenery on the upper floors.

One cannot blame the fellow for thinking the place was freewheeling.

He is so naive it has not yet occurred to him that, were Louise and I not trained investigators, we would as soon eat him as listen to him.

"So how long have you been on the lam?" I inquire casually.

He tilts his head and gazes far below. "The night sky below has dimmed and blazed six times."

I nod significantly at Louise. "Three moons ago."

"Moons? You mean suns. 'Days' would make it even clearer, Hiawatha."

"What are you doing up here all alone, son?" I say.

Midnight Louise tries not to gag when she hears my avuncular "son."

The little fellow tries to tuck his head under his wing. "Lost," he mutters in a muffled but shrill tone.

"Aw, what shame. My partner and I specialize in missing persons."

"I just wanted a glide around the Big Space."

"Who can blame you? I myself have a yen for the open road."

"What is a road?"

"A . . . Big Space, only low, flat and narrow."

"That does not make sense." He wrinkles the down on his pale forehead.

I notice he has a yap on him that is horny and curved like a lobster claw. One would not wish to be this guy's chew toy. And the claws on his unnatural two feet look pretty ragged too. Though he is small, he is no pushover.

"What is your name?" Louise is asking, grimacing to show her sharp front teeth.

He hides his head under his navy-blue vest again. "Blues Brother, tweetheart, and I do not want to hear any titters about that. My owner is a big film fan."

"So how did you get out here in the Big Space, BB?" she asks.

"Broke out. Thought I'd tool around the neighborhood. Only it is bigger than I thought, and I can't find a thing to eat except some crumbs the people leave. Also it is hard ducking below that bright, glowing ceiling."

"So how did you end up on an upper floor of the Goliath in the first place?" I ask. The seasoned operative likes to start at the beginning.

"I was imported."

"Obviously," Miss Louise notes. "Your kind of bird is not native to the US. You are an exotic pet."

BB fluffs his feathers modestly. "I like to think so too. It is the usual story: raised in captivity, sold to the first bidder, caged and asked to do stupid pet tricks, not even on *Letterman,* which might be worth it."

"No mystery why you flew the coop, but I still would like to know why the Goliath? Why not take a spin around the home neighborhood?"

"And why this floor," Louise puts in, getting my drift at last.

He cocks his small, cagy head. For such a little thing he is a pretty good stool pigeon. "I thought everybody knew. Floor twenty is reserved for pet owners, and therefore pets. The place is crawling with cats, dogs, iguanas, and exotic birds."

"So how long have you been freewheeling?" I ask casually.

"Couple of days, as far as I can tell by the unnatural light in this place. I haven't seen an outside window since I took off."

Louise and I exchange glances that play the same unspoken melody, "Blue Bird of Happiness."

"Where were you when the dame took a dive?"

"Minding my own business," BB says indignantly. "Sleeping on the twenty-fourth-floor railing."

"So you did not see a thing," Louise finishes sourly.

"I did not say that. I heard something."

My ears perk up. This is the perfect witness of the animal sort. It can hear and talk. If Dr. Dolittle talked to the animals, this bird listens to the humans.

Miss Louise cannot wait to finesse a confession from the blue bird. "What did you hear?"

"Someone chattering away near the circular perch."

"You mean this railing we are all hanging onto with our best shivs?"

He gives me the half-shut eye. "I can sleep up here. What is your problem?"

I try not to teeter, but it is difficult. "What floor were they on?"

"The free air has no number."

Oh, Mother Macaw! The fellow has a New Age streak.

"The ascending cages have numbers written above them on every level," I point out. "Surely you can read numbers. Or maybe you cannot."

"Hey! I know my numbers. My ABCs too." By now his tiny

wings are flapping and rustling up quite the breeze. "It was floor twenty and four."

I swallow a grin. Some types would send their own mothers up the Amazon to cages in Kalamazoo just to prove they knew what they were talking about.

"Which door?" I press.

"They are all alike."

"No, they are not. They have numbers too, but no doubt your eyes are not good enough to read them at such a distance."

"My eyes are as good as my ABCs." Feathers much ruffled, he takes off from the "perch," leaving Louise and me clinging for dear life with no witness to interrogate.

"You did it," she charges with a snarl. "You annoyed one of the few species of talking birds into shutting up. This must be a record even for you."

Before I can talk myself into defending myself, I note that our source has landed.

On the "perch" in front of the door to room 2488.

Louise and I bound down to the carpeted hall in sync and hasten around the endless circling hall to the elevators. Once again I bound up to call an "Up" car. (You notice that it is the senior partner of the firm who has to do all the repetitive bounding to call an elevator.)

It is empty and we dash in before the doors decide to do any truncating of our fifth (in my case, sixth) member.

Again I leap up, even higher this time, almost elbow-height on the Mystifying Max by my reckoning, to punch the button to the twenty-fourth floor. At least the buttons respond to punching which does not require that pesky opposable thumb common to monkeys and other higher forms of lowlife to operate.

Finally we race down the hall to vault up beside Blues Brother, who has puffed up his chest feathers in a futile attempt at approximating pecs and hair.

Down we look . . . ooooh, a long, long way. We spot the tiny yellow-and-black signage of crime-scene tape, sitting like a bee on the huge, elaborate flower of pulsing neon below.

"Think the cops have figured this out yet?" Miss Louise asks me.

I shrug, a mistake. I almost lose it. My balance. I decide to fall backward onto the hall carpet and throw another question up at Blues Brother.

"You said you heard something before you saw the dame fall. What was it you heard?"

"Something odd."

"Which was?"

"Pretty bird."

"Will you cut out the chorus? You must hear that tired old line as often as I am forced to listen to renditions of 'Here, kitty, kitty' from every street corner, but that is no excuse for resorting to it every time you cannot think of anything new and interesting to say."

"You do not understand," BB chirps.

Miss Midnight Louise gives a Cheshire cheesy smile you find in illustrated books by Englishmen. She loves to think that I do not understand anything.

"She did not see me, the woman who flew," BB goes on. "She was speaking to the air, and then the next thing I saw she was fluttering down, down, down, like she thought she was me. Like she thought she was a bird." One onyx-shiny dark eye quirks at the pulsing neon ocean below. "She did not land like a pretty bird, though. Pretty bird," he finishes up on a wistful note. "I wish I could go home where it is safe."

Well, call me the Wizard of Oz, but I have an idea on that score and it is not a big balloon or some shiny red pumps like my nonfur person Miss Temple would lust after.

So I nod him down to perch on my shoulder—Miss Louise is shocked to see me playing the diplomat between the species—and whisper a few sweet nothings in his feathered skullcap.

He nods and takes off.

"We might want to ask some follow-up questions," she

complains as his feathers disappear over the railing into the Great Beyond.

"Do not worry. I got his room number. And he is not about to fly this berg, as his owner is in residence."

"So what do you make of it? A bird did it? A pretty bird?"

"Well, a few other twentieth-floor pets than Blues Brother might take an illegal romp. What if a bigger Blues Brother, say a parrot, got loose? Say it landed on our victim's shoulder, or even the railing nearby. Scared her right off her feet."

"You would call an Amazon parrot a 'pretty bird'?"

"I would call a vulture a pretty bird if it was big enough, and close enough. That is just a theory, given we know that Mr. Matt did not lay a hand on that lady's, er, feathers."

"Get real, Gramps. I am convinced he could never kill her, or anyone, but I am not about to take odds that he did not give her feathers a real good ruffling earlier. I mean, the idea of the get-together was to get together."

"Gramps? Are you trying to tell me something, Louise?"

"Nothing either of us would want to hear. So what have we got?"

"A little bird who heard the dead woman talking to someone just before her fatal flight."

" 'Fatal flight.' You should write for the tabloids, Pop. Who do you think we have here, Amelia Earheart?"

"We have a room number where Mr. Matt met the call girl. We have a death the cops can't get a handle on, because it took place in flight. We have a witness who could not stand up in a court of law. And we may have a few more witnesses among the errant pet population of the twentieth floor. I propose we stake out this most interesting level and see what, or who, we turn up."

"A zoo!" Miss Louise responds with a delicate feline snort. But she does not offer any better ideas.

Call Her Madam

Alfonso and Barrett sat on Molina's visitors' chairs like the mountain and Mohammed finally come together in defiance of all laws of nature.

The mountainously overweight Alfonso overhung his chair in a pyramid of sagging Big and Tall seersucker suit. He could have been suspended in air for all one could see/guess of a supporting underpinning.

Barrett, on the other hand, was so leanly ascetic that he seemed to float above the steel-legged chair he perched on, angular elbows braced on angular knees, his putty-colored jeans and sport coat blending into the bland plastic shell that supported him.

"We know whose stable she was in," Alfonso announced as direly as a funeral director.

"Not a 'stable.' " Barrett's pleasant tenor reminded one of "Mother MacCree" crooned in Irish pubs. "Too much like the fourth at Santa Anita. The deceased was working under Judith Rothenberg's, er, sponsorship."

"Judith Rothenberg," Molina repeated to buy time to

hide her dismay. "She'll want to make a federal case of it."

"She does run to the dailies at every opportunity," Alfonso noted sorrowfully.

" 'Vassar.' " Molina noted the dead woman's pretentious working name. "I should have realized. Rothenberg still keep an office out on Charleston?"

"Nope." Barrett rustled through the pages in his card-crammed reporter's notebook. "She's in a strip shopping center now, rather appropriately. Near that new club, Neon Nightmare."

"Low profile, as usual." Molina was being as humorous as she ever got at work. "Okay. I'll handle this. Anything new?"

"A bellman has narrowed the floors Vassar worked that night down to twenty through twenty-four, north side of the atrium."

"Figures," said Molina. "Her head was facing the south side of the building. And how many hookers rotate through there a night that the bellman has caught such a solid case of Vague? Neon Nightmare, huh? Haven't heard about it. Any connection with Vassar landing on a neon ceiling?"

"It's a semiprivate club," Barrett said. "Part museum, part dance hall, and part theater."

"Isn't 'Nightmare' a negative name for a business?"

"Nothing attracts the Goth crowd of hip youngsters these days like 'negative.' They offer a multimedia experience," Alfonso put in. "Kind of like Cirque du Soleil shows, only built around neon and hip hop and acrobatics and magic and music. Small-scale stuff compared to the major hotel shows, but it's got a market niche."

" 'A market niche.' " Molina couldn't resist mocking the eternal sell that drove Las Vegas. "So does death. Okay. I'll handle Rothenberg myself."

"Think she'll raise a stink?" Barrett wanted to know.

"Doesn't she always? I'd rather have heard our dead girl worked for Hannibal the Cannibal Lecter than Judith Rothenberg."

"I hear you, Lieutenant," Barrett said, snapping his notebook shut as if he wished it were crushing a bug. "Good luck."

Molina didn't believe in luck: good, bad, or middling.

Not even now that the one call girl in Las Vegas that Matt Devine happened to draw had turned up dead in a lethal endgame of stud poker.

She found the bland off-Strip intersection where Neon Nightmare squatted unimpressively. The building was blacked out for the daylight hours: it looked like a huge version of the Mirage Hotel's volcano surmounted by an elaborate neon image of a galloping horse, mane flying, that would blaze against the night sky when lit.

Neon was odd stuff. The tubes that housed the magical, mystery gas were the lackluster dead-white of tapeworms until electricity charged through them like stampeding elephants. Then the colorless gases inside glowed against the dark like lurid chalk marks on the velvet painting of a Las Vegas night.

Neon was mostly a historical display now, not part of the New Las Vegas, which was more about squeezing money out of tourists for theme park attractions rather than gambling. Fifteen bucks to ride an elevator fifty stories up in a half-size ersatz Eiffel Tower. Twelve bucks to ride a phony Venetian gondola through a hotel lobby. Fifteen bucks to view an art display you could see for eight bucks at an established museum.

Such high-ticket prices were paying down the development costs of the multibillion-dollar new hotels that peddled culture instead of the crasser side of Las Vegas nowadays. It was still all about money, and so was a call girl operation, no matter what veneer of political correctness you slapped over it.

Like the mob that had ruled Vegas once, vice had gone corporate. Judith Rothenberg had an "office" as well as an agenda.

Molina was not impressed, but this time she was backed into a corner of her own making. If Matt Devine got painted into it by any unhappy conjunction of events, her career was history, like neon. And maybe in as blazing an inferno as the Mirage volcano.

NEW WOMAN, was the name above the door and window. Molina snorted. There was nothing new about the world's oldest profession but PR spin.

She gritted her teeth and went in, prepared to play the politician she loved to hate on most working days.

A young, anxious receptionist took her name. Molina did not give rank.

"It's been kinda . . . rough around here lately," the girl confessed. A phone line on her machine blinked. "New Woman. Miss Rothenberg's not in. I'm sure she'd be happy to speak to you. May I take a message?"

She grimaced at Molina as she hung up, apologizing to a witness of an obvious lie, "You're here about—?"

"The death."

"Oh. From the media. I'm afraid you'll have to wait for Miss Rothenberg to get back to you—"

"From the Metropolitan Las Vegas Police," Molina was forced to admit. She had wanted to stay as low-profile as Rothenberg went for the high-profile.

"Oh! I'd better . . . talk to her on this one. Just a minute."

She leaped up, revealing a skirt that suffered from an awesome fabric shortage, and skittered behind the bland door that led to an inner office.

A minute passed, then two. When the girl emerged, she assumed an air of authority that went badly with her beringed facial features and deep teal metallic fingernail polish. In Molina's observation, the more piercings, the lower the self-esteem.

She thought of her daughter Mariah's pierced ears and hoped it would stop there, but there was no guarantee of restraint for the twelve-year-old aching to go on thirty-two, and physical puberty hadn't even hit yet.

"She'll see you now."

Molina forbore comment and went into the office.

Madams certainly weren't what they used to be.

Judith Rothenberg looked more like a New Age guru, with her mane of coarse, grayed long hair, makeup-free skin, frank sun-wrinkles, and Southwestern-style turquoise jewelry.

Molina showed her shield.

"A lieutenant. I'm impressed. I expected the usual tag team of male detectives. They always love to visit my shop."

Molina was well aware of the male fascination with ladies of the evening, which was why she'd come here instead. That, and the terrible fix she was in over Matt Devine.

"This a priority case," Molina said, not underestimating the habitual expression of skepticism Rothenberg employed with police officers of any rank or gender.

"One dead sex-industry worker? Who would care? I'm grateful for the pull of your corporate masters, the hotels."

"You should be. You and your girls make a hell of a lot of money off the hotel trade."

"We call them women."

"Whatever you call them, they're call girls. I am not working vice here. I am not interested in your cynicism. I am not interested in the shining career path of the victim. I'm interested in her death, and how it happened. Any insight?"

"Vassar wasn't accident-prone, or suicidal."

"How do you know?"

"I know my employees. That's the point of them working for me instead of a pimp."

"So what was Vassar's personal background?"

"It was all in her working handle. She was a Vassar graduate who decided to freelance instead of struggling up a ladder with a glass ceiling in some corporation run by greedy white men."

"Hooking was an improvement?"

"When you work for me it is."

"What about her family? Where was she born?"

"I don't know any of that, and I don't keep records on my employees. It only provides ammunition for the police and the moral vigilantes."

"And you say you 'know' your employees?"

"Enough to do business. Their pasts are their property. I know their present state of mind. That's enough. I don't take on women with abuse or control issues."

"Aren't those the women who could most use a compassionate pimp?"

"I am not a pimp. I'm an office manager. My point is that ordinary, well-balanced, well-educated women should be free to pursue whatever line of work they find most rewarding. That corporate ladder-climber often finds she has to sleep her way up a rung anyway. For nothing."

"Somehow I thought you operated more like a dorm mother."

"No. We are all involved in a business enterprise. A business that should be legitimatized."

"Never happen in Las Vegas and the rest of the real world. A few Nevada counties that okay operating 'chicken ranches' don't make a trend."

"That doesn't mean I can't keep working at it. My employees are never coerced, they are drug- and disease-free—that I make sure of—and they're not alcoholics. They are working women in the sex industry. I pay them well, and it would be even more if I didn't have to maintain a legal fund to defend them from harassment by the puritanical authorities. Are you puritanical, Lieutenant?"

"Probably. By your standards." Molina couldn't help smiling. "You enjoy cop-baiting, don't you?"

"I enjoy harassing back a society that harasses women from the git-go, yes."

"I've read the print interviews with you. I know your position. Prostitution should be legal, regulated, and an upstanding profession. Prostitutes should either be free agents, or represented by a 'manager' like yourself, who provides a 'support system.' How you are not a parasite like any street pimp, I don't know."

"First, I'm the same gender as my workers. There's no male domination involved. Second, I do pay and protect my employees. To the wall."

"I know you've done jail time in support of your 'principles.' "

"Principles with quotes around them, Lieutenant? Your bias is showing."

"Not as much as your receptionist's thong."

"You *are* a puritan."

"No, I'm a working woman too, and women who flash their sexuality make it harder for all of us." Molina waved her hand. "Your receptionist is a billboard for your business, I understand that. But you'll never convince me that anyone using their sexuality for gain, money, or advancement isn't acting out personal issues."

"What issues is someone like me acting out?"

"Well-meant late sixties liberalism. You know, I rather agree with you. If there's going to be a sex industry, and there always has been, better it be under the control of the workers, not the middlemen. But you are one."

"I'm not exploitive."

"Maybe not, but that's an individual thing. Who's to say your successor wouldn't be? Wherever money exchanges hands for things people are forbidden to do, by civil law or social mores, corruption, brutality, and exploitation creep in."

"So you give up individual freedom to avoid the misuse of it? We're all screwed then."

Molina shrugged. "Life's a struggle. So tell me about Vassar."

"Tell me how you found out her name."

"Easy. The hotel staff. She wasn't exactly a stranger at the Goliath. Did she really attend Vassar College?"

"Attend? She graduated. Sex-industry workers aren't the dumb bunnies they're stigmatized as."

"So why did she come West and start hooking?"

Rothenberg leaned back in her chair, the usual low-backed clerk's model that gave her office a proletariat air. "I don't cross-examine my employees. I would guess that she was sufficiently good-looking that she was going to enter some field where her looks would be an advantage. Maybe she wasn't thin enough for modeling, or talented enough to dance or act. That's how I get a lot of my employees."

"She seemed plenty thin to me, except it looked like she'd had silicone and collagen enhancements. Before or after she worked for you?"

"I don't know. I don't subject these women to physical examinations."

"But their looks play a big factor in whether you . . . represent them, or not."

Rothenberg shook her head and smiled. "The employee suits the venue. For the big hotels, yes; looks are paramount. But I have employees in less elevated outlets. Some are successful, if not as highly paid as the five-star hotel workers, because they're kind and sympathetic. Many of my employees function as much as counselors as sex partners. Wealthy men, for obvious reasons, require less shoring up of their egos."

"Counselors? Please!"

"It's true. A lot of people are very screwed up about sex."

"I see the results of that every day. The lethal results. Back to Vassar. How'd she become your employee?"

"Heard about me. I've become a little notorious."

Molina grimaced at the understatement. Through the years Judith Rothenberg had tormented the law enforcement personnel and governing bodies of three cities, even enduring long jail terms on behalf of her "principles," but she was always set free by some judge. Police had learned to lay off her. She had a doctoral degree and excellent lawyers and wasn't about to be pushed around as easily as street-side madams.

And, too, the police recognized that Rothenberg hookers

were less likely to be drawn into the violent eddy of street crime. The woman did protect her own, and her business did operate more as a legitimate enterprise. Which drove the Moral Majority crowd nuts, because it did seem to prove that prostitution could be a "clean" business.

"She could have fallen," Rothenberg said out of the blue. "I don't see Vassar getting into any tacky situation. She was extremely savvy. She would 'phone home' instantly if anything seedy seemed to be happening."

"Phone home. That's just it. We didn't find a beeper or cell phone anywhere near the body."

Rothenberg leaned forward, her modest chair squeaking in protest. "No phone? All our workers have phones, and every one of them has an emergency number programmed in. All they have to do is press a button, and we know who and where, if not why."

"And then the Hooker Police go rushing to the rescue."

"Something like that. I do have my own security."

Molina had seen the bodyguards accompanying Rothenberg to court on the TV news. She favored high-profile muscle, like retired wrestlers. She knew how to direct a media circus.

"So Vassar didn't sound any alarms that night." At Rothenberg's shaking head, she went on. "Maybe the phone is still lost in that neon jungle at the Goliath. One of her shoes almost came off in the fall."

Rothenberg nodded.

Molina suddenly realized that her fears were not valid. Rothenberg would not cry murder, because everything was invested in her belief that sex for sale could be safe and civilized.

"Frankly," Molina went on, "the evidence is pretty overwhelming that no foul play was involved. There isn't an inappropriate mark on the body that couldn't be explained by a fall. The Goliath is the only Vegas hotel that has that dangerous central atrium design. She would have had to be leaning over the edge, but that neon ceiling is pretty fascinating from above. Still, I find it hard to believe that the woman was simply admiring the view and plunged to her death."

"We've never had an untoward incident at the Goliath," Rothenberg said. "Admit it, Lieutenant. Accidents can happen. Even to sex companions."

Molina allowed the sick, troubled feeling that had taken up residence on her insides to show on the outside. Judith Rothenberg took it for officialdom hating to admit that Vassar's chosen line of work was healthy, safe, and subject to ordinary worker accidents now and again.

"I won't let you sensationalize Vassar's death to make a moral point," Rothenberg added more sternly. "I won't let you use her to undermine everything she believed in, including herself."

So now the police were the stigmatizing villains, Molina thought.

Amazing how circumstances and everyone she talked to were making it so easy for her to hide the embarrassing truth and save her own and Matt Devine's skin.

As a mother and the woman who had advised Devine to take the course that had ended in Vassar's death, she knew massive relief. He would be safe. She would be safe. Mariah's future would be safe.

As a cop, she was seriously unhappy. It had been too easy to bury this fatal "mistake" to be honest or true or decent.

Her job was to do something about that, even if it hurt.

All in a Night's Work: The Midnight Hour . . .

Only one other person besides Molina knew the why and wherefore of Matt's desperate rendezvous with a call girl, and she was on the air solid from 7:00 to 11:58 P.M.

Matt called her at four in the afternoon, and they agreed to meet at the black bar named Buff Daddy's, one place Kathleen O'Connor couldn't slip into without standing out like a hitchhiking Caucasian thumb.

Matt, being anxious, got there first. The repainted Probe was the only white car in the parking lot, he noted, anticipating his entry into the club.

There were many ways one could feel an outsider. Being a priest had been one. Being an ex-priest had, surprisingly, been another. Being the only one of your race in a particular place was more external, even more obvious and alienating.

Matt just strolled in, checked to see that Ambrosia's far table was empty, and made for it without much looking around.

He sensed no hostility, just curiosity. Curiosity only

killed cats, and the last time Matt had looked he'd had no fur or a tail.

He sat down and, when the dreadlocked bar girl came by about seven minutes later, ordered a beer and a Bloody Mary for Ambrosia.

The drinks arrived much faster than the server had, and the regally red Bloody Mary seemed to make a good stand-in for Ambrosia. The chatter and buzz in the place returned to its customary pitch, while Matt waited for the absent queen of the airwaves.

Ambrosia rolled in like coastal fog fifteen minutes later, swift and casting a giant shadow.

Matt watched her approach, never having seen her at a distance before, but only in the claustrophobic halls and cubby-hole offices and studios of the radio station where they worked.

She walked with the little cat feet of Carl Sandburg's metaphoric fog, lithe and sure despite her three hundred pounds. Her bright knit tunic and pants rippled like tribal ceremonial robes. She was a lot younger and heavier and darker, but reminded him of the late sculptor Louise Nevelson, who had dressed like a living totem to some indeterminately ancient ethnic culture and who thereby went beyond that to utter individuality.

For the first time since he had awakened that morning, Matt felt a thread of hope pulling his leaden spirit upward.

Leticia Brown, aka Ambrosia on the radio, spied the Bloody Mary before she did him, and beamed.

"Is that stalk of vodka-soaked celery for me, or are you just happy to see me?" she quipped in Mae West's deep breathy tones.

"All yours."

She eyed the long-neck in front of him as she sat. "Men and beer. It's some tribal thing."

"It says we're hoping to stay sober, for the air in my case."

"Son, you got miles to go before Mr. Mike makes you sit up and pay attention."

"I know. I thought I'd tag along for your stint."

"I enjoy a live audience as much as the next radio voice, but Matt, honey, you got five hours to kill after we get there."

"I know. I'd like to kill a lot more hours." When she only sipped her drink in answer, he added. "I'd like to kill all of last night, rewind it, and erase it, only that last verb is grimly apt."

"Last night! That's right! Did you do the dirty deed?"

Ambrosia sipped the Bloody Mary through a straw, her perfectly made-up face puckered into the innocent insouciance of a fifties teen at a soda fountain.

"Did I do the dirty deed? Lieutenant Molina seems to think I did."

"Lieutenant? We talking *poe*-lice here?"

Matt nodded. "Everything went horribly wrong."

"When doesn't it, baby?"

He could only huff out a half-laugh and sip his beer. It tasted flat already, but he guessed that everything would for a long time.

"Let's go back to square one," Ambrosia declared. She was definite about everything, and that was what Matt needed now.

He nodded permission for her to direct this off-mike session of theirs. She wiggled a little as she settled into the wooden captain's chair.

"So you did what we decided was the only way out. If a stalker wants your cherry, you give him—her, in your case—used goods. Used goods. Virginity. That whole notion is such retro-think! You read about that poor girl in Pakistan, where her eleven-year-old brother violated some tribal rule by walking with a girl from another neighborhood, and the dudes in the tribunal decided the only way to make it right was to gang-rape the little boy's teenage sister, and they did it personally while hundreds of villagers stood outside and laughed? That is so not-human. I do not want to share the planet with such scum. Bunch of dirty old men panting after some young girl and coming up with fairy tales about 'honor' to make it happen. Sometimes I hate men. Just the gender. Every last one. I do. Tell me why I shouldn't."

"It's a woman who's hounding me."

"Un-natch-u-ral woman. That's who she is. Acting like a man. Like she needs to own people. I'm sorry, Matt. Sometimes I get so mad. You're not like that scum."

"I suppose any of us could be like them. If we didn't have the capacity for evil, being and doing good wouldn't be worth as much."

"Don't give me that theology. I don't want to see any evil in the world. No devils. And that witchy woman stalking you is a devil. Riding in on her motorcycle, snatching the necklace right off my neck and waving it around like a scalp before she roared off . . . one unnatural woman. And she don't even come from some crazy primitive land, you say."

"Only Ireland, and that is a crazy, primitive land in its own way."

Ambrosia nodded, and directed the last part of it at the waiter. Her Bloody Mary was a thin, watery pink in the bottom of the tall glass.

She sighed. "Ireland and Israel. Strange, besieged lands. You'd like to like those feisty people, much sinned against, but sometimes they're so stubborn you could strangle them. We were sinned against," she added contemplatively, the first time Matt had ever heard her refer to her race, "but we danced and sang and marched our way out of it, as much as we ever could."

"I can't know about that, not really."

"Nooo, you can't. And I can't really know about that poor Pakistani girl, much as I came close to her experience."

Matt nodded, acknowledging what she had confided to him during a previous session at Buff Daddy's, her childhood sexual abuse.

There she was on the radio, a disembodied voice that was mother confessor to anybody who chanced to call in.

In person she still hid behind a wall of flesh, flaunting what was pretty about herself, but keeping it to herself.

"So what happened last night that was so bad?" she was asking softly now, the pacifier of a fresh Bloody Mary sitting before her again. "Just losing it? The virginity thing? I'd like to know, since I've never misplaced mine yet."

"Me neither," Matt admitted, as he had not yet told anyone else.

The perfectly plucked and groomed eyebrows lifted without wrinkling her smooth, brown forehead. "You neither? How's that possible?"

"I got to talking to her. The call girl. I'd been assured she was a perfect pro, that there was no way I could take advantage of her. Turns out, she couldn't take advantage of me either."

"She wouldn't play?"

"Not so much that. It's when we got talking . . . you know what happens with that. You connect, whether it's over the airwaves or face-to-face. She wasn't as 'professional' as advertised. She had, as they say, issues. I had issues. So . . . . nothing happened."

"All that angst and nothing happened? I am disappointed, my boy. I may be sympathetic, but I like a good gossip as much as the next person. So that leaves you witch-bait. Still. I say you should have checked your conscience at the front desk and gone for it."

"Maybe. But then I'd have a better motive for her death. Maybe."

"Death? Whose death? I hope that motorcycle mama."

Matt shook his head. "She was there only in spirit. Everything was between me and this woman, Vassar. I left thinking it was all right. I left her the money. She understood why I couldn't sleep with her. Weird expression. It's about anything but sleep, as far as I can tell. Anyway, she didn't take my walking out on her as personal. In fact, I think she was beginning to examine some personal issues. I considered that a positive step. Maybe I was wrong."

"You jilted a ho' and hoped that she was reconsidering her lifestyle? I have heard of unreformed do-gooders, but that beats all."

"Yeah, I'm a compulsive do-gooder, all right. Anyway, sometime after I left at three in the morning, I don't know when, Vassar slipped, jumped, fell, or was pushed off the twenty-fourth-floor tier of the Goliath Hotel and fell all the way to the third-floor neon ceiling. The impact killed her."

"Holy smoke, child. You saying you're not only still a virgin, but you're a murder suspect too? That witch-woman on the bike is a double whammy, that's for sure. I'd like to send her over to Pakistan."

For a split second he actually relished considering it. "No. We don't want to do that."

"Speak for yourself, John, such as you are."

Chapter 13

. . . Maxed Out

It turns out that we turn up a not very interesting menagerie of bored and thus talkative pets on the twentieth floor of the Goliath Hotel. You would think it was the Noah Hotel and we were the head-counters for the *Ark.*

I make it one snapping turtle, two trilling lovebirds, three twitching bunnies, four porky pigs, and a python in an air duct, five gnawing ferrets, six yapping lapdogs, seven afghan hounds, eight cooing cockatiels, nine hamsters running, ten gerbils a-gyrating, eleven iguanas leaping, and twelve pampered pussums.

Unfortunately, none of them have anything significant to say, so Louise and I pad out through the kitchen again, snagging an errant shrimp and a fallen-by-the-wayside gourmet turkey burger on the way out.

We pause for a snack behind the hotel's rear Dumpster, which is camouflaged as a mini-ark in keeping with the Goliath's biblical theme.

"I must compliment you on your restraint today, Miss Louise," I say after disposing of the shrimp. I have a weakness for seafood, so I leave the turkey burger, unnatural hybrid that it is, to her. She can take it. She is a modern girl.

"How so?" she asks, patting daintily at her whiskers.

"We encountered a lot of tasty tidbits on the hoof, paw, and belly up there. I imagine during your life on the open road you must have had to dine on their cousins frequently."

"What I dine on when or where is none of your business. Certainly now that I have a personal chef I do not need to rustle up my own foodstuffs."

"So Chef Song at the Crystal Phoenix hotel is still laying down the rice bowls for you in return for his precious koi going unmolested in the hotel pond, is he?"

"Why should you care? I have never cared for carp. By any other name, and price, koi are still carp. And it is obvious that you have converted completely to health food. I saw the bowlful of Free-to-be-Feline on Miss Temple's kitchen floor myself. It is amazing that you do not lose weight on such a macrobiotic diet, but perhaps your metabolism has slowed down with age."

I am speechless. The little twit can load a couple sentences with more insults than Don Rickles can pack into a Milton Berle roast.

"Then you had better hasten back to your gourmet Asian cuisine at the Phoenix," I say finally. "I need to check on Miss Temple."

We agree to part ways and I hoof it back home, meditating on that full bowl of Free-to-be-Feline Miss Louise spotted. It is always full because I do not eat that disgusting health food, which is probably composed of compressed seaweed and sawdust. Certainly the army-green color would not appeal to anything other than a buck private and I have never considered military life.

Back at the Circle Ritz, I let myself in through the trusty French doors on the patio, having vented my temper with Miss Louise, tooth and nail, in climbing the palm tree that so conveniently shades the building.

My dear roommate is in residence at the moment, and greets me with happy little cries. I respond with unhappy big cries, and am rewarded when she opens a can of baby oysters and shuffles them over the Free-to-be-Feline in a succulent chorus line as an encouragement.

I wolf them down. Several hours in Miss Louise's company is very draining.

"Now do not eat just the oysters, Louie," Miss Temple advises me fondly. "The part that is really good for you is underneath."

That is always what they tell you and you cannot believe a word of it, whoever they are or however well-meaning they are! I am a great believer that the "good stuff" is usually right on top and easy as pie to reach for those who would take it. Observe the case of Adam and Eve, though that turned out badly, but that is only because it was an object lesson. The lesson is that you must be surreptitious in pursuing the objects of your desire. Do not just reach for them and grab them right out of the Crystal Phoenix koi pond in broad daylight.

So I manage to move a few unappetizing pellets around with my nose in such a manner that my movements could be mistaken for actually eating the things. I see that I must export a few to the wastebasket by dark of night. If I do not disturb the underlayment in my bowl, Miss Temple can on occasion get as stubborn as a Yorkshire terrier and hold back on the toppings.

After my bit of domestic undercover work, I hop up on the sofa arm to smooth my whiskers and bib.

A rat-a-tat of fingernails on the glass panes inset into the French doors alerts both me and my lovely roomie. I manage an under-my-breath growl as Miss Temple rushes to admit Mr. Max Kinsella.

When it comes to Mr. Max Kinsella, there are times when I regret that we are rivals for my Miss Temple's affections. He has much to recommend him.

I heartily approve of Mr. Max's second-story skills, his surreptitious ways, his magical arts, his limber physical condition, his penchant for wearing black and only black, his skill at keeping his lips zipped, and his impeccably effective way around the female of his species. In fact, he is a lot like me in many ways, as anyone could plainly see.

That may be why my hackles rise when he enters the picture and my Miss Temple's domicile, even though he once shared her Circle Ritz unit as an official resident.

Things change, and I am official resident now; he is visitor.

"Missed dinner, huh?" he comments, observing my grooming ritual.

"Baby oysters over dry cat food," my personal chef says.

"Scrumptious," Mr. Max comments acidly.

I flash him an agreeing glance, but not an agreeable one.

"May I sit on your tuffet, Miss Muffet, or is the House Cat going to draw claws on me?"

"Louie is just a big lovable lug," Miss Temple says, speaking from her experience.

The Mystifying Max honors me with a fleeting glance. He does not believe that for an instant, and I must say I like him the better for it.

"So what brings you out in the light of day?" she asks.

"What else? Seeing you. How's the working world going?"

Miss Temple sits down on the sofa, much closer to Mr. Max than to me. In fact, she is close enough to lick his whiskers for him, if he had any.

"Good. That Crystal Phoenix job may have been all-consuming, but now that the revamped attractions are up and running, I'm getting calls to handle public relations for big events all over town."

Mr. Max runs a few pads down Miss Temple's arm. "Are you not going to miss Elvis? I hear he haunts the Haunted Mine Ride at the Phoenix."

"Where does Elvis not haunt in Las Vegas? It used to be his town, so why not? I've got a big gig this weekend. Not your style, or Louie's, but I will have fun. It is the Woman's World expo at the civic center. Miles of stuff that bores men but enthralls women. I wonder why we're so different? Do you ever?"

"Never." Mr. Max does what I cannot, no matter how hard I try. He smiles.

"So what are you working on nowadays, besides writer's block?"

"Writer's block. I love it. It sounds so intellectual. There's never such a thing as 'magician's block.' "

"Actors 'blank' onstage sometimes."

"That is momentary amnesia. Writer's block is long-term, from what I can tell. I went online and you should see the sites that spring up from those two little words. I have never had a trendy malady before. I enjoy it."

"You would. You still have not told me what you are up to."

"I am following your clues, Miss Drew, and looking further into the Synth."

"Progress? You are making progress?"

He is by now nibbling on her neck, so I suppose he is making progress indeed.

"Some," he finally says, a weasel word that does not describe the thorough inroads upon her person he has just engineered. "Have you heard of a new club in town called 'Neon Nightmare'?"

"Sure," says my Miss Temple, retreating from the abandoned purr-in with visible effort. "PR people know all, like fortune-tellers. A strange outfit is running the place. It is part disco, performance hall, magic club, bar. If you want my professional opinion, the owners have diversified their image too much. Neon Nightmare is a cool name, though."

"*Hmmm.*" Mr. Max is miles away from Neon Nightmare.

I am contemplating a fast, full-bore, four-limb leap upon his unprotected spine, but he suddenly leans back against the sofa, foiling my purpose.

"I suspect the place has links to the Synth," he tells Miss Temple.

"Really? You really think the Synth is concrete enough to have a clubhouse?"

"Why not? An extravagant attraction is the best disguise in Las Vegas, anything extravagant is."

"What about Matt?" she asks.

Mr. Max fulfills my dearest wish and pulls far away from Miss Temple. "What about him?"

"He needs our help."

"Let him help himself. It will be good for him."

"Max! You have a compassionate side, I know you do."

"But does he have a passionate side? That is something you should think about, Temple."

"Why?" She is sitting up like a redhead someone has just called a mere strawberry blonde.

"If you want to be someone's champion, you need to know what he is capable of."

"Apparently a lot more than I would have thought!"

"Ah. Women always resent the professionals."

"No, I do not! I did not resent that poor Cher Smith, even though you were feeling so sorry for a stripper you'd never met before that you nearly got arrested for murder."

Mr. Max sighs, the gesture for which I most envy men and dogs, and I make it a point to never envy men and dogs.

"Cher was not a professional. That was her problem, and ultimately her death warrant. But you are right, Temple. We all have our knee-jerk soft spots. I am just warning you that you have no idea what Matt Devine is capable of; or me, for that matter; or Carmen Molina; or even yourself. Or, to be ridiculous, even Midnight Louie. We all harbor surprises deep within. Sometimes they are well-kept secrets from ourselves."

"I thought we were all in this together, and going to 'get together, people and love one another.' Right now. Are you trying to tell me that Matt might have murdered that call girl?"

"I am trying to tell you that he might not have. It is a fifty-fifty chance for any one of us to committing it—murder—if we are pushed hard enough, and something, or someone, important enough is at stake. And those are pretty good odds for Las Vegas. I could have snapped Molina's neck the other night when I realized you were in danger and she had to delay me by going *mano-a-mana* in the parking lot."

"But you did not. You let *her* beat you up!"

"I do not want to fight real murder charges as well as the phony ones, and my object was to get into a car and get to you. A cop car did as well as any."

"Especially since you can crack any handcuffs on the planet. Still, it must have bruised your pride to let her subdue you."

"Bruised pride heals. Dead amateur detectives do not."

"I was all right. I had your darned pepper spray. Not to mention Rafi Nadir."

"You are lucky he fled the scene. He might have been more lethal than the Stripper Killer, who was merely a sick puppy. Nadir is dangerous."

"And he once was Supercop Molina's significant other. Oh, God, this whole town is . . . a neon nightmare."

"Exactly. Just like life."

Mister Max pecks her on the cheek, a chaste gesture even a possessive guy like me cannot resent, and gets up to leave by the same circuitous route he arrived.

Sometimes you just gotta love the guy.

And sometimes you do not.

. . . The Shadow Knows

The Strip couldn't extend to the distant mountains surrounding Las Vegas, so someone had come up with the bright idea of bringing the mountain to the Strip: the club named Neon Nightmare.

From the exterior the new enterprise was a bold slash of neon and a galloping horse graphic atop a man-made peak that reminded Max Kinsella of the ersatz landmarks at Disney attractions.

He squinted at the towering façade by leaning far over the Maxima's steering wheel to peer through the windshield.

That windshield was the last protective barrier between himself and what he proposed to do.

He was planning to venture back into the world of the professional magician, planning to expose his carefully secured flanks and underbelly . . . for what?

Not for Matt Devine. He wouldn't lift a magic wand to save Matt Devine, would he? The ex-priest was grudgingly likeable, and he was a true innocent, but Max owed him nothing. No. And not for Molina. She had twisted her professional and personal life into a barbed-wire spiral of ethics and self-interest like the briar and the rose in an old English ballad. Sweet and sour turned mostly sour. He would do it for Temple, but she was on the fringe of this. No. He did this for himself, for the nagging certainty that everything bad that had happened in this town in the past year affecting the other three had something to do with him.

Call it instinct, call it ego. It was time to face the music and dance.

Trouble was, the Man of a Thousand Faces had problems coming up with a credible new identity. Elvis was too obvious to fly here. The Cloaked Conjuror's masked costume had come in handy a couple of times, but at a magician's club would only get Max stoned by flying doves if not more lethal missiles. He'd considered a mime's disguise: leotards and white-face, but the costume would only emphasize his trademark lanky muscularity, and he couldn't picture himself, even in deep disguise, with painted teardrops and a bowstring mouth.

So . . . Max sighed at his newest persona, one he would have never seriously presented to an audience. So unoriginal, but apt and useful here and now. He came to this new costume party as a glitzy Phantom of the Opera, black sequins turning the cape into a distracting, glittering carapace, the porcelain half-mask sporting an Austrian crystal jet-black bat as a tattoo over right temple and cheekbone.

With the cape he could crouch a little to hide his six-foot-four frame, another trademark he didn't want ringing a bell of memory.

No one would have heard of the Phantom Mage, but the costume was flashy enough to banish thoughts of the recently vanished Mystifying Max, who had always been both bare-faced and discreet and who religiously wore matte-black.

Max studied the building's sloped exterior, planning his entrance. It should be noticeable, but not too spectacular.

He wanted to move among colleagues, not rivals. This was a fine line: he must impress, but not over-dazzle.

For some reason he thought of Midnight Louie, a master of surreptitious dazzle if he ever saw one. Always turning up where he was least expected, and always looking like a long-lost alley cat who had happened to get lucky.

Max didn't believe in happening to get lucky. Neither, he suspected, did Midnight Louie.

He was equipped with all the bells and whistles seen on screen and stage. He could fly like Peter Pan, he could rappel down a skyscraper like Spider Man. Thing was, what to do where, and when.

The dark of night was an ally, for the building kept the neon fireworks at its pinnacle. He finally scaled the rear of the volcano's rough red stucco surface like an upright Dracula and ducked under the massive neon signage crowning the structure.

Neon required maintenance. Maintenance required a service hatch.

He found the two-foot-square camouflaged flap under the mare's running right hoof and eeled inside, pulling his cape after him like a train. Or a tail.

Immediately he was surrounded by pulsing wood and glass, the man inside an MTV video. Music, music, music. The building was constructed like a bullhorn. He was at the narrow tip, and all the bass beat came throbbing up at him like a bad dinner. Neon Nightmare was a dance club first, a magic showplace second.

Wishing for earplugs, Max let his feet find the service ladder in the dark and started down. *Hmmm.* The Phantom/Dracula would enjoy a swooping appearance. He touched the dark belt at his waist, equipped with a stuntman's gadgetry, and snapped the steel fastener over a ladder rung.

Below him the bad vibes ratcheted up to a piercing, wounded falsetto howl.

"The music of the night," as the Master had said.

Max swung out and down, into the pulse of a strobe light above a floor of writhing forms.

They looked like imps in hell, but were mostly teenagers and wished-they-were-still teenagers.

Max landed as light as a thistle-down in a swath of magenta spotlight.

He released two dozen bat-shaped balloons that sped to the building's peak, farting air unheard in the uproar. They seemed to vanish even as they fell like used condoms, unnoticed, to the floor below, to be trod underfoot.

The Prince of Darkness had arrived.

He was cheered by the drunken crowds for this tawdry, second-rate illusion, and then the dance went on. He unfastened his belt line and left it dangling invisibly for retrieval later.

By strobe light he moved from the floor to the entry area, and there he was, thank God, intercepted.

"Lounge act, or magician?" he was asked.

"A little of both. It's a cross-media world."

"Indeed," said the black-tails-attired round little man who had accosted him. "I applaud your entrance, but we are a private club. Can you pass muster?"

"I don't know the qualifications, but the place, like the music, hath its charms." Max loathed the frenetic blend of hip hop and jazz. He favored Respighi, Rimsky-Korsakov, Vangelis, and the lugubrious poetic charms of Leonard Cohen.

"*Hmmm.* May I escort you to our clubrooms? We are always interested in new would-be members."

Max recognized that the exact opposite was true, but he was here to overturn custom.

"Please do. I am not often a member of anything, but I do like your ambiance."

"Ambiance is our specialty. This way."

Max found the dance music muting as he followed the man up a spiral that reminded him of the interior of a giant conch shell. The spiraling upward path both confused and enthralled, like a fun house attraction.

The trick was the same as in a maze. The route bore only in one direction, no matter how many times it seemed to twist in another. This was a left-handed maze, perhaps in tribute to the left-handed art. Magic. And sometimes, the occult.

Max arrived at as commonplace a destination as any club might boast: a wood-paneled, four-square room at the heart of spiraling darkness.

One wall was solid glass, and it overlooked the madly lit dance floor below.

As he stepped nearer to analyze the view, he noticed other faintly lit windows onto the chaos positioned at irregular intervals in the upper darkness.

A soft whirr made him check the room behind him in the black mirror of the glass wall. A desk was rotating into view.

By the time he turned, it was in place and occupied.

A man in a business suit sat behind it in a silver mesh chair. Its spare, ultramodern shape and bristling levers reminded Max of an aluminum praying mantis. Or preying mantis? Ordinary man. Extraordinary chair. Max began to feel less melodramatic in his Phantom getup.

"New to Vegas?" the man asked.

Max nodded.

"New to magic?"

"Not quite."

"Not new to the spotlight."

"I did circus work for a while."

"Trapeze?"

"Some."

"High-wire act?"

"Always."

"This is a private club."

Max turned his head over his shoulder to regard the masses gyrating to the music unheard up here.

"That's the paying public," the man said. "They take us for a New Age disco. We are much more."

"I'd heard."

"Are you much more than you appear to be?"

"I hope so."

The man leaned back in his airy chair, steepling manicured fingers, the epitome of a businessman: overstuffed, well-suited, conservatively groomed, losing a little hair. Ultimately nondescript.

Such men never projected personalities strong enough to seem capable of running anything. Such men were always dangerous to underestimate.

"What is your name?" he asked.

"You mean the Phantom Mage doesn't do it for you?"

"Not bad. I like the Mage part. It's different. Implies real magic. You know anything about real magic?"

"I take my magic seriously, if that's what you mean. I've worked hard to make my move into the profession. I have some illusions that no one else does. I was thinking, if there's a magician's club starting up in Vegas, like the Magic Castle in Los Angeles, I'd like to be in on the ground floor."

At this the businessman laughed. "You can't. Our magician's club is as old as time, or at least as the Dark Ages."

Max tried not to over- or underreact. This is what he had been hunting. He must have managed to remain encouragingly still, neither overwhelmed or underwhelmed, because the man went on speaking.

"Alchemy, religion, philosophy, superstition. All played their parts in developing magic over the centuries until it reached our rational age."

"Not so rational that there still isn't room for wonder."

"True. And I wonder who you are and why you're here. You haven't given me a street name."

"I don't like mine. Why else would I reinvent myself?" No answer. "It's John. John Dee. As in Sandra, if you remember back that far."

"Ever been in the military?"

"No."

"Done time?"

Max paused for effect, and to hint at a slightly shady past. "No."

"You must have studied magic in its older forms to have taken the *nom de illusion* of 'Dee.' "

Max could have both kicked and kissed himself.

The bland inquisitor was right; Max's subconscious had dredged up the name of the most notorious alchemist of the Middle Ages and claimed it for his own: Dr. John Dee.

Actually, if he examined his unconscious, when he had said "John D." He'd been thinking of Rockefeller. Or MacDonald. The titan or the 'tec writer.

"I am intrigued," Max admitted, "by magic's ancient theosophical roots."

"They were also political," the man corrected, "and we modern-day offspring do not forget that."

"I am, at heart," Max said with perfect truth, "a very political animal."

"Then we may get along well together. In the meantime, allow us to consider your membership."

John Dee, aka the Phantom Mage, bowed profoundly in agreement.

The Mystifying Max recognized a kiss-off when he heard or saw one. They would try to investigate "his" background. Good luck.

He left the chamber, already planning further investigations right here at Neon Nightmare, more convinced than ever that something sinister was going on.

. . . *Play "Misty" for Me*

Even after three Bloody Marys, Leticia Brown, aka Ambrosia, Sibyl of on-air Sympathy, was as smooth and cool as chocolate-mint ice cream.

Matt watched her field call-ins and select the just-right song to soothe the savage breast. Her motions on the console were as liquid as her voice. It was a ballet in the dark, lit only by the various red, blue, and green lights sparkling like Technicolor stars in the studio's half-light.

Matt sat in with her, knowing to keep quiet. Their reflections in the big glass window were ghostly. Nightly voices in the dark were half ghosts to begin with, phantoms of the air waves. The host's voice was like a baton, urging on the shy triangle section, coaxing the violins to soar, toning the brasses down.

The words, the moves, the songs she chose to play for each caller were a ritual that calmed Matt, both unexpected and comfortingly predictable.

In the secular world, it was a bit like saying the mass.

Ritual mystery and revelation at the same paradoxical moment.

He listened to the sad souls calling in. None had a possible death on their conscience, but the anguish of their lost loves, or broken romances and marriages, their ill children and parents, wove a quilt of guilt and suffering that seemed to blanket the entire country slumbering in the dark of night across the miles.

A radio show was at once as intimate as a confessional and as public as the stocks in a Puritan village.

Matt couldn't believe he did this, six nights out of seven, for his daily bread.

The Midnight Hour remained the name of his show, even though its popularity had extended it to two hours. Beyond that it would not go. Matt sensed you needed to ration the music of night, the whispers of the soul, even when they were interspersed by tasteful, wry ads for biofeedback devices and magic crystals.

He was beginning to see the program as a sort of midnight mass offered to an invisible congregation.

Once a priest, always a priest. Ambrosia had no such formal calling. Yet there she sat, as sacred as a mountain, as certain and immovable, touching buttons, touching hearts, reaching out electronically as she never could personally, or physically.

Watching her, Matt mourned his missed opportunity with Temple. Opportunities, plural. He had glimpsed a truly personal, consuming connection, and had retreated. To what? An impersonal encounter with a call girl. A call girl. Not a person. A role. It hadn't worked either. Neither of them could be as impersonal as their ritual roles demanded. Me Tarzan, you Jane. Me pay, you dance. Me lost, you lose.

He regretted "Vassar's" death. Mostly he regretted her short life. He had to wonder what he had contributed to that. A shot of curiosity? A condescending pity?

It was easy to get maudlin at a late-night radio station. Ambrosia, pseudonym for a strong, lost soul, was a fantasy, but it worked for her and for her listeners.

Mr. Midnight was a fantasy too. Matt didn't know if it would work for him anymore. And in only two hours that simulacrum of himself would be "on." Could he still do it?

"Yes, honey, I hear you," Ambrosia crooned in her soft, maternal, omni-ethnic voice like liquid jazz. "Life hurts. All the great artists knew that. That's why we love them. That's why they always made it hard for them. Here's a little Ella for you. Go with the flow. Let go of the 'no.' Say, ye-ess to life."

Jazz. Beethoven gave him a headache. Duke Ellington gave him hope.

Ambrosia looked up at him, and winked.

The control board blinked.

A call coming in.

"Miss Ambrosia?"

"That's my name."

"No, it isn't. It's a pseudonym."

"As Miss Red Riding Hood said to the wolf, 'My, what big words your big teeth have got.' What can I do for you, honey?"

"Play 'Misty' for me."

Ambrosia's mellow eyes snapped to Matt's.

They both knew the reference: Clint Eastwood's directorial debut was a film of that very name. *Play Misty for Me* centered on a male deejay stalked by an obsessively possessive female fan.

"What a golden oldie!" Ambrosia's voice was still as smooth as whipped cream. "I don't know if it's on my play list."

"Maybe I'll call back later and ask Mr. Midnight to play it for me."

"He doesn't do music, dear. He just talks."

"Such a shame. I'd think he could play beautiful music if he set his mind to it."

"I play beautiful music. What do you want to hear besides 'Misty'?"

"Nothing. I want to hear 'Misty'."

"I'll find something just right for you, honey."

Matt waited, wondering what Ambrosia would come up with. She always surprised and always satisfied.

Her long, artificial nails twisted a dial, punched a button. Matt had never paid attention to the mechanical aspects of radio. They pointed at him, he talked. They mimed cutting their throats, he stopped. He watched a clock. He listened, got lost in the river of voices. He was a dilettante.

In an instant a sinister male voice was intoning, "I'll be watching you."

Matt knew the song, loathed it, and so did Leticia. It was an eighties hit by the Police, a stalker's anthem. The singer promised to observe every move and every breath the victim took, and tacitly threatened to end both.

Anybody who knew anything about domestic abuse recognized the stalker mentality, and the song seemed to glorify the omnipotence of the deranged rather than indict it. It was raw threat, very real. And even more threatening after 9/11.

Ambrosia's Cleopatra eyes narrowed at Matt. She was aiming a stalker's attitude right back at the caller. Both of them had instantly recognized Kathleen O'Connor, of course, who had called Matt's show before to taunt him.

Matt wasn't sure about fighting fire with fire in this case, but he guessed Kitty the Cutter would get the unspoken message: the police will be watching you.

Ambrosia made an up-yours gesture through the glass, and leaned into the mike, which was off-air now that the song was playing. "Guess your unwanted girlfriend will get the idea," she cooed into the foam-guarded metal mesh.

Matt managed a pale smile. Ambrosia had encountered Kitty only once. She didn't know how lethal the woman could be. And he worried. Kitty had already stripped Ambrosia of a necklace. This act of on-air defiance might motivate a more personal attack.

"You okay?" Ambrosia was asking Matt.

"Yeah, sure. I was hoping this would be a therapy session, though."

"That woman does need therapy. A good rolfing."

Matt's smile became a weak chuckle. Rolfing had been a trendy form of rough massage for decades. It was supposed to release inner demons. There were a lot of alternative physical and mental health therapies, but none of them addressed dealing with actual, outer demons.

Matt started thinking exorcism.

And then . . . the show rolled on. Ambrosia's usual callers lined up to make the usual requests. In their voices, as if in a confessional, Matt heard the quiver of deep emotion expressed in half sentences and long pauses. There was nothing slick about personal pain. About losing a live lover or a dead child. They weren't clever or glib, just honest. Just hoping a song and prayer would move someone's heart, maybe even their own. Matt heard the truth beneath the hope: the fatal cancer that wouldn't recede without more of a miracle than an upbeat song on the radio; the broken relationship that was obviously over with the other party, and obviously not with the caller. There were some happy calls, like McDonald's Happy Meals: warming fast food for the soul. The thanks given for a relative's recovery from a terrible car crash, for a child's progress in physical therapy, for living with/loving/having "the best" man/woman in the world.

Sophisticates might laugh at the hit parade of songs played to soothe or reflect the feelings on semianonymous display: John in Reno. Mary in St. Helens. Matt supposed people made these universal sentiments popular because they spoke to them as nothing else quite did, words and music in perfect harmony. It was a rite, like much of religion. Soul food.

And . . . after a few hours of listening, he felt better. Other people had troubles. His might be a bit more extreme, but no different, really. Guilt. Loss. Hope. Fear. Hope was always the leveler for a mountain of helpless feelings. For him, there was another word for hope. Faith.

He wondered how much of it he still had left. Perhaps enough.

Radio stations signed off by playing "The Star-spangled Banner." Ambrosia signed off her show at midnight by always playing one song. After five hours of mellow, it was an odd choice: "The Battle Hymn of the Republic."

In the aftermath of 9/11 and, personally, in the aftermath of Matt's own disaster, it seemed to strike just the right note.

She gave him a fierce thumbs-up through the glass, and then leaned into the mike again.

"The hot seat's all yours again," she said. Threatened. Affirmed.

He stood up. You do the hokey-pokey and you turn yourself about. And that's what living is all about.

. . . Men in Black Too

Max ducked into a narrow hall, and then found a service closet. The place was packed with them. No major sound-and-light show operated in an electrical vacuum.

He peeled off the Phantom Mage's mask and cloak, stripping to his naked face and black-clad form. Then he bundled the items into a ball and left them on the floor behind a pink neon palm tree.

He hoped to retrieve the Phantom Mage before he left. For now he planned to merge with the civilians packing the dance floor and in that innocent guise do some serious snooping.

If he was caught . . . hey, just a juiced night-clubber wandering into forbidden territory.

There had to be more to the building than the central neon core and the balcony offices.

At the moment, the center was incredibly loud, the crowd action more like a rave than an ordinary dance club. A deep bass beat vibrated every part of the building. Even the neon lights seemed to spit and hiss and tremble.

Then a herd of gigantic horses came galloping down from the pyramid's peak. Max studied the illusion. Giant TV screens ringed the apex, each broadcasting the image of the single external neon horse to make a herd. A vivid rainbow of colors cascaded in its flying mane and made its eyes into manic flares.

The "nightmare" of the place's title had come to life. Max had never seen neon so liquid, so mixed, so electric.

The crowd dancing below was the same, except it was also mostly under thirty. His partner of the moment was a sleek, model-tall black woman wearing tattoos and a filmy designer sari. They gyrated apart, nobody seeming to dance with anybody in particular, which suited his purpose. With every step he took, Max was moving to a wall opposite the entrance, his eyes searching through the strobe-light effect.

The control booth was probably on high, like the casinos' Eye in the Sky snooping parlors, but there had to be ground access to a physical plant, to whatever powered the hyped-up sound-and-light show.

The lower walls were covered in classic neon advertising designs. Pink flamingos. Signs announcing BAR. EATS. He stopped cold to recognize the Blue Dahlia's fabled signage, then realized that it was an outmoded design. All these pieces were vintage neon, throwaways redeemed. Neon had been what made Las Vegas hot for a long time. Now it was not. Perhaps Neon Nightmare would make it cool again. Like going through a light cycle instead of a life cycle.

The major neon companies were still in business, but now they were fabricating computerized digital light shows, like the canopy over Freemont Street downtown. The new culture-driven megahotels spurned the obvious glitz of million-dollar neon light paintings for more subtle, if no less expensive lighting effects.

Max would guess that some of the neon classics before him had been plucked from storage in the Boneyard, a lot behind YESCO, Young Electric Sign Company, one of Las

Vegas neon's founding firms. Max had visited it when scouting props for his magic act. He had found Wonderland in a wasteland, marked by such gigantic landmark icons as Aladdin's gilt lamp from the original Aladdin hotel and the gigantic Sliver Slipper. Both were studded with the dotted Swiss of lightless neon bulbs, piled together among other defunct signs like old drunks abandoned to the sun and the sand. Civic hopes foresaw a neon museum in the future. In the meantime some of the most unique signs had been dismantled and lost.

Were the Synth magicians feeling as outmoded as neon signs in the new Las Vegas? Was the Synth not some mystical ancient conspiracy but a response to the contemporary downsizing affecting every segment and part of the country?

Max noticed more men not dancing in the room, all as quietly attired as he. House security. They seemed to be looking for something. . . .

About time he quit mooning over old-time neon and found what *he* was looking for.

Then he spotted it. As always, the obvious was the best disguise. The three rectangular sides of a hot-pink neon doorway framed an actual door painted the same matte black as the walls.

Max leaned back against the space, his hands behind him feeling delicately for an opening mechanism. At last he found it, the kind of magnetic latch that responded to a sharp push by bouncing the door outward.

Clever. One would never suspect a full-size door operating on a principal designed for cheesy audio-video cabinets.

Max stepped past the neon outline to vanish into a black blob of unadorned wall. He checked out the men in black opposite. They were staring at his former dancing partner, who was doing a vintage Watusi in the center of the floor, all by herself.

All by himself, Max turned sideways and slipped

through the ajar door, pushing it only as far open as his slim frame required.

He stepped into utter darkness.

And then he heard a sharp metallic click.

Chapter 17

. . . *Unfixed Females*

What a pretentious joint!

I take one gander at the wild, neon-eyed mare galloping over the top of this pyramid-shaped building and then I ogle the black velvet rope keeping the wretched refuse of the Las Vegas Strip from pouring into the place.

Among the guards up front I recognize a figure whose very name is a curse word among my humans, Mr. Rafi Nadir, whom it was my not-so-great pleasure to spy (while he did not see me) at Rancho Exotica a couple of harrowing cases back. Still, he has done my Miss Temple a semi-decent turn a couple of times now and I cannot bring myself to indulge in my most utter loathing.

Hmmm, I wonder in my wicked way . . . would it not be interesting if his ex-squeeze, the torch singer Carmen, aka Homicide Lieutenant Molina, were to get a yodeling gig at this place. *Sigh.* (I have to think my sighs.) No such luck. She likes her anonymous moonlighting stints at the Blue Dahlia too much to go slumming at the latest hot spot.

Of course no velvet rope intended to keep out the hoi

polloi can bar Midnight Louie from going where and when he pleases. I am the koi polloi and invisible until I strike!

So I stroll among the mingled Manolo Blaniks and Nikes entreating entry with low success. I am the same color as most of their pant legs or boots or platform shoes or what have you.

I am soundless midnight fog drifting past their ankles and calves. I manage to almost sideswipe Nadir himself, who is clad in black denim, so tacky for the guardian of a supposedly upscale place . . .

In a minute I exchange the spotlighted, overheated, pushing, whining hubbub of the Uninvited for the morgue-icy, over air-conditioned, strobe-lighted cacophony of the Insiders.

In here it sounds like a herd of wild horses amplified on rock-concert speakers, and indeed a neon wave of such creatures washes continually over the walls. There is no ceiling as such, as the interior narrows to a black vanishing point.

Actually, I am right at home in the pyramid structure. My ancestors were mummified and enshrined in just such triangle-shaped tombs a couple millennia back, and there is some ancient stirring in my blood at the modern, noisome desecration of my ancestral traditions, not to mention my royal roots.

Call this place Luxor West, or maybe Memphis West, as Elvis himselvis would probably groove on it. Meanwhile, I have all I can do to keep my tootsies and penultimate member from being stomped upon by dancing humans. I cannot understand why they consider the equivalent of smashing a cockroach an exercise, entertainment, and art form. And they would not even eat them afterward! Another signpost of the wasteful Ugly American.

However, native customs are not my reason for reconnoitering this venue. Nor am I interested in the menu, at the bar or underfoot. I am interested in what Mr. Max is: any signs of the Synth.

I have heard enough about this mysterious organization

to form some notion of its composition. If we are talking hidden, sinister magicians, as opposed to home-grown, known-quantity ones like the Mystifying Max, I can think of no better candidate than the Asian Athena, Shangri-La, who entered our communal consciousness by shanghai-ing Miss Temple and myself, and most successfully making off with Miss Temple's precious opal ring from Mister Max. I always knew that opals were unlucky, but would anybody listen to me? No.

Now this makeup-masked minx (I understand the creature's performing face paint is from the Noh drama of Japan) and her familiar, the Siamese siren Hyacinth, have reappeared in Las Vegas on the grounds of the Cloaked Conjuror's secret estate. I am convinced that the Synth is emerging from the darkness to do evil. What is the point of being a secret, sinister organization if you cannot creep out once in a while and cause chaos?

So let other gentlemen of the night cruise this Neon Nightmare hunting prey of the opposite gender. I am after loftier game in order to save my significant other. If I happen to run across the winsome Miss Hyacinth in less than her usual homicidal mood, I would not object to trying to establish some rapport in whatever way possible, all in the service of the greater good, of course.

Am I glad I ditched that wet blanket Miss Midnight Louise for this assignment!

She sniffs at my *People's Court* appearance, but the fact is I came out of the humiliating episode that preceded our call for justice in very good shape. I had the latest in enlightened birth control methods forced upon me against my will.

Luckily, this gives me what James Bond would kill for, excuse the expression, a license to thrill. Like Mr. Bond's trademark martinis, I was shaken but not stirred. Unlike Mr. Bond, I am shooting blanks.

Despite knowing this, Miss Louise has no tolerance whatsoever for unfixed females, and I am very sure that neither Shangri-La nor her nimble magician's assistant, Miss Hyacinth, are in any way whatsoever "fixed."

. . . *Play Mystery for Me*

Matt took a last look at Ambrosia's beaming face through the studio glass. On the big schoolhouse clock affixed to the wall the seconds were ticking toward zero hour: midnight. That's when Mr. Midnight began answering call-in questions.

He had some of his own tonight.

Could he really be sitting here at the same table and microphone when only twenty-four hours earlier he'd been in a posh room at the Goliath entertaining the idea of losing his innocence with an intimidatingly gorgeous call girl who called herself Vassar?

Could Vassar really be sixteen hours dead?

A trick of reflection momentarily pasted Vassar's haughtily beautiful white features over Ambrosia's darkly stunning black ones.

He stared at both women, unwilling to give either of them up for dead.

But a radio show was just that: a show that must go on.

And, if he had truly listened to his own advice all these

months, he would believe that going on was the only reasonable response to loss.

The canned intro resonated in his headphones, introducing "Mr. Midnight," who brought personal counseling and humane advice to "The Midnight Hour."

Personally, he didn't feel very human tonight. Or rather, all too human. *Lord, I am not worthy.*

"Mr. Midnight?" The voices were always hesitant at first. Calling in was not easy for most, despite the numbers who did it. For people who sought the long-distance anonymity of a phone-in radio program, speaking up at all was not easy.

He had to respect his callers, even if he had trouble respecting himself for conducting business as usual.

"I'm here," he said, to encourage her to talk, to affirm something to himself.

"I am in such trouble," the young voice went on. "I don't know what to do."

Matt recalled Vassar saying very similar words only twenty-four hours earlier, after they'd gotten past the roles of buyer and seller, predator and prey (which one being which depending how you looked at their unique situation), man and woman.

Matt suddenly knew what to do. "No trouble is so bad it can't be helped by talking to someone else about it. What kind of bad is it?"

Very bad. She thought she was pregnant. She was in high school. Her boyfriend, forbidden of course, was older and wanted nothing to do with her or her condition. Her parents would never understand. She didn't dare confide in a girlfriend; she didn't have many . . . any . . . of those.

The classic story had also been classic in the New Testament. The church had resolved it with the concept of the Virgin Mary. Sadly, no other unwed mother since then had received a similar dispensation. In the Holy Land, they were still stoning them to death.

"Just once," she was saying. "Honest. I never thought . . . just once."

If there could be a virgin mother, could there be a sinless sinner? Not in any religion he knew. There could be an innocent sinner. That he had reason to believe.

He coached her into giving birth to some options: a drugstore pregnancy test. Buy it out of the neighborhood, off the Strip. If it came out positive, talk to a school counselor. Her writhing protest was clear even over the phone line. Planned Parenthood, he suggested in desperation, aware that were he still wearing a Roman collar, even figuratively, that would be anathema. But where does a girl desperately seeking impersonality go with this most personal of problems? To people she doesn't know, since the ones she does have made clear through sixteen callous years that they don't really care enough about her to inspire any kind of confidence at all. That was the real sin. It starts at home and spreads beyond to school and the larger society. Once the human hen yard decides that you are the chick to be picked out and pecked to death it only gets worse and your predictably nervous behavior only reinforces the bullying.

Matt recalled the awful incident Ambrosia had mentioned of the Pakistani teenager gang-raped by the village elders. If a pregnancy resulted, that fact would only further condemn her, even and especially in the eyes of her own family. She would be doubly dishonored. For this the God of Christians had made himself human and died by torture, to reflect and reject humans' inhumanity to humans, and two thousand years later it still went on.

His caller was sounding a little more hopeful. Not a lot. A little. She had a plan, a mission. A test to buy. Information. Maybe she wasn't. Maybe she'd go to Planned Parenthood.

Maybe, Matt thought, her self-destructive spiral could be halted by contraception. He had mixed feelings about that issue. He knew many "good" Catholic couples who had rationalized using it despite the church's stand against it. Many others had tried natural family planning methods with great or not-so-great success. Being orthodox in any religion was always a balancing act.

But given that this girl on the phone, this child, had been conditioned to not care much for herself, preventing her from having another person in her care until she had matured seemed a necessary stopgap.

"Thanks for listening to me, Mr. Midnight," she was saying, gushing, high on the idea that she had places to go, things to do, that she wasn't necessarily alone.

"A lot of people would listen to you, if you take a chance. But pick them carefully."

"I know. Not everyone is mean, is what you're saying, even if it seems that way. Chuck—" She hadn't meant to mention his name, not ever and especially not on the radio.

Matt couldn't help smiling at the notion of all the "Chucks" out there in the listening audience who were doing hasty examinations of conscience.

"I never thought I could get caught. I never thought, I guess. I need to figure out why I did that, and how not to get caught again, right?"

"You need to figure out who you are and what you want and need and care about."

"Everybody says that: figure out who you are. They never say how."

"Look at what makes you happy. Look at what makes you hurt. Think about your future, not just now. Think about what you owe to yourself, not anybody else."

"Isn't that selfish?"

"No. That's self-knowledge. We're all working on it. Every day in every way. We don't always get it right. Making mistakes is how we learn."

"Have you made mistakes, Mr. Midnight?"

"Many."

"But here you are, rich and famous."

"Not so much of either, but more than I ever thought."

" 'More than I ever thought.' Maybe that's it. Being more than you ever thought. Hey, thanks. And say 'Hi' to Elvis for me."

Matt shook his head at her parting shot. A regular listener, there even when "The King" or a darn good imitation had called in a few times. This was Las Vegas. What do you expect if you hang out a counseling shingle on the airwaves? You are going to get what you asked for. The lonely, the lost, the Elvis freaks.

"Only the Lonely." Was that an Elvis song? Maybe, maybe not, but clearly Elvis had been so lonely he had never been alone until he died that way in his own throne room.

The next caller was a crank, insisting that aliens had taken over the famed Area 51 outside Las Vegas and were all masquerading as Elvis impersonators.

God save him from Elvis freaks.

Another caller was back in the all-too-real world. She was, she said, a devout Catholic widow. But the Social Security system screwed seniors out of their earned benefits, so she was going to live without benefit of matrimony with Stanley, who wasn't Catholic and had no problem with it, so they'd both collect the SS they needed to underwrite their monthly prescription-medicine bills.

Both of them had distant adult children they would tell they were married. They hated lying to the kids, but wait until the juniors found out what prices the seniors had to put up with.

Matt heartily encouraged her. To live so long and still find the courage to bond and then pay a survival-threatening penalty struck him as the heart of social injustice.

He couldn't believe how much this job forced him to endorse positions contrary to Catholic doctrine. He was out in the real, secular world now, not within the enchanted circle of a parish. He had faced a true ethical dilemma, and come out of it more uncertain and confused than ever. Was Miss Kitty winning? Or was he coming to terms with things he had been able to avoid in his vocation? He wouldn't know until, like his first caller, he went through the process, took action, found himself.

The phone line clicked as another caller came on.

"Mr. Midnight."

The clock said eight minutes to go on his expanded two-hour stint.

"I'm here." It had become a catchphrase for his show.

The station had commissioned new billboards around town with those two words. Mr. Midnight is here for you. (*Even if he isn't here for himself,* Matt would add whenever he drove past one of the billboards.) They ran spot ads on radio stations the nation over, wherever his program was syndicated. "I'm here."

That's why he had to be here, tonight, the hardest time he'd ever put in. He should have been somewhere with Vassar, even if it was at the city morgue. Ashley Andersen, she had told him, finally, last night. Confessed her true identity. Ashley Andersen from Wisconsin. On scholarship to Vassar and never fitting in. And look at her now. Glamorous. Well-off. Scandalous. Dead.

I'm here. Sometimes. Strictly by schedule.

"Play 'Misty' for me."

Of course she would call back. Especially now.

"You're dialing the wrong show. Ambrosia's off the air. I don't do music, just chat."

Ambrosia was making frantic throat-cutting motions, but he shook his head just as definitely. Vassar's death had made him angry for her, and ultimately, wonder of wonders, for himself. Let the games begin.

"Just chat." She repeated, laughing, with a lilt.

Her voice had the loveliest trace of an Irish brogue. Nothing stage-Irish or exaggerated. Just a faint mist of musicality. Hearing her, one could almost love her instead of loathe her.

Matt held to that idea. Had Kitty the Cutter been lovable once? Or never? Was that what had shaped her?

"What's your trouble?" he asked, emphasizing the word for the Irish political conflict, The Troubles.

"Ah. It's about a man." -

"Of course."

"I gave him everything. Or the chance at everything."

"And he failed you. Just like a man."

"Well, no. He was a man. He betrayed me."

"My gender takes a beating on this program." Matt could never bear to call it a "show," though sometimes it was. "Another gal done wrong by some heartless cad?"

"Not heartless. Too much heart. No balls."

He glanced at Ambrosia. Games he could play on his own time. Raunchy language that could lose the station its license was another matter.

She shook her head, disowned any say-so on program content. This was too vital.

Matt had long since disowned the issue of cowardice. Martial arts had built up his self-esteem in that area, if not others. He had abandoned every precept of his youth and vocation to meet Vassar. Even she had understood and respected that. As he had come to respect her. Yes. That was his weapon. His assignation with Vassar had been a meeting of the minds, even the soul. Who would have thought it?

"A coward," Matt said. "Fickle. Anything else?"

"Only that he went to a common whore, snuck around on me. Thought I'd never know."

"Maybe he knew you'd know, wanted you to know, wanted you to get the idea, and get lost."

"Wanted me to know? Snuck around, I said. Danced in and out of casinos all along the Strip so no one could trace his path."

"Apparently you did."

"Well, a woman knows."

"So, forget him. You really want that kind of sneaky rat?"

"*Hmmm*. I had hopes that he would have *some* morals. His history certainly indicated that."

"So what are you going to do? Moon over this no-good guy? Confront him? He'll only lie."

"You're right. The only thing to do is to wash my hands

of him. Wash that man right out of my hair. Wash my hands of him, like Pontius Pilate."

Matt felt a chill. She knew her Scriptures as well as he did. He was to be crucified, was that it?

"Maybe," he said, "you should consider yourself lucky. This is Las Vegas. You can get a lucky break here. He obviously wasn't worth your attention."

"Obviously. He obviously was a lot more sneaky than I thought. I guess I'll just leave him alone all by himself to pay the price. There will be one, won't there?"

"For every action and reaction, there is always a price."

"Right. So this is my declaration of independence. He's off my hook. I want nothing more to do with him. Let him stew in his own juices, if he has any. I'm outta here. Will you tell him for me?"

"I think you've done it yourself, very well."

"Thank you. It's been fun. And, if you really want to do me a favor, play 'Misty' for me."

Matt was surprised to find Ambrosia "breaking" into the studio, shattering the "fourth wall." That's what actors called the invisible divide between them and the audience, and it pretty much applied to radio too. Both mediums offered ersatz intimacy.

Before Matt could answer, Ambrosia punched some buttons on the console.

The Midnight Hour closed for the first time with music, not talk: Johnny Mathis crooning "Misty." His voice was as caressing as ever. Matt couldn't believe this was the swan song to Kathleen O'Connor's obsession with him.

Once the words and music were launched and the mike was dead, Ambrosia glared at Matt. Not at him, on his behalf. "Sorry, my man. I really wanted to give that girl what she had coming to her. And that was *not* a last word from you. She don't deserve that." She smiled suddenly. "Oh, that Johnny is one mellow fellow, isn't he?"

Would that Mr. Midnight were one too.

. . . Max Outed

Not many people, especially security, carried firearms that required cocking anymore.

Max decided he had heard his almost-invisible door magnetically shutting again. Or . . . he was not alone in the pitch dark.

He stood still and listened.

No one can stand still longer than a performance-hardened magician. Perfectly still. Even his breathing slowed. His performance days were a bit too far behind him, but most of his physical disciplines had held up. He worked out daily.

In time all the tiny almost sub-sonic sounds to be heard became clear.

The faint thump of the raucous musical heart of this odd building. The occasional click, almost mechanical, that came not from a pistol-packing phantom, but from somewhere inside this dark and concealed space.

Max began moving on his treadless, rubber-soled shoes designed to leave no trace and make no sound. He felt like a mime against a black velvet curtain, moving, or appearing to move, but hardly perceived.

And then he heard a thin trail of laughter, as distant as a dream.

His hands reached further out, finding a wall.

He moved along it, swift and silent as a spider, halting the instant the wall vanished.

The slight breath of air on his mask-bare face, the touch of his fingers, told him he had reached the intersection with a wider hall.

This he went down, drawn by the sound of men murmuring, the sound increasing, murmurs becoming words. *Thurston in twenty-four . . . on Halloween yet . . . damned bastard! . . . the thugi . . . dead, I suppose. . . .*

A woman's voice came bright as a bird chirp in that basso chorus. *Cloaked Conjuror*, she said. Jeered. Laughter, mostly male. Hearty. Mean.

Max stopped moving, listened further.

More murmurs and now the convivial click of crystal. Not glass, but crystal with its higher, bell-like clarity, as seductive as a long fingernail skimming silk.

He had to be there, bare-faced or not.

Max let his fingers do the walking, those combination pads and prints so supersensitive they could feel another's sticky fingerprints on glass.

They reached out and touched something. Another door into the dark.

Max knew how these doors worked now. He gave this one a karate chop at the doorknob level, where no doorknob, where no light existed.

The barrier snapped open, halfway, truncating Max's figure into two halves, both dark.

A roomful of people stared at him as if he were an apparition. What an entrance! Now all he had to worry about was an exit.

. . . Synth Lynx

It strikes me as very odd that humans have to work so hard at having fun.

What is it all but running around the block until the day of the executioner's axe? For the mouse it is the toothsome cheese that comes just before the steel trap. For the cat it is the endless naps that come before the Final Nap. For people, it seems to be addictions, group tours, and therapy.

The scene at Neon Nightmare reminds me of a cruise on the good ship LSD. I was not around for the vintage happenings, but it recall what I have learned of the sixties: sex, drugs, and rock and roll. Just add neon and you get the general idea.

The light, sound, and action here is so manic that a dude of my persuasion strolling into the open raises no more of an eyebrow than a chain-smoking, hooka-pipe-hooked caterpillar did in *Alice in Wonderland*.

Speaking of Alice, there are no little girls in ballet slippers and full skirts here. I am seeing lots of skin, much of it tanned (one way or another), tattooed, and pierced. The same goes for the dudes.

When they are not gyrating in the flashing neon strobes on the central floor, they are hunched around too-tiny tables importing illegal smokes, tokes, and cokes of the non-capitalized kind.

I cannot feel too superior. I do like a little nip now and then myself. It has even been known to turn me head over heels, quite literally. But this is a small vice I indulge in the privacy of my own home, provided for me quite legally by my thoughtful roommate, who herself does not indulge in anything illegal other than meddling in police matters. And maybe sporting incendiary hair, an invitation to arson of a temperamental sort.

Although I understand that my Miss Temple has been snooping around such debased environments as strip clubs lately, I am glad that she is not here to see this: Mr. Max slinking along the perimeter to disappear into a door as invisible and matte black as his own attire.

Mr. Max does slink almost as well as I do, for a two-leg. I know he is investigating the premises, but it still saddens me that he must hang out among such dissolute individuals.

I decide to go forth and do likewise, however, for I have this pet theory. Okay, it is very pet and very much theory. I believe that Hyacinth and her evil magician-mistress Shangri-La are links to the Synth.

They have been turning up at the fringes of several cases like a bad dream now for months. In fact, Hyacinth has been turning up in my personal bad dreams like a case of kitty acne. (You know, that nasty black rash that shows up under the chin. No problem in my case, as black is my business, my only business, but it provokes a major depression in my pale-coated kin, believe-you-me!)

So I am determined to stick around this joint until I learn more than I should.

Granted, that is a dangerous position to be in, but if you are a solo operative, danger is often the only way to go. I may not get anywhere tonight, but at least I will see Mr. Max safely home after whatever he is up to is over.

My Miss Temple would appreciate my thoughtfulness, and I will know as much as Mr. Max does, which strikes me as a very good thing.

. . . Magic Fingers

If the people in the room were surprised to see Max appear in their concealed doorway, he was pretty nonplused himself.

It was like looking into one of those small worlds in a glass globe that could make snowflakes fall when shaken, not stirred.

The room was paneled in cherry wood and glowed like fine claret. Flames flicked against a soot-black chimney. Max noticed that the disembodied fingers of fire fueled gas logs, but otherwise the effect was British Empire clubhouse, and quite inviting.

To add to the ambiance, the men gathered on an array of tufted leather couches and Empire satin-and-gilt chairs were all in their middle years and dressed in black tie.

Only two women were present. One woman was Hispanic, perhaps mid-thirties, sleeker than a polished ebony hair comb, matte black in her own way, with pale skin like a mask, raven eyebrows drawn in perfect arches, and a wide, crimson mouth. Her eyes were as dark as tar. She too wore black tie, with a man's formal suit.

The other woman matched the age of the men present, her torso relaxed into middle-age spread, wearing a paisley turban and a black caftan. She reminded him a bit of Electra Lark, Temple's much more colorful landlady at the Circle Ritz. But her hair was concealed by the turban, and it was difficult to assign her an exact age. A middling-preserved sixty, he would think.

"I see I've not dressed for the occasion," Max said, taking the initiative. He stepped inside, bowed, and shrugged.

"You weren't expected," the Hispanic woman spoke in a husky tone that outrasped Temple's slightly foggy voice.

"Nor were you," he answered with another slight bow. Max immediately, from some impish impulse, decided to nickname her "Carmen."

They regarded each other, the assembled magicians, for Max recognized faces that went with familiar posters. These were long-established magicians. One could say over the hill. Steady, reasonably well-known professionals who had not, and never would, front a major hotel act in Las Vegas.

The good old boys. The pre-pyrotechnic crowd. Performers who didn't have a gimmick, as Gypsy Rose Lee and her stripping sisterhood had found essential. His kind of magician, really. His youthful idols.

They were the Synth.

Of course.

He had found them.

Or had they found him?

Old-fashioned though they were, it wouldn't do to underestimate them.

"How did you get in?" a Colonel Mustard type asked from the fireplace.

"Who are you?" Carmen demanded, her strident voice overriding the duffer's.

Max answered the old fellow first. "I blundered in. I'm a magician. I find a door with no visible hardware, I play with it, looking for the trick. Magic fingers." Max lifted and waggled his own particular set of those useful appendages. "Every puzzling thing I see is an illusion I have to figure out. It's my vocation. That's all there is to it." He turned to the Spanish rose with thorns. "I was known, at one time, as the Mystifying Max."

Of course they all knew that. He was a renegade. A true solo artist. Everyone knew of him, and no one knew him. And he was one of them. A professional magician of the old school.

"You vanished," Carmen observed with an Elvis-like S-curled lip.

"I gave up the art, for a while." Max paused. "It's changed. Now it's more fashionable to mock magic than to practice it."

That was the party line, of course. Yet he believed it enough to sound sincere. He had grown up in the old traditions. Even if he hadn't been forced to flee after the murder at the Goliath over a year ago, he had already begun to wonder if he could move fast enough for the shell game that magic in the media age had become. Or if he even wanted to.

Heads were nodding around the room, grizzled, balding heads. One belonged to the man who had interviewed the Phantom Mage and said, *Don't call us; we'll call you.* Apparently Max had not lost his touch for changing his personality, his stance, his mentality with each new role he played. Max winced internally. Problem was, now in his own persona, he wasn't playing the role as much as he should be. He hadn't identified with this generation; he had revered it. Now, he wondered, had he joined it?

The older woman's turbaned head also nodded, as much in sorrow as in agreement. "Magic isn't what it used to be," she added in the fruity, post-menopausal tones of an Ethel Mertz.

Max took a deep but shallow breath, so no one would notice. He would be accepted here. He realized that meant they thought he was passé, that they had no reason to think he might not be as disgruntled as they were.

An upsetting thought. Not that he had finessed them into accepting him under false colors, but that they knew his performing persona and found it quite logical that the Mystifying Max should be part of a retrograde magicians' coven, driven by dissatisfaction and bile, angry at progress, set on preserving the past at any cost.

Could it be that truth was the best disguise?

"Come to the fire," Colonel Mustard invited.

The invitation triggered a memory. Sparks, the man's performing name had been. Cosimo Sparks.

"Have some brandy," suggested the turbaned woman, lilting her thinning eyebrows and a snifter at the same time.

There was something familiar about her, but he couldn't quite attach it to a time or a place.

"Czarina Catharina," she introduced herself. "I did a mentalist act."

He nodded. He had seen the posters in Jeff Mangel's on-campus art gallery at the University of Nevada at Las Vegas, and she wasn't among them, but a mentalist wasn't quite a magician. The professor had died surrounded by the posters he had preserved, but now Max was surrounded by many of the famous faces immortalized in those very posters, a Who's Who of . . . forgotten magicians, bypassed headliners, outmoded prestidigitators.

The potent brandy seared his lips, making him jerk like a false reading on a lie detector test graph.

"Strong stuff," Carmen noted with a contralto laugh.

"No," Max muttered. "It's strong stuff meeting a roster of a World Magicians' Hall of Fame." Oddly, he meant it.

His hand shook slightly as he lifted his brandy snifter and inhaled the high-proof perfume of Hennessy XO Special. He had liked to think he had retired, forcibly, from his profession, pushed by an inexplicable murder into flight. He didn't like to think he had also reached a dead end.

"World Magicians' Hall of Fame! There's no such organization." Sparks barked like a discontented seal. "It's all commercial tie-ins nowadays. Make a Lear jet disappear on live TV. Make the Seagram Building crumble on cable TV. We might as well be terrorists as illusionists."

"You were always too subtle," Czarina noted sadly, "to survive."

Her words struck a chill like a dagger to Max's heart. He had consoled himself that he had retired because his primary career, counterterrorism, had finally made his cover profession useless. But the fact was he had been a magician first and foremost, from his preteen years, and now he was among his own kind, who faced his own kind of extinction, and they were his enemies. They were the Synth.

Max couldn't help it. He took a deep, sighing breath.

Carmen rose and stalked toward him. "You are one of us, aren't you? However, or why ever you 'blundered' in here, it was no accident. You have come home."

An undercover operative could not have asked for an easier "in."

A fellow magician could not have imagined a harder task.

He was in like Flynn. Like Errol Flynn, Mr. Swashbuckler, he would have to play many parts, and some of them, he saw now, might break his heart.

. . . *Playback*

Hand it to Leticia, Matt thought. She never fully relinquished the Earth-mother persona of Ambrosia.

She walked Matt out to the parking lot. The 2:00 A.M. sick-green parking-lot lights turned the black asphalt gray and made a knot of female fans waiting for Matt look jaundiced.

"Safety in numbers," Leticia declared. "Don't you linger after all the sweet young things get your John Hancock and leave."

Matt eyed his white Probe, looking pea-green in the lights, and nodded. He could edge over to the car while signing the station photographs and they could all skedaddle without risking a close encounter with Kitty the Cutter.

The slam of Leticia's car door assured him that she was sealed away from any motorcycle raids. He thanked his gushing fans and signed, moving toward the car.

Sweet young things they were not. More like sweet middle-aged things, women whose faces wore the worry lines of hard work and hard times. People with higher educations and high-paying jobs took their insecurities to psychoanalysts and trendier alternative practitioners. Radio listeners let it all hang out, Matt had discovered, the same phenomenon that drove the tabloid TV show phenomenon and kept Jerry and Ricki and company in clover.

He was just a local phenomenon in a second-tier media. He liked it that way, and hoped that Kathleen's unfond farewell broadcast on his show meant she was really out of his hair.

He was signing on the Probe's fender now, straining to keep some light on the photograph so his penmanship was at least recognizable.

There was one last customer, an immensely overweight woman with the optimistic beaming eyes of a child. Seeing such doomed outcasts always made Matt hurt for them. Everybody faces rejection, but not everybody is a walking advertisement for it. She did everything wrong: carried too much weight, wore circus-size polyester, had her brown hair crimped into some shapeless frizz, a bad complexion, thick-lensed glasses in bad frames, and bit her fingernails down to the bloody quick. Did the Almighty have no mercy sometimes? Couldn't He have given this female equivalent of Red Skelton's Poor Soul some natural advantage? Just one.

Her smile. She brought the signed photo close to the crooked-framed glasses, read what he'd written, and smiled. Her teeth were perfect: small, even, white as snow.

"Gee, thanks! That's one thing I'm good at. Devotion. Your 'devoted listener.' I just love radio. It lets you imagine anything."

And off she toddled, happy.

Matt leaned against the car door. There ought to be an Individuals Anonymous group for people who weren't thin, confident, good-looking, and socially smooth.

They should spend their time reinforcing their self-esteem, instead of pursuing autographs from people like him who looked like they had it all together and certainly didn't.

He breathed deeply. The air was the exact temperature of his body. Breathing seemed to be swimming in a puddle of warm, unscented night.

Was she really gone, out of his life, Kathleen O'Connor? But before he could breath free, something fell from somewhere, out of the corner of his eye, a piece of air-lifted paper, whatever. It looked like a falling woman, Vassar slipping downward in the hollow core of the Goliath Hotel at an hour when everybody else was wafted upward in the glass cages of hotel elevators.

A pale figure stepped out of the radio station building's one-story shadow.

Matt straightened, tightening his fingers on the car keys in his pocket.

He'd been dreaming when he should have been following Leticia's orders and getting himself out of the deserted parking lot.

The figure was slight, light-colored, and coming toward him.

For a moment he fantasized the ghost of Vassar.

Then he feared it was Kitty.

Before he could act on any instinct: stand or run, the figure had come too close to avoid.

"Matt? You are Matt Devine?"

He hesitated, unwilling to give anything of himself away again.

The figure stepped closer, into the wedge of green light that shed a lime pall over Matt and his white car.

He was relieved to see it was a man.

Most people would fear male muggers. Matt feared a female one.

"Who are you?" he asked.

"Don't you recognize me?"

This invitation to inspection had Matt trying to pin a label on a cipher. The guy was maybe five-five, pale-skinned, no Las Vegasite. Balding hard, but only in his . . . mid-thirties, maybe? Mild-looking. No mugger. So what was he, then?

"It's Jerome," he said.

Jerome. Okay. Didn't ring a bell. Or did it?

"Do I know you from somewhere?"

"St. Vincent's. And I guess I've changed. Used to have a mop of hair. That's the way it always is with us bald guys; heavy on top at the beginning, cue balls by the time we hit the late twenties. Your hair seems to be hanging on."

"Yeah. I guess." Matt didn't think much about his hair, except when it needed cutting. It had never occurred to him that cutting was a privilege. "St. Vincent Seminary?"

"In Indiana. We were there. Together."

"Jerome. Jerome! Uh, Johnson, wasn't it?"

"Still is."

"Sorry. Las Vegas is so far away from all that."

"Is it ever."

"What are you doing here?"

"Here? Right now? Or here in Las Vegas?"

"Both, I guess." Matt looked around, realizing their vulnerability. "You have a car. Want to go somewhere?"

"I have a Geo Metro. Sure, but I don't know the places yet."

"Why don't you follow me to the first fast-food joint we hit? They'll have chairs and coffee."

"Kinda like an AA meeting."

"Yeah." Matt immediately wondered if that was Jerome's problem. Because he had to have one. People from your past didn't turn up unless they did. Look at himself, turning up in Cliff Effinger's present. And now Effinger had no future at all. Ever. Anywhere.

I'm dangerous to know, Matt wanted to tell Jerome Johnson from St. Vincent's. *You don't want to go anywhere with me.*

The man reeked of the Midwest. He could have been an extra in *Fargo*, but he'd come a long way to be in this parking lot. Matt couldn't turn him away.

He got into the Probe, started it, watched in the rearview mirror for Jerome's vehicle to wheel in behind him. It did, a toy car on spindly wheels, looking as insubstantial as the man who drove it.

Why? Matt wondered.

Johnson had obviously come here trying to make a connection. St. Vincent's was an Ice Age ago to them both. So much water had melted under the church's medieval bridge since those days. So much had happened to them both. Jerome today had not worn a collar. It didn't mean he had left the priesthood too. Lots of priests nowadays dispensed with obvious religious labeling. But Matt sensed they had something in common. That was why Jerome had looked him up, had approached him in this disconcerting way. The only way he could have found him was through the radio persona, and even then he would have had to have tried hard.

Matt pulled onto the deserted street, watching for motorcycles, but more worried about the unassuming man in the very unassuming car behind him.

Matt didn't like surprises from his past any more than he liked surprises from Max Kinsella's past. In that case, he had ended up stalked by a madwoman. What did this sad little guy want from him? More than Matt could or would want to give, he'd bet.

Lose one crown of thorns, gain another. God help him.

He drove, half an eye ahead on the highway of lit signs fifteen feet above the street level, half an eye in his rear-view mirror, not only scanning for the headlights of Jerome's little car, but for any other following vehicles.

Nothing.

Matt suddenly swung the Probe's steering wheel up the usual Strip center rise and dip designed to discourage speedsters. A Wendy's he remembered only when he saw the big lighted sign.

He took a slot between two mammoth SUVs near the front door. Jerome found a place in the street-facing row behind him.

They entered together, suddenly lit by night-bright restaurant fluorescents.

It was awkward standing in line to order, strangers surrounded by strangers, not wanting to make small talk because there was none. Between graduates of the same seminary there was only large talk.

They found a fairly crumb-free table for their plastic trays and sat near the window, where they could watch lights stab the night ad infinitum. It was like a fallen universe, a big city street at night, with galaxies of signs touting 24/7 enterprises and the small satellites of cars cruising by continually.

The black-backed window faintly reflected their faces, neither particularly recognizable.

"So how did you find me?" Matt asked, stripping the flimsy paper jacket off the straw for his Sprite.

"Just . . . luck. I saw the billboard. Or one of them."

"Those miserable things! Hype. But the radio industry is a media business, and it's all hype. What were you doing in Las Vegas?"

"I work here. Live here."

"Really? You ever go to the ex-priest meetings in Henderson?"

Jerome lowered his eyes to his tissue-wrapped burger. Grease was soaking through like giant raindrops. "No. I . . . I felt no need."

"I don't go myself. I just was surprised that there were enough of us in Las Vegas to get a group together. So you are . . . ex, then?"

Jerome nodded as if not happy about it. Or about admitting it. Matt said, "There are almost as many 'exes' as 'ins,' these days."

"I know. I heard about you."

"What?"

"Nothing bad. Only that you'd gone through the whole laicization process. I didn't. I just . . . walked away."

"I guess that's the norm."

"You were never the norm. In seminary, I mean. You were always different."

"Different? Me? How?"

"You kept to your studies and yourself. Oh, you played sports, did the community thing, but it was like you were never fully there."

"I felt pretty grounded."

"You never—" Jerome sucked on his own straw, as if swallowing his next words. He was drinking a cola, and Matt wondered about taking in all that caffeine so late at night . . . so early in the morning.

"I never what? I'm used to having my failings presented to me. Seminary, you know."

"You didn't have any failings. We all figured you were the one who'd never leave. Except I—"

"You what?"

"I never bought that, even though you always seemed like you were really meant to be there. I always felt you were escaping your past, but I had to honor what you were trying to be."

Trying to be? Matt wondered. Was he still trying to be something unreachably honorable? Not a priest, but a celibate. Would Max Kinsella consider honoring him for his . . . restraint with Temple? Would he be having this conversation with Kinsella ten years down the pike?

But this was now, and that was then, and it was disturbing news.

"All? You were *all* talking about me? I didn't talk about you."

"Maybe that's why—You didn't know what was going on. Did you?"

"I like to think I'm fairly observant."

"But then."

"But then . . . we were kids. We were engaged in a very serious course of self-examination and study."

"I used to admire you."

"Used to?"

"I mean, back then, when I was just a kid. I was two years behind. You don't remember me, do you?"

Matt tried to, and then he tried to think of a way of

lying and saying he did without actually lying, but Jerome cut through all that.

"I not only had hair then, but I had glasses." He looked up from his burger. He had pale blue eyes, rather soulful. "I wear contact lenses now. I don't much want to be what I was back then."

"It's understandable."

"Is it? How can you say that when you don't understand?"

Matt felt irritation scratching like his long-lost clerical collar. He'd finished a draining night shift at work; he was at worst a suspect in a murder and at best responsible for a woman's suicide. And now he was expected to make small talk with someone he didn't even remember from a time he wanted to forget.

And who expected him to do this? He asked himself. He did. He smiled wryly, at himself.

"I've got a lot on my mind, and, no, the brain is not turning back the album pages very efficiently right now. Doing a live radio show is terribly draining. I'm told by those who know that there's a natural 'let-down' afterward. It's not my best time."

Jerome swallowed, not any food or drink, just his own very visible Adam's apple. "Mine neither. I'm not an after-midnight kind of guy."

"What's your job?"

"Day shift, obviously. I'm a picture framer." He shrugged. "Guess it's an outgrowth of all those Sacred Heart paintings the old folks at home had framed on the walls everywhere. You can't outrun your own history."

"No. You can't." The words cut Matt like a razor.

His own history was getting pretty lurid. He wondered what Jerome would think if he knew his old seminary schoolmate had been with a high-priced call girl just last night. Matt checked his wristwatch with a spasm of guilt. *This time last night he had been talking to Vassar. She had been alive.*

"I don't mean to keep you up."

"It's not you," Matt said hastily. This guy looked like people were always ducking out on him, and Matt didn't want to add that guilt to the load he already carried. "I was thinking of a . . . friend."

"There's someone—?"

"Someone? Oh. No. I'm single."

Jerome nodded, looking a little uneasy.

"Something wrong about that?"

"No. Only it's obvious—"

"What?"

"That you're committed to marriage, since you equate being single with having no significant other."

"Yeah, I guess. Listen. We haven't seen each other in years and we weren't even in the same class. I don't get—"

Jerome took a deep breath. "You never knew, did you? I kinda hoped it was that way, that one of us got out unscathed."

"Knew what?"

"What was really going on in seminary."

Matt felt the burger bites in his gut congeal with cold, as if slapped with an ice pack. *Oh, my God, was this about the nightly news?*

"If I was so ignorant, why are you looking me up?" he asked.

"I was hoping to find someone who escaped. Who got clear. If one did, it makes the rest of it, the worst of it, better."

"One! Are you saying it was that prevalent?"

Jerome shrugged, sucked on his straw even though only a few drops of melted ice water migrated up his straw. "Maybe not. It just felt like it. To us."

"Was it peers, or instructors?"

"Both. Kind of like those British public schools used to be, maybe still are. Bullying and boys on boys. I think now it was all about authority, not sex. Sex was just the excuse."

"I don't want to hear this."

"Why, when telling is the only redemption?"

"Why tell me?"

"I—I always admired you. I hoped you'd escaped what I couldn't. It's important to me to know that you did."

"Yes, I did. At St. Vincent's. I could swear that on a Bible in a court of law, but, Jerome, I didn't escape it elsewhere. I was at St. Vincent's because I was running away from the abuse at home. Not sexual, thank God, but abuse."

"You were abused?"

"What kid hasn't been, to some extent, by someone at some time?"

"You believe that?"

"I've seen that. No family is perfect. Every generation has its own axe to grind. We all get sandpapered with someone else's issues. And we go on."

Jerome nodded, and neatly wrapped most of his burger in the tissue for disposal.

Matt hadn't managed to eat much either. Not so much because of Jerome Johnson, but because of Ashley Andersen, both Upper Midwest babies in a world far colder than a North Dakota blizzard.

"Maybe that's why no one messed with you," Jerome said meditatively. "I remember you working out those martial arts moves, alone. You were like . . . oh, Luke Skywalker in the first *Star Wars* movie, remember? Looking for the Force in yourself. I never thought it might be because . . . you looked invulnerable. Like nobody should mess with you."

"They didn't. So maybe my past made me less likely to be abused. It didn't feel like it then."

"And now?"

"Now I'm strong in some ways, and weak in others. Hey, we're human, yes?"

"I always . . ."

Jerome no longer seemed capable of finishing a sentence, and Matt, the stressed-out Matt who'd seen a bitter enemy make mincemeat of his life and more importantly of his conscience, was growing impatient with this stumbling loser who had nothing better to do than to look him up. The blind leading the blind was not Matt's current goal.

"I always . . . liked you, especially," Jerome said, finally raising his limpid blue eyes to Matt's again, brimming with something unfortunately quite readable.

Holy Mother of God. Help me now and at the hour of my death, amen.

The Morning After: Fast Backward

"In bright and early, Lieutenant?"

"Always, Chet. So are you."

"Yeah, but I got a great job. This is better than Eye in the Sky at any Strip hotel. This is Eye in the Sky central for all of Las Vegas."

"This" was Chet Farmer's wall-to-wall wired domain, stacks of audio and video equipment, a gray/black wallpaper of knobs and switches and dials.

The high-tech surround would have creeped Molina out, but Chet thrived in it like a spider in an electronic/digital/computerized web. There was a bit of the arachnid about him anyway: long bony limbs and such poor eyesight that he had to wear half-inch-thick lenses in heavy-framed plastic glasses despite living in the age of thin high-power optical lenses that gave everyone else a cosmetic edge.

There was no way to avoid describing Chet as a nerd, but he was a happy nerd. That was the blessing given to nerds along with extreme myopia and a socially-challenged existence.

"I need to see the Goliath tapes."

"Sure thing." He spun in his mesh-seated chair to pull some labeled tapes out. "Must be a sensitive case."

"Just hard to call. Why do you say 'sensitive'?"

"Su and Barrett both checked these out. Separately. And now you're here."

"Glad to hear they're on the job. Either one come up with anything?"

"Nope. Just a lot of faces and bodies milling through the casino and lobby area."

"I'll take another look. New eye, new ideas. Say from six to eight P.M. You make that look so easy," Molina said, envying the ease with which Chet played his electronic game board. "I had to let my twelve-year-old daughter take over the VCR at home. She's teethed on computers since third grade."

"That's cool. We can't afford any more computer-phobic generations. Do you know my folks don't e-mail?"

Chet was on the cusp of forty, Molina figured, so his parents must be senior citizens baffled by debit cards at the grocery store.

"At least I have a job where I have to keep up on some modern improvements," Molina said. "Try the hotel registration area first."

"Okay. There's the time in the lower right-hand corner."

Molina watched the broken LED numerals flick through their predictable round.

If Su and Barrett had seen nothing, maybe nothing was to be seen. Certainly Vassar hadn't checked in at the front desk. But Matt Devine had, and she wanted to know if he had been caught on tape. It was possible he hadn't. The tapes were pervasive but general. It would be easy to miss one person in the constant flood of bodies through a major hotel during the evening hours.

And, of course, Su and Barrett only knew to look for Vassar and anything "unusual."

She forced herself to focus on the front desk clerks. Matt

would have had to pass through the lines leading to one of them.

That was the one given she knew, that no one else did. Who the man was that Vassar had met.

The tape was black and white; no point wasting color on pure surveillance. It made finding Matt's very blond head harder. A lot of silver-tops came to Vegas and in black and white blond was white.

Something familiar flashed past her eyes. "Stop!"

Chet froze the screen instantly.

"Can you go back in slow motion?"

"I can make this thing do everything but cook, Lieutenant."

"Slow motion is good enough, Flyboy."

Chet grinned. The images began running backward in a staccato fashion, as jerky as if a strobe light were flashing somewhere above them.

A man who had walked out of the camera's view backstepped reluctantly into focus again.

"Stop there." Molina leaned inward, studied the figure from the same bird's-eye view as the camera. His face was foreshortened, his shoulders exaggerated. She caught her lower lip in her teeth. Rafi Nadir? She'd only seen him close-up once in recent years, and a lot of Middle-Eastern men came to Las Vegas, enough that the security lines at McCarran Airport snaked through half the terminal nowadays. Was it him, or just your average possible terrorist?

"Want a close-up?"

"Yeah. Lower left-hand quadrant."

Magically, the screen expanded to a larger blur of bodies.

Rafi? Rafi had been at the Goliath that night? It was possible. He was quite the man about Las Vegas, from what she had gleaned.

"That enough, Lieutenant?"

"Quite enough. Go back to the overview and run the tape forward."

"Nobody good, huh?"

"Nobody good, right."

No good, period. Molina brooded. He had gone downhill since L.A. Downhill and edged into quasi-legal territory, at the least. Not all cops stay the course, but they don't have their futures written on their foreheads either. She had the uneasy feeling that Rafi's downward slide, if graphed, would exactly parallel her upward climb, in rank at least. It had not started out that way.

All the while her eyes were scanning the images flowing past the registration desk. The time read 6:10, the seconds fleeing like suspects.

Ten minutes, then she sat forward again.

Chet read her body language and immediately stopped the tape, reversed it, froze it.

Molina checked the time, then noted it down in the small notebook she carried in her jacket pocket: 6:23. And Matt Devine waiting at the brass stands that kept people from rushing the desk clerk.

What had nailed him was that he was looking around, constantly. Hunting Kitty the Cutter. If you knew to look for a hunted man, and Barrett and Su had not, it was easy to spot that bobbing head amid the sea of bored, nodding heads.

She nodded at Chet herself, okaying him to continue the tape, and watched Matt approach a desk clerk, chat, flash a roll, wait, study the page her computer spit out, hesitate, chat some more. The woman smiled. He was changing his room number and the woman smiled. What an operator! Mr. Charm. Irritate an overworked functionary and have her eating out of your hand anyway.

He did everything she had suggested.

"Stop."

Again the taped world obliged thanks to Chet's quick trigger finger. Molina studied every single soul in the frame, maybe seventy people. Nobody recognizable. No Vassar. No Kitty. No Rafi.

Nobody to see Matt Devine check into the Goliath Hotel for a date with death.

Nobody but the eternal Eye in the Sky and anybody with access to studying the tapes.

"Forward," Molina finally ordered.

Docilely, everyone on-screen sprang to life again, shuffling forward in line, slapping credit cards to marble, jostling each other, hanging back behind the registration line watching. . . .

Son of a biretta!

Molina's hands tightened on the hard plastic arms to keep herself from leaping out of her chair, but the control geek at the monitors sensed her excitement.

"Got it!" Chet caroled.

Even in black and white, there was no mistaking that head. Black as night, towering over the common crowd.

Max Kinsella had been at the Goliath Hotel the evening that Vassar had died, long before she and he had tangled in the Secrets parking lot and before Temple Barr had met the Stripper Killer face-to-face in another parking lot.

The ultra-modern letters on the frozen tape read 6:26.

Molina was doing some fast mental math.

Was there any way Kinsella could have escaped her custody and gotten back to the Goliath in time to interfere with Vassar in a fatal way?

Yes. And the bastard would even have had time to visit his heroic ladylove on the way.

If Kinsella could fly as a suspect, Matt was off the hook, and so was she.

But no. She and Matt would still have to reveal their roles in the whole charade, and who would believe the tale of Kitty the Cutter, woman of mystery?

Still. Kinsella had been there. She knew it. She had evidence. It would be worth something. Sometime.

. . . Gone for Good

Matt awoke, so early that the light wasn't sluicing through his bedroom miniblinds, and panicked.

Yesterday had been Sunday and he had missed mass.

The instant overpowering, guilty surge was an old altar-boy reflex.

Matt knew it had been Sunday. He knew he had missed mass. He had deliberately missed mass.

After the Saturday night he planned had turned out, he hadn't figured out how to go back to church. Was he a lamb of God or a leper? Did he need confession, and if so, exactly what sins should he confess? For the first time, Matt understood the constant internal agonies of over-scrupulous Catholics caught up in an obsessive-compulsive round of self-doubt.

Father, forgive me, for I may have done something wrong sometime, like maybe now by debating just what is confessable and what is not.

Often Matt had been secretly impatient with their endless, tiny, tedious venial sins, then had joined their self-abasement and assigned himself penance afterward. Now that his mind was splitting hairs, too, he began to see the torturous thumbtacks of self-incrimination that pinned these overanxious souls to a rack of worry and insecurity.

Okay. Yesterday had been Sunday. Today was Monday. A new week. Vassar was two days dead instead of one. Molina was digging into a new week's worth of investigative work. He was, what, eight hours into being promised release—paroled but not pardoned, if you will—by the call-in lips of Kathleen O'Connor? Could you believe a psychopath? Wasn't the impulse to want to believe them just another way they wrapped you up tighter in their own sick scenarios?

Nothing was sicker than his feelings about Vassar's death.

Matt sat up, his bare feet on the wood floor, which felt slick and cool.

Somebody must miss Vassar. She hadn't lived, or worked, in a vacuum. Maybe he could find out who. Tell them, him or her, about her last hours, which hadn't been too bad really . . . or was that hubris?

Matt shook his head, trying to make sense of the crowded hours: Vassar, and then Molina breaking in on him at home with such awful news, and next Temple, asking questions he didn't want to answer. Then Leticia babysitting him through the lonely hours live on radio, and Kathleen calling to say he was free, and finally Jerome, Jerry Johnson from seminary, showing up in the parking lot with fifteen years of baggage invisibly dragging behind him, expecting Matt to help lift the load.

Punishment, he supposed, for trying to turn against years of conditioning.

He got up and trudged to the shower, sloughing his *gi*-pajamas. Martial arts-wear as sleepwear. Was there some underlying statement in his habits? Did he need to be on guard even as he slept? Especially as he slept? Yes.

Hot water, then cold may have cleared his head, but not his heart.

Dressed, Matt went into the main room, not surprised that the hour was too early for anything except extra z's.

Maybe he would drive somewhere, to an all-night fast-food place. Eat breakfast as the sun rose over the mountains at the valley's eastern edge.

His wallet and keys lay on one of the small cube tables that formed an impromptu coffee table in front of the sofa.

He swept the items up, designated for opposite pants pockets, then stopped to study the key ring.

Something was different. Wrong. Missing.

His heart leaped to the top of the Mount Charleston, seeking the first rays of sun.

It was Monday morning, and Kathleen O'Connor's worm Ouroboros ring was gone. The bad news was that sometime in the recent past she had been in his rooms, had moved among his things, perhaps even while he slept, to accomplish the sleight of hand of the missing ring. The good news was that, for the first time, he truly believed that she had given up on him.

Liberation felt uplifting, like a good confession. Like saying the Apostle's Creed and starting a whole new day, a whole new life.

But one man's liberation was often another's loss.

The snake had left Eden.

Where was it slithering next?

. . . *Jailhouse Hard Rock*

"Okay," Molina said, shaking the multivitamin energy drink-to-go on her desk.

Breakfast.

Everyone in the room was eating on the run, or on the meeting break: Alfonso, Barrett, Su, and Alch.

Alfonso had a McDonald's cholesterol special on his lap, sausage and cheese predominating. Barrett munched a sports nutrition bar. Su had coffee from the Office Urn of All Sediment and an Almond Joy candy bar. Alch, he went for a Weight Watchers bar, munching in time with Barrett.

Molina eyed her troops, aware how their very differences, physical and psychological, made them good partners. Too good for this case that cut so close to her own bones. Yet she had to do her job. Or seem to.

"I saw Rothenberg," Molina announced. "Vassar was her girl, and Rothenberg believes that her girls are too mentally, physically, and socially healthy to off themselves, or to get offed. She won't be yelling police incompetence if we just bury this investigation. Case closed?"

"No way," Su mumbled through three hundred luscious calories that would not put an ounce on her tensile little frame, Molina reflected. "A call girl dies. Chances are ninety-to-one it's murder."

"No evidence," Alfonso countered.

Molina took a deep breath. It was now or never. Do her job or save her rear.

"I don't like that bellman with Alzheimer's," she said. "The kind of tips they get for playing matchmaker, I don't believe he never noticed a thing."

"Lots of that sort of traffic at a big place like the Goliath," Su said. "I doubt those women even remember the faces they saw the night before, and they get paid plenty."

"What do you suggest?" Alch asked Molina. Morrie always recognized when she was leading a horse to water.

"Bring the bellman in. Sweat him. Let me know when you're ready."

Alch nodded.

Barrett spoke up. "Whatever the bellman says, there's not a mark on her that wasn't caused by hitting neon at eighty miles an hour. Some bruises, a lot of internal damage. She could have dived. But Rothenberg has a political stake in representing hooking as safe and sane."

Molina nodded, waiting for their respective partners to bow in.

"It's not good PR," Alch offered, trying not to look lustily at Su's half-eaten candy bar. "A dead call girl when you're a national spokes*woman* for hookers' rights to choose? Rothenberg might know more. Maybe somebody was moving in on her operation. It's pretty passkey. The girls are gung-ho about wanting to do what they do. An old-school pimp would be a wolf among sheep."

"Interesting," Molina agreed. "Rothenberg's bled the local media for all the feature stories she can get. She might be ripe for plucking, and her girls too. Vassar might have been approached first to change handlers."

"What if she went for the idea?" Su asked, sitting forward on a chair she already perched on like a sparrow.

"What if she'd been recruited by someone else, and Rothenberg saw her libertarian utopia looking shaky? Would she kill to defend it?"

"Even more interesting," Molina granted. "And then there's the string of deaths of near-apparent women of the night. You know which ones I mean?"

"Yeah." Alch burped. That Weight Watchers bar must have been heavy consumption for him. He shrugged apology, but was too jived on his idea to blush for his social sins. "First there was that woman's body dumped at the Blue Dahlia parking lot. 'She left,' was painted on the neighboring car. Yours, as I recall, Lieutenant."

"You don't have to remind me, Morrie."

"Right. Anyway, Su and I solved that one. Some weirdo had killed her for *not* being a shady lady, can you believe it?" he asked Alfonso and Barrett.

"And there was that young stripper, Cher Smith," Su put in. She was competitive with her elder, Alch, even though, or especially because, they were partners. "We lucked out when her killer tried to attack a strip-club costume-seller who was armed with pepper spray."

"Right," Molina said too quickly.

The less anyone dwelled on *that* recent episode the better she'd feel personally. The fact was that a mere civilian had lured and trapped the killer, pathetic as the murderer had turned out to be.

"We've still got one outstanding," Su noted unhappily, folding her candy bar wrapper into very tight, neat origami.

Buddha bless overachieving third-generation Asian-Americans, Molina thought.

"That's the broad," Alfonso said, Egg McMuffin sticking to his teeth, "they found in the church parking lot about the same time as the Blue Dahlia dame."

God bless old-time cops of whatever ethnic heritage who never let go.

"Gloria Fuentes," Barrett added with narrowed eyes, "was no shady lady. She was a retired magician's assistant. Sure, they're all legs and cleavage, but this lady was over the hill, pardon me. She'd been out of the performance game for years. Hell, her main magician, Gandolph the Great, had quit performing to sniff out fake mediums years ago. She was no spring chicken, and she died in a church parking lot, for Gawd's sake, not in the parking lot of a trendy restaurant-nightclub like the Blue Dahlia, pardon me, Lieutenant, for your patronage."

"The Blue Dahlia hasn't had any crime calls except that one," Molina noted.

"But that was a doozy. Murder One," Barrett chortled.

Yes, chortled. Molina turned to Alch, whose insight she could always depend upon.

" 'She left,' " he intoned. "That was the phrase painted near the body in the Blue Dahlia parking lot, and that was the phrase that appeared during the autopsy of Gloria Fuentes's body, like invisible ink finally showing up. I think those murders were connected."

"We nailed the Blue Dahlia perp," Su objected, pulling a second Almond Joy from the pocket of her size-zero navy silk jacket.

Alch's salt-and-pepper head shook doggedly, like a wet Old English sheepdog's. "I think they were connected, all right, but not necessarily by the same killer."

All jaws stopped munching.

This was a radical suggestion.

Molina bowed her head, or maybe merely nodded, at Alch.

Encouraged, he went on. "Maybe it was a copycat killing. I mean, there we have it, in the Blue Dahlia lot, the phrase 'She left.' How basic can you get? Every woman who's involved with an abusive man, what is her death all about? She left, he got homicidal. It's predictable."

"We've never found a suspect for the Fuentes case," Molina pointed out.

"But," said Alch, perching on the edge of his chair a lot more uncomfortably but no less eagerly than Su had on hers, "the same words turn up relative to Fuentes *after* the body's in *our* custody. *She left*. Same old overcontrolling bastard's complaint, only someone got into our system, into the morgue, mind you, to send that message. What did Gloria Fuentes leave? Anybody know? Anybody look into that?"

"Lived alone, past sixty," Su said.

"You're young," Alch returned. "That doesn't mean she couldn't have had a man in her life."

"Or a child," Alfonso said. "Sometimes a kid gets threatened and the mother gets drawn into something uglier than she's ready for."

Amen, Molina thought.

"Her 'kids' would have been out on their own, older than me," Su said.

"Doesn't matter," Alch returned. "Kids are always kids to their parents. But I checked Fuentes out. She *was* single, had no known boyfriends, no known kids. Once she left the stage, she did a little magic act for civic groups around town, kids' birthday stuff. She didn't even have anyone to leave anything to in her will. It all went, what there was of it, to some magician's retirement home."

"Funny. She'd been a looker. Somehow she ended up alone," Alfonso meditated, chewing his high-fat cud.

"And dead," Barrett said. "If this is a cold case, I say we look deeper. Fuentes may not have been a lady of the night, but you point out yourselves that the woman at the Blue Dahlia led a respectable life, she was just murdered like a stripper or a call girl. Maybe we got a killer who's not too good at telling the difference."

"Gloria Fuentes," Molina said meditatively, as if caressing the idea. Her troops would jump on that train of thought, she knew. "Alch is right. We haven't dug deep enough into her lifestyle, present and past. The words 'She left' showing up on her body smacks of magic tricks."

Su jumped in with both size-four feet. "And Vassar could have 'left' too. We don't know that she wasn't dumping Rothenberg and all her principles."

Molina nodded, though she didn't believe it. Rothenberg's girls didn't leave; they retired.

She quashed a surge of triumph. Nasty as the neon ceiling death was, it was redirecting her detective's attention to the one definitely magic-related death that had hit the town since Max Kinsella had left a year ago and come back last fall.

If *she* had to hang out on a limb, that son of a . . . psychopath should too. And she might finally find a case that tied him to all the mayhem and murder in this town that was still floating loose.

That would be worth her own personal and professional jeopardy, all due to the misguided impulse to help Matt Devine escape from between a rock and a hard place.

Molina frowned, thinking of his particular problem. Kathleen O'Connor. She'd have to pursue that lead herself. None of them would be in this mess without that femme fatale operating just out of sight, sound, and reach of the law's long arm.

Maybe not even the Mystifying Max Kinsella.

. . . Sudden Death Overtime

"You may have wondered," Temple said, "why I've called you all together."

"Two is 'all'?" Max asked dubiously.

Matt was too polite to question the obvious, but his expression of stubborn silence agreed with Max's for once.

"Well, Louie is here also," Temple said.

Everyone glanced at the large black cat that formed the only barrier between Max and Matt as they shared the small living room sofa. Given Louie's size, it was a considerable separation.

Louie, knowing he was being discussed as all cats do, did a tarantella move and extended his long black furry legs. Then he showed his claws, curved them artistically into the open-weave upholstery, and yawned, as if to say: *I could rip this fabric to shreds, but I am being the little gentleman and am restraining myself for my Miss Temple's sake. So you two guys better follow my example and keep away from each other's throats, tempting as they may be.*

Temple eyed her gentlemen callers. She perched on the edge of the chair facing the sofa, her feet not quite touching the floor, as usual. She hadn't seen these two men juxtaposed often, and here and now it was obvious that they were Night and Day.

Max was Night, long and lean, attired in magician's black from the hair on his head to raven-glossy black Armani loafers on his feet. Matt was Day, not as tall but more solid, blond from the hair on his head to the suede loafers on his feet. In a fashion parallel of the Civil War ballad of the brothers on opposite sides, one wore black and one wore blond, instead of blue and gray.

Matt was more classicly handsome than Max, but Max had more presence.

Neither one was in the least shabby. *Okay, girl. Down. Speak, Lassie, speak! What are you trying to tell us*?

"I am not Nancy Drew, Miss Marple, or Jessica Fletcher," Temple said. She was red, from her hair to her lucite-heeled Stuart Weitzman Dorothy-in-Oz scarlet pumps.

"Great," Max noted, glancing at Matt. "One's underage and the other two are definitely overage, if not for you, then for me."

Temple and Matt blushed in concert.

"Go on," Matt encouraged her. He was a great facilitator.

"But I am a mean hand with a ruler and a pencil, so I've resurrected my table of the unsolved murders I made before the Stripper Killer was caught, and I added Vassar."

Temple slapped the template in question down on the coffee table.

"And I made copies." She handed them, after a second's hesitation, first to Max, then to Matt.

Midnight Louie glared at her.

"Sorry, boy. I do have an extra."

This she placed on the sofa by Louie's large black paws. Her human companions shook their heads.

WHO	WHEN	WHERE	METHOD	ODDITIES	SUSPECT/S
dead man at Goliath Hotel	April	casino ceiling	?		Max
dead man at Crystal Phoenix	Aug	casino ceiling	?	Resembled Effinger	?
Max's mentor, Gandolph	Halloween	séance	?	Cause undetermined	assorted psychics
Cliff Effinger, Matt's stepfather	New Year's	Oasis	drowning		2 muscle men
Woman	Feb	church parking lot	strangled	ligature	arrested
Cher Smith, stripper	Feb	strip club parking lot	strangled		arrested
Gloria Fuentes, Gandolph's assistant	Feb	church parking lot	strangled	*"she left"* on body in morgue	?
Prof. Jeff Mangel	March	UNLV hall	knifed	ritual marks	the Synth
Cloaked Conjuror's assistant	April	New Millennium ceiling	beating or fatal fall	masked like CC or a TV show SF alien	?
Vassar, call girl	May	Goliath Hotel	fatal fall	after seeing Matt	Kitty O'Connor Matt

"Hey!" Matt spoke first. "You not only added Vassar to the list of dead people, you put me in the suspect column."

"Along with Kathleen O'Connor. And Max is first in the list with the death that started it all at the Goliath, so it's only fitting that you should finish up the list to date with Vassar's death at . . . the Goliath. Anybody see a pattern here?"

"Temple," Max explained, "the karma of heading and finishing up the suspect list is lost on the suspects in question."

"This suspect list reflects both who *we* might think is responsible and who the *police* might, or do."

"Don't use a euphemism," Max growled. "You mean Molina. Say it."

"I'm also saying that I'm no expert, but given what's happened, I think we better get our acts together and figure out the who, what, where, when, and why of these deaths and what Kathleen O'Connor is up to before we're all finessed onto Death Row."

"She's my problem," Max said, glowering. "I knew her first."

"You mean in the Biblical sense, I assume," Matt added.

Temple chalked up one point for the mild-mannered ex-altar boy.

"In every sense," Max said, not sparing Temple the truth.

His glower did not diminish. His arms remained crossed on his chest, a classic posture of self-containment. Max hated being here with her and Matt, Temple knew, and with Midnight Louie. He hated group anything, which at least made him a very unlikely candidate for an orgy. He was the original lone wolf and had gotten too used to it, certainly for their communal needs now, and maybe for his own good.

"You're not the issue here," Temple said, catching Max's eye. "Matt is."

"Only because Kathleen can't find me."

"Is that ego, or analysis?"

"Analysis." Max glanced at Matt, not unsympathetically. "Look. She's following a classic pattern. It's older than Devine here, and it's older than me." He uncrossed his arms to prop them on his knees and lean forward, speaking only to Temple, as if he had to justify himself and the past only to her.

"Here's how it goes down with the likes of Kathleen O'Connor, even when you're both seventeen. You meet her. You think it's chance, and later you see that she put herself in your path. With you," he added as an aside to

Matt, "the introduction was shocking, but she's older now, and hasn't time to waste. So you got the razor to the gut, a flesh wound, so you'd know she could inflict any kind of wound she wants, when she wants, on whom she wants."

Temple frowned now. "So she was always a psychopath?"

"A shrink would probably argue that label," Max said. "More like a sociopath with a heavy case of narcissism."

"What's the difference?" Temple wanted to know.

Matt answered. "Both a psychopath and a sociopath lack a conscience. They don't feel hurt, so they hurt, just to see what happens to people who do feel. A narcissist is always trying to prove the world stupider than she is. In a way, a narcissistic sociopath is worse than the average psychopath. She can pass in normal society."

"Where'd you learn that?" Max asked, sounding impressed.

"Confession," Matt said shortly. "They're expert manipulators, and they love to manipulate all that's solid and sacred."

" 'Solid and sacred,' " Max mocked. "Wouldn't go over in a personals ad."

"Cut it out, guys!" Temple said. "This woman has ruined both your lives. You want to snipe at each other, or get her?"

"Get her," Max said without hesitation.

Matt temporized. " 'Get,' sounds so hostile. She needs help."

"*You* need help, can't you see that?" Temple exploded. "That's what she's done to you. She's made you into a murder suspect, and you're worried about her, for heaven's sake."

Max's frown was back. "Temple's right. It's the same pattern. Half a lifetime ago, while I was dallying with Kathleen on the riverbank, my cousin Sean was walking into an IRA death trap. And you, ex-Father Devine, once suggested that might have been deliberate manipulation on

Kathleen's part: seducing me and killing Sean at one and the same time, killing one man . . . boy, really. . . . and condemning the other to permanent Purgatory because of it."

"Purgatory?" Temple asked.

The two men were staring at each other, ignoring her, speaking the same language for once. Catholic. Guilt. Only for one it was the Irish and the Troubles and for the other it was the Polish and the family dysfunction.

"It must have been hell for you," Matt said, "given how I feel about Vassar's death, and she wasn't a relative, an innocent, or anyone I even knew."

"Still is."

Matt's mouth tightened. "Then Temple's right. We have to find this woman, stop her."

"All we know about her today," Temple put in, "is that she ran across Matt several months ago somehow and can't let go. How? And why?"

"Simple," he said. "Talk about poetic justice. My hunt for my stepfather drew her attention. I distributed these photos of him with my contact information. That's when she showed up here at the Circle Ritz, by the pool when I was working out. She thought I was a contract killer looking for him."

"What does that tell us about her?" Max asked.

"That she expects the worst of everybody," Matt answered. "If we knew why, we might know how to get to her."

"No," Temple said. "It tells us that she wouldn't have found you, Matt, if you hadn't been looking for Cliff Effinger. It had nothing to do with you, Max, not then. Sorry."

He shrugged. "My own sociopathic narcissistic streak is shattered."

"Effinger's the key?" Matt said doubtfully. "He's dead."

"But he wasn't then, Temple said. And why is he dead now? He was killed. By someone. Molina nabbed a couple of thugs who for the rap, the guys driving that semi when the drug bust was made, but even the police didn't have enough evidence to charge them with Effinger's murder."

"And that bust *was* tied to your and Louie's kidnapping," Max said, "from the Opium Den stage."

"When," Matt put in, "that lady magician Shangri-La used Temple's ring in a disappearing act and it vanished." He didn't quite look at her. "Until it turned up on a murder scene Molina was covering."

"I love the way everybody knew about my ring being found, except me." Max's frown escalated into a glower.

Temple took a deep breath. "*I* didn't know this until just recently."

Max glanced at Matt, immediately realizing what she meant. Matt knew about the ring being found long before either of them. He could only have been told by Molina, and he had kept that from the two people who had a right to know what had happened to the ring, the man who gave it and the woman who accepted it.

"The point is," Temple said to break the awkward silence, "that the ring was found near the dead magician's assistant, who was killed at the same time as that other body was dumped at the Blue Dahlia. Her name was Gloria. Gloria Fuentes. Gandolph's retired assistant."

"Who's Gandolph?" Matt asked.

Neither Temple nor Max answered him. They were staring at each other, lost in the implications.

"The question is," Max told Temple, "was the ring left there to implicate you, or me?"

"Temple, obviously." Matt ran a hand through his blond hair as if unconsciously pushing away an encroaching headache. "Even Molina's not so obsessed with arresting the great Max Kinsella that she'd blame you for the death of anyone simply connected with magic."

A silence. They were three, but there were islands of knowledge between them shared by only two, and perhaps in some case by only one. Time to build bridges over troubled water.

Temple focused on Matt. "Gloria Fuentes has a more

direct connection to Max than mere magic. She was the longtime assistant to Max's mentor, Gandolph the Great."

The news jolted Matt. "Wasn't that the fellow killed at last Halloween's Houdini séance? And now you tell me this guy's retired ex-assistant was killed only a few months later?"

"Yes." Max was terse. "You see what Molina could do with those facts, given her hard-on for charging me with some crime or other."

"So—" Matt was perking up from the funk he'd been in since hearing the shocking news of Vassar's death. "That ring being at Gloria Fuentes's death scene was a double whammy for Max, only Molina didn't know it. Doesn't know it?"

"No, thank God." Temple grimaced. "And don't you tell her. That's why I didn't invite her to our heart-to-heart. Even though she's up to her shield in your recent foray into the local sex industry, she has no idea of how badly someone is out to get Max. It has to be Kathleen O'Connor."

"Why?" Matt demanded.

"She doesn't let go," Max put in. "I also reacted to Sean's death differently than she expected. Guilt, she got that, an endless peat bog's worth to wallow in. But I went undercover in the IRA, found out who bombed that pub, and turned them in, remember."

"That's right. You were reared Catholic yet you betrayed the IRA."

"I would have betrayed the pope to get the ones who killed Sean." His eyes narrowed at Matt. "You can probably dig that. You were pretty hot to find your evil stepfather. Didn't you ever want to wring his neck?"

Matt nodded. "And now I'd like to wring the neck of whoever hurt Vassar."

"You, ah," Max said cautiously, "can't offer any insight on her last hours on earth?"

"Nothing except that she was alive and well when I left her."

Max refrained from asking how well, for which Temple gave him full credit. The conversation was getting unbearable for all-parties involved.

"I realize," Matt said, looking steadfastly at the top of the coffee table, which was littered with sections from two days' worth of newspapers, "that inquiring minds want to know what happened between Vassar and me. Sorry. No comment."

"What did Molina say to that?" Max asked with his best Mr. Spock raised eyebrow.

"Nothing. She never asked."

Max suddenly laughed. "I love it! You shut down Molina on a case where her own hide is at stake. I've heard of Teflon politicians, but you, Devine, have a Teflon sex life. Nothing sticks but mystery."

"Yet," Matt said. "She hasn't asked me yet."

"And if she does?"

"I tell her the same thing I tell you: no prurient details. Vassar deserves better than that. She deserves a heck of a lot better than what happened to her, however it happened. I didn't know her like a cousin, but I did get to know her enough to realize that."

Another awkward silence.

Temple broke in with her best nonintimidating small wee voice. "Can you tell us, Matt, if you had any reason to think she *might* commit suicide?"

He stared at the pages of newsprint again, one bearing a small front-page story about a plunge to death at the Goliath. Then his eyes met Temple's.

"I don't know. She had . . . issues. Doesn't everybody?"

"Amen, brother," Max agreed. "Okay. If I'm reading this right, you don't know yourself whether she jumped or was pushed, and you're the last known person to have seen her."

"Yes."

"When exactly was the 'last time'?" Temple asked, eyeing the newspapers.

"Four A.M."

"So you spent, what, six hours with her?"

"More like eight. Call it a shift, if you like."

"I'm not calling it anything," Temple said carefully. "You must have gotten to know her . . . talked . . . in all that time."

He nodded.

"Tell us about her," Max said in a surprisingly calm voice. "She's just a role to most people in a town filled with hookers and call girls and boys and private dancers. Tell us about her, not about what she did for a living."

Matt nodded, seeming to welcome the chance. He leaned back, clasped his tanned hands around one khaki-clad knee. The casual pose couldn't disguise the darkness in his voice.

"Molina . . . misrepresented her to me. Not her fault. She gave me the best advice she could."

"*Humph!*" Temple couldn't resist inserting. "You didn't hear anything of the kind from me!"

"I heard it from you, though," he said with a glance at Max. "And Leticia at work. Everybody said this was the best thing to do."

"Not me," Temple said.

Matt finally met her glance. "I wish to God now I'd listened to what you *didn't* tell me to do. Anyway, Molina swore that this level of call girl would be smart, comfortable with herself and her . . . job, impersonally personal, the solution I so desperately needed. And I don't think even you"—he eyed Max—"know what it's really like to have Kitty O'Connor on your case, day in and night out. She was beginning to seem omniscient."

"Like God," Max suggested, "or your own conscience. The Hound of Hell. Impossible to flee."

"And she'd made enough threatening gestures at females I knew . . . Mariah, even Electra, that I was pretty paranoid and ripe for her manipulation. And for drastic solutions." Matt shook his head. "The idea was that she couldn't track me to a call girl the bellman sent up, and I ran all over Las Vegas to lose her."

"Not enough," Max said. "I saw you go into the Goliath that night."

"You!"

Max managed to shrug indifferently and look sheepish at the same time. "I knew Kathleen was stalking you. I wanted to catch a glimpse of how she looks today. You did a damn fine job of trying to lose a tail. If I hadn't known you, I might have lost you."

"Max!" Temple didn't mean to sound exasperated, but she did. "Are you telling us you were at the Goliath, that you saw Matt going into the hotel?"

"It was earlier in the evening . . . sixish, wasn't it? Right. I followed him in, checked the surroundings. Certainly didn't see Kitty O'Connor, and then I split, because I was worried about you and the Stripper Killer. If I'd been able to stay . . ." He nodded at Matt. "I might have been curious enough to hang around after you left and seen something. So we get to share the riches of guilt this time, if that makes you feel any better."

"It doesn't and I think you know that. Misery loves company is a sop to the poor of heart."

Another silence.

Temple felt like someone trying to herd a glacier toward the Tropic of Cancer.

"So what did you see, Max?"

"I saw our fair-haired boy check in and go up in the elevator. I saw no one who looked like Kathleen, or Kathleen in disguise, but it's been almost twenty years, Temple. She could look like your grandmother by now."

"She doesn't," Matt said dryly. "You saw the sketch."

"Wouldn't it have been weird," Temple speculated, "if Vassar had been Kitty the Cutter?"

"You mean," Max said, getting it at once, "if she had followed our man Flint into the Goliath and arranged to ring his bell, metaphorically speaking, when the bellman ordered a call girl. That would make her dead, and I can't say I'd be sorry."

Matt shook his head at their lavish scenarios. "Vassar

was a tall woman; Kitty was petite. You can't fake that."

"How petite?" Temple asked.

"A bit bigger than you."

"Oh. I always imagine her as bigger than life. Like Wonder Woman."

"No," said Max, "she's a wee bit of a thing, rather like a plastic explosive." But he was thinking so hard he was frowning again. "It's possible Kathleen was there. Certainly she could fool me after all these years. It's possible she followed you to the room and killed Vassar after you left. Did you notice anything suspicious?"

"Everything felt suspicious, everybody I had contact with was out of a B movie. The accommodating desk clerk, who let me pay cash for a room and then change the number at the last moment, all by the book according to Molina, by the way."

Max grinned meanly. "She sure knows how to read the wrong side of the law for such an upstanding policewoman."

Matt went on, as if needing to relive each sleazy step toward disaster. "And there was the lurking bellman, happy to pocket a big tip to provide X-rated entertainment. It was like some hokey formula. I felt unreal."

"I've got a news flash for you, Devine. Hiring a hooker is not a 'real' experience."

"I know that. I can't believe I listened to everybody, including you, and did this. I thought you worldly sophisticates knew what you were doing."

"We don't. And we just look worldly. It's all an act, Devine. Magic. Don't believe in magic. It's not real."

"Vassar was more real than any of you," Matt commented bitterly.

That hurt. Temple felt it like a punch to the stomach. She hadn't led him down this particular garden path . . . but she could have made the whole charade unnecessary, she knew that now. And that was another punch to the gut.

She got back to business to hide the pain. "So. No sign of Kitty the Cutter knowing where you were and who you were with. She couldn't have passed as the bellman. Or was he short?"

"He was," Matt said with a certain spine-stiffening motion. "But so was the waitress who brought dinner. I never thought of that. She was . . . petite."

"Could she—?" Max asked.

"That is such a repellent idea, that woman spying on me even as I'm going to lengths she drove me to . . . I suppose she'd like that. What would make a person want to destroy another person?"

"Why did the fundamentalists attack the twin towers?" Max asked. "Envy. They can call it religion or politics, but it's envy and fear. Kathleen is like that. She hates innocence. She hates freedom. She hates anyone with a zest for life."

"Why?" Matt asked.

"Why you?" Max retorted. He sighed. "You trigger her most negative emotions. Don't feel guilty about it. But I did. I was seventeen. You're . . . seventeen, too, don't you see? Kathleen's getting too old to find true innocents cluttering the landscape. I'm too burned-out for her. You're fresh meat. She can really do a tap dance on your head. Let her bring you down, and she's won. Unlike most of Las Vegas and some people of our acquaintance, I don't care to know what went on between you and the dead woman. That's irrelevant. It's what went on between you and the dead woman and Kathleen O'Connor, don't you see? With her, it's always a triangle."

"An unholy trinity," Matt said slowly, "as it was that night: Vassar, me, and Kitty O'Connor rolling in a room-service tray."

Temple felt a certain satisfaction. She had brought the two men together to shake loose some facts, ideas, and maybe solutions.

She hadn't expected it to be pretty, and she hadn't expected to enjoy it. It hurt to watch Max's self-protective cynicism and Matt's injured innocence jousting as if they were each other's worst enemies when their real antagonist, and the truth, was still out there.

And whatever had happened, or had *not* happened between Matt and Vassar, the call girl's sudden death had made her a permanent fixture in his life, and that of anyone who cared about him Which, Temple thought sourly, included her, dammit.

. . . *Homicide Alone*

Molina stood inside and pushed the garage door opener control, waiting until the single wooden door shook, rattled, and rolled all the way shut.

Nobody like a cop to follow home-safety rules. No neighborhood cat would slip under *her* closing garage door undetected, not to mention the odd, escaped serial rapist.

When she went through the door into the kitchen, locking it behind her, the house felt cool, dim, and suspiciously silent.

Then she remembered. Mariah was at an after-school game followed by a team pizza party. Some lucky parents with regular hours or even an at-home mom would be dropping Mariah off from a minivan around eight P.M.

So not even Dolores, the trusty neighborhood nanny, was here.

Molina wasn't used to an empty, quiet house.

She draped her jacket over the back of a kitchen chair and pulled the paddle holster from her back waistband, heading for the bedroom to deposit it in her closet gun safe.

Even with Mariah not there, she never left her weapon unattended for a split second.

A sudden thump from the living room halted her instantly.

Only Catarina or Tabitha, thundering over the hardwood floors, slipping and sliding, on almost-year-old paws. The tiger-striped kittens had become cats, but still could revert to an adolescent romp.

"Hi, girls," Molina greeted them as they charged past, one only two feet behind the other.

No answer. Their bowls were full of dry food and they didn't need to make up to her for dinner.

Actually, she was glad they were growing up and settling down. Kittens were appealing and fun, but layabout adult cats were better medicine for the frazzled police professional.

Many of Molina's peers were unwinding in a laid-back cop bar right now. She glanced at her watch. 6:05 P.M. She could have actually stopped by for once. Except that having made a habit of heading home to kid and kittens had made her a stranger in a familiar land. So had her rank. Face it. She was not a party person.

Ah. Mariah was gone. No need to listen to that pulsing, rapping, mewling, screaming rock/rap radio station. Save her from preteens going on thirty!

Molina backtracked to the living room, moved the dial to the easy-listening station she had once kept tuned in, and waited until "Sitting on the Dock of the Bay" came drooling over the airwaves like a cool mint julep spilling between the cracks of an overheated wooden porch floor somewhere over the rainbow where bluebirds sang and crickets chirped and sap ran.

Ah. She stepped out of her loafers, worn because their low heels did not intimidate male coworkers shorter than she. She picked them up by the heels and carried both shoes and semiautomatic pistol toward her bedroom.

She paused at the open door to Mariah's bedroom.

The same bright chaos as always. Textbooks in canted piles under discarded clothing scattered around the room like the Scarecrow after the Flying Monkeys had gotten through with him. Mariah could never decide which look-alike shapeless T-shirt and baggy pants were coolest of them all. Posters everywhere of sinister, pouting males and females masquerading as singers. If she'd seen these punks when she was walking a beat she'd have arrested them on suspicion of juvenile dysfunction. Stuffed toys enough to almost hide the state of the unmade bed.

Nothing straightened up as promised: "Tomorrow, I promise!" And tomorrow and tomorrow.

Molina shook her head and smiled. Better an untidy room than a messy head. And Mariah's head was still mostly straight on. So far.

She moved the few steps down the hall to her room. So quiet now.

Maybe she would have a drink before dinner. There was a bottle of aged whiskey that had aged even longer in her kitchen cupboard waiting to serve in Christmas egg nogs. Somehow she never had time to have adults over for Christmas.

She paused at her bedroom door, remembering the crowded, noisy Christmases of her childhood in East L.A. The tiny bungalow crammed with tearing kids tearing wrappings off a Technicolor mountain of presents under a skinny balsam Christmas tree draped in miniature piñata figures and huge pinwheel-striped lollipops from the Christ child to every kid under twelve in the house, and there were tons of kids. Her eight half-brothers and -sisters, for instance, all younger. All kids still, and she, Carmen, had been older, an adult early, more their nursemaid than their sister, even when she had been only nine, or seven, or even five.

They danced around her imagination now, her half-brothers and -sisters, black-haired, black-eyed sprites with adorable faces . . . that needed constant wiping by her of food and tears, depending on the day or the occasion.

She loved them all . . . and it would be a cold day in hell before she would want to shepherd more than one kid, Mariah, to adulthood again. She'd been a mother most of her life. When she'd become the first in her family to go to college, a two-year college, it was more a betrayal than a cause for celebration.

Molina . . . Carmen . . . sat on the bed, gun and shoes sitting beside her, symbols of everything that had gone right and wrong in her life.

She so seldom had time to think. To remember. Now, even shattered images of Rafi Nadir washed over her in the dead quiet.

She couldn't seem to control the memory flood. Was she drowning? Drowning in guilt? Or just stranded tired and alone for once? Sitting on the dock of the bay, on the tree above the flood, waiting to be rescued.

No. She rescued herself. Always had. She didn't sit around waiting for anything. For anybody.

She started singing counter to the living room radio, softly, in harmony. It was odd hearing her own voice without accompaniment, without the boys in the band behind her.

She sighed. It had been too long since she'd dropped in at the Blue Dahlia to add the words to their music. Dolores was always available. She should do it again soon.

Sittin' on the dock of the bay. Something, something *away.*

She saw Vassar spread-eagled on neon, stripped and dissected on stainless steel, a twelve-hour transformation, from pinned butterfly to laboratory frog.

She shook her head, shook the image away. There was no reason she couldn't contact her family now, though it had been so long.

Except that Rafi would have known, and he wasn't about to let her go. And maybe, maybe, she was just as glad he'd forced her to run away, start a new life alone. With Mariah when she arrived.

She had been mired in her own unhappy history. Always the half-breed. Her mother's one unforgivable mistake, that she'd tried to undo eight times until she had died of it.

By then Carmen had been in place, knowing she was a mistake, apologetic enough to make up for it, tending her mother's whole-breed brood, loving them, hating herself.

She shook her head. That was so long ago. Why was she thinking of it now?

Of course. Rafi. He was like the recurrent nightmare in a slasher movie, Michael or Jason, never quite dying, always popping up to revive the terror. A franchise attraction.

Molina stood up. She was a big girl now, in every respect.

If Matt Devine had anything to do with Vassar's death, she would find out and arrest him. If Rafi found her and Mariah, he would be sorry. If Max Kinsella crossed her path again, in the wrong place at the wrong time, she'd stop him no matter what it took. If Temple Barr was in mourning for the two men in her life, let her weep and wail.

If she, Carmen . . . no, Molina, had to destroy her career to bring down a murderer, so be it.

She went to her closet, opened the door, dropped her shoes on the floor, moved to turn the tumblers on the safe.

Something elusive and soft brushed her wrist.

She started to push it aside.

It was velvet. Midnight blue velvet, a limp, 1930s evening gown, Depression era; sleazy and soft and irresistible.

Molina frowned at the Blue Dahlia side of her closet with its meager column of vintage gowns. Carmen wasn't here anymore, but her wardrobe was.

Blue velvet? God, she was losing it. She'd forgotten buying that one.

Or did she just want to forget? Not only the ancient past, but the recent one, all the way up to encouraging Matt Devine to make a date with destiny.

. . . A League of Her Own

Matt had spent his working life on a phone for over a year now: first at the hot line and now at WCOO radio.

He was used to calls being urgent, to surprises, to communicating well despite the distance and the lack of face-to-face contact.

Now he was hanging on hold, waiting for the phone to be picked up again after a long, frustrating attempt to make contact.

He supposed calling the FBI might be like that.

"Matt!" boomed a confident and somewhat superficial voice.

"Frank," Matt echoed, determined to control this conversation.

"What can I do for you?"

"I'm afraid I still need information on that woman terrorist, Kathleen O'Connor, only this time it might involve murder."

"I came up dry last time."

"I know. I believe in try, try again."

"What's the murder case?"

"Mine."

"What?"

"Well, it cuts two ways, if you recall how Miss Kitty introduced herself to me a few months ago."

"Humor does help, Matt. Yes, I remember. She cut you. Razor, wasn't it? Odd weapon for a woman."

"She's an odd woman. She's been stalking me."

"Why?"

"Because I was there? All I can glean from what she's said, which I don't entirely believe, is that she has a grudge against priests."

"You're an ex-priest."

"So I told her. It doesn't seem to matter to her."

"I know she's been a thorn in your side for some time. What's happened to escalate matters?"

"First, she started physically threatening my friends and acquaintances. Women, girls, old women, it didn't seem to matter as long as they were female."

"You are talking major-league obsessive."

"Yes." And Matt hated doing this sort of talking on the telephone. Despite a bug-free apartment, he still had the slimy sensation that someone was listening. It could be a hangover from his radio talk-show history, or just knowing that the FBI probably recorded everything.

"I wish we could talk in person."

"Can you come out here?"

"Not right now."

"Then shoot. If it's not a matter of national security, this is a safe line."

Matt grimaced. That wasn't much of a guarantee, but he needed solid answers, not speculation. Besides, he had confessed so often to Father Frank Bucek when they were both in seminary, Frank as instructor, Matt as acolyte, that pulling back now seemed foolish.

"Okay. This woman made it plain: my virtue, or their lives."

"Nasty. I assume you took measures."

"I tried to. I got as much advice as I could—"

"From whom? You didn't ask me."

"I'm . . . sorry, Frank. Guess I was embarrassed."

"What? That some woman was so infatuated she'd blackmail you into submission? You and Brad Pitt. Don't be an ass, Matt. It's like that out here in the real world. There are guys who would envy you."

"That's like telling an eighty-year-old woman she's lucky to be raped."

Silence on the line. Long silence. "You're right. I was being cynical. It gets that way, if you see enough. Sorry. It works both ways. Stalking is stalking. So what advice did you get?"

"It was clear she wanted to destroy what I had taken out of the priesthood, my celibacy."

"Odd fixation. Odd woman."

"I know. So, my . . . friends . . . all urged me to lose my virtue and thereby my value to her."

"It makes sense, but this is a senseless woman."

Matt nodded, even though Frank couldn't see the gesture. "The solution they came up with was that I take advantage of Las Vegas's reputation as 'Sin City.' I was to take a circuitous route along the Strip, get a room for cash and then change the number, at an upscale hotel, and hire a high-class call girl to do the job, make me unfit for my stalker."

Frank chuckled. "Surely an expensive way to go. Did it work?"

"Yes . . . and no."

"I'm on tenterhooks."

"I bet you are, you old married man. I bet you love hearing my odyssey of unwanted sex."

"Maybe. It's an interesting theological question: for love of your fellow man, should you submit to carnal knowledge, once against your vocation, and now against your free will and inclination only? If you were a woman, say St. Maria Gorretti: virgin, rape victim, and martyr, the answer would be a resounding yes. But the Church is a bit more ticklish about male self-sacrifice."

"Apparently not in seminaries."

"Whoa! Where did that come from?"

"A former St. Vincent's alumn who approached me. That's not what I meant to call about, but he says there was a lot of abuse back when we were there. Was there, Frank?"

Another silence. "God, I hope not."

"You don't know? You were an instructor, a confessor, a mentor."

Silence. "I . . . honestly don't know. Did you see it?"

"Maybe. But I didn't know enough to recognize it."

"You never—?"

"No. I'm told I was fairly unapproachable by then."

"Ah, yes. Mr. Angel-face iron man. Not unapproachable, really, just closed like a work-in-progress freeway. I knew you were chewing on family issues. I respected that. Leaving you alone to do it seemed the best course. That work out?"

"Eventually."

"Good enough. So you came through unscathed."

"I thought so, but if others didn't, then there's no honor in that, is there?"

"No. It's hard enough to outgrow your childhood and your past, then you learn that it was all corrupt. I wasn't, Matt. I was as shit-faced innocent as you were then. That's no excuse."

"Yes, innocence never feels like enough of an excuse. She's dead, Frank."

"Whoa again. We're out of the seminary here. Who?"

"My . . . salvation. The invulnerable Las Vegas call girl. She fell to her death in the hotel atrium after I left."

"Fell."

"Archangels fall. She could have been pushed."

"And you take the fall. Well, my money is on your stalker. She would be the kind of jealous bitch to teach you both a lesson for trying to get around her."

"That's why I need you to dig deeper, Frank. I know this woman was an IRA operative. She may have been very clever, very undercover, but she was loose in northern Ireland as Kathleen O'Connor about seventeen years ago. She had a second career squeezing money out of very wealthy Irish-Hispanic men in South America after that. She must have left some kind of trail. With the emphasis on foreign infiltrators now, surely you can find something on her. She isn't a ghost."

"No. I remember running a search already. Are the police on your tail for this call girl death?"

"Yes . . . and no, I think. Remember Molina?"

"Sure. Good cop."

"Well, she was one of those who advised me to take the call-girl route."

"No kidding. She must be sweating it now."

"She won't let me get away with murder if she thinks I did it, no matter what."

"I know. Good cop. Got a few hang-ups too, but, hey, it's what makes us all interesting. So . . . you join the mile-high club with that call girl?"

"Mile-high—?"

"Those Las Vegas megahotels are said to be halfway to heaven."

"Frank."

"I know. None of my business. You do see, though, don't you? If you hadn't made a fetish out of chastity, if you'd failed like a billion men and a few thousand priests before you, you wouldn't be in this mess. You wouldn't have had anything to lose."

"You really believe that now?"

"Yeah. For women and for men. It's a form of control, don't you see, Matt? And no one can control you if you can control yourself."

The paradox had Matt's head spinning.

It was trying to control himself that had gotten him into this out-of-control situation, after all.

"You're reasoning like a Jesuit," he complained.

"Come to think of it, being an FBI agent is a little like that. Anything else I can help with?"

Matt shook his head, then realized he was on the phone and needed to say something.

"No. Not for now. Just find out something—anything—on Kathleen O'Connor."

. . . *Glory Days*

The glossy photo Alfonso slapped down on Molina's desk made her blink for a moment.

What did she want with a vintage photo of Dolores Del Rio?

"Fuentes," Alfonso explained without being asked. "About forty years ago. A looker." He pushed the highly colored portrait aside to reveal a full-length black-and-white cheesecake shot beneath it. "Her calling card was her legs, though, not that face. She did a lot of product posing in L.A. before she ended up in Gandolph the Great's magic act." Another photo: gorgeous Gloria with an ordinary-looking youngish guy who was already showing a little too much chub for the camera.

"Were they friends, lovers?" Molina asked.

"Coworkers. Barrett dug up a bunch of old-time magicians. They've got this old folks club going at the local barbecue now. Meet every Tuesday, only we got a membership list and made some rounds. Everybody said Gandolph—real name Garry, two R's, Randolph as in Churchill—"

"Again your easy erudition amazes me, Alfonso."

He shrugged modestly. "I try to know things that might come in handy, and you never know what might come in handy in our line of work. Anyway, they were colleagues. Buddies. That's all."

"She didn't outlive him by much," Molina commented, moving the glamour photo front and center. The body on the autopsy table with the words "she left" scripted under her rib cage hadn't even hinted at such past glory as this. Dish to dust.

"Now that might be funny," Alfonso said. "Old Gandolph dead under uncertain circumstances on Halloween, his former assistant strangled to death only months later in the parking lot of a church. Odd part is, she wasn't churchgoing, the ex-neighbors in the apartment building were sure of that. It was kind of an unofficial retirement home for ex-performers, that place: cheap, a little rundown like they were, kind of a community, though, and they kept an eye on each other."

"Is this stuff in the original reports?"

"Some. Some Barrett and me made up." He grinned.

Molina knew he was referring to the Abies' mysterious ways of squeezing new facts out of old cases.

If they could wring some fresh suspects from the Fuentes case files, it would create enough of a flutter in the department and the media to let Vassar die a natural death in the news.

"So how did she get to a church parking lot?" Molina asked.

"Someone was trying to look her up a few days before she died. A mysterious stranger."

Alfonso enunciated the final phrase with relish as he sat on the plastic shell chair in front of Molina's desk. Plastic wasn't supposed to groan like wood under massive weight, but this chair managed at least a squawk. Maybe the steel bolts were giving.

"Any description of this mysterious stranger? Was he tall?"

"Got someone like Barrett in mind, Lieutenant?" Alfonso flipped pages and shook his head. " 'Fraid not. Middling kind of guy: middle-aged, middle-height, middle-weight, but dressed in a hooded sweatshirt and loose running pants, light gray, like he had come from the gym. Kept his hood on too, so he could be bald as an eagle or as hairy as Elvis on top. Wore sunglasses, so his eye color is a mystery too."

"Just asking for her?"

"She had an unpublished number, so her address wasn't in the phone book. He was asking for her apartment, but nobody would tell him. They look out for each other at the Iverton Arms."

"The place sounds like a time warp."

Alfonso nodded. "Retired performers live in the past. You should have seen the old ladies fawning over me, inviting me in for pastry and a photo-album session of their clippings from the days when they were cuties instead of Medicare patients. Not so many old guys in residence. Guess my gender isn't in it for the long run."

"Maybe too many cigarettes and pastries," Molina suggested.

"Always the diplomat, Lieutenant," Alfonso said blithely.

Three ex-wives and a series of police doctors hadn't gotten him to change his habits or his profile in thirty years. One remark from her wasn't going to do it now.

"That's more than we got on Fuentes the first time around," she noted approvingly. "You and Barrett keep on it."

"And what about that call girl, Vassar?"

"Alch and Su are backgrounding her. It's a little tougher. Rothenberg's employees don't offer the police pastry and photo albums, more like zipped lips and the bum's rush."

"I thought you softened her up yourself."

"The city attorneys haven't softened her up in fourteen-years. What makes you think I could do it?"

"I thought maybe woman to woman—"

"Sisterhood means zilch when you're on opposite sides of the long lean line of the law, Alfonso. I just wanted to know what she thought about the death."

"And?"

"Oddly complacent. More concerned about making a point that it was unlikely for a seasoned call girl to get hurt, or underestimate a john with designs on throwing her off an atrium railing. She's all politics."

"Want Barrett and me to do some digging there?"

"Higher placed minions of the law than you and me have done that for years and came up with harassment suits and ACLU press conferences. Besides, the Goliath death is iffy, at best."

Alfonso stood, taking a stab at pulling his belt up over his ballooning belly. "If the words 'she left' show up on this Vassar's corpse, though, let me know."

"You and half the force."

All in Another Night's Work: Split Personality

Max was finding his new double identity, established on an impulse, quite handy.

He was back at Neon Nightmare on a crowded Friday night in his Phantom Mage persona.

Given the circus of acrobats, dancers, and magicians who performed nightly at the place's pinnacle and then came down to earth when their gigs were over to mingle with the audience, the Phantom and his hokey half-mask fit right in.

Max knew he was like a moth drawn to flit around the fatal flame the Synth threw off, but the building was itself a maze that demanded further exploration before he could hope to penetrate to the heart of the labyrinth, the Synth and all its works, and its workers.

What he didn't learn now by clandestine explorations, his own self could return later to learn by subterfuge.

So he began at the bar, buying a drink and moving along it to entertain its patrons with a card illusion, an instant manifestation of a filled glass, a silk-flower bouquet, whatever cheap tricks would make him a familiar and accepted figure in their midst.

He gyrated out onto the dance floor a time or two, thankful that the music's volume made conversation impossible. The place was a mime's paradise, actually, a high-volume meat market for the young and the restless, transient singles in search of momentary connection.

After ninety minutes another breath-defying bungee-trapeze act was flashing through the neon stampede high above. Drums beat like pounding horse hooves, so loud they made the floor shake and teeth ache and almost impinged on sanity.

During this perfect distraction, Max turned the white side of his mask to the wall and slunk along it in search of a door to an area he had not yet investigated.

The place was as riddled with hidden chambers as a Swiss cheese. He still hadn't erected a mental map of the place, unusual for his swift and certain skill at 3-D visualization.

And the doors were the same seamless built-ins that could only be cracked like a safe in the pitch dark: with the help of sensitive fingertips in finding the fulcrum that controlled the swing mechanism.

A piece of wall became a door under the pressure of his fingers. Once cracked, it remained only ajar. Max tried to listen for any sound beyond it, but the chaos of the nightclub concealed it and also filtered through now that it was open. Best he dart within before the sound leak betrayed his snooping, and explain himself to anyone inside later.

Not only doors opened at his fingertips, but a cover story was always a moment's inspiration away.

But the area beyond the door was empty and dark, and when Max pushed the door's opposite point, it swung smoothly shut.

He moved quickly, feeling the limits of his particular box of darkness with his hands and feet. As long as he expected anything—unseen stairs leading up or down, sudden openings, a demanding resident or guard—he would be surprised by nothing.

Voices murmured faintly ahead to his left. Probably the club room of the Veteran Magician's Society. The Phantom Mage was an upstart to them, and would not be as welcome as an established act like the Mystifying Max.

He almost chuckled aloud at how easily he could approach the Synth from two different personas, now that he had found their hideout.

But that was just it. Had he truly found the Synth? No one had mentioned the name during his introductory interview three nights ago. Max guessed that they were a front organization, and that not all the members even knew about the Synth.

Still, Rafi Nadir's presence outside the club Wednesday night was a bad omen. First he shows up in Las Vegas and gets his ex-girlfriend Molina's paddle holster in a snarl. Then he shows up at the TitaniCon science fiction convention as a hired guard in alien guise. Then he's out at Rancho Exotica in another semiofficial role. Next he's in a strip-club parking lot just in time to see Temple attacked by a serial killer. Then he's hired as security at the Cloaked Conjuror's secret estate. Now, here he is at Neon Nightmare. True, men who take muscle jobs move around like pawns on a chessboard, busy as beavers while the more powerful people behind them move glacially slow, preferring to sacrifice the front men rather than their own safety.

But Nadir was turning up like funny money in a Monopoly game.

Max's fingers, which had never left the smooth sheet-rocked walls and had felt every taped seam, again encountered one of the featureless doors. The pressure points changed from door to door, never turning up in the same predictable position, as a doorknob would. He stretched high and low and finally found the right spot.

Low-level light outlined the rectangle of a slightly open door.

Max eeled inside, finding himself in another comfortably clubbish room, but this one offering a wall of Eye-in-the-Sky television screens reporting from various spy points throughout the building.

The seat before the console was a burgundy leather wing chair. Max sensed this was a recreational watching post for the most part. He sensed the mind of a nonsexual voyeur. A dilettante of surveillance, who enjoyed the power of looking out over this dark and neon-lit realm. Not that the board couldn't be manned by a serious surveillance team if necessary.

He quickly checked all the camera locations so he would know what to avoid on his next visit.

A half glass of wine sat on the cherry wood console. He came near, sniffed like a dog. A dessert wine, sweet and expensive.

He could picture some enormous Nero Wolfe of magical misdeeds sitting here overseeing his hidden realm.

Enough theorizing! Time to leave before the oeneophile returned.

Once again in the dark beyond a closed door, Max waited and listened, then moved farther into the building.

Suddenly, a grid of hot pink glowed ahead of him.

Moving along the wall he almost felt a part of, Max discovered the passage widened. A giant blocked his path.

Elvis, maybe nine feet high.

His white suit glowed, accented with garish magenta and indigo lightning bolts and the famous Taking Care of Business initials: TCB. Indigo streaked his hair and his hot-pink guitar had strings of poison green.

He was executed all in neon, of course.

Max moved out of the dark and into a neon Wonderland. Behind Elvis lurked a red neon shoe big enough for a potion-expanded Alice, dotted with patriot-blue stars. A neon lion boasted a mane that lit up in alternating strands of orange and hot pink.

The place was a hidden museum of neon. Max moved among the gigantic figures, noting that most of the styles seemed to date from the advertising art's heyday, say the fifties and sixties.

After the concentrated darkness behind the scenes, Max felt he now inhabited some Technicolor dreamscape. A galaxy of neon icons loomed over him, reminding him of fabulous dreams he had as a child, when illuminated pinwheels of planets and galaxies in the night sky spun just above him and he could only gaze in wonder. He'd never forgotten those dreams, and had never had them since. Sometimes he wondered why, wondered what he had lost, what all children lost.

Yet here this universe of forgotten neon silently winked on and off, lighting up a space as vast and dark as a jumbo-jet hangar. Who would imagine Neon Nightmare harboring such a huge hunk of neon paradise?

Max rarely played the tourist.

He never blinked at the neon icons on the Strip, although he admired their gorgeous chutzpah. Those signs, the Flamingo Hilton's chorus line of hot-pink feathers, the Four Queens's glittering card faces downtown, were the showgirls of the Strip, bejeweled, beplumed, bedazzling. Living in Vegas, you quickly came to take them for granted. Maybe you even wanted to apologize sometimes for their blatant appeal.

And then you saw the gathered impact of outmoded neon signage and suddenly realized what the Strip had lost when it went upscale during the Steve Wynn years. Sheer visceral fantasy.

It surprised and bewitched Max, and for too long.

He heard more than the low sizzle of neon tubes, but a distinctive shuffle. Not Elvis shuffling his neon blue suede shoes, but smaller men moving on soles as soft as his own, like cats in Hush Puppies.

Max spun, looking for a black wall he could blend into despite the neon turning night to day all around him.

He glimpsed the figures then. All in black from sleek hooded masks to gloved hands, to slippered feet. Ninjas from a hokey martial arts movie, small, wiry men as agile as grasshoppers.

Hokey didn't matter. Intention did. And this crew was out to nail him.

Max darted into the neon jungle all around him, behind Elvis, around the lion that roared in all the colors of the rainbow.

There were four, maybe five of them, separating instantly to pursue and trap him.

The Phantom Mage wanted to remain precisely that at this point. It was one thing if this false persona had been caught snooping at Neon Nightmare. It was another thing if he were to be caught and unmasked as Max Kinsella. With one blow, both of Max's options for infiltrating the Synth would die. And he might too.

So he played tag with these anonymous denizens of the neon night until he could double back, slide through Elvis's wide-spread legs with a patented knee dip, and scrabble into the black, unlit corridors that had led to this carnival of nervous light and ambushing darkness.

Max ran from a Neon Nightmare into a maze, a labyrinth. The labyrinth. The Minotaur was his shadow, but it had fractured into mini-Minotaurs in pursuit.

The bull-beast thundered behind him. Its name was Uncertainty. History. Myth. Loss. Treachery.

The dark was his brother. The dark was Sean, lost in time and treading the endless moibus strip of Death, always turning back upon itself until it almost became Rebirth. The worm Ouroboros.

Who would have thought this place was so big and intricate? A kind of Hell, learned only by running the length and width and breadth of it.

Which, of course, was endless. Hell is other people, Jean Paul Sartre had said. But what did he know? The French found Hell in endless politics. The Russians in endless bureaucracy. The English in endless colonialism. The Americans in endless self-analysis. The Jews in endless longing. And the Irish? In endless self-destruction.

He was Irish and expected to impale himself upon his own image, except the dark offered no reflections.

If they caught him they would kill him.

It was the ultimate race. Not against time, or history, but against enemies.

He had once welcomed enemies, when the thought of them made him one with his dead cousin. *You killed my cousin, my brother. Come, kill me if you can.*

They could. Max was old enough now to no longer consider himself immortal.

And he had a life now, or a half-life, like all radioactive matter. Temple was most of that half. He thought of her learning that he had been caught and killed . . . and decided that he could not be caught and killed. Maybe they'd just catch him. Maybe the chase was enough. So far it hadn't been for Kathleen, but for these unknown men so far away in time and space . . . Maybe.

He couldn't rely on it, so he dodged the dark's sharp unseen corners, raced past easy exits never knowing of their existence, drove himself deeper into darkness, like a screw into hardwood.

He ran by instinct, no longer knowing anything.

His wind was going, and his resilience. He was blind, out of control, everything that he had fought so long from becoming . . . from going back to.

Someone panted in the dark. Himself.

And the unseen pursuers.

He paused to find a wall and flatten himself against it. This labyrinth was their construction. It was meant to trap intruders like midnight flypaper. They were the spiders; he was the fly.

Finally he would hit a dead end, and they would have him.

He moved forward. Backward? He heard their rustling clothes, the secret almost-silent slide of hidden doors, the thud of feet and heartbeats, his own.

He was running wild, irrational. Lost. Everything that

could, would fail him. How to capture control again, which he had mastered for so long?

No time.

No time.

Keep running, thinking, losing.

Animals who allowed themselves to be herded, died.

He was being herded and he knew it.

Then fresh air assaulted him like the soundless crack of a whip. The crack of a door, rather.

He saw a scimitar of light, felt claws clutch his forearm.

He was being drawn in, into light or further dark.

A force slammed him against a wall and the door behind him clicked shut.

The light was an illusion, a hissing, dying thread of false fire. A magician's trick.

"Follow me," a whisper rasped, as a hand pulled him forward into more dark.

It could have been anyone's hand, or whisper. Kathleen O'Connor. The Cloaked Conjuror. The ghost of Harry Houdini, or Elvis, for that matter. What an act that would be! Unbidden thoughts of a really wild comeback stage show jousted in his brain. What if he based an act on bringing back ghosts? He could do Elvis . . . Houdini had been a much smaller, more muscular man, but he'd done a damn good imitation of him at the haunted house . . . No! This was not about his performing future. This was about escaping his consuming past.

In the dark.

This was about escaping Neon Nightmare before the Synth found him and put a name to their nemesis.

Chapter 31

. . . *Neon Babes*

Naturally, I am the Ninth Ninja in this low-budget stalk-a-thon at Neon Nightmare.

Finally! Tailing Mr. Max has paid off.

I knew something sinister was going on at Neon Nightmare, and tiptoeing through the tulips of neon blossoming in the secret warehouse has not only introduced me to a set of human ninjas, but reacquainted me with the nightmare ninjas from my own dreams.

The place is not only crawling with human agents of the amorphous Synth, but with Miss Hyacinth's own nonet of Havana-brown hit men.

So while Mr. Max is eluding the human variety, I am sidestepping the determined pursuit of the feline assassin, times nine.

It is not the first, nor, I imagine, the last time.

Even as Mr. Max is whisked away by a strange dude in a hooded robe, rather like a monk, I am dashing back into Disco Central to vanish among the crowd.

Interested as I am to encounter the ninja brigade again,

I really crave to cross whiskers—vibrissae is the technical term—with that Siamese siren Hyacinth.

Miss Midnight Louise, being caught up in a post-hormonal hurricane, kicked her can during our previous case, but I am sure that I can get much farther with her by less violent means. In any case, I would rather make love than war.

I decide to hang out by the bar, as that is where the single babes congregate.

I must admit I create quite a sensation.

An unescorted dude of my ilk is the cause for much comment in such a place, and the chicks really like to pat me on the back.

So I strut back and forth on the black glass bar top, accepting tribute and admiration. They are particularly fond of stroking my tail to the very end.

"I'll buy the dude a saucer of White Russian," one lonely lady yells over the chaos at the barkeep. Her would-be escort snarls into his frozen margarita, but what is a mere guy compared to a well-furred Casanova?

Anyway, there I am, lounging on the bar, licking up a luscious concoction of cream and Kahlúa, thinking of my friend of the same name, a performing panther of great elegance, when I hear a hiss at my rear.

Either I have a personal problem, or there is a snake or flat tire on the premises. I opt for the snake.

When I turn my head and look down at the floor behind the bar, I am confronting a pair of gleaming, red predatory eyes.

Not even a Sears catalogue could have delivered so fortuitously, back in the days when Sears had catalogues, which only goes to show how many lives I have enjoyed.

"Missster Midnight Louie," the apparition breathes.

"Misss Hyasssscinth," I respond in kind.

My human hostess withdraws, fearing a hissing and spitting match.

Often an irresistible attraction looks like that at the onset.

"Fancy meeting you here," she says.

"Nothing fancy about it. I came because I thought this

was the kind of flashy joint you would be hanging about."

"So you think I am 'flashy.' "

"Not at all. I think you are a show biz kind of girl."

"Really?"

"Indeed. Your career is on the upswing. Not only a cable sci-fi show, but some possibility of a product endorsement. Obviously, you have your paw on the pulse of the modern entertainment media."

"And you want to resume your role as a cat food spokesman?"

"I would not be averse to it."

"So you had nothing to do with that spitfire who invaded the Cloaked Conjuror's headquarters and dared to cross claws with me?"

"That chit? Obviously a low-class upstart. I did try to prevent that grudge match, you recall."

"I recall that you offered to go some rounds with me yourself."

"Can you blame me?" I ask, flexing my brow whiskers like Tom Selleck. We both are luxuriously haired, you know.

"Are you saying your offer was a gallantry, rather than a challenge?"

"Gallantry is always a challenge," I respond.

"So you have no ulterior motive in making my acquaintance."

I allow my ears to flatten and my expression to become downcast. "Alas, I do have an ulterior motive. I cannot resist a foxy female."

"Then come down here and we will do a little line dancing."

Of course I cannot resist an invitation, or a challenge, from an unrelated female.

I leap down, only to find that Miss Hyacinth has pulled a disappearing act. Not so strange for a feline doll who assists in a magic show. I decide to play her game of hide-and-seek, so I ankle out from behind the bar, where I am at the mercy of the gyrating feet on the dance floor.

No sign of Miss Hyacinth, but a lot of foot-stomping is

going on. In fact, I am being subjected to such a fever of Saturday night feet, even in the relatively static arena of the bar area, that I finally loft back atop the mirrored black surface, which reflects the constellations of panicked neon mares in the heights above us all.

Now I understand what I am experiencing: a kind of psychic stampede. To my keyed-up senses, it is as if these humans are a cat colony in communal heat. Thanks to the efforts of the Ladies of Spaying, among my kind that sort of thing is dying out, but here it is in full, rampant bloom.

I strut along the bar in a direction opposite to my first fling up here, finding dudes wearing backward baseball caps (loathsome fashion!) and the fedora as occasional as the shaved head, knocking back obscure beers, high-octane lemonades, and trendy coolers.

Not many dames line up at the bar on this side, as it seems to be a dudely kind of place, what with a TV perched above the liquor-bottle wallpaper blaring out some sports contest, but one lady does attract my notice.

She is sitting artistically behind a martini glass, that sublime inverted pyramid shape that spells sophistication and a nodding acquaintance with my ancestors' favored sepulcher.

I ankle over, rubbing against a half-dozen sweaty longnecks on the way.

What attracts me is the luminous color that fills her classic martini glass. Ah! I cannot rhapsodize enough. It is the liquid, lurid green of the Queen of Cat's eyes, Bastet herself. It is the Green Fairy of absinthe gone nouveau noir. It is as modern as the blinkers on a well-bred Chartreuse cat.

The lady in question, and in a place like this, the "lady" is always in question, attracts my attention next.

Other than Miss Temple, a feisty ginger-bit of a Tortie to me, I am not much impressed by human pulchritude.

But this lady is well-matched to her sour green-apple martini. Her hair is as black as the sheen in my coat at its most well-licked. Her eyes are the blue-green of the Divine Yvette, my absent ladylove, at her most imperious Persian princesshood. Her lips on the short straw stuck in the opaque drink like a tap into a poisoned apple skin, are, well, to coin a phrase, grapefruit ruby-red. Her skin is the dead-white of an albino and hairless Sphinx cat.

All in all, she is a Technicolor treat.

I boldly stop before her and yawn, so she can observe my glossy black coat, so like her hair . . . my blood-red tongue, so like her lips . . . my lettuce-green eyes, so like her poison of choice . . . my shark-white teeth so like her pale, satin skin.

I am eye-to-eye . . . indeed, eyetooth to eyetooth with, of course . . . the living inspiration for the sketch of Kathleen O'Connor, aka Kitty the Cutter. (My thankfully absent roommate does have such a way with words!)

They say a cat may look at a queen. They also call unfixed female cats queens. They also call jealous and vicious women "cats." I think I have Miss Kitty's number.

I stare into Miss Kathleen O'Connor's aquamarine eyes.

"What have we here?" she asks loudly enough that only I may hear. "A tomcat on the town? Would you like a drink?"

I do not respond, but she raises a pale finger topped by a scarlet nail, and in two shakes of an innocent's lamb's tail, the bartender presents me with a saucer of the same vile green liquid she imbibes.

I deign to run a paw across it, sniff the result, then shake the excess onto the black-glass bar.

Miss Kitty laughs. She has claimed even my kind's name, as if evil had an inbred feline bent. I owe her for that one too.

"You Las Vegas boys," she says soft and low, "are all alike. Thinking you know something, but too . . . discriminating . . . for the real world."

If I know who she is, does she know who I am? How could she? I am an undercover operative. I am as discreet as a poodle in Paris. What could she know about me?

She leans close, sips from her straw, blows the words at me as if she expects me to understand. And I do.

"Tell your friends—and I know you have some, big boy—I

have some myself. Tell your friends that I said 'Hello.' I don't know quite how you will go about telling them that. Perhaps it is just as well. Anyway, kiss them good-bye for me."

I have a thousand questions, most of them starting with, "Are you really leaving my associates alone?"

I do not admit to human "friends." (Miss Temple, of course, is different. She is much more than a friend. She is my tender little filet of solemate.) And I certainly do not "talk" to humans, friend or foe. I stand alone among my kind in knowing more of humanity than I would want to. This particular piece of it I would like to toss into the pool in front of the Mirage's volcano attraction during mid-explosion, but even though she is a petite little doll she is too big to throw for a loop here or anywhere else.

So I content myself with hissing in her voodoo martini and stalking off without a word.

Sometimes it is better to leave to fight another day.

. . . *Wizard!*

Another whip-crack sound of an unseen door opening. Night air and parking lot lights slapped Max's senses silly.

He felt like a tomb robber slipping out of Cheops' pyramid at Giza. A dark figure urged him forward, and soon both were ensconced in . . . an aged Volkswagen Beetle.

Shades of Tomb Raider? Hardly.

Yet, behind them, shadows of the Synth were pouring from the black pyramid of Neon Nightmare while the titular horse was screaming in neon rainbows above it all.

His guide revved the VW and putt-putted them into a dark corner of the lot, where they parked between the looming screens of a Ford Exasperator and a Lincoln Aggravator.

Great. If he'd wanted a getaway driver in a midget clown car he could have called on Temple and her new Miata.

Or maybe not.

He eyed the driver, a hunched figure in black rather like

Sister Wendy, the Episcopal nun-cum-art-expert on public TV.

Max was getting very tired of mysteries inside of enigmas inside of puzzles.

"I don't need a chauffeur," Max said finally. Grumpily.

"You need a friend." The simple answer paraphrased the old Carole King song.

"No." Max was certain. "Friends are excess baggage."

"So I taught you," the raspy voice answered. "But I was wrong. Terribly wrong. I'm sorry."

Not many people had ever said "I'm sorry" to Max Kinsella.

There was only one person, maybe two, he needed to say "I'm sorry" to. One was Sean, his dead cousin. The other one was dead too.

Or was he?

Max turned to eye the obscure figure.

Magicians were good at obscuring things, even and especially themselves.

"You saved me back there," Max said.

"You needed saving," was the answer.

"We all do, but I especially needed it half a lifetime ago, in Ireland. Only one person applied for the job."

"He must have been a masochist."

"He was a genius."

"Thank you." Said modestly.

Max twisted in the cramped seat to see better, as if a change in position could penetrate the veil of mystery.

"Garry?" he asked. "Gandolph? It's you? You're alive?"

"My greatest and most cowardly illusion. I'm sorry. I never meant to deceive you."

"The hell you didn't!" Max pushed open the car door, stepped out at full length, and still didn't top the Lincoln SUV at his back. The parking lot was quiet now, pursuers faded back into their bizarre building. "You old fraud! You . . . faked your own death. What are you, a Houdini for the

New Age set? Did you plan on reappearing and snagging a major hotel gig, or what?"

The lumpy form struggled out of the driver's seat to confront his pupil.

"It wasn't planned. At least not my death. You fret over a death in a foreign land long ago. I now know your pain, pardon the cliché. Can't you guess what happened?"

"Wait." Max ground his bicuspids and his brain cells at the same time. If Gandolph was alive, and he definitely was, then . . .

"You were dedicated to unmasking false mediums," he said. "That required a false persona. You were always good at disguises. But you needed to be better. So . . . you did what a lot of magicians have done for stage work. You hired . . . a double."

Gandolph's head nodded in the dark.

"A double," Max repeated. "And your double died at the haunted house séance. You didn't expect that."

"Never. I never would have allowed another person to risk life or even limb on my behalf. I merely wanted to lurk behind the scenes, as you yourself did that night. Quite a brilliant impersonation of Houdini, by the way. You are nothing like him, in physique or in magical style."

"Thank you. But I also have you to thank for thinking you were dead all these months. You didn't warn me."

"How could I? I expected my double to survive the séance. I would never have hired a stand-in for my own murder! I never dreamed the Synth would be so irritated by my existence."

"So it *was* the Synth!"

"The Synth has a thousand heads, and they are all Magic."

"Magic is an illusion."

"So is death." The figure so short and squat stepped forward to doff its hood.

Max looked down into the grandfatherly face of the late Garry Randolph, now come back to life, wondering if he should pinch himself, or his mentor. Was Garry really alive and back? Yes!

It had been almost two decades since he'd read *The Lord of the Rings,* Tolkien's epic fantasy. If he remembered correctly, Gandalf the Gray, whose name Garry Randolph had folded into his stage persona almost forty years ago, had been lost in a deep cavern and presumed dead.

Only he had returned.

Now Garry had pulled that same mind-boggling trick and Max was as bedazzled as any wannabe magician.

Not until now, seeing Gandolph alive again, had he understood, or admitted, how much the older magician had meant to him, alive and dead. He had an ally again, a mentor. Someone who talked his language, the bilingual tongue of magic and counterespionage.

Like the company of the Ring, he felt energized again by the notion of a stout companion. Garry was more than that, though, he was all Max had left of family. And he was alive!

There'd be plenty of time now to figure out who had wanted Gandolph dead, to unravel the Synth and all its works, to track down Kathleen O'Connor—Garry had known her, seen her, as a girl. She wouldn't intimidate him, as she had Matt Devine and Temple and even Molina, long-distance.

He realized he had felt the same sense of betrayal at Garry's presumed death and resurrection as Temple had felt at Max's own disappearance and return. You can't condemn a man for avoiding you because he was a walking death trap, not even Matt Devine.

Max smiled broadly and held out his cloaked arms. "Welcome home, maestro."

The old man embraced him with true feeling. "Welcome to the endgame, rather. My home is your home now, I've learned that, and it was what I intended. Yet I dare not appear as myself until all my enemies are unmasked."

"They're my enemies too."

"Then we have even more in common. Come on, let's

go chew over our pasts and our futures until our damn jaws ache and we know we're alive because it hurts. Let's go . . . home?"

For once Max found himself stunned into silence. He had never dreamed that a live Garry Randolph would return to the house he himself had occupied alone for many months, a recluse and a hermit and a hunted man, brooding on ghosts.

He had never dreamed another human being would urge a retreat to any place they could both call "home."

It felt incredibly good.

He was so . . . unusually jubilant that he almost forgot where he was.

Something skittered past his ankles: large, dark, ratlike.

Or was it a shadow that fell between the bolts of flashing neon from the neon mare high atop the building's distant peak?

Whatever it had been, it recalled Max to himself, to here and now, and to danger. He stood there in the guise of the Phantom Mage. Now he should make like his name and vanish.

"We should leave separately, and ensure that no one follows us. Let's meet at the house."

"Delighted to, my boy!" Gandolph hustled back into his low-profile car and started the engine.

Amazing, Max thought.

Garry Randolph alive. Investigating the same shadowy entity that he was. Now they'd get somewhere!

Time for him to make the first step. Swirling his theatrical cape around him, Max stalked away like Dracula repelled by the whiff of garlic toast.

He could hardly wait to lose this persona and this place and rejoin forces with Gandolph.

Yes!

. . . Torn Between Two Tails

Some shamuses have all the luck.

Not Midnight Louie.

Here I am, as undercover as a dude can be at the Neon Nightmare. I have just made contact with the Woman in the Case.

I have previously seen Mr. Max Kinsella slinking around the joint, although he has been as invisible as a flea on a tweed suit for the past hour or so.

I am frantic to keep these two natural enemies apart, though they have not seen hide nor hair of each other in years, and I am mad to trail both of them as they separately (I devoutly hope) leave this place.

There is only one entrance and exit that I know of, the velvet cordoned-off door guarded by the goons up front.

That does not mean there are not other doors, used for service purposes.

Miss Kitty is still holding down the bar like a forties film fatale.

Mr. Max is still AWOL.

I pace beside the bar, blending beautifully with the black high-gloss floor that reflects the clientele and offers me further cover. Who would notice me when you can eyeball Victoria's Secret thongs on half the babes in the room?

The noise that passes for music nowadays is louder than a chorus of queens in heat, and the smoke and mirrors and neon of the dance floor is interfering with my night vision.

I decide to slip out the front door for a bit of fresh air while I figure out what to do.

And then whilst I am in the act of successfully slipping and the clamor and commotion inside is fading into a bad dream . . . I happen to notice the two muscle men I am ankling behind.

There has been a changing of the guard since I came in, and one of them is now Rafi Nadir, the indomitable Miss Lieutenant Molina's ex-squeeze and no friend of Mr. Max, although he has a soft spot in my heart for coming to the aid of my Miss Temple recently.

That does not mean that I cut him any slack in the hired hood line.

But I am really perplexed now.

I slip along the building's foundation and the row of trendy metal and neon cutouts of Las Vegas's favorite flora, palm trees and cacti.

They are spatters of Technicolor chalk and I am the soft unseen canvas of a velvet painting behind them.

Apparently I am not soft and unseen enough, however, for I hear a hissing sound.

I pause, ready to leap left, right, or up. Snakes do not faze me but I cannot stand these timer-operated sprinkler systems they have around here that can drench a guy to his toe-hairs.

Before I can execute a Kitty Kong move I am tapped on the shoulder by a set of delicate feminine shivs. That is to say that they dig in like a hellion with hangnails.

"Say, Pop. Chill out. It is Number One Daughter."

"No Charlie Chan–speak from you, Miss Louise. And you presume."

"Of course I do. I am a professional investigator now, *non*?" She sits down beside me and directs a narrow glance to the guys at the door. "Who is that dude you gave the evil eye to on the way out?"

I guess a partner should know the cast du jour.

"That, my inquisitive sneak, is one Rafi Nadir, aka Raf. He is a shady character around town, but I have it on eyewitness testimony—mine—that he helped my Miss Temple collar a crook who was threatening to close down her windpipe not two nights ago."

"So he is a bad guy with one gold star to his credit, but only from you and your girl-tortie roommate."

"Right."

"Okay, he is not the reason you are dithering around here outside Neon Nightmare. What gives?"

"What gives is why *you* are dithering around here outside Neon Nightmare. I at least have been inside."

"This rave and mosh scene is not for me. Hard on the eardrums. Truth is, I came across Mr. Max Kinsella a couple hours ago and decided to tail his Hush Puppies until they cried Uncle."

"He wears Hush Puppies? Mr. Max?"

"Do not sound so wounded. No, he remains the sartorial fashion plate you know and loathe. His shoes are Bruno Maglis, which, as you know, have served many a celebrity, but they are as silent-soled as plain old sneakers. One whiff of his footwear and I knew he was someone to watch."

" 'Sartorial,' Louise! That is a big word for a street kit."

"Listen, I can sling around anything you can, including vocabulary."

"Whatever. I have determined that Mr. Max is indeed inside. Somewhere. I also have a dame I wish to tail. I was just wondering how to go in two directions at once, or serially, but perhaps you can solve my dilemma."

"Of course I can solve your dilemma, and any other cold cases you have hanging around. We are not Midnight, Inc. for nothing. Speaking of vocabulary, that was actually a rather clever idea of yours, Pop."

"Thank you, Louise. Now—"

I gaze aghast at the open door to Neon Nightmare.

She is limned against the interior neon like a silhouette of evil incarnate. Miss Kitty O'Connor.

"Something got your tongue, and eyeballs? Ah." Miss Louise perks up her ears and the hair on her hackles. "Some hussy, I see."

"If you see her, can you tail her?"

"Like her thong bikini."

"She will have transportation."

"So do I." Louise snaps out her shivs. I hear them bite sandy Las Vegas dirt.

"Go, girl," I order in the day's vernacular.

I hardly see her blend into the dark, but one of my problems is now Miss Kitty O'Connor's problem. She has set all my human friends atremble, but I send her my heartfelt sympathy. Miss Midnight Louise is one fierce tiger to have on your tail, and I ought to know.

All right. I decide on a stroll around the foundation of Neon Nightmare. Above me the mare in question ripples with a blaze of neon . . . magenta, indigo blue, yellow, red, and purple.

I detect no obvious exits and end up near the main entrance again . . . just in time to see the figure reminiscent of the Cloaked Conjuror appear in the parking lot with a swirl of cape and a glimpse of white-face.

That hokey Phantom of the Opera getup has never fooled Midnight Louie. I hotfoot it along behind Mr. Max's striding feet. Rats! Miss Louise is correct. He wears sound-softening shoes with the exquisite redolence only found in Italian leather goods. From Caesar's sandals to Gucci loafers. So far has Rome fallen. And its vaunted arches.

As I expect, we soon pussyfoot up to a black car parked on a side street.

As Mr. Max swirls aside his theatrical black cloak to enter the driver's side, I dive into the entrance to the backseat. Thank heaven for black car interiors.

Instantly the engine throbs slightly under my feet. I extend my shivs into carpeting as I prepare for takeoff. I do not expect Mr. Max to linger.

He does not disappoint me. I am hurled forward, then back as the car accelerates smartly, before settling down to cruising speed.

So black is the night, and the car, that I risk peering over the backseat.

Mr. Max is pulling off the mask and loosening his hair with his fingers. He has no more idea that I am hitching a ride on his wagon than that his most bitter enemy had been indulging in Martian-green martinis at the Neon Nightmare bar.

I wonder where he was during that interlude. Wherever it was, he is now in a more distracted mood than I have ever seen him indulge before.

Streetlights cast bright prison bars over our moving vehicle. He drives fast, smooth and sure. I find a thrill catching in my throat, for I am certain that this time I will know what my Miss Temple knows and has not seen fit to share with me: where the Mystifying Max goes to ground. His home turf. The hideaway that even Lieutenant Molina has not been able to find.

What a night!

I am so jubilant I brace my shivs on the backseat's upright portions to glimpse the streetlights shining above.

I see one particular light pierce the rear window and then slide across the car's ceiling like a luminous serpent.

I frown. Streetlights flash by at a downward angle.

This was an *upward* light.

Risking discovery, I ratchet up the backseat upholstery until my ear-flattened head can see out the rear window.

The moon has fallen from the sky, or maybe the horse from Neon Nightmare is on our trail.

A single wild bright eye follows the car.

The Neon Nightmare is a cyclops?

I blink as the expanding ball of light rakes my delicate irises, turning my pupils into spikes.

We are being tailed by a one-eyed monster.

Luckily, considering my kind and my color, I am not superstitious.

I immediately realize our peril.

It is a motorcycle that follows us, and Mr. Max is obviously thinking of other things. In fact, I hear him chuckle to himself. He is daydreaming when a nightmare is on our tail. *Tails!*

I am along for the ride, after all.

The lone light winks shut.

I cannot see it, but I hear the faint vibration of a growling motor gaining on us.

Our vehicle suddenly slows, then turns. And turns again.

Mr. Max is heading home.

He must head elsewhere.

I leap atop the passenger seat back, howling my warning.

The car swerves as Mr. Max glances in his rear- and side-view mirrors. I see his eyes focused like black laser lights.

The car swerves again, executing a neat 180-degree turn so we are facing in the opposite direction.

Actually, I am facing the rear of the car, for I have been unceremoniously hurled into the foot well of the passenger seat, my shivs stapling nylon carpeting to keep myself from bouncing around a lowly space spiked with odd bits of gravel and scented with asphalt and used gum.

When the car stabilizes, I claw my way to the top of the passenger seat to see. There is nothing behind us but blackness.

I glance into the driver's seat.

Mr. Max glances at me, but does not seem to really see me.

And then we barrel down the side streets in a zigzag pattern that would make a sidewinder snake dizzy, and suddenly we are shooting onto an entrance ramp to a freeway. Our speed matches the flow of traffic and then increases. And increases.

We weave in and out of lanes, passing every vehicle except, thank Bast, a highway patrol car. I see the single glare of the motorcycle headlight illuminating the car ceiling. Still we speed on. Soon we have slipped the surly bonds of the Nevada posted speed limits and left city and traffic far behind. And still we dodge the single light that clings like static electricity to every move we make.

Finally we screech into another 180-degree turn and immediately Mr. Max hits the gas so we are racing back in the direction from which we just fled, right into the light that has never failed to follow our every maneuver.

There is only one outcome for this showdown. High impact.

I no longer fear our one-eyed pursuer, but I think Mr. Max is trying to lurch me loose from my death grip on his interior upholstery, which is one of my favorite aromatic materials, leather.

Good luck.

It will give before I do.

. . . *Going to the Devil*

Max hit the brakes until they screamed in the desert night like a puma. He turned around in a wide U on the deserted highway and retraced his path.

It had been the ultimate game of "Chicken."

Maxima and Ninja at full throttle into each other.

Max had never wavered, but he was armored by a car.

Now he brought that car to a full stop and jerked the gears into Park. He hurtled out the passenger door, not bothering to shut it or think about anything but who and why.

Las Vegas was flatter than the proverbial pancake, but the car-motorcycle chase had driven deep into the desert where dry washes veined the landscape like seams in a golfer's face.

The motorcycle, maneuvering to both dodge and confront a car that had just executed a sudden 180-degree turn, had spun out on the gravel, skittering over the concrete in the restless desert wind.

Max ran to the edge of the arroyo fifty feet from the

highway—that's how far the motorcycle had sailed through the air—and looked down into the darkness.

Nothing to see now, but if the gas tank blew . . . he pulled out his cell phone, then realized it would leave a trail and snapped it shut again. Better find a pay phone at the nearest gas station, which might be miles away.

He slammed himself into the front seat and drew the door shut like a bank vault behind him.

He had forgotten what, or who, he had glimpsed in the car during the last, few, desperate seconds of maneuvering. The car seemed empty as he raced alone over unlit asphalt, eyes on the faint dotted line of the two-lane highway. The creature, black as a skunk, was gone now. Midnight Louie, believe it or not. Or not. Or had it been a racoon? Something black and masked about the face. He had only glimpsed it as a scrabbling form in the dark.

On the other hand, he had no doubt about the motorcycle rider, who had reacted a split second too slowly to his latest evasive maneuvers. That was the way of war and races: move fast or spin out permanently. He couldn't be dead sure of that person's identity, but he had a gut feeling exactly who it was: the elusive easy rider who had creased his scalp with a bullet weeks ago, who had been dogging Matt Devine at the radio station, who had sailed into an unexpected off-road experience.

He doubted that any emergency vehicle he could call to this site could save anything, not even a guilty conscience. Still, he memorized the first highway marker he came to, and pushed the pedal to the floor. The Maxima leaped like a jackrabbit to the charge as he aimed for a faint line of gas-station neon maybe five miles away.

. . . Roadrunner

Ouch! There is nothing out here but cat-claw cactus and it is digging directly between my toes on every step.

It was no big decision what to do when Mr. Max played spin-the-bottle with the motorcycle and won, brakes down.

As he bailed out of the car to check on the damage, I bailed out right behind him.

I stare down at the dried-out wash, gazing at one red taillight.

It is not the motorcyclist I fret about. I knew who it was and I am not sorry to see Mr. Max decide to leave, and no doubt find an anonymous phone upon which to report this fatal accident so long overdue. I know how this dude thinks: like I do, were anyone human ever to realize that I do think.

Right now I am thinking that if Miss Kitty O'Connor has truly clawed her last, I am not about to let any tears soak into my best black lace jabot. She was not exactly a friend to me and mine.

However, I have one nagging worry. Let us just say that I have a nagging nagger nowadays. The last thing I did in delegating power this evening was to tell my junior partner to tail Miss Kitty O'Connor. I do not doubt my order was heeded.

Ergo, Miss Midnight Louise was likely on the motorcycle when it made its Evel Knievel leap to fame and future forensics examination.

Well, one cannot have an associate gasping out her last on the sere desert sands. Since nothing I would or could manage to do with a cell phone can offer an iota of good at the accident scene, I hurl myself down the crotchety incline, avoiding cacti all the way.

Such a path is hard on the unprotected pads, let me tell you. I had never expected to be an upside-down pincushion, but it is in that condition in which I finally catapult to the bottom.

My nose tells me my first worry is well placed. Raw gasoline is one of the strongest odors on the planet, and it hangs in a nasal miasma over the crash scene.

One spark and everything in the vicinity is instant barbecue.

So I pause before approaching nearer to observe the scene.

The motorcycle is on its side, a spray of broken-off accessories pluming over the sand. Broken glass sparkles from the moon-glow high above.

The rider lies fifteen feet away, limbs turned at angles even the most agile alley cat could not manage while in a living, breathing condition. The helmet has rolled like an obsidian pumpkin to the foot of a huge Joshua tree cactus a couple yards away.

"Louise," I call plaintively.

Something in the distance answers me with an arpeggio of yips ending in a howl. Coyotes. I wonder if Mr. Max will return to the accident scene, or if he will only lurk at a distance, as I would, to see the ambulance come and go.

Probably. I pause by the fallen figure's head. The skin looks dead in the moonlight and snaky threads of black hair cross the forehead and cheek. Some of them, I sniff on closer examination, are tendrils of blood.

I paw delicately at the motionless mouth, my shortest hairs unstirred by any breath or breeze.

It is a still night in the desert, in more ways than one.

I do not hear any feline complaints either.

Nervous as I am, I must approach the fallen vehicle. If Louise had hitchhiked a ride with Kitty the Cutter, she would have needed to do what I have done before: ride in a saddlebag.

One of these handy black-leather pockets faces up at the star-pocked night sky. I examine it with mitt and nose and even tongue. Its exterior buckles are closed. I doubt the dead woman would have overlooked Miss Midnight Louise inside and buckled her in.

Next I bend down and explore the side of the bike crushed against the ground. The scent of oozing cactus juice is even stronger than spilled gasoline at this level.

I find another saddlebag, a twin to the first, crushed flat under the motorcycle's metal side. I sniff for blood, but can't overcome the gasoline reek. It is like trying to smell lilies of the valley when gardenias bloom next door.

There is a sudden scrape behind me and the sand shifts under my feet as I leap two feet into the air, execute a 180-turn like Mr. Max's car, and face the wilderness.

I make out a silhouette cresting the dry wash.

Oh, Great-grandmother Graymalkin! It is a lone coyote.

Now, eating nightly is a serious matter to this breed, which has been hunted to hoped-for extinction by humans and yet still manages to scrounge a living from the few uncivilized acres of desert left to its kind.

Actually, my money is on the coyote in this primal battle, but in these circumstances I cannot afford to let my finer feelings stand in the way of my survival skills.

And a coyote is at least twice my size with teeth at least six times the size of mine.

I know from many street brawls that it is not size but attitude that determines who comes out on top. However, an opponent who is perpetually starving to death and who can only look on one as fresh meat is an extreme case it would be better to avoid than get physical with.

So I prance sideways, my back up and fur fluffed to porcupine fullness.

The coyote tilts his feral head in the universal canine gesture of puzzlement. I am sure that the hint of quills is not welcome to a desert-living breed who must grow up on regular snoutfuls of cactus spines.

Either cowed or simply shocked by my performance, he edges down into the wash a good ten yards away from me and soon is nosing at the recumbent form of the former Kathleen O'Connor.

Much as I would like to tell Miss Temple (could I tell Miss Temple anything) that I had witnessed Kitty the Cutter being eaten by coyotes for the sin of persecuting Mr. Matt and Mr. Max, I cannot allow the death scene and the corpus delecti to be tampered with before the ambulance comes.

"Ah, Mr. Coyote, that is not prey for you. The body is several rungs up the evolutionary ladder from you. It is always bad policy to eat your betters. They tend to retaliate. Not that I speak from personal experience, mind you."

He does not even lift his head at my whimpered protests, but paws at Miss Kitty's dead hand. There is no doubt that it is dead, for if it were not, no way would it sit still for playing patty-cakes with a coyote.

Mr. Coyote snuffles disgustingly at the corpse, then lifts his head to sniff the scents emanating from me.

There is no way to turn off my natural perfume, any more than I could deactivate the hypersensitive nostrils on a canine creature.

So it is time to let this bozo get a big whiff of my attitude.

"You do not want to mix it up with me," I warn him in a low growl. "I am not your usual lost domestic feline. I am big-time muscle in Las Vegas, and I am out here on a case. Mess with me and you will lose a major sense."

His hackles bristle in response and there we are facing off.

It is in the silence that holds while we bluff each other with our badness that a thin, watery wail pierces the darkness like a cactus needle.

First I think siren, but this time the dog is ahead of me. Its ears prick, its head lifts and off it goes bounding along the meandering trail of the dry wash.

I bound after. Ouch! The ground is littered with Christmas tree needles if a Christmas tree was ever a saguaro cactus. Some are the length of knitting needles!

I limp after, Mr. Coyote being a speedball who can use years of canny desert experience to avoid the prickliest pear plants.

I arrive to see him rubbing his nose in the sand and pawing at it with both front feet.

There is a puddle of shadow on the ground that the moonbeams do not deign to illuminate and every raised hair on my shoulder blades tells me that it is Miss Midnight Louise and that she is dazed or injured, or else she would be standing upright and spitting like a kettle at 4:00 P.M. high tea.

. . . Neo-Neon Nightmare

A high, thin keening ripped through the darkness.

Max had run the car off the road, turned off the lights and the engine, and waited.

The siren grew louder and shriller until it sounded like an alley cat in heat. The flashing red and blue lights of the squad car leading the ambulance slowed at a distant mile marker, then spurted ahead.

Max grew impatient when the squad car stopped, a pale blot gleaming like a beached whale carcass on the desert darkness.

"There, you idiots," he whispered. Trained by both his apparent and his secret vocations to precise observation, his eye had already detected and pinpointed the darker patterns at the bottom of the wash that were a motorcycle and a body.

Soon, though, the officers and ambulance attendants were stumbling alongside the rim of the dry riverbed, their high-power flashlights illuminating mesquite bushes and prickly pears.

Finally the lights danced over the high-gloss sheen of a motorcycle flank. They converged in a clot, one man going back along the highway to direct the ambulance driver forward . . . for more efficient pickup of the victim, the body.

Everyone was scrambling down the incline now. One of the cops held them back while a pair of EMTs rushed to the blot that was Kathleen's body. They bent over her, applying tests and remedies. The gurney was half carried, half rolled over the rugged terrain.

Max grunted soft appraisal. The major activity on the scene would obscure any traces he might have left, and with his unmarked soles they would be few.

The tire tracks his car laid on the asphalt as he had spun around wouldn't erase. Come daylight, when an accident investigation team hit the scene, they'd implicate a car and driver in the outcome. His Maxima was history. He'd leave it at one of the designated drop sites, and walk away. One call, and it would be picked up minutes after he left it. Within hours, it would be in another part of the country getting crushed in an auto graveyard.

Max ran a hand over the passenger's seat. He'd had this car longer than any for a long while. Temple had ridden in it several times. He'd miss it. Then his palm stroked several superficial slashes in the leather. On the other hand, the hitchhiking critter . . . Midnight Louie, maybe? . . . had scarred the upholstery beyond repair anyway.

. . . Death Trip

"Get away!" I howl at the coyote.

He interrupts his pawing at the shadow of Midnight Louise to gaze at me, puzzled. Puzzlement is a canine characteristic we felines never descend to.

"This is not human carrion," he half whimpers, half growls, "as you warned me away from before. This was a four-foot."

I do not know if the word "carrion" or the verb "was" irritates me in Big Cat proportions.

Either way, I go screeching sideways at him, bouncing on my toes like Bruce Lee on hot coals, my coat hairs all at attention.

That is enough to back him off two steps. "Take it easy, little guy."

And that is another incentive.

I leap straight up, shivs out, and come down at an angle, extremities thrashing. I nick the nose.

"Hey!" The bozo buries his injured snout in the sand, his forefeet pawing at the sting.

While he is on his knees, I rocket past and kick sand in his eyes.

"No fair!" he whines.

While he is still on his knees and now blind, I leap again and land on his back, taking a good toothy grip on his hackles.

Now he springs straight up.

"*Ow-ow-wow-wow-ow*," he cries.

He tries to buck me off like he was a bronco and I was an old cowhand, but this galoot has spurs on every limb and I use 'em, digging in. I am going for a very big silver belt buckle here.

He is turning in tight rabid circles now, and I must admit my own head is getting quite a workout, but I hang on for dear life.

Suddenly Mr. Coyote comes panting to a dead stop.

His head hangs so low I am in danger of using it for a ski slope were I not hanging on tooth and nail, literally.

"If you let go," he offers. "I will."

"There is nothing you have ahold of, except stupidity."

"I will go off, leaving you and this cursed spot alone," he growls between gritted teeth.

"Sounds like a good idea. If you try to pull anything silly while retreating, I will really get nasty."

"Wolf's honor," he says, invoking his bigger, stronger brother in absentia.

"Lion's honor," I say, loosening first one shiv, then another.

Finally I drop off, still on all fours and ready to rumble.

Mr. Coyote's appetite has lost its edge, even if my shivs have not. (Nothing better for sharpening than a little raking and clawing.)

He is backing away, head and tail lowered. "What did you say your name was?" he asks just before he turns tall and runs.

"Louie," I answer. "Midnight Louie. And I like my opponents shaken, not stirred."

With those words the coyote turns so fast it could eat its

tail like a certain worm Ouroboros I have heard discussed around the Circle Ritz . . . and disappears.

I do not take long to stand there and congratulate myself. An unpleasant task awaits at my unguarded rear: somehow I must conceal Miss Midnight Louise from the oncoming human retrieval team so that she can be interred later among her own kind, with appropriate honors.

Had I not assigned her instead of me to tail Kitty the Cutter, I would be lying there dead in the dust . . . sand, rather.

I begin to understand Mr. Max's long-held regrets, and even Mr. Matt's more recent ongoing angst about the lady known as Vassar. We guys have it tough. Because the world relies on us to be in charge (except for some female exceptions, who are in the minority of exceptional females), when something goes wrong we tend to take it too personally. Guyness is a heavy load to carry, but I have just acquitted myself at the peak of it in facing off the coyote.

Miss Louise would be proud of me, were she still here.

With this thought I steel myself to turn and face something even worse than a ravenous coyote: my dead partner.

Before I can add action to thought, I hear a rasp behind me, then another.

No! More desert scavengers! What are they? Whiptail lizards? Kangaroo rats? Rattlesnakes? I will take them all!

I whirl around, prepared to battle a legion of creepy crawlies, but find the night still and dark behind me.

The puddle of shadow is all that remains of Midnight Louise—rather like the dark puddle the Wicked Witch of the West came to in *The Wizard of Oz,* but the parallel is purely visual. I make no comment on the personality of the late Miss Midnight Louise vis-à-vis the WW of the West—the puddle is still as motionless as an oil slick.

I approach. A guy has to do something when his partner is killed, but what? I have hounded off the desert dog. I guess I need camouflage first. I spot a lacy tumbleweed blown up against a prickly pear. That is it! It will be light to drag over and will hide ML's resting place from the prying humans about to descend on this site of tragedy and death.

At least my former partner took Kitty the Cutter down with her! I grasp the tumbleweed by the thick stem and drag it over. It catches on every cactus needle betwixt its lodging and Miss Louise, I swear.

At last I lay it carefully across her.

The desert wind starts to lift it up, up, and away.

I cast myself on it to hold it down . . . ouch!

Again I hear the furtive rasping noise, but there I am spread-eagled on a tumbleweed, trying to keep it from escaping its duty as a makeshift headstone.

Rasp, rasp. Enough with this rasping! My nerves are irritated already. One more rasp, whatever you are, and I will eat you!

I have in mind, of course, a desert mouse. I would not eat a desert rat. You never know where they have been.

And then the earth moves.

Or, rather, the tumbleweed does.

Who could imagine it? Midnight Louie thrown by a mere tumbleweed?

But tossed aside I am, like balsa wood.

I come up sucking sand and squeezing my eyes shut against a sleet of grit.

If that coyote is back, I am kitty litter!

Blind as a kitten I struggle to my feet, game for Round Two.

The rasping noise I have been hearing has escalated into a spitting sound.

There are lizards who attack that way, I have heard. Euw! Talk about not fighting fair.

I bat my eyelashes as if I were the Divine Yvette at home plate (bizarre as that image may be), but still I cannot see past the dark and grit and the, ugh, spit that have sewn my lids shut as if I were on some embalming table.

Finally, though, I see the tumbleweed heading into the dim distance like the bouncing ball on a set of on-screen lyrics.

I gaze down at what I presume to be ground and the

denuded dead body of my former partner, not to mention my questionable next of kin.

It is gone!

Well, it depends if you believe in the dead walking.

Me, I do not.

On the other hand, I have seen Elvis, and more to the point, Elvis has seen me and been very cordial.

I feel and pat my way around the crime scene and find nothing but cactus quills for my pains. And I do mean pains!

The only conclusion is that the night gust that ran off with the tumbleweed also whisked away the earthly remains of Miss Midnight Louise.

She was only a slip of a girl, like my Miss Temple, I think maudlinly.

Nothing much holding her to earth but her determined shivs, and my poor Miss Temple only has them on two, not four feet, and only through artificial implementation.

I am getting quite choked up, what with the sand and dust and unhappy thoughts of my two female associates.

I have saved Miss Temple's skin more than a few times, but in this case I have sent Miss Louise to certain death, as it turned out.

Whoa is me.

I stagger back to the human crime scene, my perked ears hearing no sirens yet, hearing nothing but the vast, empty desert and the vast, empty echo of my guilt.

The motorcycle and rider remain a macabre still life on the wild desert floor, flesh and machine separated by death but complicit in death.

Finally my vision has cleared except for an odd blurring.

Poor Miss Louise. She only did what I had told her to do.

Why did I not choose to tail Kitty the Cutter? I am always one for the dames anyway.

Why was it not me whose fresh furry corpse was jostling even now through Joshua trees and saguaros and cat-claw patches?

Well, I might not be jostling, being somewhat too heavy even for a Kansas-strength tornado to sweep up. Face it, Toto was a wimp as well as a dog. Midnight Louie would not go gently onto the Yellow Brick Road, let me tell you!

So if I had gone with Kitty the Cutter, I would be alive and kicking, as I have so recently proven, and Miss Louise would be in the safe custody of Mr. Max, who was wise enough to keep clean away from this messy accident/death scene.

Poor Louise! She was not so bad, even if she was not likely any relation. I bow and shake my head at the vagaries of life, and death.

A sudden cough to my rear interrupts my sober vigil.

"Do you mind?" a raspy, faint voice asks.

I glance first to the still form of Kitty the Cutter. She is not moving.

I glance second all around me in a 360-degree circle.

And I see that the puddle has been wafted near the downed motorcycle.

I approach with caution. As well I should.

The puddle lifts a spiky head and then lifts a lip to bare sharp, white fangs.

"First," it says, croaking, "you send me on a death trip. Then you try to plant a tree on my spine. Then you let a dust devil have its way with me."

I race to the talking carp pool as if it were a mirage of the Crystal Phoenix. It must be Louise! A live Louise!

Well, it is a head lifting from the desert floor, and not by much.

I am a one-cat emergency technician team. Quickly, I assess the situation with a realistic professional eye. One kit down, pretty flattened. Just a few centimeters off from road kill.

Her eyes are glued shut from sand-dust. Her once coal-black coat is as mouse-colored as a computer accessory. She looks like a radiator brush that has been sent through a corkscrew backward.

Obviously, some good nursing care is needed, but the

only good nurse I know is my Miss Temple and she is miles away.

Looks like it is up to me. We dudes are not good at this TLC stuff.

I grit my teeth, bend down, and begin licking the dust off her eyes and face. Arrphg. Tastes like a gravel pie.

However, I come equipped with a tongue that is the equivalent of number 80 sandpaper. Do not call me Easy Rider, call me Rough Rider.

It is tough going. It strikes me that my task is not unlike licking afterbirth off a newborn kit. That is women's work!

However, the hardened operative must be prepared to save lives, however necessary, as well as to kick posterior.

Speaking of kicking posterior, at length it becomes necessary for me to lick posterior . . . it is bad enough when I must do this chore on my own self.

However, in time I have Miss Midnight Louise shining like a new pair of patent leather Mary Jane shoes. Now if she can only make like a pair of shoes and get up and walk. Miracles of that nature not even a professional tongue can achieve.

At least her peepers are open and she is looking around.

"What happened?" she asks, like they do on the TV shows.

"Well," says I, sitting down and aware that my much-tried tongue would rather keep silent. "It looks like Miss Kathleen O'Connor ran off the road and took you with her. Apparently you were in the left saddlebag, which is under the fallen motorbike, so it is a wonder that you survived."

"Your deductions are accurate only so far," she retorts.

Yes, even half dead, Miss Midnight Louise can dredge up a retort.

"I was in the left saddlebag, as you speculate, but when I sensed some trouble and peeped out, I saw Miss Kathleen ready to take a run at Mr. Max and his vehicle, and the semiautomatic she pulled out from her black leather motorcycle jacket. I decided desperate measures were called for.

So I scrambled out of the saddlebag onto the back of her seat—"

"You rode pillion on a speeding motorcycle?" I demand incredulously.

"I do not know what pillows have to do with it. It was as rough as a roller-coaster ride out on the seat at eighty miles an hour. But I managed to climb her back and rake her neck, thereby disrupting her aim and unfortunately her driving sense, sending her and the motorcycle and myself into an off-the-road soar that ended as you see it."

I am speechless.

I sit down and manage to dig up enough spit to wet a mitt and sweep it over my worry-wrinkled brow.

I cannot believe it.

According to her testimony, Miss Midnight Louise has single-mittedly brought down Kitty the Cutter.

"Louise," I say, when I think I can speak. "You are telling me that you stopped Kitty the Cutter from shooting Mr. Max?"

"That was the general idea."

"Then you . . . you killed her."

"No," she says faintly. "I have never brought down prey that big. Maybe a bulldog or two—"

"I tell you, the dame is dead. Iced. Offed. I had to keep a coyote from eating the remains."

"The same coyote you did your Karate Kid act on?"

"You saw that?

"Heard it. Thanks for the eyewash, by the way."

In the distance, I hear a car motor approaching.

"We have to get you out of here."

" 'We' is not an operable option."

"It will have to be." I regretfully examine my rescue handiwork. "If you cannot walk, I will have to do the sled-dog routine. Too bad I rousted that coyote. He could be useful now."

"I would never accept assistance from a yellow-bellied dog."

"Dogs are not so bad once you teach them a few manners."

"Going soft in your old age, Daddy-o?"

"Quite the contrary. I am about to give you the rough ride of your life. Now keep still and think of England."

"Huh? Why would I think of England?"

"I hear it is the thing to do in unthinkable circumstances."

With that I bend down and take the loose skin at the nape of her neck in my strong teeth.

There is only one way to get her off the scene of the crime that will soon be crawling with curious humans. I must make like a mama-cat and move my litter of one.

. . . Ghosts

Max watched the ambulance attendants finally bully the loaded stretcher up the incline and toward the waiting open mouth of the vehicle's rear. Its occupant was slid in as unceremoniously as a corpse slammed into a metal drawer at the local morgue.

In the momentarily lit ambulance interior, Max could see people bending over Kathleen, fussing, hooking, injecting, intent on coaxing life back until all options had been exhausted.

He had once bent over Kathleen. Only once, long ago. The memory seared like acid. What had been a moment of deliriously innocent guilty pleasure had become years of intense regret.

Would that regret finally die with her?

Max hoped so. He'd advised Devine to "get over it," knowing that it had been impossible for himself. Maybe he could finally take his own advice.

Or find someone to make him take it.

The ambulance raced away screaming, the squad car ahead of it.

The fallen Ninja gleamed in the soft moonlight, elegant as a polished onyx tombstone.

Motorcycles were dangerous toys. Ask the man who had owned one. Helmets or not, admit you rode a motorcycle and your health insurance rates would soar. But Max wished he owned the Hesketh Vampire now, a fast, screaming motorcycle that would take him back to town as if he were mounted on a banshee, able to hear not one thought thanks to the distinctive high-velocity howl that gave the bike its macabre name.

The Maxima would not attract attention. It would purr back to town and move quietly into its preordained stall, like a docile horse. It would move to its imminent destruction, unnoticed, and shrink to a cube of crushed metal and glass and bits of cat-cut leather. It would have no history, leave no trace.

It was not interesting anymore.

When the lights of the Strip made a luminous dome on the black horizon, Max hit the number programmed into his cell phone and designated the drop point, the parking ramp of a major Strip hotel, in the slot marked for hotel executives only. It was always empty and no one questioned that.

Max walked out through the ramp, passing the occasional couple heading for their cars, too self-involved to notice him.

Sometimes it seemed too easy.

He walked the endless way to the Strip, amounting to maybe four city blocks in a town that didn't sport billion-dollar hotels as big as airports. He caught a cab to within two miles of his house, then walked home like a sneak thief casing the neighborhood, avoiding lights, jumping privacy walls, cutting through unlit backyards, until the last unlit backyard was his own. He entered the house with a key through a hidden door.

Safe at home. Just like a baseball player who's hit the ball out of the park.

He moved through the large utility room, past the unoccupied maid's room and bath, into the black-as-pitch kitchen.

Someone turned on the overhead fluorescent lights, a dimmer switch that made no sound and spun up to maximum brightness in one smooth flash.

Max spun around to maximum alertness, never taking a visitor for granted. Who knows. It could have been a ghost. He got one.

"I know I should have waited for you to arrive," Gandolph said. "I shouldn't have let myself in either. You might have changed the security measures."

"I thought I had."

Gandolph smiled, waggishly. "I managed not to trip any of them. I haven't lost all my marbles during my . . . exile. You look terrible, Max. Is this a bad moment for a reunion? What took you so long? Where have you been?"

"Back in Ireland." Max opened the huge Zero-king stainless steel refrigerator and pulled out a beer. A Harp beer. "Want one?"

"Beer is not my druthers, dear boy. Why do you think I bought Orson Welles's former house? Like him, I am a gourmand. Wine, brandy, perhaps the not-too-trendy liqueur when I'm in a mellow mood. No beer, ale, or stout of any sort."

Max twisted off the cap, drank deep. "All that is still here. Help yourself."

The older man disappeared into the adjacent wine cellar and came out reverently bearing a bottle.

Max took and uncorked it for him.

"My arthritis thanks you." Gandolph lifted the ruddy wineglass to the light to savor it visually before he tasted it.

Max reflected on arthritis, the unspoken reason why Gandolph had given up the practice of magic to concentrate on unmasking false mediums. When had it hit Gandolph, the stiffening of fingers once so nimble? Somewhere in his early fifties. Max might be heading in the same direction. Who knew? He'd been out of contact with his family for so long, for their own protection, he didn't even know what maladies ran in their genes, what he might expect. He was as good as an orphan.

"Max, lad," came Gandolph's cajoling voice, warmed by his first savored sip of the Chardonnay. "You're brooding. That's a genetic predisposition of the Irish more ingrained than a love of liquor and even more dangerous. Don't think. Talk. What's happened?"

"There's bad news and worse news. Which do you want first?"

"Bad before worse."

"Actually, I think my bad is your worse, and my worse is your bad. Did you know Gloria Fuentes was dead?"

"Gloria! No." Gandolph sat on a kitchen stool. "I haven't seen her in years, of course. Odd how you can work together so closely with someone, and once the act is retired, lose touch. And I was dashing about the country looking for mediums. When was it?"

"A few months ago."

"Only a few months?" Gandolph shook his head. "And me back in town just in time to miss seeing her alive. Poor Gloria. She wasn't that old. I hope it wasn't cancer."

"It was faster. Gandolph, somebody strangled her in a church parking lot. Do you know what she'd be doing there?"

"Oh my God, what a tragedy! Why was she there? Going to church, I assume. Just because she worked onstage in fishnet tights didn't make her a showgirl. She loved her work, but when it was over, she was out of the spotlight. Had a gaggle of nieces and nephews she doted on. She'd been retired for years. They did catch the killer?"

"No. Do you think her death could be related to the attempt on your life?"

"I don't see why. Once I retired, we lost touch. I was like you, pursuing the trail of ghosts that were hard to find, and I was darn hard to find myself. If this is the bad news, what is worse?"

"Worse for me than for you, I think." Max sat on a kitchen stool and told him about Kathleen O'Connor's terrible accident and probable death, as if he were at the village pub chatting up the friendly barman.

"The emergency crew was working on her, of course," Max finished up. "But it looked like frantic revival efforts in the face of inevitability. I'm convinced she's gone."

Gandolph's round face grew long and he shook his balding head several times.

Baldness. That was another thing Max didn't know would come to him soon or later or never. He was beginning to feel age hovering behind him like Elvis's ghost, closing down his future.

"Terrible," Gandolph was muttering. "A terrible . . . accident? I can't quite call it that. She was still pursuing you, after all these years?"

"Me. And others in my place. Innocents, as usual. She liked to torment innocents."

"I remember her. Prettiest lass in Londonderry. It couldn't last as I remember it, of course, that beauty."

"It did," Max said shortly. It had been too dark in the desert to see Kathleen's face as other than a light-and-shadow-kissed mystery, and now he would never see it again. "Others saw her more recently. A sketch had been done from memory. Her beauty had matured, that's all. Grown, not faded."

"Hearsay, though."

"I believe the source, an impeccably honest source." Max smiled to recall just how hopelessly honest Matt Devine still was. Momentarily, he envied him. "I'm glad I never saw her again, Garry. I can't think of that lovely young girl without seeing a death's head superimposed on those treacherous features. Sean's skull, sans crossbones."

"You didn't see her at the accident scene."

"Too dark."

"But you're sure it was her, sure she's dead."

"What other woman would pursue me on a motorcycle? Someone else had seen her riding one earlier."

"She rode a bicycle in Londonderry, like a country lass."

"She was a country lass then. She had moved up in the world. You don't know. . . . You remember Sean and me trying to trip each other up while we both played court to Kathleen. You know what happened."

"A sad, sad thing, Max. You can't blame yourself for winning the lass over your cousin, or for him being alone that night in a Protestant pub that was bombed by the IRA."

"No, but I can blame Kathleen O'Connor. I've since met someone she was plaguing, stalking really, here. And when he heard of how I knew her, and where, and what happened, he had an interesting diagnosis for it all. He thinks she knew the pub would be hit and that Sean would be there. He thinks she enjoyed dallying with me while my cousin was being murdered, that she relished the guilt I would bear for the rest of my life."

"That would be unthinkably evil, to plan that sort of thing, and she was just a young girl. Who is this 'someone' who thinks such terrible things?"

"My impeccably honest man, an ex-priest that she targeted as a victim when she couldn't find me."

"An ex-priest? No wonder. I couldn't believe you'd tell just anyone your sad history, especially the undercover implications."

Max laughed, not happily. He drank some more beer. "Oh, Gandolph. Oh, Garry. You and I exited Ireland together all those years ago, and mostly worked together until you retired a few years ago. You were a stepfather to me, in magic and in espionage, but you can't know what's happened in Las Vegas in just the past year. This man, this ex-priest, is my new Sean, my cousin and my rival, and my fellow victim of a fatal woman. If he weren't so honest I'd feel free to hate him, but I can't."

"He rivaled you for Kathleen?"

"In terms of competing for her deepest hatred, yes. It

was shocking to see her find another to bedevil, to be almost unfaithful in her hatred. But . . . there's another woman too. I had to leave Las Vegas for almost a year to keep some hounds on my trail away from her. She met him in the meantime."

"Ah. So they are now a pair."

"No. She took me back, but it's different, isn't it? If I hadn't been able to come back—"

"They would have been a new couple?"

"Maybe. I can't be certain. I don't think they can be either."

"Just as none of us can be certain why Kathleen played the game she did, right up to the end. It went way beyond aiding the cause of Irish freedom. That was only a pretext for her."

"Agreed. But since her reappearance—and she left me alone for all those years—I've had to wonder what triggered her return. And return she had."

"She Who Must Be Reckoned With," Garry mused. "Ghosts are like that. Supposed ghosts, I should say. They have unfinished business and cannot rest, so say the mediums. There's a certain psychological attraction to the notion that the dead wait around for justice to be served."

"Kathleen served up injustice."

"Perhaps not in her own mind. What a puzzle and homicidal round we began in Northern Ireland."

"I began."

"No. You were in the middle, that's all. As all innocents are, caught in the middle. You were just a boy."

"Are any of us 'just' anything? I was . . . programmed to hate the 'other,' the 'wrong' side, as in all sectarian wars. I found my soul mate in Kathleen O'Connor. We were made for each other, drawn to our most opposite extremes. Now she's dead, and I don't know what to make of myself anymore."

"Dead? Kathleen? No, lad. Such ideas never die. They infect. For a time she revitalized the movement, single-handedly, with her hatred and her . . . well, whatever she had in full measure."

"But *you* are alive. I never expected that."

"To my discredit. I would rather be dead in my own place than alive in another's."

Max thought. "I can't say that of myself. Yet."

"Then you have a future."

He studied Gandolph. Once he had believed the older man could never be wrong.

Now he knew that anyone could be.

Even, for a split second of inattention or blind fury, Kitty the Cutter.

The Morning After: Foxy Proxy

Temple stood stock-still in the middle of the crowded convention aisle, people brushing against her every five seconds, their excited hubbub echoing to the top of the cavernous space.

This hubbub had a definite soprano tinge. One might even call it shrill. If one were sexist. Luckily, there weren't any of those sort around here. It wouldn't pay.

Temple inhaled the very mixed bag that scented the air-conditioned environment. There was a smorgasbord of odors from the food booths and latte bars, from exotic or even erotic massage oils and hair spray. She hadn't done PR for a major civic-center event in a few months. Her feet, once hardened to miles of concrete underfoot, now throbbed beneath her despite the concession of thick-soled and cushy clogs.

She had finally found time to venture out from the press room. The media had come, saw, and conquered, shooting miles of film that would show up on local and regional

TV, and as far away as Los Angeles, Phoenix, and Chicago.

Temple's résumé was rosy with new praise from the organizers, but she wasn't one to blush at getting quote-worthy recommendations. A freelancer lived or died by word of mouth.

And the subject of her reentry into major convention business was so up her alley. It was the annual Nevada women's show, a combination sales exhibition and pajama party, crammed with booths on time-saving gadgets, amazing beautification products, clothes, jewelry, and legerdemain: false nails, false hair, false push-up boobs, false teeth . . . ah, no, not that quite yet, but falsely whitened teeth.

This was an unabashedly girly event and Temple was an unabashedly girly girl. If it was good enough for a buff but disarmingly petite little number like Buffy the Vampire Slayer, it was good enough for her. So she'd had no trouble revving up the media on all that was new and exciting in a Woman's World.

Working this convention was the equivalent of a Mental Health Day off from work, times seven.

Now, on Sunday, the last day, she ambled among the exhibits, even paused to decide if a lifetime of never being able to tie a decent-looking knot could indeed be redeemed by a handy-dandy gadget called "Scarf-It-Up!" Exclamation free of charge.

For her, even exclamation marks couldn't redeem butterfingers.

She moved on, fascinated by a display of glittering minerals in small plastic towers, fairy dust for female faces. The women who manned the booths (paradox intentional) spotted her staff badge and immediately offered elaborate demonstrations and yummy freebies, which she took. For journalists that was a no-no, but PR people needed to know how the items they promoted worked. It was on-the-job research. Right, she thought, tucking a clever zebra-fabric mini-tote with miniature samples of lip gloss, eye cream, and nail enamel into her usual Goliath-size tote bag.

She loved being back in business.

But this was the exhibition's last hours on the last day. When the Sunday sun went down, the magic booth-city of ideas and products would vanish like the dropped flyers littering the aisles.

Tempting words blared from the papers ground underfoot along with the rainbow wink of glitter: Renew. Glamourous. Recharge. Easy. Cheap. Miraculous. Magic.

Temple found her wandering eye snagged by a glittering tray of rings. Inexpensive costume rings, but, hey, a girl could always use a cocktail ring. So she often thought in department store aisles, but she had never ever bought one.

These were cubic zirconia, she guessed, set in gilded sterling silver. "Vermeil" was the formal name for literally gilding the costume jewelry lily. A girly girl could always scope out rings, just because.

One. This one. It reminded her—sharply—of the ring Max had given her last Christmas, which already seemed half a lifetime ago.

She paused to stare at it. Amid gaudy "diamond" solitaires too big to be real, this was the only classy design, the setting angular and intriguing. One large stone, a moonstone maybe—it couldn't be a real opal—was offset and set off by twinkling diamonds. Cubic zirconia, or name-brand substitute.

Temple felt a compulsion to buy the thing. Was it merely because it looked like the ring she had lost so soon, surrendered to an onstage magician who had vanished with it never to reappear . . . until the ring had turned up weeks later at a murder scene. Apparently it had gone from Temple's hand, to the mandarin-nailed claw of Shangri-La the magician, to the plastic evidence baggie of Lieutenant C. R. (Cruella de Rottweiler) Molina.

Temple's fingers hovered over the ring.

"Don't be shy. Try it on," a hyper-happy (harpy?) female voice urged.

Temple, bewitched by the ring, didn't even answer, but did as suggested.

The ring glided over her knuckle (third finger left hand) as though made for it. It settled into the groove between her middle and little fingers like a baby into a cradle.

"How much?" she asked.

"Ummm. Thirty-eight ninety-five."

Gee, $38.95 to reclaim a dream, a memory, a moment. Not a bad bargain. But it wasn't really like her ring. Her memory must have already decayed a little. She knew she couldn't be sure. Still . . .

"Thirty-two. It's the last day of the expo."

Thirty-two! Well. Temple stared at the ring on her finger. It seemed to belong there. Her other hand dug in her tote bag for her wallet. At thirty-two cash would be okay, and the exhibitor probably would be spared a percentage to the credit card company.

"It's lovely," the woman said, sealing the bargain. "Made for you."

The real ring, the original, had been lovely, and the way it had been presented had been even lovelier, that Temple remembered exactly. Poor Max. His best intentions of six months ago had turned into hash again, like all best intentions. Not his fault. Not hers. Just . . . life and all its accidents.

Temple stuffed her change, five bucks plus some coins once tax had been added, into her tote bag and turned away.

"Wait!" the saleswoman urged. Her beautifully manicured hand reached out to push a small hot-pink moiré box into Temple's tote bag. "The box is free; might as well take it."

"Thanks!" That's what Temple loved about girly events; they were brimming over with bonuses and free gifts and little touches you didn't expect.

She glanced again at her hand, fanned her fingers, enjoyed the ring resting there like it belonged, like it had always been there.

She didn't dare tell/show Max. He would recognize it for the cheap imitation it was. He would remember the ring he had given her in every detail. She just remembered it in her emotions, and that seemed close enough. Better than nothing. It was her secret, this ring. Her secret and her souvenir.

The next morning was Monday. Temple awoke with Midnight Louie sprawling across her stomach. He felt like a very bad hangover.

"Louie!"

One lazy green eye slitted open. He deigned to regard her, then shut the eye again.

"Louie! You are an avalanche and I am an innocent Swiss village. Move! Off!"

He responded as all cats do to vocal commands. He didn't even bat an eyelash. And he had them. A lush line of jet-black a Supermodel would give her cheekbones for.

Not even a wink.

"Louie! I had a very big weekend. I don't have to go to work today, it's true, but I have a lot to catch up on."

Louie yawned and allowed himself to roll over. In so doing, he rolled right off the minor hump Temple's body made in the covers and onto unoccupied comforter.

She polished his head with her palm. "Sorry, boy. I overslept. I need to be up and doing!"

He yawned his response to that declaration and shut his eyes again.

Temple twisted herself into a pretzel trying to exit the bed without disturbing a hair on Louie's Olympic-broad-jump-length body.

"Ow!" Temple complained when she had kinked her feet onto the floor in a position preparatory to rising and shining.

She really didn't want to get up any more than Louie did, but . . . she had people to rouse and perpetrators to pursue.

The ring winked at the morning, catching her eye. She'd have to be careful to wear it for herself alone. In the daylight it looked so . . . tawdry. Maybe dreams deferred were tawdry.

Her tote bag sagged against the wall by the bedroom door. She remembered the cute little box the saleswoman had given her for the ring. Time to put the things of a child away. She'd inter the ring in the box and bury it at the back of a dresser drawer, where all tarnished memories dwell.

Temple dredged her tote bag and all its ill-gotten gains from the floor and probed its chaos with her right hand. Her fingers finally curled around a tubular object. Either a freebie lipstick or the box in question.

Tiffany it wasn't. Temple stuck in her thumb and pulled out a plum-blossom special, a lurid taffeta-wrapped box looking super-tawdry in broad daylight.

She opened it to reveal a cheap foam pillow pierced by a horizontal slit.

Only this hole-in-one was already occupied. By a ring. An ersatz gold ring, very large and very plain, of a snake . . . or a worm, or an eel, or something else icky . . . biting its own tail.

Was there a message there? Hmmph. Free box and free ring. Bingo. Goodie.

The new ring was way too big to fit even Temple's thumb—she tried—and it didn't sport the slightest dusting of rhinestones to give it star quality.

For a moment she wondered if the saleswoman had lost a valuable item. Naw. Like the ring Temple had bought on a whim and a prayer, this ring was also, utterly . . . worthless.

She set both rings away in the bottom dresser drawer, under the scarves she had bought and been given over the years—and had kept because it seemed rude and even cruel not to—and had never used.

Because she never had, and never would, learn to tie a knot worth letting anyone actually see.

Dead Certain

"You've never been in an autopsy room before?"

Matt stared at Molina. "You mean when I was a priest? No. Nothing happened in my parish that called for that."

"Yeah, visiting the morgue is pretty uncalled for, isn't it?"

She flashed him a wry smile, as if they were in this together.

And they were, in a sense.

"Now," Molina said, holding the steel-and-glass entry door open for him, like a good hostess. "It looks pretty regular up front. Reception desk, chairs, etcetera etcetera. Just brace yourself. Every step farther in gets more like a new TV show hybrid: *ER* blended with *The Twilight Zone*, if you remember that golden oldie."

"Reruns," Matt pointed out. "Who could forget Rod Serling and his spooky series?"

"This place isn't exactly 'spooky,' " Molina paused to tell him. "It's way too clinical. That's what'll get to you. The utter ordinariness of dead and dismembered bodies.

Not like a crime scene, which is a sort of origami nightmare you have to figure out. Here, it's all clear. Dead and about to be buried. Think you can handle it?"

"I've done funerals in my time, Lieutenant."

She regarded him with a gaze as icy as a vodka gimlet. "You identified your stepfather's body here. I remember that. No gentle remote viewing booth for this one. You'll see her on cold stainless steel and she won't be prettied up."

"Why? Why did Effinger get the opening-night curtain presentation and why does Kathleen O'Connor get none of the frills?"

"Body's too fresh. No time. Besides, we know there are no relatives to find. When I asked, not even your friend Bucek could come up with anything on her through the FBI. Don't let Grizzly Bahr ghoul you out. He's just a sawbones. Literally."

Matt then followed her to the reception window, where a perky young thing with highlighted hair shaven to look as if crop circles had set up permanent residence on her scalp handed them clip-on VISITORS tags.

Matt pinched a bit of cotton knit with the alligator clip, also stainless steel. He hated to tell Molina, but he was ready to see Kitty O'Connor, mistress of the edged razor blade, laid out on another metal surface.

Mercy?

He only had to think of Vassar, and he felt none. He was as cold as dry ice.

They went through doors and down hallways. They passed people in lab coats with matching tags, only these bore names.

"I nicknamed him 'Grizzly,' " Molina said abruptly, "because it fit his last name and his attitude. All MEs are weird. Death is their daily bread. Maybe they're reincarnated hyenas, but they laugh about it a lot. Don't be put off. Bahr knows his stiffs."

"Why are you worrying about me?"

She stopped. Fixed him with a Blue Dahlia gaze only

she could level. "Sometimes you wish someone dead. Usually you have reason. Sometimes you get your wish. Don't freak on me."

"I never wished Kitty O'Connor dead."

She resumed walking through the bland, confusing halls.

He could pick it up now, the faint . . . unpleasant . . . smell. Death with an orange twist. Vaguely kitchen, vaguely crematorium.

"I didn't," Matt said, his stride lengthening to keep up with the tall lieutenant. "I wanted to talk to her more than anyone, I think."

Molina turned, vertical forefinger pressed warningly against her lips. "The Iceman cometh."

Matt stopped to look around.

A pair of double doors burst apart to birth a form as forceful and burly as John Madden commenting on a football game. The vaunted "Grizzly" he presumed.

Grizzled was right. Bristling gray eyebrows, piercing gray eyes driving a physique once powerful and now larded with midlife excess.

The old lion. Still clawed. Not sleeping tonight, not an instant.

"Who's Dr. Kildare, the intern?" he growled at Molina.

"He may be able to identify the body."

"Will he pass out?"

"I don't know," she said. "Shall we find out?"

"Let's." He lifted a clipboard and ran his restless gaze down it. "This is the easy rider organ donor, right? Unusual it's a woman. Motorcycles! Might as well take arsenic as an appetizer. If I had a thousand dollars for every dead Marlon Brando–wannabe that came through here, I'd be retired in Tahiti."

"Brando made it there," Matt put in.

Bahr stopped, turned on him, quieted like a rearing black bear in a Grizzly Adams movie.

"I don't want to be where Brando is. It's a saturated-fat paradise. Me, I'm all muscle. Come along, son, and see the bifurcated lady. She's a sight. Must have been one while alive, but now she's autopsy Annie. Follow me."

He blasted through another pair of double doors, and by now Matt couldn't escape the pervasive odor of the working environment: decay.

He tried not to breathe too deeply, but even shallow breaths brought the heavy bouquet of rotting flesh.

The room was like a lab: big, inhabited by stainless steel tables, sinks, and equipment. People seemed superfluous in here. Matt accepted the clear safety goggles and latex gloves Molina also donned like a seasoned astronaut used to looking like a parody of a person.

Matt ran a prayer through his overactive mind. For the dead. For Kathleen O'Connor, who had been somebody's precious baby once.

She lay on a stainless steel bier, naked.

Matt realized that he had never seen a naked woman before.

But she wasn't a woman now. Death made her unreal, a department-store mannequin glimpsed in an unfinished window-dressing set.

He kept his eyes on what he was here to see: her face. Was this truly her? Was she truly dead? And gone.

She looked tiny, fragile on that large steel bed.

Odd that she had hurt him with a small steel blade.

Now the blades had been at her. Her torso was seamed like a Raggedy Ann's body. Her stuffing seemed to have been removed, and returned, like Scarecrow's after the Flying Monkeys had dispersed him.

Her face, though, was whole, such as it was. He couldn't say the same for her head, and avoided looking above her eyebrows. Raven eyebrows. Her eyelids were shut and her cheekbones and chin bruised and scraped. Somebody's child had taken a great fall.

"Motorcycles," Bahr snorted. "Hate 'em. Make hash out of my bodies. She wore leathers, so the limbs are pretty solid, what's not broken. But the face . . . restructuring by Gravel, Inc."

Matt sighed, then was sorry he'd exhaled. He'd have to inhale sooner, and ingest the air of decay.

"Is it her?" Molina asked.

He'd forgotten about her in the presence of Milady Death.

Was it?

Kitty had been vital and certain, threatening and powerful. This . . . corpse was none of that. It wore a skullcap where the surgeon's saw had sliced through her cranium. She was like an Egyptian prince, her vital organs removed and weighed and stored elsewhere.

Still, beneath the matted raven-black hair, behind the abraded facial skin, Matt saw flesh as white as snow, lips as red as blood, eyes as liquid as Caribbean waters . . .

"Her eyes," he said aloud.

Molina held up a plastic baggie. It contained, not the furtive glimmer of Temple's opal-and-diamond ring from Max Kinsella this time, but two pale, flat gemstones, aquamarines when he bent closer to look.

"Colored contact lenses," Molina said. "She wore them. Like her archenemy, the Mystifying Max, Miss Kitty altered her eyes. Their natural shade was gray-green, if you believe romantic coroners like Grizzly here."

Bahr hawked out a laugh as another man might expel phlegm.

"The eyes have it," Molina went on. "Contact lenses. Vivid blue-green. Looks like the lady couldn't make up her mind. Was she blue, or was she green?"

"Green," Matt said. "She worked for the IRA."

"Or maybe Ralph Nader," Bahr put in. "You do know her, then?"

Matt wasn't sure that his relationship with Kitty O'Connor could be described as "knowing."

He tried for the objective eye. Saw long, narrow neck. Pale skin paler now in death. Small determined chin. Slightly upturned nose. A pretty girl without the hatred that made every feature sharp and feral. She should be handing out appointment cards in an office somewhere, a dentist's or a chiropractor's.

All the anger that had propelled her, made her vivid, living, had left her.

She's gone. She left.

"Is it Kitty O'Connor?" Molina asked, unconsciously shifting into the neutral reference that remains demanded. It. The remains.

He glanced over the entire figure again, this time seeing something like a spider on one of her prominent hipbones. Even as he thought somebody should brush away the trespassing insect, he caught his breath as he realized the black blot was a tattoo. Of a serpent swallowing its own tale, just as Kitty's lifelong flirtation with death had finally been consummated. The worm Ouroboros celebrated in the unwanted ring she had given him, and taken away.

Only she would bear such a mark.

"Yes," Matt said.

"You're sure?"

"I was sure when I walked in. But I needed to make double-sure. It just seems . . . impossible."

"She was mean, but she was mortal."

He nodded. That terse epitaph fit his stepfather too. But Cliff Effinger plainly had been murdered.

Kitty had not died so obviously. Could mere accident have claimed her when bitter opposition could make no dents on her stainless steel soul? Anything was possible.

Including the fact that his worst enemy was dead, that he was free.

Free to live out the legacy she had left him: a lot of atypical acts, enough guilt to ensure Purgatory for eternity, eternal regret for another life lost.

He heard Molina and Bahr conferring, as if Kathleen O'Connor's dead body were just another conference table to gather around.

"A couple of odd abrasions on the nape of the neck, almost cuts," Bahr was saying.

"*Hmmm.* Know what I'm thinking?" Molina asked.

"Women can get those from abrasive labels at the back of the neck. I'll check out her clothing."

"—the only anomaly, and it's a minor one for a spinout into a dry wash like this," Bahr's voice was grumbling.

A spinout in a dry wash. It sounded like an epitaph for a frustrated and wasted life, Matt thought.

A hand closed on his arm.

Molina's.

"We can leave now," she said.

Matt wasn't so sure you ever left Grizzly Bahr's realm, not once you had seen it.

"Good job," the man himself said, grinning. "You didn't upchuck once. Disappoint an old man, will you? Out of here, then. You've graduated Ghoul School with honors."

Sweat Shop

"What's the story on the man with the golden arm?" Molina asked Alfonso later that morning. He stood before her desk with a manila folder in his hand and a Cheshire-cat smile on his well-used face.

"How'd you guess?"

"I assigned my detectives to sweat a possible witness who's clammed up. First you'd do a thorough background, which I assume is what fattens that manila folder in your hand. Next, I told you to let me know when you had him ready for the ropes. And here you are bright and early Monday morning."

"Awesome, Lieutenant. You're wasted behind that desk."

"Tell me about it."

"Yup. You got it. Guy's name is Herb Wolverton. Energetic, strong for his size. Was in the merchant marine years ago. Can lift hefty luggage as easily as he can pocket hundred-dollar bills. 'Retired' to Vegas from Biloxi, where he had accumulated quite a rap sheet, all petty stuff but as long as an octopus's arm. Drunken brawling, gambling . . . and it used to be illegal there unless you were on a licensed riverboat. Nothing felonious, just cantankerous. Had a chip on his shoulder, old Herb did, and it turned into a brick when he drank.

"Anyway, vice was no stranger and when he hit Vegas eight years ago he settled down to work his way up as a bellman. Since he'd been used to greasing his palms in Creole town, he fit right in. Real accommodating to anyone with green palms."

"What have we got on him that we can use?" Molina rose and headed into the corridor for the interrogation rooms.

Alfonso's grimace exaggerated his hangdog features as he caught up with her, huffing slightly. "Not much. He's threatening to call a lawyer, but we keep telling him we're just interested in his testimony as a witness. I have a feeling this guy is real scared, but I can't tell of who."

Molina quashed an urge to correct him. Whom, it was whom. She'd told Mariah that at least a couple hundred times.

"Alch and Su in?" she asked instead.

"Yeah, but Barrett and . . ."—maybe he had read her mind—"and I brought him in."

"Still, I'd like you and Su to do the interrogation. Alch and Barrett and I can watch."

"Me and Su? We're not partners. We don't know each other's moves."

"Exactly. I want to shake this clam up until he burps up a pearl or two. An edgier interrogation just might do it. And we're investigating the death of a woman. Su might make him feel guilty, subconsciously at least."

"Psychology, Lieutenant? Guys like this only know fists or rolls of cash."

"Humor me," she advised, not remotely sounding like anyone who knew a thing about humor.

Alfonso got the idea and shut up.

Barrett was holding up the wall outside one of the

cramped interrogation rooms when they arrived. Molina sent him to round up Alch and Su while she and Alfonso slipped into the adjoining room with the two-way glass every suspect knew was there. It still came in handy. Observers could spot things interrogators might miss in the heat of the Q & A, and the sense of unseen hovering watchers unnerved all but the most hardened criminals.

When the three detectives arrived, Molina had to explain her thinking again. What she didn't tell them was that detective teams could get like old married couples, if there was any such thing nowadays: so used to each other's ways life was a sleepwalk. Complacent. Much as they all grumbled about the unusual pairing, Molina noticed Alfonso and Su sizing each other up as they went next door to meet Herbie Wolverton, boy bellman.

They made a Mutt and Jeff combo, no doubt, with gender and racial differences accenting the unlikely pairing. Wolverton would be distracted by the odd couple. A distracted witness was an unintentionally frank witness.

"You don't make this guy for a killer?" Alch asked, turning a chair around and straddling it, his chin balanced on the plastic-shell back.

She understood his paternally protective attitude toward Su (much resented by Su but good for sharpening her edge). Differences, not similarities, made a detective team cook, Molina had discovered. And maybe marriages. You can't learn anything from a clone of yourself.

She settled into her own uncomfortable chair, intrigued by the show she had set in motion. She realized that Herb could reveal facts that would lead to Matt Devine and ultimately to her. So be it. She wondered what would persuade a bellman to shut up so completely when all he had to do was describe the usual comings and goings on an ordinary bought-and-paid-for night shift in Las Vegas.

It was all up to Alfonso and Su, unlikely partners: unearth information, and maybe bury their lieutenant.

Herb Wolverton was already unhappy, an excellent sign.

He fidgeted on his own plastic hot seat, sitting at the

plain table with the tape recorder its only accouterment.

Molina could have studied the rap sheet in the manila folder Barrett had given her, but she preferred to write her own scenario, then do a reality check.

He was around thirty-five, a well-used thirty-five. Over-muscled the way some short men will get, but still a boyish and jaunty carriage. Aye, aye, sir. Yes, ma'am. His freckled face was surfer tanned. Although not stupid, he had allowed youthful potential to decay into mere canniness.

His blue eyes darted doglike to Alfonso and Su, Su and Alfonso. The big sloppy man unnerved him. That kind of St. Bernard confidence had always escaped him. He'd had to be wiry and shipshape to get some respect. Su . . . oh, he'd seen a foreign port or two and he liked those delicate Asian ladies. Just his size. He could be a courtly fellow if he wasn't feeling threatened.

"Ma'am," was his first word, with a nod to Su. He almost rose from his chair, but Alfonso gestured him down. Down, boy.

The tension was already riveting. Herb ached to charm and disarm Su, the appealing toy Pekinese. He knew Alfonso could crush him if he wanted to, hardly knowing it. He didn't know Su could too. But she would know it.

Fox terrier, yes. Aggressive but eager to please. Already conflicted and now . . . scared.

Molina could smell his fear through the two-way glass.

Alch leaned forward. "Someone's got to him good."

"But who? This guy is combative, a scrapper."

"Small potatoes," Alch noted.

"Right," Molina agreed. "He's not used to a town like Las Vegas, running on major juice. You think a former client of Vassar's, some big mojo guy, resented her profession? Tried to claim her?"

"Anything's possible," Alch said, "when you're dealing with Sex in the City, especially this city. Mr. Big, is what you're suggesting. Vassar was a prime piece of real estate. Wonder if Rothenberg has dealt with that before, having girls so classy the clients get possessive?"

"We'll have to ask her," Molina said, "but first our team needs to have a go at Herbie."

Beat policemen often referred to suspects by childhood diminutives and Molina had adopted the habit. Infantalizing suspected perps reinforced their own shaky sense of control. Made the Bogey Man into Little Mikey. It was a self-deluding ploy, but must have served a purpose. The police were so often impotent when it came to the courts and defense attorneys. Only place to show muscle was on the streets.

"Mr. Wolverton." Su sounded as demure as she looked. "I've gone over your rap sheet. It's pretty minor. I'm guessing that you'd want to cooperate with the police in a capital murder case."

"Capital murder?"

"Well, it's possible that the victim was held against her will in the hotel room. That would be kidnapping."

Wolverton's frown aged him a decade. "I don't think . . . Vassar, she was always a pretty savvy lady."

"You knew the victim then?" Su inquired as if making chitchat at a garden party.

"Yeah, sure. She was a regular. Came and went all the time. Classy act from entrance to exit. But not my type," he added, as if fearing admiration might be mistaken for obsession. "Too big."

Alfonso weighed in lazily. "It wouldn't take much strength to push a tall woman over that chickenshit balcony. Those stiletto heels she had on? Would have made her unstable. Tippy."

"Look." Wolverton licked his lips and eyed Su. "My job is to see people up to their rooms, drag in their luggage, turn on the air conditioner, get ice if they want it, show 'em which way the faucets turn. Then I'm outta there."

"Didn't you forget something?" Su asked gently. Too gently.

"What? What'd I forget? It's my job, for chrissakes, not yours. I know my job."

"The tip." Su brushed her middle finger over one of her

exotically plucked brows. "You got good tips, didn't you?"

"Yeah. Great tips. Everybody was happy with me. Why not? I am a happy guy."

"Most Happy Fella," Alfonso put in a like a genial uncle. A little too like a genial uncle. Like a godfather.

Herbie jerked his head, loosening taut neck muscles. "It's a pretty good job. I meet some very interesting people."

"But you really get tipped for what you don't do," Alfonso insinuated. By now he was smirking like a fellow transgressor.

Wolverton glanced at Su. "I don't get it . . . 'what I don't do.' "

Alfonso rested his forearms on the table and leaned inward, taking up more than half the surface, edging into Wolverton's space.

"A happy fellow, a good citizen, would report solicitation instead of profiting from it. Las Vegas ain't no chicken ranch down the highway. That stuff is illegal here."

"Everybody does it. Why are you on me about it?"

"Because you're lying," Su finally interjected. "What red-blooded male could forget what room Vassar went into and who was in it? The tip for placing her with a customer must have been big."

"Su," Alfonso remonstrated, "you're forgetting one thing. Maybe Herbie here isn't a red-blooded male."

"Hey, I'm as red-blooded as any hunk of meat out there. But it's a business, see. Faces come and go in Las Vegas like everybody's on a merry-go-round. There's no point in remembering something you'll never see again. Besides, I dig girls, not guys. Why would I take inventory of just another john?"

Alfonso leaned closer. "Haven't you had any famous check-ins?"

"Yeah. Ah, Mel Gibson one time. And Rod Steiger before he died. But they didn't want call girls, I remember that. Most other people are pretty anonymous."

"Why do you use Judith Rothenberg?" Su asked out of the blue.

"Why not? Her girls are clean and classy. You never have trouble with a Rothenberg girl."

"Until now," Sue pointed out. "Is that it? Are you paid to keep quiet if anything goes wrong? Is Rothenberg taping your mouth and your memory shut?"

"Naw, she wouldn't have enough pull to make me risk my skin."

"Who would?" Alfonso asked.

"Nobody. Nobody's bribing me, I swear it. I got a good deal here. I make enough to get along, and if you don't like how I get my biggest tips, face it; it's just business in L.V. Even you guys have to hype yourself up to make a periodic hooker roundup, and then you go for the street types."

"We don't do that," Alfonso said softly. "We don't mess with any of that. We are homicide detectives, Herbie. I don't think you get how big this case is."

Sweat was glistening on his forehead now, Molina noticed, but the boyish blue eyes remained bulging and defiant.

It wasn't treats that made this dog go; it was threats. Someone had scared the shinola out of him.

Su's narrowed eyes announced the same conclusion.

"She's got it," Alch murmured with satisfaction.

"Got what?" Barrett asked, annoyed. "This guy responds to force. Look at how Alfonso's got him crowded half off his own chair. As nice a job of creeping intimidation as I've seen in a while."

"Exactly," Molina said. "So what force is big enough to shut him up even when facing that kind of intimidation?"

"Money," Alch said. "A lot of money."

"Someone with more force," Barrett said.

"Right, Barrett." Molina threw Alch an also-ran smile. "This guy has seen Godzilla. Otherwise he'd be squealing like Randy the Rat. Money wouldn't keep him mum on a murder case, if we've got one."

"And he's scared enough to make me think we do," Barrett said.

Now Su was leaning into the table, but only slightly, her shoulders tilted, her air just a trifle big sister. "You were the only one, Herb. The only one to peek into the room where Vassar's assailant waited. I know a big tip wouldn't keep you from making the guy. I know you called Vassar to that room, that you take your job seriously and you wouldn't want anyone messing with some classy lady you had sent up to her death."

"Shuddup!" Wolverton clapped his hands over his ears. "I didn't see no monster lurking behind that door. Nothing to remember. An ordinary guy, all right! I forget faces like that eight days a week. One ride up and down in the elevator and I couldn't remember my own mother's mug. You don't know what it's like. Faces, faces, hands, hands, bags, bags. Even hundred-dollar bills get to look like ones. I'm telling you the truth. Nothing registers."

"Except johns who want high-dollar suites," Alfonso pounced, "so they can abuse high-dollar call girls."

"Maybe, but I read the paper too. You guys didn't find any marks of violence on the body. Maybe the woman fell, huh? Maybe she just fell."

"Or jumped," Su put in.

Herb Wolverton jumped at the suggestion. "Yeah. Who knows how these broads really feel about what they do? I mean, sometimes I gotta tote and haul for some arrogant prick that makes me feel two inches tall. It goes with the territory, but the turf can be pretty mean. I shrug it off, but someone like Vassar, whose services are more . . . personal. It might get sick, you know what I mean? She might . . . get driven into something she hates herself for. So, yeah. She could have jumped. But I don't know. I wasn't there."

"And you don't *know* where you weren't, because you can't remember the room number she went into on her last visit, or a thing about the looks of the guy who opened the door." Alfonso's tone was scathing.

"No. I can't." Wolverton was not caving into anything, intimidation or angst.

"The mob, do you think?" Barrett asked Molina on the other side of the window glass. "Vassar could have been some godfather's favorite, and it could have gotten ugly, like Wolverton says. He doesn't look like a guy who'd cross organized crime."

"Organized crime is so corporate in this town nowadays," Molina objected. "And if he'd had the bad luck to really tread on some old-time neanderthal toes, he'd be buried in the Mojave by now."

"Yeah." Alch stood and turned his chair back to face the two-way mirror. "It doesn't make sense: Wolverton 'forgetting' every detail and still being here to not tell the tale. Something scared him, and it wasn't mob, or muscle. It was worse."

"I agree," Molina said, standing too. She caught both their glances and didn't let go. "Your partners did a great interrogation job, but they're up against something that's got this guy whammied. We'll watch his bank account for a bribe, see if he does anything unusual. Or if . . . he really does have a lousy memory."

The men filed out, discouraged, meeting their partners in the hall for mutual head-shaking.

Molina went next door, shut it, and confronted Herb Wolverton.

"My name is Molina. Lieutenant. You know something we should. So whatever you're afraid of, be more afraid. We'll be on your case too. You owe money, you're afraid of goons. Be more afraid of us. You owe Mr. Big a favor, you're afraid of a grave in the sand. Be more afraid of us. There's something else out there that gives you the heebie-jeebies. It's not anything to worry about. Worry about us.

"That's it. You can go now. Back to the Goliath and the happy fellah job. If you really want to."

Wolverton took a few moments to think over standing up. When he did, his eyes took in her Amazonian measure.

He edged to the door, and Molina opened it.

He looked up, and up, at her.

And then he made his last stand.

"Vassar was about your size, Lieutenant. And she's dead."

He scurried into the hall. Molina stepped out to watch him run the gauntlet of her unhappy homicide detectives.

He avoided eye contact and hastened to push the elevator button, visibly fidgeting while it creaked its way to their floor.

Something, or somebody, really bad had scared him.

That was her first thought. Her second was that it had scared him enough to "forget" a face as movie-star memorable as Matt Devine's. Good luck for Carmen Molina. A puzzle for Lieutenant C. R. Molina. It would be intriguing to see whether self-interest or professional curiosity won this game of cat and rat.

Wake-up Call

"Okay, honey," Ambrosia was crooning into the mike as if the gray foam sound-muffler was toasted meringue ready to be eaten, "here's a little something to cheer you up."

The upbeat anthem of "Raindrops Keep Fallin' on My Head" percolated over the radio speaker as Matt stepped into the studio and closed the door.

Right now he was trying to converse with Leticia Brown *between* the raindrops . . . during the three dead-mike minutes that a song or commercial break would take before she had to get back on the air as Ambrosia and talk to the people.

"I can't believe it," she repeated as she stared at him. This had been her mantra during their tête-á-tête through the previous song too. "That *she-witch* is really dead? Like melted? Tall pointy hat and all?"

"Melted away. Out of my life anyway, and anybody else's. Forever."

"You almost sound disappointed."

"Sorry, you mean."

"No, I say what I mean. I'm not like those poor uncertain souls who call you and me. You sound *dis-ap-pointed.*"

"Why would I be disappointed?"

"A body can get used to being persecuted, you know. That's not uncommon. At least someone's paying you attention. That's better than being invisible. If you know what I mean."

"I do. It's called 'playing the victim,' and it's common to oppressed people. You believe I was doing that?"

"I don't know. All I know is you're entitled to a little meanness after all the spite and spit that was aimed at you. Celebrate your freedom, boy! Wiggle you ass like the football playcrs do in thc cnd zonc. Spikc a football. Stomp an ant. Be not nice."

Leticia shook her shoulders in what Matt had seen described as a "Watusi" dance move. Given her three-hundred Spandex-draped pounds and the fact that she always wore heavy shoulder pads no matter the outfit, she did look a bit like a linebacker for the Amazon Large League.

"Any man's death diminishes me," he quoted John Dunne.

"That was no man, honey. That was *an e-vil wo-man.* I never play anything that downer for my dear little lambs, but there is a song about women like that. That is the worst species of demon on earth."

"No mercy?"

"No mercy. Be a little human for once. Gloat like the rest of us."

She suddenly leaned into the mike and cooed to it as if to a baby. "Now isn't that better, sweetie? Sadness should run away to the corners of your vision like raindrops on a windshield. Is it all better now?"

"Better," the listener repeated.

Who dared argue with Leticia/Ambrosia? Darn few.

Her smile was a union of Cheshire cat and Crest Whitestrip as Matt backed silently out of her domain. It would be his cocoon and his hot seat soon enough. He glanced at the schoolhouse clock on the wall: time writ big and simple, boiled down to Big Hands and Small Hands and the slender, restless Second Hand.

He wondered if you had a secondhand conscience when you were supposed to take pleasure, or relief at least, in another person's passing.

The listener's voice coming over the speaker was a woman's now. Women always sounded a little breathless and young on speaker systems. The microphone exaggerated higher vocal tones, and had since the talkies had come in and made a falsetto of matinee idol John Gilbert. Remember him? Not much.

This woman caller also sounded hesitant, unused to dialing radio programs.

"I guess I can ask for a song dedicated to someone," she said.

"Ded-i-cated to the one you love." Ambrosia quoted the old song, talking the melody in perfect rhythm. Rappin'.

"It's for someone named . . . Vassar."

Matt's heart stopped for one too many times in the past few days.

"Vassar," Ambrosia echoed. "A classy lady, I take it."

"Very classy."

"School friend?"

"You could say that. She's . . . dead now."

"Aw, sorry, honey child. Well, I think I can find a song that'll talk to the both of you, even now."

Carole King's "You've Got a Friend" came over the speaker, but Matt barely heard it after automatically identifying the tune and the lyric.

He was busy doing a mental post-mortem on the voice of the woman who had requested a song in Vassar's name. Was there anything of Kitty O'Connor in it? No. It was a softened American accent, friendly but monotone, with still a sobered bounce beneath the syllables. Someone really in mourning. For someone named "Vassar."

Matt headed posthaste for Mike's tech booth.

"Who is that? Where'd the call come from?" he asked.

Mike eyed the rectangular gray screen on the telephone and shook his ear-muffed head. "Cell phone or pay phone, no caller I.D. on this one. Or maybe he knew the code to turn off the originating number. Oops, gotta fade and then it's your two hours on the air, dude."

Matt backed out of the booth, silently shutting the door. Somehow he had known that this call would be haphazard, untraceable. At least the request hadn't been phoned in by Elvis from who-knows-where. Two stars to the right and straight on to morning. Elvis had always been a Lost Boy, if not Peter Pan himself.

Leticia was already standing, pushing back the studio chair, making way for him.

"I like that," she said. "Ending my show on a sad note but with an upbeat tune. Paradox is what they call it. Makes for good tension on radio and in the *thee-ay-ter*. Miss Carole King. What an album *Tapestry* was. We are Woman, hear us roar. At least now and then. Here. I kept it warm for you."

She wasn't kidding. Leticia pushed the leatherette-upholstered chair his way. He knew the surface would be obscenely hot from her overflowing bulk.

Cocoon or womb? Sometimes Matt wondered which better described his show and his nightly workplace.

He donned his headphones and sank onto the chair, spun it to face the mike. No music. His show had no music to face, only faceless voices, the music of the night. Lone wolves howling in the dark.

Oh, wait. He had theme music. He waited for it to fade, and then only his voice conducted the orchestra of regret and fear and pain and hope that came cascading over the airwaves every night but Monday. The Midnight Hour. His. Two hours actually, it had become so popular. Would someone crash his party tonight now that the name of Vassar had been invoked? But Kitty O'Connor, the only one with nerve enough to masquerade on live radio, was dead meat now. Wasn't she?

* * *

With Kitty officially dead, Leticia didn't linger after her show to protect him.

She headed home.

Matt fielded calls and touchy ethical questions and borderline schmaltz, his mind only half on his job. No one claiming to be Vassar phoned in. Not even anyone pretending to be someone else who could easily *be* Kitty O'Connor. Not even a *bad* Elvis impersonator. For a moment he wondered if Elvis was a rock-'n'-roll Gospel guardian angel who had vanished once Matt's personal demon was dead.

Whoa! Such speculation was not solid theology. And Elvis had faced plenty of his own demons, especially one falsely-named Colonel Tom Parker who had outlived him as obscenely long as he had plundered Elvis's earnings and his artistic soul.

Kitty O'Connor as an Irish Colonel Parker, now that was a thought!

Meanwhile Matt had tired, sad, earnest voices to answer. He did the best he could while still caught in his own tired, sad, earnest confusion.

At last the two hours were finally over.

He could go home knowing that Kitty O'Connor would never trouble his life, work, or mind again. At least not in person.

The parking lot was deserted except for Mike's souped-up Honda Civic and his own bland white Probe. Lights shone unwaveringly. No distant motorcycle throb threatened the night.

She's gone.

Ambrosia played that song often for left-behind lovers.

I have to learn how to take it.

Matt had never comprehended that one could miss an enemy, or miss watching for an enemy, rather. He was like a soldier in No Man's Land. Armed but not dangerous to anyone, because nobody was there. Trudging through mist that looked haunted, but was disconcertingly unoccupied.

Except that he was used to bogeymen, and women, leaping out of the dark in the radio station's deserted parking lot. Now they might be all ghosts: Clifford Effinger . . . Kathleen O'Connor . . . Elvis. Vassar? *You've Got a Friend.* Really?

A woman was waiting by the one lit parking light.

Matt felt his heart stop again, although his feet kept on trudging.

There was no running away from ghosts, he'd learned that much in Las Vegas.

This one stepped forward in female form, hair black as tar, skin pale, lips rosy, eyes unreadable in this bogus light. "Hi," she said, shy and not shy. "You're Mr. Midnight, aren't you?"

He nodded, not bothering to deny the hokey handle. A "handle" was an air name, he had learned since working at WCOO. *We Care Only for Others.* Yeah, right. And ad revenue.

She offered the night a breathy laugh as an apology. "I'm sorry for botherin' you, but I didn't know how else to reach you."

"Knowing how to 'reach' people is always a problem," he said.

"I know. I do . . . outreach work myself. Kind of what you do, but face-to-face. Sorry." She stepped forward, thrust out a hand. "My name is Deborah Walker. Deborah Ann Tucker Walker, to be specific."

He looked at her outstretched hand, heard her stretched-out name, and couldn't help smiling, especially at the soft, Southern grit in her voice. Deborah Ann Tucker Walker could not be put off, not politely, anyway.

"Mr. Midnight," he said, shaking hands. Her palm was soft as dough, but his own palm detected the small calluses of the dedicated housewife or craftswoman.

"You don't have to give your real name," she assured him. "I give mine only because I have so dang many of them. Not to my credit or shame. Just fact. Married twice, once too long. I got past that, and then I tried to help other women who couldn't. Not too different from what you do."

"Not different at all. What do you need?"

"Your time. And I think *you* might need me, rather than vice versa." She smiled, widely. "I'm not used to dealing with celebrities. Not too many of them came through Alabama, exceptin' Jimmy Buffet."

"What are you doing here? I mean, in Las Vegas?"

"My second husband moved here to follow his job. 'Whither thou goest' and all. I was a Quaker for quite a while, but I do believe in my Scriptures."

"A Quaker? For a while?" Matt couldn't help sounding intrigued.

She grinned. "I'd like to talk to you about a mutual friend. If I tell you about being a Quaker, would you tell me about being a Roman Catholic priest?"

He paused. The station sometimes broadcast his past as a program hook, usually in press releases, but not on the air. Not every night for the world to tune in on. They liked Mr. Midnight to be a nondenominational man of mystery. A mini-me for the masses.

"Only thing open is fast-food joints," he warned.

"Shoot. I like slow food. But I can adapt to anything."

"I bet you can. Where's your car? You can follow me to Tinker Bell or Ronald Colman Donald or Warren Burger King."

"Tinker Bell would be good. I always liked to eat fairy mushrooms."

"Right."

He got into the Probe, keyed up the motor, and waited for her car, a Honda Civic he had mistaken for Mike's of all things, to pull in behind him.

What was it about the WCOO parking lot? Central Casting Central? A séance site for the Las Vegas universe? An alternate Elvis nexus? Did everyone show up here, at least once? For their fifteen minutes of fame? Too bad his had lasted so long.

* * *

"Thing is," she said, sucking on the straw in her chocolate malted milk, "it was the best success I'd ever had, and the worst."

"Vassar," he repeated, to make certain.

"Right. Vassar."

"You called in the song for her on Ambrosia's show! How did you know her?"

Deborah frowned. "Do you ever really know someone like Vassar?"

"I didn't," Matt confessed. Confessed. He knew what that word really meant. Sacramentally. He didn't fool around with it. He didn't expect a former Quaker to get it.

But she did.

"Well, I didn't really know her either, even though we talked a lot. Who could?"

"I only saw her the once."

"I saw her several times, but I wasn't gettin' anywhere."

"Anywhere . . . where?"

"Well, I was like the AA buddy you don't want."

She tilted her head as if posing for a Glamour Shot mall picture. Matt had to remind himself that Southern courtesy was real, even if it had been parodied so much that it looked phony.

"Vassar didn't want you in her life," he said.

"No, sir. Not at all. Oh, she did . . . and sometimes she didn't. I just tried to be there for her, all the time."

"Some people are fragile," he agreed. Wrong again.

"No, Vassar wasn't fragile, exactly. She was . . . spooked? That the word? So tough, some ways. I envied her. I really did. But we Southern women are like willows. We bend. Too much, too long. I don't much know how to deal with Blue Northers, I admit it. You know what a Blue Norther is?"

"No—"

"Well, it's a storm, you see. Comes out of nowhere, but usually the North. It's blue like a Yankee uniform. Dark, sudden, sweeps everythin' away before it. Don't look so worried. I'm not a reactionary. I'm a modern woman. I've been up, and down, and up again. Anyway, it's unpredictable, but you know when it's there, a Blue Norther."

Maybe that Norther had swept Kathleen O'Connor away before it, Matt thought. She was from Northern Ireland, a Norther kind of woman, icy, sudden, unpredictable. Dead.

"Anyway," Deborah Ann said, that being a favorite introductory word, "I've been volunteerin' for an outreach program for fallen women. Only we don't call them that to their faces. For vertically challenged women, if you get my drift. Oh, you're finally smiling, Mr. Sober Face. I don't blame you. Listenin' to Other People's Troubles is the opposite to usin' Other People's Money. No fun."

"So you made contact with Vassar. Knew her."

"Contact! That's somethin' that electrical outlets do. People get to know each other. Vassar wasn't easy, but she was . . . innerestin'."

"A hard case."

Deborah laughed, softly, like she did everything but think. "You could put it that way. Not easy to reach. Defensive, the shrinks would say."

"What would you say?"

"Hurt some. Not about to be disappointed again. Like you? Like me? I reckon we all have been hurt some."

"Did you know what hurt Vassar, why she'd do what she did for a living?"

"No. I've learned what it must have been like. She'd tell me about her clients sometimes. They didn't sound much different from the guys you could end up marrying. Some guys were sweet and lonely, she said. Some thought they could own you. A lot just wanted no-strings stimulation and release, one step up from a blow-up doll."

"Blow-up doll?"

"You don't know what that is?"

"Would I ask otherwise?"

"Don't get testy! And if you don't know, I'm not gonna tell you. I can see why Vassar liked you."

"If you won't tell me about a blow-up doll, why are you telling me about her?"

"Because you knew her."

"Not much. Not for long."

"Doesn't matter. How long. How much. What matters is, how . . . real. Anyway, I was tryin' to be her phone buddy. I'd get her on the line—she always called me, and hung up on me too, when she was done for the time bein'. She'd get me on the line and dribble out the teeniest bit of a question. Need. Want. Aggressive, she was. About what she was doin'. But not really."

"Do you know what I was seeing her for?"

"No, sir. I imagine you were a client, is all."

Is all. A client. Of a call girl. Matt tried not to hear himself described in the terms that applied.

"Anyway—"

Matt thought that he would strangle the next person to use that opening expression.

"I was gettin' nowhere with Vassar. I mean, what do I know about fancy northeastern schools? She'd been there. Hadn't been happy there, but she'd been there. Had a chance to be everythin' upscale: northern, snooty, ed-u-cat-ed"—just there she'd sounded like Leticia—"*so-phis-ti-cat-ed.* A natural woman. Only it didn't really feel natural, and Monday night she called me. She phoned home, bless her, my little ET. I can't tell you how happy I was to see her need me for the first time. Call it an addiction, but it's my kind of happy. I like to be of service, is that so wrong? I like to help people rather than harm them. Now that is not cool in an MTV world. That seems to be . . . embarrassin', in some way, don't you think? No, you don't, you like to do the same thing, don't you?"

"No," Matt said automatically, embarrassed. Then he listened for the cock to crow. "Yes."

"Yes. Of course. Here's the thing. She called me from some fancy hotel. What hotel in this town isn't fancy, right? It was . . . oh, the wee hours of Tuesday."

"Early Tuesday? What time?"

"I don't know, exactly. Her call woke me up. Whatever you might be thinkin', I'm a decent woman and in bed before midnight."

"Then you don't listen to my show. Program."

She looked really embarrassed. Almost blushed. "No, sir. I'd never heard of you or your . . . program, until Vassar mentioned it during that call."

"She knew who I was?"

"She was a fan! Before and . . . um, after the fact."

Matt winced to consider what the "fact" Deborah Ann referred to so blithely might be.

"Anyway . . . that's when she told me all about you. She was so excited."

"She was?"

"Oh, yes. You were a celebrity, but, best of all, you listened to her. I'd never gotten to Page One with her, but you put her on Page Eighteen. She couldn't wait to see me the next day. She'd made up her mind. She'd start raging in the middle of being ecstatic. Said her last client before you was a prick. A real pig. But you weren't. That showed her something. You showed her something. She was going to do something with her life. She wasn't sure just what, but somethin'. She was going to leave."

"Leave? Las Vegas?"

"No! The Life. You know. Hookin'. She was lookin' at it in a whole new way. Something you said. Lotta somethin's you said. I couldn't get everythin' she was sayin'. She talked so fast. My, but she was hyped. I'd never heard her so excited."

"Happy? Are you saying she was happy?"

Deborah Ann sat back to consider, then sipped on her straw. "Don't know any other way to describe it."

"She wasn't in despair?"

Deborah stared at him. " 'Despair'? Honey, that girl was so high she must have been wearin' platform mattress springs. I'd never been able to get beyond that worldly wise attitude of hers. So teenage, really. Anyway—"

"Yes, anyway?" Matt was getting impatient. Blue Norther impatient.

Deborah Ann leaned into the table, closer, so only he could hear her, as if anyone would eavesdrop on them at a Taco Bell.

"It doesn't make sense. No, sir. The woman I talked to was a happy camper. I don't see her . . . killing herself, that's all."

"And then what happened?"

"Well, we were cut off."

"Cut off?"

"Right. Or cut out. Cell phones will do that to you, you know. You have a cell phone?"

"No. I probably should have."

"You should. A very handy sort of thing."

"But you had one, and Vassar had one, and the line was cut."

"It's not a line, I don't think. More like . . . air. There was a lot of echo while we talked, and then . . . She was gone, that's all."

"Never said good-bye?"

"No."

"Never said anything more?"

"No."

"Did you hear anything more?"

"No. Just an open line. And . . . a kind of cackling, cracking on it."

"Like a person?"

"No!"

"Like what?"

"Like nothing, that's all. We were cut off."

"That's what you came to tell me? She didn't hang up. You were cut off?"

"No. I came to tell you that you converted Vassar. Sorry, I have a Southern Baptist mentality when I'm not reverting to my Quaker sojourn. She was out of that life. Born again. She was going to talk to me some more. You did it. That's what I came to tell you. I didn't know who or what you were, or why you bothered to talk to her, given the situation, but she said enough that I knew I ought to tell you. It's not every day a person does a good deed. I'd been trying to good-deed that woman into her senses, and somehow you just cruised along like any ole customer and did it, all by your lonesome. I thought you'd like to know, ought to know, that she'd been a new woman when she died. 'Cuz she must have died not long after that, accordin' to the newspaper, if you can believe the newspaper."

He nodded. Vassar must have been standing in the hall, near the railing. He remembered leaving her there, insisting she didn't want to go down in the elevator. She wanted to think.

So instead she'd gone down on an invisible downdraft of air.

Apparently.

Converted, she had floated like a butterfly, an angel, to her death twenty-one stories below. Called her counselor and then dived.

It didn't make sense.

Deborah Walker had come forward because she wanted to make sense of it all.

But everything was only more confused. Nothing was clear.

Except . . .

Vassar had left him happy. In a good mood. Not suicidal.

And she had been cut off.

Not only in her life, but on a cell phone.

Something had happened.

What?

Or had . . . someone . . . happened?

Kitty. Kathleen O'Connor.

Did she watch? See Matt leave, an undefeated Matt?

See Vassar euphoric, dialing what passed for a girlfriend, crowing about what had *not* happened?

Had Kitty then pushed Vassar over the literal edge?

Happiness would madden a killjoy personality like hers. Anyone's happiness.

So Matt had managed to kill Vassar with kindness.

One way or the other.

Crime Seen

We have returned to the twentieth floor.

Miss Midnight Louise and myself, that is. (She insisted, though she still limps, and I objected.) But we have returned.

Midnight, Inc.

Tonight, call us Murder, Inc., for we are determined to lay all questions to rest, and any spare call girls too.

"I am convinced," Miss Louise says, "that we have missed a key point in this case."

"We?"

"Well, I do not know where your brain has been on leave, but mine has been very unhappy with our conclusions thus far. Are you not concerned about the testimony of the parakeet?"

"Parakeets are not exactly Supreme Court judges."

"But they talk, and they listen. Consider the last words heard by the bird on the scene addressed to the victim. 'Pretty bird.' "

"So? That may say something else to me than it does to

thee. You, that is. I mean, that 'keet had a bird brain. It was used to hearing certain phrases. Nothing more natural that it should eavesdrop on humans and hear its own lingo."

"Or a human lingo as characteristic as its own."

"Like, for instance?"

"Like, for instance, 'Pretty bird.' I recall that 'bird' is a pet name for a nubile human female in the British Isles."

"We are not in the British Isles here, in case you did not notice!"

"But someone else, the perpetrator, might be from the British Isles. After all, what are the British Isles but England and—?"

Miss Louise nods encouragingly at me, as if I am a dull student in need of encouragement. I know my geography, and take pleasure in reciting it for the upplty chit.

"And Scotland, where they favor sheep in plaid clothing," I grudgingly admit.

"And—?"

"And Wales, which they let maritally unfaithful princes take their lad-in-waiting names from."

"And—?"

I hate the unremitting logic of the female inquisitor. Thank Bast the Inquisition was more prone to interrogating rogue females than incorporating them. Imagine Joan of Arc as a prosecuting attorney! Miss Louise does a pretty good imitation, and she is only a feline and not at all saintly, not to mention singed around the edges.

"And . . . northern Ireland," I concede.

"Exactly! And where does Kitty O'Connor hail from?"

"Northern Ireland. But you cannot believe—"

"I can believe whatever I discern. Who else would be standing here at the balcony edge but Kitty O'Connor, crooning 'Pretty bird' to the lovely American call girl whot 'ad just made Mr. Matt 'istory for the foiled purpose of said Kitty the Cutter."

"Whew. You females play hardball. Which is what I gratefully still have, thank Bast!"

"I am not interested in the intactness of your anatomy,

old dude. I am making a point that if Miss Kitty was around and about that night, and annoyed that Mr. Matt was stealing a march on her plot to disgrace him by disgracing himself first, she might take it out on the poor call girl he called upon: the 'Pretty bird' she hated more than even herself, or she would have never fixated on undoing a mere male, who are undone by the very nature of their gender to begin with."

Well, these are fighting words, but I do not know where to begin. So I decide to build my case. It does not take much, simply calling a few witnesses who are already hanging about the place.

I could say I just put my lips together and whistled, but the fact is we hep cats are never much good at the wolf whistle game. It takes a certain canine swagger to pull off.

So instead I merow to the ether and hope that a thing with feathers will answer my call.

I am answered in spades: one turtledove, two French hens, three Budgerigars, four calling birds, five cockatiels, etcetera, ad nauseam. You would not think so many feathered friends inhabited the twentieth floor of the Goliath Hotel, but then you would not think, would you? Best to leave that to experts, like myself.

I call my first witness. Literally.

"Did you see a tall young lady on stilted heels pausing by the balcony?" I inquire.

"Tweet."

"Please repeat that response in English for the jury."

My jury is a twelve-part-harmony team of various feathered friends.

"Yes. Pretty bird," says Blues Brother on cue.

I flash a triumphant glance at Miss Midnight Louise.

"So the phrase, 'Pretty bird,' is pretty common to the avian world," I follow up like the sharp legal wit I am.

"Yes, sir, Mr. Bird-biter," the little 'keet answers.

I pace impressively before it. "So it was indeed a bird that called Miss Vassar to her death?"

"No, sir," says the 'keet.

"What do you mean, 'No, sir'?"

He fluffs his feathers and bites his toenails and works on various unmentionable portions of his underlayment, and then he sings again.

"It was a cat, sir. A feline person of the pet persuasion. I saw it."

"A cat, sir?"

"Indeed, sir."

"Would you repeat that for the jury?"

"Indeed, sir, repeating is my business, my only business."

By now I have gone farther than any defense attorney would, save for O. J. Simpson. If only there were a dog in the case to lay all the blame upon. Kato, my Akita friend, wherefore art thou?

"What cat?" I demand.

"Pale-colored, with a little dark feathering. Very attractive for a fur-body. Seated. Upon the balcony. The human lady in question was on her cell phone, but then she noticed the balancing act occurring not five feet away from her. She was most distressed."

"How distressed?"

"She abruptly terminated her conversation, 'Pretty bird,' and reached out to extract the cat from the railing. Well, you sir, being a cat, can understand how unfortunate that misguided good Samaritan gesture was."

I say nothing, for to do so is to incriminate my breed and my brethren of the court. And mostly myself.

"Pretty bird," mourns Blues Brother. "She reached so far and then farther. The fickle feline jumped down to the floor. The poor human female leaned over the railing and fell down to the glass ceiling far below. Pretty bird. Bye-bye."

I stand astounded. And corrected. No one killed the little doll known as Vassar except her own soft heart.

She died trying to rescue one of my kind, albeit a pampered, perfumed kind.

Joan of Arc indeed. The name Hyacinth comes to mind.

At least Mr. Matt is set free by my kind's obligation.

This was an accidental death. The only Kitty involved was the unknown feline fatale balanced on the balcony.

Ah, my anonymous Juliet, how fatal thou art.

Wake

Matt thought he must be dreaming, but he had thought that a lot lately.

There came a tapping, as of someone gently rapping . . . not on his or Poe's chamber door, but on the glass of the French doors to Matt's patio.

He ignored it as an audible hallucination.

He was two stories up. His patio was a pathetic thing compared to the other units' outdoor areas. It remained as he had found it: furnished by one dusty white plastic lawn chair. Temple's patio was a whimsical mini-Disneyland of potted plants and creative seating. His was a wasteland. His private garden was miles away at the Ethel M chocolate factory, filled with sere, thorny cacti.

Tap, tap, tap.

There wasn't even a tall tree nearby to scratch a branch over his door glass. The venerable palm in the parking lot ended by just tickling the underside of his balcony.

He supposed Midnight Louie could have leaped up to his balcony from the palm tree, but Midnight Louie would never knock, or scratch, or mew for entry. Matt didn't know much about cats, but that much he knew about Midnight Louie.

So . . . nothing was there. Nobody was there.

There was barely anybody here, Matt thought, still reeling from the past few days' events.

Rap, rap, rap.

Matt rose from his red-suede vintage sofa and moved to the balcony patio. The absence of curtains made his figure the well-lit star on an obscure stage, he knew, while the anonymous tapper on the patio remained in the dark, invisible.

He wasn't afraid of the invisible, so he jerked one of his French doors wide open, daring cutthroats, sneak thieves, and random murderers to have at him.

In the soft Mercurochrome glow from the parking-lot lamp, he spied a black form balanced impeccably on the narrow wrought-iron railing . . . not Midnight Louie, but Midnight Max.

Matt regarded his visitor, reflecting for the first time that Max reminded him of Flambeau, the master thief in a Father Brown story, those genteel literary exercises in crime, punishment, and Roman Catholic theology by G. K. Chesterton.

Balanced like a mime-acrobat on the railing, Kinsella waved his current calling card: the tall black-labeled bottle of amber liquid with which he had apparently leaned forward to rap on the glass.

Despite the skill of such a trick, Matt recognized that the bottle was whiskey and that Kinsella had already been drinking from it.

"Top of the evening to ye," Kinsella greeted him in a stage brogue. "Mind if I come in?"

Matt did mind, but he was too curious to refuse. Before he could nod, the magician had untangled himself from the iron railing and vaulted into the living room in one liquid motion.

"To what do I owe—?" Matt asked, omitting the phrase

that usually followed those words: the pleasure of your company.

Max Kinsella evoked many feelings in Matt, but companionability was not one of them.

Kinsella didn't answer directly. *Did he ever?* Matt wondered.

Instead he held the bottle up to the central ceiling fixture. The glass was such a dark brown that almost no light penetrated it.

"This," Kinsella announced, "is the finest Irish whiskey in the world, Bushmill's Millennium at a hundred dollars a bottle, and the Irish distill the finest whiskeys in the world. The word 'whiskey' is Gaelic in origin, did you know that?"

"Yes. It means 'water of life.' The Irish also have the finest addiction to alcohol in the world."

"Ah. Not a tad of the Auld Sod in your soul."

"Polish-American."

"So you're a beer man."

"I don't drink much of anything."

Kinsella shrugged, quirked an eyebrow, and flourished the bottle in one fluid gesture.

He set the bottle down firmly on one of Matt's discount-store cube tables. "I suggest you owe yourself a sip of Heaven now."

"Heaven isn't to be found in a bottle; more often Hell is."

"True, and I'm generally abstemious. A man in my line of work can't afford smudged senses."

"Are you referring to magic or spying?"

"Either. Both. However, this is an occasion, and I suggest you join me in an uncharacteristic elbow-bend. Where are your glasses?"

"Kitchen," Matt said, bemused.

Kinsella was not drunk, as he had feared, but he was in a strange, forced, bitter mood.

He was now peering into Matt's cupboards and apparently displeased by what he saw.

"Not a lead crystal glass in the place. You can't set up housekeeping without a pair of glasses worthy of the occasional drink of kings. Well, these gas-station jelly jars will have to do."

"I don't have any such thing." Matt moved to defend his possessions.

Max had whisked two short thick glasses from the cupboard to the counter. Now he was rattling in the refrigerator in search of ice.

"Not a sliver, not a cube. 'Tis more fitting that we take it neat, anyway."

"Why should I drink with you?"

"It's better than drinking alone?" Kinsella paused to reflect. "You can't have me doing that, can you? Besides, we have something to cclcbrate."

"You don't seem in a very celebratory mood to me."

"We Irish are deceptive. We laugh when you think we should weep, and weep when you think we should laugh."

Matt took the glass Kinsella handed him, holding two inches of amber liquid as richly colored as precious topaz, the expensive, genuine article, not the cheap yellow citrine or smoky quartz that was passed off for it. He could already inhale the rich, sharp scent of aged whiskey.

Suddenly, he did wish for crystal glasses. Life needed its rituals and its ritual vessels.

By now Matt was ready for a drink. He lifted the glass and took a swallow: hot, burning in his throat like bile, yet strangely soothing.

"Is anybody ever allowed to sit on this?" Kinsella was still holding his glass, saving it, and staring at the long red sofa.

"It's a Vladimir Kagan."

"Here's to Vladimir." Kinsella lifted the lowly glass and drank.

"You can sit on it," Matt said. "I sit on it all the time."

"Designer sofa, rare whiskey, barware by Martha Steward," Max enumerated.

Matt sat in front of the cube table Kinsella had not

claimed, realizing that the magician had purposefully mispronounced Martha's last name, not liquorfully.

The play on words reminded Matt of Martha from the New Testament: that bustling, somehow frantic female fussing so compulsive that even Christ had urged her to slow down and smell the roses. Comparing domestic diva Martha Stewart to her New Testament namesake made for an interesting take on America's Queen of Clean and Possibly Mean. Were successful women always assumed to be shrews? Or did success make shrews of us all? Matt wouldn't know. He sipped more whiskey. It tasted stronger than swallowed perfume would smell, and he didn't much like either.

Kinsella was lounging in a corner of the Kagan as no one else who had ever sat on it had dared to do, including himself. For all its provenance and rarity, it was a demanding, stylish seating piece and wasn't the least bit comfortable. Like Kinsella himself.

"You look to the Kagan born," Matt admitted.

Kinsella chuckled. "We're both magicians, in our way. Our game is not to make you feel comfortable, but challenged, uneasy. Do I make you feel uneasy?"

"Sometimes."

"Not all the time? Shame on me."

"To what do I owe the honor of this visitation?"

"It's not an honor. It's a . . . bloody wake."

"I still don't get why you're here."

"This is a wake, after all," Kinsella noted. "For that you need a priest."

"So you think an ex-priest will do in a pinch."

"Why not? An ex-Irishman will do."

"So whose wake is it?" Matt was half afraid his bitter visitor would produce Vassar's name.

"All of ours?" Kinsella sat forward, cradling the whiskey glass in his hands. "She's . . . gone. Dead. Our Martha Stewart of the soul, giving us no rest, rearranging our priorities, redecorating our psychoscapes. To Kathleen." He raised his glass. "To Kitty the Cutter. To our survival on the occasion of her death. I often thought she would kill me, but I never dreamed . . . she would die."

"An eternal enemy offers a certain stability," Matt said, slowly, amazed by how true his words were only as he articulated them. "Why else is there the Devil?"

"You should know. You're thinking of Cliff Effinger."

"No. I didn't cause his death. At least I hope not. I mean, not specifically, but by looking for him, I might have attracted the wrong sort of attention to him."

"Devine! *Effinger* attracted the wrong sort of attention to *himself*! He was a royal loser. A royal pain in the ass to everyone who encountered him. You were his stepson. You had certainly felt the back of his hand. Don't go all goody-goody on me and tell me you regret his death."

"I do. You know what he said to me once, here, in Las Vegas, when we met again as adults? He said his abusive ways in my childhood home had done me a favor. He claimed he had taught me what the world was really like. I think it was like that for him, as a child, and he really did believe that was the way to rear a kid, to know how hard and cold the world can be."

"So did you learn anything?"

"From coldness and hardness, no. But maybe from him, finally. Not what he wanted me to know. I found that inside he was small and afraid still, trying to be the big, rough person he thought it took to survive in this world."

"He was a loser."

"So was Jesus Christ."

"Spare me! Next you'll be asking mercy for Kathleen O'Connor."

"Someone has to."

"You won't admit you're relieved she's dead?"

"Yeah, sure. Who wouldn't be? But *you* won't admit you're sorry she's dead. That's what this is all about."

"Me? Sorry?"

"She's been in your life longer than any person you know. Longer than your dead cousin. Longer than Temple."

"What do you know of me and who's been in my life?"

"Only bits and pieces. But Kathleen, Kitty, was *your* demon longer than she was mine. Granted, she dug in her heels and really hounded me, but it was all misplaced obsession. I was a substitute for you, for the young you she had known years ago in northern Ireland."

"I'm glad she's dead." Kinsella lifted both his glass and his eyes in a defiant toast.

"It's your right. I can't argue with it."

"You're not glad."

Matt considered. In his worst moments he had imagined killing her to save others, but that was fantasy. The reality was that he felt relieved that Kitty wasn't here to drive him to the end of his wits and his integrity. But anyone's death as the price of his deliverance? No.

"Christ died to save our souls," Kinsella said. "Would you wish that death undone?"

"That was different, preordained."

"And wasn't her death preordained? She must have harbored a secret death wish, pushing people to their limits, maybe hoping someone, sometime, would have the guts to kill her for it."

"You didn't."

"No."

"I didn't either."

"So God did it for us."

"It's too easy to attribute things to God, miracles or revenge."

"Still. . . . A toast to God, for justice literally above and beyond the call of duty."

"I don't think God requires toasts."

"Don't underestimate Him. He gets them in mass every day."

"That's blasphemy."

"That's what they said of Jesus. 'He blasphemes.' "

"Irreverence then. And comparing yourself to Our Lord is more of it. Don't argue the Testament with me."

"Why not? What would we argue about? Temple?"

"You're trying to pick a fight with me. Why?"

"I'm not." Kinsella put his glass down next to the bottle. "I'm trying to talk to you instead of tap-dancing out an unwanted conversation, which is our usual routine. We have a lot in common. Too much probably, but the one thing we really have in common from this moment on is Kathleen O'Connor's death. I'm not as happy about it as I should be, and you're not as relieved as you should be. Aren't you drinking?"

"Sure. We Poles are as prone to depression as the Irish anyday. Our homeland has been trampled under by centuries of invaders, we've been forced into exile and immigration, and beyond that, we're the butt of Pollack jokes. At least Irish humor is always warm beneath the barbs."

"I'll give you that." Kinsella touched glass rims with Matt. "Pollack jokes are meaner than Irish jokes. It's damned unfair."

Matt let the whiskey that was likely older than himself trickle down his throat. He was surprised that Kinsella would concede anything to him, even something as trivial as the denigrating ethnic humor sweepstakes, when Kinsella surprised him even more.

"Speaking of which, I don't usually revert to ethnic stereotype," he said, eyeing the bottle.

"And you don't usually come looking me up."

"No. This case seems to call for it. I have, after all, a confession to make. I think I killed Kathleen."

Cherchez La Femme

So I hear this tapping as of someone gently rapping on my . . . chamber pot, not my chamber door!

I open my snoozing eyes. I am resting in Miss Temple's office, where I can get some peace and quiet of a night instead of enduring constant tossing and turning in the bed, my dear roommate's specialty of late.

My litter box is only a few feet away, and someone is clawing the heck out of it.

No one is privileged to use Midnight Louie's privy but Midnight Louie!

I am up and hissing like a radiator in an instant.

"Mine!" I yowl, advancing on the equally instant high heels of my fighting shivs.

"Relax," comes an all-too-familiar drawl. "It is a long walk over from the Crystal Phoenix and I needed a pit stop. It is all in the family, right?"

"If you are speaking of a professional family—"

"Any other relationship involving you would be unspeakable," Miss Midnight Louise responds.

"Our spats aside, what are you doing up and about after your recent six rounds with the Mojave Desert? Do you forget the extreme difficulty I had dragging you to the highway, then hitching a ride back to town in the back of a squad car, no less? Talk about a risky undercover assignment, that was my top job, mitts down."

"I am as stiff as Miss Kitty the Cutter at the moment," she admits, "but pampering will only delay my recovery. If I had been hit by a car near Twenty-fourth Street where the wild things hang out, no one would have stirred a whisker for me. Up there in Feral Country it is move or die."

"I got you safely back to the Crystal Phoenix, did I not? And speaking of 'knot,' that is what all my muscles were in after squiring your semiconscious form around half of Clark County."

She pussyfoots over and sits beside me. "You are the usual unsung hero, Pops, but that is the lot of an undercover operative. Speaking of which, I have been thinking."

"Apparently this is such a rare occasion that you must get up in the middle of the night and hotfoot it over here without even remembering to use your own facilities."

"Everything is such a territory issue with dudes. If you all could get over it we would have world peace."

"Then what would there be to do? Sit on our assets and clip coupons?"

"Whatever." She yawns.

I stifle a comment that such a young thing should be in bed by now. It sounds too solicitous and I would never like to be mistaken for solicitous. It ruins my image.

"So what is so earth-shaking that you need to ankle over here and play Oriental sand painting in my executive bathroom?"

"Something in Blues Brother's testimony has been bothering me. I think we should visit the twentieth floor of the Goliath Hotel."

"And risk all those bird droppings again?! They fly around unfettered up there, you know. I personally do not think your looks would be flattered by a bird poop chapeau."

"Please, Pops! No need to get vulgar. We have dodged the airborne missives so far. There is something I really think you should know. Unless, you believe the savvy operator prefers to remain in the dark about some things."

"Of course not. I am only in the dark if I know it." *Wait! That did not make sense. Oh well, no need to tip off the kit.* "So you want me to hike back to the Goliath on a whim of yours?"

"Who knows?" she asks coyly, buffing her fingernails with her tongue. "You might thank me for it."

Well, that does it. The chit is insinuating that she knows more than I do. I will not sleep the rest of the night worrying about that possibility anyway.

So it is that Midnight, Inc. Investigations creeps out of the well-lit comforts of the Circle Ritz, down a callused palm tree trunk, and out into the warm and well-populated Las Vegas streets.

By now we have made breaking into the Goliath and its bank of elevators an art form, if I do say so myself.

Miss Louise snags a fallen gaming chip in the casino and carries it by mouth to the elevator area.

I lurk behind the ever-popular ashtray, here an embellished column mimicking beaten copper.

"Look at that!" cries the obligatory tourist. "A cat with a chip in its mouth."

Better than a cat with a chip on its shoulder, lady. Those are called lions and tigers and leopards.

So little Miss Louise trots into the elevator car, the object of all wonder and admiration, and I slip in after her and cringe in a dark corner where even the security camera can't see.

"And what floor do you want, little lady?" the man tourist asks Louise with a wink at his wife.

She sits solemnly and stares straight ahead, but I realize that she is meditating deeply, mentally intoning the desired floor number like any superstitious gambler silently pleading for a roulette number to come up. With us cats, it works.

The man winks again at his wife while his forefinger taps

a random elevator button. "Will that do, Miss High Stakes?"

He has, of course, hit twenty right on the nose. If only he was so lucky at the gaming tables. It occurs to me that Miss Louise and I might get quite a racket going in that area, but the thing is we know where we want to go here, though nobody human would believe it, and in a gaming situation we would know no more than anybody what numbers would come up. Unless the great and powerful Bast would deign to let us in on it. Naw, Bastet is into mummy cases, not casinos.

Anyway, the tourist couple exits long before we do.

"I could have hit the right floor with one bound after they left," I tell Louise.

She spits out the five-dollar chip as if it were a live mouse. "By then the elevator would have been called to some other floor, and we would have to justify our presence again. This is better. Here is our floor now."

I edge out of the open door behind her, hunting for airborne pollution.

Sure enough, a flash of blue and white above reveal that Blues Brother is out and about for the evening.

I duck behind an ashtray just in case.

Miss Louise sits and curls her long fluffy train around her petite feet.

"I have been thinking," she says, "about the bird-brain cat whose high-altitude antics lured the pitiful Miss Vassar into teetering death."

"Balancing on these railings at this height is folly," I agree, "but we did it."

"In the course of an investigation. This other feline was merely being stupid. Therefore, I have come to an interesting conclusion I am eager to test on the firm's senior partner. Are you ready?"

"This does not involve further shenanigans with the railings?"

"No, merely some subterfuge with the hotel rooms."

"Oh, well, if humans can manage that sort of thing all the time, we can do it."

So we begin. Of course my superior leaping skills are called upon to produce a thump against the hotel-room door that approximates an actual knock.

I am soon huffing and puffing like a hungry wolf, or coyote. Many of the residents are not at home, but are out having a good time on the town, unlike myself.

Miss Louise sits by the railing casting an assessing eye at the floors above.

"Try twenty-eighty-eight," she suggests.

"If this is an exercise in games of chance," I say, "I am about to run out of patience and breath."

"It is only a theory," she answers with a shrug that riffles through her ruff.

I am not eager to plead middle-aged spread to Miss Midnight Louise, so I jump and thump again and at number 2088 am finally rewarded with an answer.

But what an answer!

"Ye-es?" carols a sickeningly sweet human voice that also manages to be shrill and unpleasant.

I gaze, eye-level, upon a pair of hyper-extended insteps balanced on shoe heels thinner and taller than a knitting needle.

I cringe in horror. Miss Louise has led me into the lair of my worst enemy, worse even than the evil Hyacinth and her maniacal mistress Shangri-La.

I am at the stiletto-heeled mercy of Savannah Ashleigh, erstwhile actress and would-be destroyer of my masculine charms.

Luckily, she is apparently as blind as a bat while relaxing at home without her contact lenses and stares out over the atrium asking "Who was there?"

Between her oblivious ankles—and I do not know how ankles may be oblivious, except that Miss Savannah Ashleigh's indeed seem to be that way—wafts a wisp of smoke and fur and Persian perfection I have seen before.

It wafts right out into the hall, and there remains as Miss Savannah surrenders and shuts the door.

"Yvette!" I cry, stunned by her beauty and presence yet again.

She weaves herself around me, her black-tipped silver fur coat and mascara'ed aquamarine eyes weaving me into their spell. Hyacinth who?

"What have you been up to?" I ask, thinking of her pet food commercial contract.

A sardonic voice interrupts my idyll. Miss Midnight Louise.

"Up on the railing, I think? So, Miss Yvette, did the pretty lady try to pet you, did she try to lift you down and fall over the edge herself?"

"Pretty lady?" Yvette fluffs her ruff, which surrounds her piquant little face like an Elizabethan lace collar. "I do not know what you mean. I have been out of the room when my mistress is sleeping or gone. She often forgets to lock the deadbolt, ugly name! She leaves the bigger brass prong set inside the door to keep it ajar when she goes down the hall for ice, which is frequently. Thus I am free to slip out and take the air."

"Did you 'take the air' on the railing a week ago?" Louise demands in her usual surly tones.

The Divine Yvette answers with her usual sublime patience. "I may have. I like to watch the sushi on the wing. This is not the *People's Court,* miss, I am not obligated to answer. Is that not right, Louie, *mon amour*?"

Well, what can I say to that? "Enough of this grilling, Louise. Miss Yvette is not a suspect in anything."

"If enticing a human to her death is not a crime, then I suppose she is not."

"Yvette?" I growl. "Not Yvette."

"A 'pale cat with attractive dark feathering' on the railing. Sounds like a shaded silver Persian. You heard the bird. Eyewitness testimony and he even talks so humans can understand him."

"Yvette, did you see the pretty lady seven nights ago?" I ask in my turn.

"What is time to me? I did take the moving box four floors up, where someone did pick me up and got their naked oily hands all over my recently laved fur. I was able to leap away, like mist. These humans are so clumsy. I remember that mindless mimic of the air, that morsel on wings, crying "Pretty bird!" As if I were chopped liver! I escaped back into my room to restore my garb to proper order. What wrong is there in that?"

I cannot speak.

The Divine Yvette is the feline femme fatale who apparently lured the ill-fated Vassar into her penultimate act of mercy that became an inadvertent dive.

It was an utter accident, of course. On both their parts. But I cannot deny that Vassar acted from the nobler intent, my admired Yvette from the baser one.

Still, one can understand that an oft-pawed beauty might naturally rebuff even an attempted rescue.

I glance at Miss Louise, who is sitting by offering the sour demeanor of Judge Judy to the proceedings.

"The human female only tried to rescue you," I tell her. But the Divine Yvette is as blind in her fashion as her self-absorbed mistress.

"I did not need it," the Divine One says pointedly. She flounces back to her door, where she begins to paw with her declawed right mitt, making a nerve-grinding *shwshshs shwshshs shwshshs* sound.

I sit bemused. Then I hear a thump behind me.

Miss Midnight Louise is now balanced on the railing board, looking down.

"Off!" I order.

"There it is."

"What?"

"Miss Vassar's cell phone. It had to have fallen with her, but it caught in the fork of that potted Norfolk pine tree on the level below."

I jump up beside her. Two can play at this game, which some would call "chicken."

Sure enough, I spot a small oblong of dull silver metal, a cell phone in a pine tree. If that cell phone could talk . . .

but of course it cannot. And of course the police will never discover it up here.

"Get down from there, Louise. We have seen our job and done it."

She obeys me, leaving me momentarily speechless.

Behind me I hear Miss Savannah Ashleigh's door open.

"You naughty kitten!" she admonishes the Divine One. "How did you slip out?"

The door closes, and I realize I have neglected to turn to capture a last glimpse of that vanishing plume of fur, of summer and smoke.

Miss Midnight Louise is shaking her head as if a flea, or two, were cohabitating in her ear. Perhaps witnessing the Divine One's sublime indifference to her own role in a recent death has shaken my partner, for she says to me out of the blue, "I did not mean to kill her, Pop. Just to distract her from taking out Mr. Max."

"You are discussing a woman nicknamed Kitty the Cutter. Not only that, in this instance she was a rogue driver. Innocents could have been killed. And do you think she would have hesitated to run you over if you had gotten between her and Mr. Max's car? You were the backseat driver on that 'cycle. She was out of control. You did what you had to do."

"Still . . . I have never killed anything that big before. And humans are supposed to be the superior breed."

"Every breed is superior in its own mind. There are inferior humans just as there are inferior cats, hard as that is to believe. But none of that matters when it comes down to an issue of life and death. Mr. Max"—here I swallow my territorial pride for the first time in my nine lives—"is a dear friend of my Miss Temple, and I should hate to have my roommate in mourning for the next millennium if anything untoward should happen to him. You did the right thing. You did what I would have done."

"Gee, thanks." She gives me the skeptical green-eyed slit. "I have never before considered 'what you would have done,' to be any standard worth aspiring to."

Before the terrible import of those convictions quite clear the hurdle of my overworked brain, Miss Louise gives me a quick lick on the chops.

"But I may have to reconsider my standards," she says. "Such is life and death, I see, on the mean streets of Las Vegas. Thanks for the buggy ride, Daddy-o Dearest."

I shudder to think what Miss Louise's memoirs will have to say about me. I had better get started on my own, pronto.

Callback

The phone rang. His phone rang.

Matt stared at Kinsella. Max had killed Kitty? Was it possible?

Yes. They were old enemies.

"Better answer," Kinsella suggested, seizing the Bushmill's bottle by the neck for a refill.

As if Matt, a Polish beer man according to Kinsella, would hog Irish whiskey.

He got up and went to the bedroom phone, the only one he owned. Yet. He could smell a cell phone in his future, but at least now he still had a very unportable model and could use it as an excuse to escape the unthinkable. Was he entertaining a confessed murderer in his living room? Wouldn't Carmen Molina be enchanted to know that?

"Hello."

"Matt. Am I calling too early for out there?" asked Frank Bucek's vibrant ex-teacher voice.

"No. We're awake and at 'em out here."

"That three-hour time difference is annoying. I have to

remember not to call at the crack of dawn when it's midmorning here in Virginia."

Not just Virginia. Quantico. FBI headquarters. Matt wondered what the place had got its name from.

"I have something," Frank announced.

He'd always boomed out sermons and homilies in the priesthood, hadn't allowed any mumbling among the altar boys. Nothing retiring about Father Frankenfurter.

"On . . . the woman."

"On your persecutor. Kathleen O'Connor. No 'Kathy,' for her, at least not with the IRA."

"I asked you to look into her months ago, and you didn't find anything."

"Ah, Matt, me boyo. That was before nine-eleven and the IRA began playing ball-o with the English and American authorities. Can you believe it? The enormity of the World Trade Center attack gave the IRA pause. They'd been in peace negotiations anyway, then said publicly that the scale of the attack on the U.S. was so extreme that they would never bomb Britain again."

"They're terrorists."

"Yes. Who believed them? And of course they have their hard-nosed elements who will never give in or never give up mayhem. But, by and large, begorra, they've been as sincere as you can expect of reformed terrorists. And . . . they're cooperating with the authorities, so this time I finally got some information on the bane of your block, Kathleen O'Connor."

"She's dead."

"What?"

"I just identified the body. A motorcycle accident."

"And it was her, for certain?"

"I saw her face. It was scraped and bruised, but hers, no mistake. I identified her on the coroner's examining table."

"Ouch. I don't like those places. They make you not quite believe in immortal souls, seeing all those mortal remains so still and shattered and such dead meat. So you're sure."

"Yes, but I'd still like to know more about her."

"I don't know much more. They admitted to knowing of her, but said that she had long ago become a rogue agent."

"How do you become a rogue IRA terrorist?"

"You don't take orders, for one. The biggest no-no. That's true of any para-governmental agency."

" 'Para-governmental agency'? We've got them too?"

"We've got everything we need in a modern, dangerous world. And sometimes it isn't enough. Anyway, Kathleen went off on her own years ago. Would send money home. They tagged her as working South America, the Irish-Latino community there, which is almost as big as the German-Latino community, aka the Hitler has-beens. She sent them money periodically. They didn't ask where it came from or where she was."

"So she supported them, and followed her own agenda, unsupervised."

"They didn't want to supervise her. Found her way too unstable for terrorism. A kind of Fury. Who's the mythological creature with the serpents for hair—? God, my memory. Methuselah doesn't sound right. Too Biblical."

"Medusa. That's Greek."

"Right. Miss O'Connor was a human Medusa to them. Every lock of her raven-black hair was sheer poison to touch. Apparently some of them tried."

"Raven-black?"

"Yes. They say she was a beauty the way an honorable death is beautiful. A terrible beauty, to quote the poet. Were they right?"

"Maybe. Her eyes were plastic and her face was . . . eroded . . . at the end. It wasn't a beautiful death."

"Yes, we did use to say that in the church, didn't we? 'A beautiful death.' I don't see much of those in the FBI. I suppose one thinks of a very old person, fading away without pain and faithfully shriven. Does that much happen in our Alzheimer's, post-HMO world anymore, do you think?"

"No," Matt said. "Nothing much beautiful in the way of death happens out here in No Man's Land at all."

"Extreme Unction we used to call it. I loved that phrase. It put Death in a caliph's tent with serving men and girls. Extreme. Unction. The Final Anointing. Extreme Unction. Now it's called Last Rites. Loses in the translation, doesn't it?"

"The church has lost a lot in the translation lately, including respect and dignity. Do you . . . let on what you used to be?"

"Not recently. Everyone's eyebrows lift. 'One of those.' We were blind. I'm glad I left, and I'm glad you finally left, Matt. That you're out of all that scandal."

"Not quite," he said ruefully. At the shocked silence on the phone line, he added, quickly, "Now I'm only suspected of adult heterosexual misconduct. What a relief. It's all right, Frank. I'll survive."

"Better than Kathleen O'Connor."

"So there was no report of her operating in the U.S."

"She disappeared on them, after all these years. And, frankly, they were just as happy to have such a loose cannon out of the way. I'll report her death, and your confirmation of it. She left no fingerprints anywhere, was just a rural County Clare girl who went north to Londonderry and found a cause. What made her so lethal, we'll never know."

"No."

Matt hung up, thinking that Kitty the Cutter was still pretty lethal to his circle of acquaintances.

An image of her body on the autopsy table flashed into his mind, including the spidery tattoo on her naked hip. No final anointing for her, except with the medical examiner's scalpel, and he probably used much more brutal instruments.

For a moment the official description of the sacrament of Extreme Unction flashed before Matt's eyes too; he'd looked it up again only recently: the anointing with oil specially blessed by the bishop of the organs of the five external senses (eyes, ears, nostrils, lips, hands), of the feet, and, for men, of the loins or reins; while saying "Through this holy unction and His own most tender mercy may the Lord pardon thee whatever sins or faults thou hast committed by sight, by hearing, smell, taste, touch, walking, carnal delectation." *Carnal delectation.* The phrase had always stuck with him, even though anointing the loins is generally omitted in English-speaking countries. He never forgot the section ending: "and it is of course everywhere forbidden in the case of women."

Apparently anointing female loins was itself an occasion of sin. Now he would forever associate a tattoo of the worm Ouroboros with "carnal delectation." He wondered if attending a woman's autopsy was a confessable sin.

Having delved his own possible weaknesses, he returned to the living room to minister to Max Kinsella, possible self-confessed murderer, but the sofa was empty . . .

. . . except for Midnight Louie, who had taken Kinsella's place.

Matt stared at the big black cat and the big black cat stared right back at him.

Was Kinsella a shape-shifter?

Or was it Midnight Louie who pulled all their strings?

The tomcat yawned, showing pearly whites.

Oh, the shark, dear, waits closer than you think.

Suitable for Mourning

Max so seldom called ahead to advertise one of his patented surprise appearances that Temple couldn't help feeling a frisson of dread when she picked up the phone and it was not only Max speaking, but he was asking if he could come over.

Max? Asking? After all, he had once called the Circle Ritz and this apartment home. Temple really didn't mind him popping in unannounced. Unpredictability was one of Max's many charms, at least to her.

"I've been out carousing," he warned her.

"Carousing?" Another surprise. Max drank only with meals, and only with happy meals, like with her.

"With Matt Devine."

Surprise number three was a throat-choker.

Max. And Matt. Together. Over a friendly glass of . . . something? What could they possibly have in common to talk about? Besides her.

"You're not coming over," she asked, "with news I'm not going to like, are you?"

"Like what?"

"Oh, that Molina has eloped with Russell Crowe, or that Rafi Nadir is an undercover agent for the IRS, or that you're going into the priesthood."

"Would Molina eloping with Russell Crowe be good news or bad news, in your opinion?"

"Half and half. He *is* a major movie star, but he's also spoiled and cranky and immature. Actually, it would be a heck of an entertaining match: Gladiator vs. Xena the Barbarian Princess Cop."

"Sounds like a play card for the World Wrestling Federation. No, nothing that worthy of *Access Hollywood.* And why would I enter the priesthood at this scandal-ridden time?"

"For the surprise factor?"

"I've got enough surprises right now that I don't need to go looking for trouble. And I've got a bottle of very good Irish whiskey, mostly full."

"Max! You're not driving with an open bottle! If the police—"

"Relax. My car is right in your very own parking lot and nudging up next to an extremely curvaceous little red Miata with its top disappointingly up."

Temple ambled to her French doors and slipped out onto the patio, from where she could see her parked car, which was *why* she tried to park it there. A prized new possession needed to be always within easy view.

She glimpsed a new black car beside it, wondering how long it had been there. A while, if he had been visiting Matt. *Why go back to the parked car to call her?* she also wondered.

Max was in his favorite element now, the dark, and leaving other people in the dark too.

"Are you going to come up in the elevator like a Real Boy?" she asked.

"Of course. I'll even knock."

"No, ring the doorbell. It's a lovely chime. I don't hear it enough."

"You might want to put some Leonard Cohen on."

Uh-oh. That was Max's brooding black Irish music.

They closed the conversation quickly. When Temple went back into her living room, Midnight Louie had pulled a Max and sat still as a statue in the middle of her coffee table, looking as if he had been there for generations.

She smoothed his black-satin head as she went to the kitchen and rooted out the heavy Baccarat crystal glasses suitable for premium Scotch, Irish whiskey, and terminally spicy Blood Mary mixes, yum-yum. Max didn't call her his Paprika Girl for haircolor reasons only.

The doorbell rang through its leisurely melody. Like the era of the building, the fifties, it had time to slow dance through even a practical purpose. That was an era when women in high heels waltzed through domestic chores with vacuum cleaners and single strings of pearls around their necks.

Domestic chores didn't have that quaint glamour anymore, but Temple swept open the door with the panache of that decade's leading ladies, Loretta Young or Donna Reed.

Max leaned against the doorjamb. Like many really tall men, he favored the disarming slump. Tonight, though, he just looked tired, not insouciant.

"I've got the best glasses down," she told him.

He swung through the door, planting the whiskey bottle on a nearby countertop. "We don't have to drink this."

She eyed the four inches ebbed in the bottle. "You and Matt did that much damage? I guess I deserve an equal crack at it. You wouldn't have brought the medicinal stuff if you didn't think I'd need it."

"I need it," he said shortly.

"You don't 'need' anything addictive. Never have."

"Never have been where I'm standing now."

"Then sit down. I'll pour. Neat, I presume, the way the bloody British take it."

He nodded as he passed her the bottle and she uncapped it, pouring the ruddy-amber whiskey three fingers deep in each elaborately etched glass. It glistened like amber, and Temple supposed that many once-living things had been entombed in more than one glass of hard liquor. Entombed and resurrected.

"How can I sit down?" Max demanded.

She came bearing a glass in each hand, and peered past his indignation-stiffened form to Midnight Louie sprawled like the world's biggest Rorschach inkblot on her pale sofa.

"We move the cat. He was sitting on the coffee table just a minute ago."

"He must have known I was coming," Max complained, taking the glasses as Temple bent to lift Louie in her arms and return him to his tabletop post. "I don't know if I much like him listening in."

"It's not like he cares what we say, Max. He's a remarkably sensitive animal, but I doubt that English is his second language."

Max stared silently at Louie in answer. His stare was returned in kind: intense, challenging, immobile.

Temple had the oddest feeling that man and cat could talk to one another, but that the relationship was decidedly wary.

The staring match ended when Louie rose, jumped to the floor, and stalked off into the office.

"He knows when he's not wanted." Temple went to the portable stereo to let Leonard Cohen's monotone bass throb through the room. She shook her head. "If your stare didn't do it, that music would have. Not exactly anything to cuddle up to."

Max sat dead center in the sofa and claimed one glass for a hasty sip.

"So how," Temple asked, sitting beside him, "was Matt? Is he getting over that poor woman's death at all?"

"He's got other things to think about now. So do I."

"The bad news you said was only half bad."

"It depends on how happy you are to hear someone is dead."

"Someone . . . I know?"

"In a manner of speaking."

"Not just Vassar."

Max shook his head. His hand didn't shake as he lifted the glass to his lips again, but Temple sensed that it might have if he had allowed such a thing.

"Who? Max, tell me now. I can't stand this waffling around. It's so unlike you."

"She's gone. Kathleen O'Connor. Dead."

"Kitty the Cutter dead? Not possible!"

"Believe it. Devine ID'ed her for Molina this morning, and besides, I was there when it happened. She's in cold storage at the medical examiner's facility, waiting for next of kin to claim her. There won't be any. Only enemies."

"Dead? After making all our lives so miserable? People like that don't just . . . die."

"Effinger did."

"Yes, but you're sure it's her? Both you and Matt? And Molina buys it?"

"The medical examiner buys it. It's undeniable. Even your Midnight Louie witnessed the accident."

"Louie! He was out earlier, but . . . when?"

Max shook his head. "Not today. Two nights ago."

"And no one told me?"

"Not our fault, Temple."

"You speaking for Matt now, too? Mr. Zipped Lips?"

"Not our fault," he repeated. "We had a lot to do. I had to call emergency personnel from a phone that couldn't be traced to me, dump the Maxima, and stay low. Devine had to answer Molina's summons and go stare at the dead body. We haven't much felt like talking to anyone human in forty-eight hours, or like explaining ourselves."

"Or how you feel about this," Temple added shrewdly. "Dead. For you guys it must be like . . . the twin towers falling. No. More like the upside-down world turned right-side up again, like gravity has reversed itself."

"Yeah," Max held the whiskey glass in both hands before his face, as if it were a fire capable of casting warmth and light. "Her evil pull was like some counterforce I was so used to fighting that I've lost all energy to stand on my own. She was out there somewhere. I'd sensed her hatred for so long, it almost seems unnatural to live without it in the world."

"Kind of how Matt felt about his abusive stepfather."

Max nodded. "Given a nemesis like either one of them, you start to wonder if you don't deserve it somehow." Max looked at Temple for the first time, straight on. "He must have thought about killing her, you know. Before he tried Vassar. He knew he could. He had enough martial arts training to do it. And she . . . was a small woman. Perfectly killable, except you'd become her and then she'd go on anyway, wouldn't she?"

"Matt? It crossed his mind to kill? How can you be so sure?"

"She threatened everyone he knew and cared about. It crossed his mind. Mine too."

Temple took a deep breath. "So that's what you two talked about, your homicidal impulses?"

"We also talked about our mutual guilt."

"For thinking that way, and then getting your wish?"

"For being that desperate. And then, Fate steps in and kills her for us. And now we're feeling guilty because Fate had the guts to do what we didn't."

"Max, start from the beginning. How did she die, and when, and how on earth was Louie present?"

"It began Sunday night, at Neon Nightmare. I have no idea how or why your cat was there, but he ended up in my car."

"Your car?"

"Yeah. The backseat. Must have eeled in when I left the club. Anyway, I was being my usual paranoid self, checking for any car that might be following and . . . thinking of other things, I admit, when that wildcat of yours comes clawing over the leather seat back into the front passenger seat, yowling and generally ripping cowhide."

"Ooh, your car," Temple sympathized as only the owner

of a new vehicle with a costly leather interior could. Of course hers had just a little leather because it was just a little car. Call it a Baby Bear car. "Louie knows not to scratch the furniture. I can't imagine what got into him."

"It didn't take imagination. It took glancing into my rearview mirror, which I'd ignored after a few cursory checks because I was busy thinking about something else. There was a motorcycle on my tail."

"A motorcycle? Wow. A motorcycle? It was Kitty?"

"Apparently. It was dark, the street was ill-lit. She was riding a black Kawasaki Ninja and she wore black leather and a helmet."

"Then it didn't have to be her."

"No, but it made a lot of sense that it was her. I think she made me at Neon Nightmare. I've been going there, hanging out."

"Why? It's a hot new club, but—"

"It's where the Synth meets."

"You're sure."

"Sure? I've joined them. They welcomed a passé magician like myself into the fold. They assume I'm not working because I can't, that I despise the likes of the Cloaked Conjuror, who gives away trade secrets. That I'm bitter and washed up by the newest trends in mega-magic, i.e., raise the *Titanic* on national TV and then make it disappear again, all in an hour minus forty minutes of ads. They may be right."

"So now you're mourning your career as well as the death of an enemy."

He quirked her a smile. "I'm mourning change, Temple, the first sign of dawning middle age."

"What is Matt mourning?"

"A good question. A lot more than I am. His duel with Kathleen was fresh; mine is decades old. He followed Molina's sage but cynical advice right into a death trap . . . he'd almost feel better if it had been his death rather than Vassar's. I brought that over to cheer him up, but even the whiskey of kings couldn't lift his depression."

"So you dove right in with him."

"Momentarily." Max's smile grew as slender as he was. "There is some good news. Think about how Kathleen died."

"In a motorcycle accident?"

"Doesn't that answer some dangling questions?"

"She had an *Easy Rider* hang-up? Wait! Way back when . . . when you got back from California looking up Rafi Nadir for Molina, someone on a motorcycle took a shot at you while you were driving in that convertible you had then. It was her?"

"Seems logical. I suspect she'd been looking for me since she hit town. Luckily for me, she only caught that one glimpse of me, and took advantage of the opportunity."

"Luckily for you, she only grazed your scalp."

"Rush hour on the Strip is not the ideal venue for target practice. But it wasn't me she only had eyes and wheels for. In his cups, Devine confessed that he's been . . . haunted for weeks by a motorcycle-riding phantom. It was definitely Kathleen, he said, when she attacked his female producer at the radio station, but at other times he swears it was—are you ready? An Elvis impersonator. He doesn't believe in Elvis or his ghost, of course, so he's convinced these manifestations were just darn good imitations."

Max grinned again, so crookedly that Temple suspected he wasn't telling her everything. She returned to the slow process of getting things as straight as she could.

"So Kitty didn't see you again after that sniping incident on the Strip until she spotted you Sunday night at Neon Nightmare. You've been going out in public too much again, and several times with me. It's my fault."

"Don't go all Devine-ish on me, Temple. Taking the blame for other people's actions can get to be a bad habit."

"You feel it too, don't you, Max? That someone died because of you, even if she was out to get you. Lord, Matt has his soiled madonna on his conscience, and you have your Irish Fury. You Catholic boys are a mess."

"I'm not going to weep for Kathleen O'Connor. She had a lot of years to get into something better than using a passionate cause as cover for her own twisted hatreds. And I guess I'd rather she crashed and burned chasing me than Devine. I can handle it better. His plate of guilt already runneth over."

"Tough guy," Temple teased, realizing as she said it that he'd always had to be that to survive. Tough enough as a mere teenager to seriously annoy the IRA. Toughness wasn't muscle, or age, or any gender. It was something in your soul.

"So you're sure she's dead?"

"Why even ask?"

"You hadn't been able to lose her in seventeen years. She had grabbed onto Matt like a vampire bat and wasn't about to let go. Who'd expect somebody that . . . tough . . . to let go of anything, most of all her life?"

"If she knew about Devine's appointment with a call girl, she may have been furious that he had eluded her. Then she had the good luck to spot me at Neon Nightmare. On that lonely desert road, one thing was certain: she wasn't going to let me escape with a grazing this time. She was literally hell-bent for leather to catch me from behind. If your nosy cat hadn't been in my car, and hadn't been determined to shred my leather seats, I might not have noticed her until she'd gotten close enough to shoot something . . . the tires, the window glass, me."

"But instead—"

"Instead, thanks to Midnight Louie, I saw, did an immediate one-eighty-turn so my headlights were blaring straight at her. I'd hit the high-beams while the Maxima was skating around. You know how things slow down in a car accident, even one you avoid? How it is absolute slow-motion, with these snapshots of images as sharp and large as if they were on a movie screen?"

Temple nodded, remembering. "I've had the occasional close call. Once I almost hit a squirrel that had decided to run across a street in front of me. I hit the brakes, but I can still see the little critter in every detail, stopping crouched on his delicate hind feet, trying to decide whether to run forward or back."

"What did he do?"

"Ran back."

"That's a squirrel for you, dithering and then retreating. That's why so many get run over."

"Not this one. I slowed the Storm enough to miss him, and the oncoming cars saw me braking and slowed down themselves, so he was sitting safe on the curb by the time I looked again."

"It was like that, except Kathleen didn't retreat. I saw her in my headlights. That 'cycle looked like one shiny big black bug bristling with armor. RoboRoach. Her own single headlamp almost blinded me. She swerved at the last moment to avoid a head-on collision, not because she cared about damaging any car or motorcycle, but because I'd survive it and she wouldn't.

"We were already out of town near the Great Nothing of Darkness. She went careening off into it, then I saw her red taillight bobble like a UFO headed for Venus. It arced upward. The front wheel must have hit a pretty big impediment. The little red light sailed up and then fell down so far it disappeared. That's when I knew that she had landed in a dry wash."

"Was it very deep?"

"Ten, twelve feet probably. Not so deep unless you're diving helmet first into the hard sand at seventy miles an hour."

"You're sure she's dead."

"I'm not, personally. Logically, she had to be. The person pulled out of that gully was sirened away by the EMTs, but they always have to try. Devine saw the body, and swears it was hers."

"How close did he see it? In a viewing room like where he ID'ed his stepfather?"

"Naked on an autopsy table. It doesn't come any more revealing than that. They'd even taken out her contact lenses. Blue-green. That was the wrinkle she developed after Ireland. Her eyes were hazel-green."

"She meant something to you. A lot."

He didn't quite look at her. "Kathleen was sweet, charming. So . . . unspoiled compared to the Material Girls at home. So dedicated to a cause. Sean and I had to pretend it was a contest between us, winning her. But it was first love, for both of us."

Temple kept silent, knowing from her older brothers how early boys learn to disguise softer feelings beneath a kind of brusque, rude energy.

Max went on without prompting, as if her comment had released the floodgates of the past instead of tears. "After Sean's death, when I turned on the IRA to punish his killers, I always thought Kathleen's apparent love had turned to hatred because I'd betrayed her cause. I always felt guilty about that, regretful that my thirst for justice, or vengeance, had come between us, that it was my fault.

"Only when Matt Devine came along recently, the 'innocent' ex-priest, and blithely suggested that Kathleen had set up Sean's death did I understand that he was right, that hatred underlay everything about Kathleen, that she had charmed us into infatuation and goaded us into competition. Do you know the story of Maud Gonne?"

Temple shook her head.

"I was into everything Irish then. Maud Gonne was a beautiful nineteenth-century Irish actress, but first and always she was a relentless patriot. William Butler Yeats, the poet, fell madly in love with her, wrote plays and poems for her, said her beauty 'belonged to poetry, to some legendary past.' She refused all his many marriage proposals. He wasn't as fiercely committed to the Irish cause as she required. His last poems memorialized the fruitless beauty of a bitter, angry woman."

"When did you first start calling yourself 'Max,' after your string of given names?" Templ^ asked carefully.

His glance was tender, grateful, recognizing the intuition that had guided the seemingly irrelevant question.

"Michael Aloysius Xaviar. After . . . Kitty and Sean's death and my blowing the whistle on the IRA, I needed a new identity. Max it was."

"So you haven't been called 'Michael' since." Temple didn't indicate "since" when.

"Not since then. Her. Until now." He looked at her again, smiling. "It's time to put away the things of a child, including delusions. We have more modern mysteries to solve."

Temple decided it was also high time to let Max escape back into present conundrums. "Like why both you and she had a knack for high-tech disguise."

"Hardly disguise, Temple. Merely effect. I guess she and I liked to stage-manage our own images. Maybe that's what drew her to me."

"What drew her was that you had a conscience. That's the one thing you and Matt have in common."

"Me, the seasoned man of magic, illusion, counterespionage? You think I have a conscience?" He spoke lightly, self-disparagingly.

"Second only to Matt's, which is way overdeveloped. That's why you were both her victims."

He leaned forward to finally pick up the glass and take a long swallow. "You may be right. We'll never know, will we?"

"Probably not. Who's going to bury her?"

She didn't often startle Max, but this time she had.

"Hell, Devine can bury his wicked stepfather, I can do as much for Kitty the Cutter. I'll do it."

"How? You don't exist."

"It will be a challenge. And it will be a good Catholic interment, priest and all." He savored the idea like aged whiskey. "Perhaps I can find her something white and bridal to wear, like a Communion dress. She would have loathed it. Thank you, Temple, for suggesting a ritual of closure for her, and for me."

"Are you going to invite Matt?"

"The less he dwells on her, alive or dead, the better. I

hate to say this, but be gentle with him, Temple."

She eyed him incredulously.

Max shrugged. "He was naive and he got nothing but well-intentioned bad advice. I didn't help him as much as I could have and I can pity anyone who's been the object of Kathleen's distilled ill will. It's an inbred poison, like any venomous serpent's. He wouldn't let me say I'm glad she's dead, but I am relieved she is. A lot of lives will go easier now, and who knows who would have attracted her lethal attention in the future."

"I'll let you say you're glad she's dead. Some people are destroyers. They're just evil, like serial killers. And a lot of them are running around loose in society like ordinary people, poisoning reputations and spreading gossip and lies. I guess we can't kill all the liars and sociopaths, but we don't have to pretend they add anything to the world but unnecessary pain."

"Granted. Kathleen was a disease, and she's been cured. She must have been scaldingly unhappy to have caused so much hurt. That's why I can be glad she's dead. She's better off that way, I'm sure."

"Someone too ill to live, I'm not sure Matt would ever accept that."

"He has to, because she *is* dead now. She's gone, Temple. I can feel it, as I've never sensed it before. That era is over."

"And so, where does that leave you?"

"Personally, I'm not sure yet. Professionally, as a provisionary member of the Synth."

"You mean you can concentrate on finding out what role they've played in the column of murders on my table? Max, they could be as dangerous as Kitty."

"Of course, but they'll never have the ancient hold on me that she did. Sean is finally at rest. His murderer lies in the same dark, cold ground, the universal ground of planet earth. We are left to walk upon it until our turns come. I plan to make the most of mine."

* * *

Louie only ventured out from the office when Max had left, leaving the whiskey bottle for long-term interment in Temple's liquor cupboard, which boasted one half-empty bottle of Old Crow, a vastly inferior brand.

It was like the old English ballad of the briar and the rose, Temple thought, setting the new bottle next to the resident one. Two opposites united. Like Max's macabre and touching image of his young cousin Sean sharing Mother Earth with his conniving murderer by proxy, the youthful Kathleen O'Connor.

Speaking of thorny relationships, they were all surrounded with briar and rose combinations: Matt and Molina; Temple and Molina; Matt and Max; Temple and Matt . . . more than one modern woman could contemplate at a single sitting.

"So," Temple told Louie, standing up.

The Leonard Cohen CD had long since played through and she had switched to the local golden oldies radio station, avoiding any temptation to dial in WCOO. It was only 11 P.M. anyway.

"You ruined Max's interior upholstery," she told Louie. "I thought you knew better than to sharpen your claws on furniture. You've left mine alone with not even an admonition."

Louie shook his head and then licked busily at the hair just beneath his chin, a sure sign he was annoyed with her. Usually this gesture was only evoked by a fresh influx of Free-to-be-Feline in his bowl.

"I suppose your actions drew Max's attention to his pursuer, but how and why on earth did you get into his car in the first place, and why were you at Neon Nightmare in the *first* first place?"

One of Louie's ears flattened, and he sparred at it with a well-licked paw, as if to say, *Can I really be hearing these inane questions*?

Temple examined him a little more closely. His fur had

been licked up into cowlicks all over and the hairs stuck together in a punk rocker's spiky look.

Louie had been off doing a major cleanup, which made her wonder what kind of mess he had gotten into. Could it be any worse than what Matt or Max had managed in the past few days?

Naw. . . .

Night Music

"I've got," Matt said into the phone, "a witness to Vassar's death. Where do you want to hear about it?"

The line went dead for about half a minute. Then came a deep sigh. "I haven't the slightest idea."

"I can go anywhere now, see anyone. She's gone. She left the planet."

"Do *not* use that stinking 'she left' phrase. It's connected to too many murders for my peace of mind."

"This one wasn't a murder."

"Say you and your murky witness."

"My murky witness will be your solid witness. Trust me. I'm no more in the mood for fairy tales at this point than you are."

"A solid witness, you say."

"We're both off the hook."

"Then 'It's a Grand Night for Singing.' That's a song title, by the way. Oldie but goofy. Come to the Blue Dahlia at ten-thirty. Think a half hour should get you to the radio station on time?"

"Sure. I'll come early and catch your act. I do think you have something to croon about tonight, Carmen."

"I hope so, Devine. You owe me that at least for my sterling dating advice." Said sardonically.

Matt smiled after she hung up. For once he would be the bearer of good tidings.

Matt always found it amazing what people did to distract themselves from tension. He prayed. Temple bought wildly impractical shoes. Max Kinsella performed magic tricks. Lieutenant C. R. Molina sang.

And she did it very well.

Tonight she wore blue velvet, forties style. Her voice was blue velvet whatever she wore, dark, midnight deep, and plush.

The voice was a gift. Matt's vocation as a priest had forced him to sing the mass, to intone responses. He had managed to execute that narrow-range singsong respectably, but that was all.

Secretly, he had visited Baptist congregations, wowed by the vigor, faith, and musical pyrotechnics of their choirs. Plain song would always hold a pure, medieval attraction, but the passionate musical joy of the black congregations struck a chord in him that maybe only Elvis would understand, now that Matt had been forced to understand Elvis.

Most torch singers caught the reflected sensual glow of the flames their lyrics celebrated. Molina was a cerebral singer. Her voice was something apart from Carmen the Performer. You couldn't get a crush on her even while she crooned Gershwin's "I've Got a Crush on You." That made her an even more fascinating performer. The audience sensed something held back from them. Matt had heard that the secret of great acting was to always hold something back, leave the audience craving more. Something more to come, if only you can wait long enough, hold the applause, and . . . wait for the fireworks.

But even Molina's vintage performing wardrobe was somehow didactic. This forties gown, that silk blue Dahlia above one ear perched on an out-of-period Dutch cut that was vaguely twenties decadent at the same time it was schoolgirl fifties. Her only makeup was dark lipstick, Bette Davis style. And Davis had been many things on the screen, all of them magnificent; sometimes the neurotic, but never the Vamp.

Matt ordered a deep-fried appetizer and a drink and gave himself the luxury that Molina never had given herself: thinking about her as a person, rather than a profession.

The trio behind her had suddenly become instrumental only.

Matt realized his dining-out Scotch was a drizzle of memory over ice cubes and Carmen was offstage. Time for him to "strike up the music and dance." To her tune, of course.

Even at the Blue Dahlia, Molina was somehow in uniform.

Matt left a nice tip on the table and got up. He headed for the hallway and the second door on the right, straight on till morning, where her tiny dressing room was.

He knocked, and was invited in.

It was here she . . . they . . . had hatched the scheme of sending him to a professional call girl to lose the virtue that Kathleen O'Connor had wanted to capture for herself. As if one could acquire another's virtue. As if virginity was a condition rather than a state of grace.

"Here we are again." Molina acknowledged their mutual complicity in the call-girl scheme, gesturing to the round-seated wooden chair he had used before.

He watched her expression in the round mirror of the vintage dressing table. She hadn't turned to welcome him, and he understood that. Guilt between even casual co-conspirators was as much a barrier as the one between performer and audience. Every stage comes equipped with an invisible "fourth wall," a division that is only in the mind of both performer and audience. A barrier.

"What do you have for me?" Molina had finally turned around, her workaday tone neutralizing the persona of Carmen.

"A way out. For both of us. Vassar accidentally fell to her death."

"Says who?"

"Says the woman who was on the cell phone with her at the time, the woman she called after I left the Goliath suite."

"Woman?"

"A volunteer counselor. I have her name, address, rank, cell phone number. She's real, Carmen. She has a convincing explanation for Vassar's death, and it wasn't either of our faults."

"Some woman? How did you find her?"

"She found me."

"The radio station. Your show. That attracts nuts, don't you know that by now?"

"So does your profession."

"So be mad. I was only trying to help you."

"Your advice was impeccably hard-headed. It was just wrong for me. And for Vassar, as it turned out."

"What do you know about a call girl? There was semen in the body. If not yours, whose? Hookers, and especially high-end call girls, won't lick a stamp without a condom these days. It does make one wonder about her previous stand. If things had gotten tight and you'd hadn't been contacted by your convenient phone witness, I'd have had to ask you for a sample. Where does that fall on the spectrum of sin? Probably venial, compared to actual copulation. You didn't even screw her, which was the whole point. Did you?"

"No. I didn't even screw her. And that was the whole point. I was the first person who didn't even screw her. Can you understand what that might mean to someone like her?"

"Maybe." Said sourly. Molina was clinging tight to her professional distance. Compassion was an enemy to a cop.

"So what's the latest story on Vassar's last gasp?"

"You and that coroner. Always cynical. Always laughing at Death in fear of Death laughing at you. I've got good news. At least to me and my conscience. Vassar was happy, okay? She didn't regard me as a flop. We made talk, not love, and sometimes talk is better than sex. I felt better for talking to her. Apparently she felt better for talking to me. She called this counselor she'd been avoiding right away. Deborah Ann Walker. She came to WCOO to find me and tell me that. Nice lady. Like Vassar. They were both classy ladies. The hooker and the reformer. Not so different, after all. Maybe the lady lieutenant figures in there somehow. Carmen, I know you tried to help me. I tried to do what you said. I failed. I chickened out. And that seems to have made all the difference. To Vassar anyway. And to me. I didn't need to 'lose' anything about myself. I needed to give something more to someone else."

A knock on the door. The barman with a tray. Two Scotches on the rocks.

Molina waved him in and him out again. She drank from her glass before resuming the conversation.

"This Walker woman was on the phone with Vassar *after* you left her at the Goliath?"

"She was on the phone with her just before Vassar fell."

"Then where's the frigging phone?"

Matt outstared her sudden fury. "That's your job, to find it. My job is to tell you the truth you don't want to hear. You didn't do me any favors with your advice. But it worked out in a strange way, after all. I'd give right now what I was so desperately trying to keep Kathleen O'Connor from getting to get Vassar back, but I can't be sorry I met her. I can't be sorry I . . . failed to be a good customer. I'm glad I was a better friend."

Molina pushed a hand through her unmussable hair. "You and Vassar, making fools of us all. Kathleen O'Connor *and* me. You're right. I was fighting O'Connor through you and Vassar. I had convinced myself that this would heal everybody's ills, you and the call girl. I was acting like a goddamn social worker instead of a cop. Here's the hardened call girl. I send her an ethical man. Here's the beset ex-priest who actually cares. I send him to a woman who regards sex as richly rewarded therapy. A marriage made in Heaven, right? Except I no longer believe any marriage is made in Heaven."

"That's where you went wrong."

Carmen/Molina glared at him, saying and singing nothing.

"You were right. Vassar and I were very good for each other. That's what Deborah's testimony tells me. We were both better off for meeting each other."

"Deborah." Molina pulled the fake blue Dahlia from her hair, tossed it onto the dressing table. "That's the name of a judge in the Old Testament, isn't it?"

Matt nodded.

"And she's your witness to Vassar's last words?"

Matt nodded again.

Molina sighed, rested her head on her hand, which was braced on the dressing table pillar. "Don't you see why I interfered? Kathleen O'Connor was every sexual predator I never caught. You were my . . . Mariah. My innocent daughter who's growing into the real world that hides scum like that, whatever the gender. I wanted to see you safely through adolescence, Matt. Maybe the means were cynical, but the intent was . . . honest."

"I know."

"You know?"

"Sure. You and me, we're dinosaurs. True. Our work, our vocations, require us to live up to public images, rigorously honest, severe, sexless, perfect as our Heavenly Father is perfect. Recognize the dogma? Except we're human. We want to preserve what's innocent in us, but we can't afford to live by it in the real, ugly world.

"So I know where you're coming from, Carmen. Strict Hispanic Catholic family. Or Polish Catholic family. High standards. Impossible standards. Still, if you don't go for the top, you'll settle for the bottom. That's the problem with religious absolutism: there's either bad or good. Perfect or imperfect. You either sin or you don't. No middle ground. No gray. That's not what Jesus preached in the New Testament. His bottom line was compassion, which abolishes the black and white and leaves only the gray and the benefit of the doubt. That's why they killed him."

"Abolish black and white from the law enforcement profession and anarchy would reign."

"Maybe so. Maybe not. I'm just saying we can both be thankful that nobody killed Vassar, not even us. It was a stupid accident. I left her standing by the railing overlooking the atrium. Deborah heard her cry out and then the cell phone clattered and buzzed, but it didn't shut off."

"Someone still could have come up behind her and pushed her."

"Maybe. But I don't think so. Deborah says she was exhilarated, hyper. She more likely . . . turned around to lean against the railing, lost her balance on those high-rise heels."

"You realize what you're telling me? That a call girl was deliriously happy because you *didn't* sleep with her. Not much of a personal advertisement."

"Do I care? I'm deliriously happy I didn't have to act against my conscience myself. Can't you accept the gift of a free conscience? That doesn't come along every day."

"No." Molina turned to the mirror to wipe off Carmen's camellia mouth with a tissue. She turned back to lift her glass toward him. They tapped rims and sipped.

"I have to play Devil's advocate so I don't buy every fairy tale I might want to believe. I'll have that atrium scoured for the cell phone. Of course someone could have spotted and taken it by now. Still, if this Walker woman's testimony holds up then we're both in the clear. My career and your freedom. We were gambling for pretty high stakes."

Matt nodded and sipped again, feeling relief tingle all the way to his fingertips.

"Only two things bother me," she added.

"Two things?"

"Rafi Nadir and Max Kinsella."

"Kinsella and Nadir? Who's Nadir?"

"Ah—" Molina waved a dismissive hand. "A pick-pocket around town. Different case. Anyway, I personally checked the Goliath videotapes. They show you checking in. And they show Kinsella hanging around the registration area about the same time."

Matt knew his face showed utter, unfeigned shock. What was Max doing there? Right then?

He was so shocked that he only vaguely understood that Molina the cop always had to have the last suspicious word.

He was very glad that he had not mentioned Kinsella's presence on the even more recent death scene of Kathleen O'Connor, which had not yet entered Molina's official radar.

But it could, if anyone had seen both Kinsella and O'Connor at Neon Nightmare.

Melting

Temple was curled up on her couch with Midnight Louie, watching a really bad Boris Karloff movie. Karloff, of course, was never bad, but some of his later films were.

She couldn't sleep.

Hi-ho the witch is dead, the wicked witch is dead.

She had actually broken out the Midnight Louie shoes, which really didn't go well with her Garfield T-shirt-cum-nightgown.

Glittering white crystal high heels with the image of a black cat on the heels were not the done thing to wear with cotton knit, although almost anything went in Las Vegas.

She gazed down at her bare insteps surrounded by the elegant dazzle of Stuart Weitzman custom pavé shoes. Elegant, gorgeous, even improbable shoes invariably made her feel better.

High heels were a little girl's stepping stones to adulthood. Maybe adulthood was something as simple as losing a shoe and gaining a prince, or accidentally killing a witch and gaining a magical pair of red sequin pumps. Then killing one on purpose later.

Temple had to admit that she had a prince, or two, in her life, and a witch or two, as well. She also had to admit to herself that she hadn't wanted Kitty dead, not really, although maybe the woman was dead because two men were determined that Temple wouldn't be hurt by her. In olden days, women were thrilled to have men fighting for their honor and their lives. Temple wasn't thrilled with the uneasy guilt she felt now. She was particularly queasy about Matt's unspoken willingness to sacrifice his most personal well-being for her. Oh, he was concerned about a host of other women in his life, but they were all incidental, weren't they? And she wasn't. Had Max guessed that? Of course. He wasn't a jealous man, but he had always been worried about Matt since he had returned to find a new neighbor in Temple's building and life. She couldn't complain about either man's sincerity in thinking of her safety, but she wished she weren't so darned guilty about, and impressed by, both of them.

Nowhere in the book of fairy tales did it mention two Prince Charmings. Come to think of it, both Max and Matt had been involved in the retrieval of the glass slipper, aka the Midnight Louie shoes. Modern life, not dreams, was what fractured fairy tales are made of, Mr. Ariel.

So now, fairy tale-wise, one witch was dead. An evil witch who had looked as glamorous as Glinda the Good Witch of the North in the Judy Garland movie, all Southern-belle skirts and glitter and magic wand.

The evil witch was a bony hag in a pointed hat with grossly striped stockings and granny lace-ups in villainous black. Why, then, had she wanted the ruby red slippers? For the power they conferred, of course, but maybe somewhere in her evil black cinder of a heart she had simply coveted something beautiful for its own sake.

Temple had to wonder if Kathleen O'Connor had coveted innocence that way, Max's teenage chastity, Matt's post-priesthood delayed-adolescent possession of the same. Kathleen had wanted to destroy both boys. Men. And maybe she yearned for the very innocence she sought to destroy. Maybe it was her own.

Two women dead only a couple of days apart. The mysterious call girl (to Temple anyone who followed that line of work would always be mysterious) and the mysterious stalker-girl.

And here she was, trying to avoid either extreme, trying to be a real girl the way Pinocchio ached to be a real boy.

Three clicks of her heels and maybe she could be back home in Minnesota, where call girls were few and under wraps and wicked witches froze their long noses and toes and peaked hat tips off.

But, no, she couldn't leave the Emerald City of Las Vegas yet. There was still too much to solve about herself and everyone around her.

She was too melancholy to move on. She glanced at the sparkling shoes on her feet. Her high-heel addiction had always been the bravado of a short girl, a small woman. I am walking on hot spikes, hear me roar. Except I'd rather whimper sometimes.

But didn't everybody?

Even Vassar. Even Kitty the Cutter.

That's what got to Temple. Between them, these women so different from her had forced two men she cared about to the bitter edge, making them commit to unwanted sex in one instance, and unwanted death in another. You couldn't ask for any more dire consequences.

Was her gender really so destructive? Or so frustrated?

And then there was Molina, gloating over it all like a legal vulture bent on picking away at everybody's bones and insecurities.

Temple watched Karloff's cadaverous features in his black-and-white world. Films were better before color. So was newspaper photography. Color cluttered up the scenery, distracted the eye, made everything a moral morass, shades of the rainbow.

Midnight Louie stirred against her hip, uttered a cross between a meow and a purr.

"You're right, boy. I'm in a very bad mood tonight. I guess cats don't have moods. Just territorial disputes."

He seemed to nod as he licked away at one forepaw, head bobbing up and down.

It was pretty bad when she was discussing her emotional state with a cat. A large, intelligent, amazingly handsome cat, but a cat nonetheless.

A knock came on Temple's door. Her eyes streaked to the clock on the portable stereo. Eleven-fifteen. Who on earth . . . Max had already been by.

She rose and clicked over to the door, peering through the tiny peephole.

The hall was dark and the sidelight only distorted the view.

She opened the door but kept her chain lock fastened.

"Matt!"

The mechanism resisted her fingers for a moment, but then her door was wide and he was hesitating on her threshold like a Fuller Brush salesman, if there still were Fuller Brush salesmen.

"What is it?"

"I've got to get to work," he said, "but do you have a minute?"

"Sure. Come in. What's going on?"

"I had to tell you some good news."

He was checking out her apartment, spotting Louie still on the sofa—looking most annoyed at losing his lap pillow—hunting for signs of Max, she supposed.

"Are you alone?" he asked.

"No. Louie and you are here. That's all."

He paced a little in the entry hall. "I just wanted to let you know, so you wouldn't worry."

"What, me worry?"

"You've been doing it. I can tell. I've just seen Molina."

"This should stop me worrying?"

"At the Blue Dahlia."

"Worse and worse."

"And I told her that I heard from a counselor of Vassar's, who was on the phone with her and probably heard her fall. After I left. It was an accident, Temple. Molina knows that now."

"An accident. How . . . great. I mean, not great that she fell, but . . . for you."

"Yeah. For me. For Molina."

He stopped, ran a hand through his blond hair, turning into a punk bedhead. Looked at her.

"Vassar . . . died . . . planning to reinvent her life. Oh, God."

"A happy death," Temple said, remembering the phrase from somewhere.

"A happy death," he repeated. "I've got to get to work. I can't be late . . . what am I now, some kind of White Rabbit? Oh, Temple."

"Aren't you glad? If I understand all this, no one's to blame for Vassar's death and even she was upbeat at the time. That's the way I'd like to go, that everyone would, fast and happy."

"Fast and happy. Better than slow and sad, that's right. Temple."

"Thanks for telling me, Matt. I won't worry now. Not much." She didn't lie well.

He glanced down, and frowned. "Why are you wearing those shoes now? It's almost midnight."

"Maybe I was expecting Prince Charming." She didn't know why she'd said that, except that she was mistress of the flip quip and she was feeling a very confusing need to be inappropriately flip at the moment, her and her tiny feet and big mouth . . .

Matt put a palm to his forehead as if he was trying to play mind-reader, or hold his thoughts in. But it didn't work, because his next words came out of left field, the left field of his inner anxieties.

"I didn't sleep with her."

"You don't have to tell me this. I mean, it's none of my

business. Except . . . maybe it's relevant to the case."

"What case?"

"Well, all of them. The unsolved cases. The things that are none of our business. Except Molina's. So . . . who?" Temple wanted to be very precise on this fact.

"Who what?" Matt was looking more confused now than she was.

"Who didn't you sleep with? Besides anybody in the past seventeen years."

"Seventeen? How do you get seventeen?"

"Well, from since you went from high school to the seminary."

"You've been keeping track of my non-sleeping-with timeline?"

"Well, I just have a mind for these details. So you were going to tell me. Who."

Matt shook his head, sufficiently distracted that the information no longer felt so horribly personal. It was about a "case," after all.

"Vassar. It didn't work. Molina's plan. Not for me. Not for Vassar."

"Oh. But she didn't kill herself."

"No. Not that. Not because of me. Someone still could have . . . but it's not likely. It was *all* an accident. An accident, Temple. All of it."

She nodded, continually. "I understand. You'd better go now. The show."

"The show." He joined her in nodding and stepped into the hall.

"Drive carefully," Temple caroled after him like her irritating Aunt Marge, whose cautionary tones she had not heard in twelve years, thank God.

"I can't believe I said that," she muttered to Louie, who had risen and was now rubbing his black satin legs against the rough Austrian crystal sides of her shoes.

Temple had never wanted to know, and *not* know, something so much in her life. Now that she knew, she didn't know what to make of it, what to make of Matt thinking it was important to tell her what had happened, and not happened between him and Vassar. As a friend, she was glad he hadn't been forced to go against his conscience. As a neighbor, she was glad he felt free to confide in her, although he had seemed somewhat constrained to talk just now.

As . . . whatever, she was relieved. And scared.

She leaned over and gazed hard into the Emerald-city-gleam of Midnight Louie's eyes.

"And have *you* anything momentous to confess concerning your sex life, or lack of it, and any recent involvement in violent death you might have had?"

The cat gazed solemnly back, and kept the usual mum.

Midnight Louie Picks a Bone

I am flabbergasted.

Appalled.

Outraged.

Imagine my very own collaborator springing such a surprise on me.

I refer, of course, to the untimely death of Kathleen O'Connor.

I grant you that Miss Carole let me be first on the death scene, but I am not that crazy about inspecting the corpus delicti, especially if it is nothing I can eat.

Ultimately, not even a coyote was willing to pick Miss Kitty's bones, which I suppose is something of an epitaph. Too bad nobody will write it on her tombstone, though I doubt she will have one.

A mystery woman to the end. And that is another good epitaph gone to waste.

I am really coming up with them.

At least I do not have to compose any final words for my

partner, Miss Midnight Louise. It would really shrivel her whiskers to know I had the last word.

I must say that the kit has benefitted from her association with an older, wiser mentor, as no doubt Mr. Max will from the return of Gandolph the Great. She is a little distraught about causing a human death, though who is to say that a minor cat scratch really tipped the balance. I have had to explain to her that we are predators by nature, despite living on the handouts of human cuisine, in these, our latter decadent, domesticated days.

Still, she shows an oddly unspecieslike regret about her role in Kitty the Cutter's demise. Perhaps she has caught something from Mr. Matt, with whom she briefly resided when she first showed up on the scene.

My one regret is my longtime resolution never to speak to humans. It kills me to know how Vassar died and not to be able to set assorted consciences at rest. But it is too late for me to lower myself at this late date. And, in fact, I do not know if I could talk to them anyway. I have never tried and have always found other means of communicating my druthers.

Sometimes, I believe, it is good for humans to not know the answer to every question. Life, and often death, as I tell Louise, is like that.

She is not impressed.

Louise is like that too.

Very best fishes,

Midnight Louie, Esq.

For information about getting Midnight Louie's newsletter and/or T-shirt, contact him at *Midnight Louie's Scratching Post-Intelligencer*, PO Box 331555, Fort Worth, TX 76163, by e-mail at **cdouglas@catwriter.com**. or visit the Web page **http://www.catwriter.com.**

Carole Nelson Douglas Explains

In my defense, Louie, even I did not know that Kathleen O'Connor was leaving Las Vegas, and in a fatal state.

In books, as in life, as you point out, accidents will happen. If you miss her forbidding presence, it's partly your own fault for putting Max wise to the tiger on his tail.

In fact, since you are the only individual (I will not say "person") in Las Vegas who knows what really happened to Vassar and the only one who knows why Kitty the Cutter crashed and died, I should think you'd be pretty pleased with my most recent portrayal of your detecting skills, even if you have to keep them to yourself.

I am also pretty sure, though, that your new-found maturity won't outlast the inbred charm of your big bad attitude, anymore than Kitty's death will end the mayhem, murder, and ongoing angst that Las Vegas is famous for.

Look for

Cat in an Orange Twist

By Carole Nelson Douglas

Now available!
From Tom Doherty Associates

Turn the page for a preview

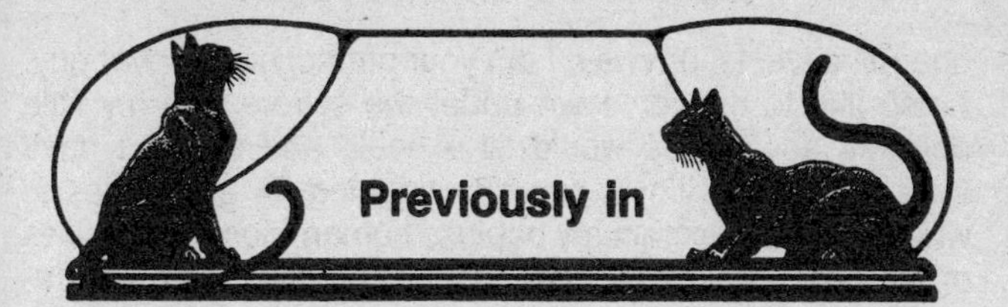

Midnight Louie's Lives and Times . . .

I have always been what you might call an afishionado. Those large, fancy Asian finsters called koi, in particular, tickle my palate. I like to snag my own. Literally.

So when I hear that feng shui is coming to town, I figure Las Vegas is getting some new variety of finned delicacy. No such luck. Feng shui, I learn, is something between a trend and a religion, and Las Vegas is always religiously trendy, so it is a big deal here.

Naturally, my lively little roommate, the petite and toothsome (even though she is of the human species) Miss Temple Barr is up to her Jimmy Choo rhinestone-buckled ankle straps in this shui-phooey business. She is, after all, a freelance public relations specialist, and Las Vegas is full of public relations of all stripes and legalities.

I should introduce myself: Midnight Louie, PI. I am not your usual gumshoe, in that my feet do not wear shoes of any stripe, but shivs. I have certain attributes, such as being short, dark, and handsome. Really short. That gets me overlooked and underestimated, which is what the savvy operative wants, anyway. I am your perfect undercover guy. I also like to hunker down under the covers with my little doll. My adventures would fill a book, and in fact I have several out. My life is just one ongoing TV miniseries in which I as hero extract my hapless human friends from fixes of their own making and literally nail crooks. After the dramatic turn of events last time out, most of my human associates are pretty shell-shocked. Not even an ace feline PI may be able to solve their various predicaments in the areas of crime and punishment . . . and PR, as in Personal Relationships.

As a serial killer-finder in a multivolume mystery series (not to mention a primo mouthpiece), it behooves me to update my readers old and new on past crimes and present tensions.

None can deny that the Las Vegas crime scene is a pretty busy place, and I have been treading these mean neon streets for sixteen books now. When I call myself an alpha-cat, some think I am merely asserting my natural male dominance, but no. I merely reference the fact that since I debuted in *Catnap* and *Pussyfoot*, I then commenced to a title sequence that is as sweet and simple as *B* to *Z*.

That is when I begin my alphabet, with the *B* in *Cat on a Blue Monday*. From then on, the color word in the title is in alphabetical order up to the current volume, *Cat in an Orange Twist*. (*Yeow!* I do *so* detest citrus!)

Since I associate with a multifarious and nefarious crew of human beings, and since Las Vegas is littered with guidebooks as well as bodies, I wish to provide a rundown of the local landmarks on my particular map of the world. A cast of characters, so to speak:

To wit, my lovely roommate and high-heel devotee, Miss Nancy Drew on killer spikes, freelance PR ace MISS TEMPLE BARR, who has reunited with her only love . . .

. . . the once missing-in-action magician MR. MAX KINSELLA, who has good reason for invisibility. After his cousin SEAN died in a bomb attack during a post–high school jaunt to Ireland, he went into undercover counterterrorism work with his mentor, GANDOLPH THE GREAT, whose unsolved murder last Halloween while unmasking phony psychics at a séance is still on the books.

Meanwhile Mr. Max is sought by another dame, Las Vegas homicide LIEUTENANT C.R. MOLINA, mother of preteen MARIAH . . .

. . . and also the good friend of Miss Temple's handsome neighbor, MR. MATT DEVINE. He is a syndicated radio talk-show shrink and former Roman Catholic priest who came to Las Vegas to track down his abusive stepfather, MR. CLIFF EFFINGER, who is now dead and buried. By whose hand no one is quite sure.

Speaking of unhappy pasts, Lieutenant Carmen Regina Molina is not thrilled that her former flame, MR. RAFI NADIR, the unsuspecting father of Mariah, is in Las Vegas taking on shady muscle jobs after blowing his career on the LAPD . . .

. . . or that Mr. Max Kinsella is aware of Rafi and his past relationship to hers truly. She had hoped to nail one man or the other as the Stripper Killer, but Miss Temple prevented that by attracting the attention of the real perp.

In the meantime, Mr. Matt drew a stalker, the local girl that young Max and his cousin Sean boyishly competed for in that long-ago Ireland . . .

. . . one MISS KATHLEEN O'CONNOR, deservedly christened by Miss Temple as Kitty the Cutter. Finding Mr. Max impossible to trace, she settled for harassing with tooth and claw the nearest innocent bystander, Mr. Matt Devine . . .

. . . who is still trying to recover from the crush he developed on Miss Temple, his neighbor at the Circle Ritz condominiums, while Mr. Max was missing in action. He did that by not very boldly seeking new women, all of whom were in danger from said Kitty the Cutter.

In fact, on the advice of counsel, i.e., AMBROSIA, Mr. Matt's talk-show producer, and none other than the aforesaid Lt. Molina, he tried to disarm Miss Kitty's pathological interest in his sexual state (she had a past penchant for seducing priests) by attempting to commit loss of virginity with a call girl least likely to be the object of K the Cutter's retaliation. Except that hours after their assignation at the Goliath Hotel, said call girl turned up deader than an ice-cold deck of Bicycle playing cards. So did he, or didn't he? Commit sin . . . or maybe murder.

But there are thirty-some million potential victims in this old town, if you include the constant come and go of tourists, and everything is up for grabs in Las Vegas 24/7: guilt, innocence, money, power, love, loss, death, and significant others.

All this human sex and violence makes me glad I have a simpler social life, such as just trying to get along with my unacknowledged daughter . . .

. . . MISS MIDNIGHT LOUISE, who insinuated herself into my cases until I was forced to set up shop with her as Midnight Inc. Investigations, and who has also nosed herself into my long-running duel with . . .

. . . the evil Siamese assassin HYACINTH, first met as the onstage assistant to the mysterious lady magician . . .

. . . SHANGRI-LA, who made off with Miss Temple's semiengagement ring from Mr. Max during an onstage trick and has not been seen since except in sinister glimpses . . .

. . . just like THE SYNTH, an ancient cabal of magicians that may deserve contemporary credit for various unsolved deaths around Las Vegas.

Well, there you have it, the usual human stew, all mixed up and at odds with each other and within themselves. Obviously, it is up to me to solve all their mysteries and nail a few crooks along the way. Like Las Vegas, the City that Never Sleeps, Midnight Louie, private eye, also has a sobriquet: the Kitty that Never Sleeps.

With this crew, who could?

Expiration Date

"Well, as I live and breathe! Or maybe I don't."

Temple looked up from her trudge across the condo parking lot. Albertson's plastic grocery bags dangled from her every extremity. She'd been thinking, however, less of cabbages and more of furniture kings, her next freelance public relations assignment.

"Electra."

There her sixty-something landlady stood like somebody's favorite fairy-godmother-cum-conscience, arms akimbo on broad muumuu-swathed hips.

"Let me help you with those bags before you break a fingernail," Electra said.

Temple stopped, happy to let Electra strip her of assorted burdens. She hadn't seen Electra Lark in what seemed like ages, given all the clandestine excitement in her own life lately.

Apparently that was a major omission, because something was radically different about Electra. For one thing, she looked fifteen years younger.

"Electra. Your hair is *brown.*"

"Well, aren't you the ace detective! Correction. My hair *used* to be brown."

"And so it is again. Hey. It looks great this way. And what did you mean by 'maybe you don't' live and breathe?"

Electra leaned close as they resumed plodding toward the side door of the Circle Ritz apartments and condominiums, a round '50s building that was, architecturally speaking, as charmingly eccentric as its owner.

"It seems this old place is haunted."

"Haunted? Oh, I don't think so, Electra."

"Don't believe in ghosts?"

"Not here."

By now Electra had tugged—and Temple had elbowed—the door open and they squeezed through together.

Inside, the hall was cooler, but not much. Summer had not yet turned Las Vegas streets into one big sizzling Oriental wok.

"Why should the Circle Ritz be immune from ghosts?" Electra asked.

"Because I live here and I really don't need another complication in my life right now."

"You live here. Isn't that amazing?'

They had reached the small but handsome lobby. Electra pressed the up button for the sole elevator with one elbow and the expertise of a longtime resident.

"I *don't* live here?" Temple was getting alarmed.

Electra's usual mode was unconventional rather than cryptic. She'd always used her snow white hair as a palette for a rainbow of temporary colors to match the vivid tones in her ever-present muumuus.

Brown was alarmingly ordinary for one of Electra's expressive bent.

"Is this your subtle way," Temple asked, "of trying to kick me out? You can't. I own my place. On the other hand, you *could* kick out Matt Devine. He only rents." As if anyone would ever want to kick out Matt Devine.

"Matt who?"

"Electra! You're acting ultraweird. Maybe Miss Clairol has gone to more than your head. The moment I dig my key out of my tote bag and let us in, I'm going to fix a cup of tea or a snifter of brandy and find out what's going on with you."

"Funny, I was planning to ply *you* with brandy, if you have any."

Temple temporarily transferred some grocery bags to Electra's arms while she plumbed the jumbled depths of her ever-present tote bag. The keys surfaced tangled around a giant can of paprika. Some of her purchases hadn't fit into the six bags she could conceivably carry.

She dropped the paprika into a bag in Electra's custody, then unlocked the door.

She never glimpsed her own place without an internal sigh of satisfaction. No "unit" in the Circle Ritz was the same, another aspect of the vintage building's charm. Temple's place was Mama Bear size: medium, partly because it had been bought for two.

The Baby Bear–size entry hall showed views of a black-and-white kitchen just the right size for Goldilocks and, farther in, the pie-slice-shaped living room. Its handsome rank of French doors led to a small triangular patio. Off each side of the main room were two bedroom suites with tiled baths. One of them served as Temple's home office, because for the year that Max had lived here openly, no way did they need separate bedrooms.

Temple's current live-in roommate sprawled on the off-white sofa dead ahead. Okay, he was often lazy, but he always looked good, which was more than some of her women friends could say about *their* slacker layabouts.

"That's no ghost," Temple said, admiring the black hairy body lounging so fluidly on her furniture.

Electra snorted. "I've seen more of Midnight Louie lately than I have of you. And he's a real Houdini when it comes to slipping in and out of this place."

"I've been busy." Temple proved it by heading for the

kitchen to unload her week's worth of the Craven Cook's convenience foods, frozen stuff first. "And why do you need to ply me with anything alcoholic?"

Electra unloaded canned and dry goods onto the tiled countertops in silence. Nothing in the Circle Ritz had ever been updated except the owner's hair color.

The rhinestone-festooned Felix the Cat clock on the wall swung its molded black plastic tail back and forth, telling time as quietly as a cat.

Temple finished stowing the refrigerated foods, then turned to the still-startling brownette beside her. "Weird how radical 'ordinary' looks on you. Would Dr Pepper on ice in my best Baccarat glasses stand in for the brandy I don't have?"

"Absolutely. I've squeezed out some the world's deepest, darkest secrets over Dr Pepper. So misunderstood."

By the time they'd iced their soft drinks and headed for the living room sofa, Midnight Louie had obligingly moved to the white faux goathair rug under the coffee table. There he lounged like a *Playgirl* centerfold in desperate need of a full body waxing.

"This is nice." Electra leaned back into the neutral-colored sofa cushions.

Inspired by her recent research into decor, Temple decided she really needed a fashion-forward seating piece with as much ooomph as the red suede '50s couch she had found at the Goodwill for Matt, a floor up.

Electra wiggled into the cushions. "I do like sitting down with a tenant in one of my units. Unwinding. Not worrying about ghosts."

"First, explain the hair. I've gotten used to the Color, or Multicolor, of the Week, but . . . brown. Who wants to be brown?"

"Brown is back, big-time." Electra hefted the mahogany-shaded soft drink in her glass. "And sometimes you've been fashion-forward for long enough that you yearn for some stability. Like tenants you know and occasionally actually *see*."

"I'm getting the idea that you think I've been running around town too much. You are not my mother, Electra."

"Heaven forbid! My own kids were enough to get educated and out on their own. It isn't just you, Temple, dear. That darling boy Matt Devine has been even more of a ghost around here than you lately. And when I *have* run into him in the parking lot, 'run' is the word for it, as in 'hit and.' He doesn't stop and chat like he used to, or offer to help me with something. He just skedaddles like I was Typhoid Mary in a toxic muumuu."

"Don't take that personally," Temple advised, although she certainly had when it first started happening to her. "After all, he's got that night-shift radio counseling job. Doesn't exactly get him out and about early in the day. And now there are out-of-town speaking engagements. So he's been a bit distracted lately. The price of being a semi-celebrity."

"Distracted, hell. He's been avoiding me. And now you are too. Plus, you're making lame excuses for him. Why?"

"I felt the same way, Electra, until I realized all that Matt had going."

"He's always been busy, but never . . . aloof. I'm worried about him. Something is wrong."

Electra's frown accentuated two of the amazingly few lines on her face. Even the darker hair color didn't age the plump contentment of her features. Temple guessed Electra had never been a pretty girl, but she was heading toward being a gorgeous old lady.

She almost leaned over to pat Electra's hand . . . and tell all. Only there was so much to tell and it really wasn't her story to spill.

"Matt's all right," Temple said firmly. She wished she really believed that.

"And then there's my favorite phantom," Electra said ominously. "He's running on a short leash."

Temple glanced to the cat-shaped rug that was rubbing its permanent five-o'clock-shadowed jaw on the toe of her Via Spiga pump.

"Louie has always been a night person. He's proven he can take care of himself, and then some, and he's not reproducible."

"Not *that* phantom. I mean Max."

"Oh."

"Oh. *Hello?* Pardon my slang, but you and he did buy this place together. As far as I'm concerned, he's been AWOL since he vanished a year and a half ago. 'Absent without Leave.' Without my leave, if not yours."

"Electra, I really can't discuss why Max moved out, or why he didn't move back in, actually, when he . . . turned up again. I keep up the mortgage payments, don't I?"

"I don't care about the mortgage. I care about you. Here I have this attractive young career-gal tenant who has associated with two of the—well, in my age group, the word was 'eligible,' but I'm sure you young things have a much raunchier way of putting it nowadays . . . hot hunks?—guys to hang out at the Circle Ritz, and she seems to have lost both of them sometime, somewhere, somehow."

Temple tried to answer but the "hot hunks" phrase had temporarily muted her.

"Oh," Electra went on, gesturing widely enough to make Louie jump up as if she held a hidden treat in one of her hands, "I knew Max was still my Invisible Tenant. What a second-story man! As good as Louie at discreetly eeling in and out the place, which one would expect of a professional magician. They never can do it the easy way."

Electra peered owlishly over the titanium rims of her often present reading glasses. "I don't know if that applies to *everything* about them, but we'll let that go. Anyway, Max's hide-and-seek act added some Cary Grant caper charm to the place. So romantic. But he hasn't been eeling in and out, or out and in, like he used to. Matt's been vague and distant. And you've been looking way too worried for a natural redhead for far too long."

Temple heard her out, turning the cold crystal glass in her palm. Electra had put her flower-appliquéd fingernail on the unflowery bottom line: Temple and the two men might have faced extraordinary dangers in the past few months, more might still be facing them, but the upshot was that Temple's personal life wasn't very personal at all anymore. With anyone.

"I don't mean to depress you, dear, but I'm worried. Max I enjoy worrying about. I know if he gets himself into a tight corner, he'll get himself out of it, and you along with him. But you and I know that Matt's background doesn't exactly equip him for living in city full of sex, drugs, and rock 'n' roll. I would hate to see that sweet boy get into something he's not ready to handle."

"Ex-priests are more resilient than you think."

"You think so, dear?"

"I hope so. Listen, Electra. I can't say much about it, but you're right. We've all three been under tremendous pressure. I don't want to scare you, but it could have touched the Circle Ritz. Even you. Now I think, and hope, it's over. Or the worst of it, anyway."

Electra sat forward.

"I really can't say more."

"A tiny hint of what kind of danger you're talking about might help my insomnia. You know, up in the penthouse I can see a lot of comings and goings. Not that I snoop on my tenants, of course. You're saying you've kept me in the dark because it's 'good' for me? Honey, ignorance is never bliss."

Temple bit her lip. She recognized the truth of Electra's reverse aphorism. She owed her an explanation. So she spilled the bizarre beans everybody had been keeping secret from each other for too long.

"Matt had a stalker. But it's over now. Definitely over."

"A stalker? From his radio job? Media personalities attract nuts sometimes."

Temple shook her head. "That's what's been so . . . awkward. The stalker was someone who wanted to harass Max but couldn't find him."

"How would he find Matt, then? They have nothing in common but you. *Oh*."

"That's why they've both stayed as far away from me as they could. They didn't want the stalker finding me. And the Circle Ritz."

"Nothing in common but you and the Circle Ritz?" Electra looked down at Louie, who rewarded her attention by performing an impossibly long stretch that torqued his body in two opposite directions and showed off all of his, er, undercarriage.

"Amazing," Electra mused as Louie's yawn showcased sharp white teeth and crimson tongue. "Was this stalker a woman, by chance?"

"Yes. What an amazing deduction, Electra. The vast majority of stalkers are male."

"Deduction, phooey! I just remembered seeing Matt down by the pool months ago talking to some strange woman. I don't often see strangers in the rear pool area."

"How strange was she?"

"Not strange weird, just strange as in 'unknown.' She was a knockout, actually. Wore a jade green pantsuit, more formal than you usually see in Vegas, especially poolside. I couldn't see her features very well, but she had Louie coloring."

"Louie coloring?"

"Naturally black hair and lots of it. Red lips, not natural in her case; white teeth, maybe helped along by bleach. I'm guessing she had green eyes like Louie too. The two of them made a striking picture near that oblong of blue water, that's why I stopped to study it. Matt so blond and lightly tanned and so very unclothed, she so white skinned, yet boldly colored and overdressed. That's what struck me, how pale she was, as if she never went out in the sun. Not a native, that's for sure."

Temple, mesmerized, contemplated the vivid picture Electra had painted. She'd never seen the woman in the flesh tones, in Technicolor, but that's how the lively Electra always thought. Even Janice Flanders's "police" portrait had been executed in charcoal gray. Executed. Strange word for the act of making art, but apropos in this case.

"Kitty the Cutter." Temple murmured the sobriquet she had given the woman months before.

Electra hissed out a breath and sat back. "That bad, huh?"

"Her first attack was her worst."

Temple supposed that Matt's lightly tanned body still carried the scar. Not that she was into dwelling on Matt's lightly tanned body. Kitty, though, had been into ruination, all right. She felt a surprising surge of anger.

"You say it's over," Electra was prodding.

"It's over. She left. She's gone."

"*Hmmm.*" Electra sounded properly skeptical. "She must have left a lot of damage in her wake. So both men had to stay away from you for your own protection."

"Kitty was a jealous god. If she was after a guy, nobody female close to him was safe, not even Molina's daughter—"

"*Lieutenant* Molina?"

Temple nodded.

"I thought you two haven't gotten along ever since Max disappeared and the lieutenant was questioning us all. She seemed sure he'd been involved in a murder at the Goliath Hotel the night he vanished."

"We don't," Temple said. "Get along. Then, when she was persecuting Max, and now."

"You poor thing! Trying to hold the fort with all this going on. No wonder you're so confused about your love life."

"I'm not confused about my love life, I just haven't had much of one lately." Temple clapped a hand over her mouth.

"Oho! Now it comes out. I wasn't born in those exciting days of yesteryear for nothing, dear. You are blowing opportunities left and right, girl."

"I'm not blowing them, circumstances are. Max can't get married—"

"Why not?"

"For reasons I find reasonable."

"And Matt can't do anything *but* get married, I imagine, given his Church's strict position on everything carnal. No wonder everyone has been so cranky lately."

"We have not! Been cranky. Just stressed."

Electra chugalugged the last of her Dr Pepper and stood. "Disgraceful. All this sex on TV, sex on the Strip, sex on the billboards, and here we have three healthy young people who can't seem to get around to it."

"This is all so none of your business, Electra. You don't know the whole story."

"Whoever does? When you figure it out, tell me. I'd like to see two people in this unit again."

"You're such a romantic."

"Even if it's only you and Molina."

"Electra! That's outrageous."

"Not the way things are going around here. Give my regards to whichever phantom you see first. Adios, Louie."

With that Electra let herself out. Temple considered shouting denials after her, but rose, went to the French doors, and opened one onto the balcony patio.

Her plants looked a little droopy. The pool, kept filled year round, glistened like a huge, wet, emerald-cut aquamarine in the sunlight.

Now Temple was seeing phantoms: Matt and the strikingly described woman Temple had never met, but who had bedeviled the lives of two men who were important to her.

Electra had stirred up a lot of ghosts in the process of complaining about them.

Temple turned to regard her familiar rooms, running reels of her memory back and forth, pausing on certain indelible pictures.

Max's fingerprints were all over this scene. On the stereo system, in the kitchen, the bedroom. They'd lived together here for six ecstatic crazy-in-love months, flirting with marriage but not quite saying so. Temple moved suddenly across the room, causing Louie to scramble upright at full alert.

In her bedroom she went straight to the row of louvered closet doors.

The soaring chords of Max's favorite Vangelis CDs seemed to ricochet like musical bullets off the walls.

Digging in the deepest, darkest corner, she pulled out the last remaining performance poster of the Mystifying Max, the one Lieutenant Molina had insisted on borrowing after she'd deduced, merely from the blue-toned sweaters he'd left behind, that Max's compelling cat-green eyes were contact-lens enhanced.

It always galls to have an enemy tell you something you should have known in the first place.

Temple unrolled the glossy poster. Max the professional magician emerged, the top of his thick dark hair first, his devilishly arched Sean Connery the Younger eyebrows, then the phoney but compelling green eyes. He was wearing his trademark black silk-blend turtleneck sweater, long-fingered hands posed like sculpture on each opposite arm. Max was six four and sinewy, as strong and lean as steel cable, an aesthetic athlete. He wasn't handsome in a classical sense, but he didn't have to be. Sexy was good enough.

And for an all-too-few long, loving months, it had seemed that he was all hers.

Temple let the poster roll up like an old-fashioned window shade. *Now you see him. Now you don't.*

One week he was admitting her into his undercover life, like a partner. The next week . . . vanished again, without ever leaving town. Something had happened on the night Matt's stalker had died pursuing Max's car. Something that was taking Max away from her. Something that, if it kept on, might be taking her away from Max.

She'd seen fire and she'd seen rain, and she'd stood by him. Electra had just reminded Temple how hard it was to stand by a phantom. It had been that way after Max had first disappeared, when big, bullying Lieutenant Molina had badgered Temple to crack like the small-boned, petite woman she could be mistaken for.

Hah! That'll be the day, copper! Even two ham-fisted thugs hadn't done that.

No, Temple's key problem wasn't Las Vegas's hardest-boiled female homicide lieutenant. It was Max. Always and ever the charmer, always and ever impossible to pin down.

Temple put the rolled-up poster back in the corner of her closet, her fingers brushing soft black jersey in the dark. The Dress. The rather out-of-date dress. For a vintage clothing aficionado like Temple, nothing was ever really out of date. Not even the stuff in her refrigerator that she always seemed to get around to only past the expiration date.

The Dress. Max had been back again, then, in Las Vegas and in her bed. But. Matt Devine had been there when Max hadn't, and something got cooking there. He'd seemed so safe for a white widow (with a significant other gone, but not legally pronounced dead) like Temple: ex-priest, handsome as hard candy, nice as someone else's big brother, and too ethical to take advantage of any woman. Perfect prom date. No unromantic groping. No danger.

Except that one time, after his vile stepfather's funeral. Funerals always let out the demons. The phantoms of the past.

On her sofa. Temple walked back into the living room. That one. Broad daylight. Matt's fingers on the long bright hard row of black buttons up the center of That Dress.

Something happening. Oh, very definitely. And definitely to her taste. His too.

Temple sank into the cushions, reliving those—ha! Bring on the film noir flacks—"forbidden moments." She could sure see why they were forbidden. Way too addictive.

So. Did Matt really mean it? Feel it? Of course. But did he want to? Maybe not. Did she? Maybe not . . . oh, yeah. But she was spoken for. And very nicely too, when Max was around to speak for her.

But he hadn't been, not lately.

And he hadn't told her why. A poster is a poor excuse for a man, even a charismatic one.

Temple squinched down in the cushions and picked up her cell phone from the coffee table. She would try calling Max one more time today.

Her phone bleeped at her and shot a little message graphic into her heart.

Message. From Max? All her internal mutterings faded. At last.

She pressed the right buttons and then a couple wrong ones, and groused aloud and tried again, putting the phone to her ear.

"Hey, Little Red." Max's baritone vibrated through the earpiece. If you could sell that on the Web via spam . . . "Sorry we've been playing phone tag. That is definitely not what I'd like to play with you. Too much has come up for phones. I'll be in touch when I can. *Ciao.*"

Something soft and sensuous stroked her forearm. Temple looked down. Midnight Louie had silently lofted up next to her. His long black tail was just barely swiping her skin.

Temple gritted her teeth.

Electra had been right. Midnight Louie was the most constant and attentive male in her Circle Ritz life these days.

Did relationships have an expiration date too? And how far past that date did you dare nibble on the past without getting poisoned?

Tooth and Nail, Feng and Claw

"Well, Louie, what do you think? Am I feng enough to satisfy the Queen of Shui-ba?"

Huh? Since when did my daring and darling roommate, Miss Temple Barr, consult me on fashion matters?

I am a gentleman of the old school, from my polished nails to my formal black tie and tails that is a blend of Fred Astaire and gangsta record mogul.

One can never go wrong wearing black. Perhaps Miss Temple's crisis of confidence in the mirror is because she is wearing silver.

I do love those burnished sea shades, though. The memory of glints of gold and silver—the shiny-scaled koi that swim in them—reminds me of my dear old dad, Three O'Clock Louie. He retired to Vegas a while back from a Pacific Northwest salmon-fishing boat.

There is nothing golden—or fishy—about my Miss Temple, however. She has red-hot cinnamon fur, *yum-yum*, and baby-big steel blue eyes. She also is heir to the sad human fate of wearing a union suit that is all skin and virtually no hair, like the unfortunate Sphinx breed of my own cat kind.

Today Miss Temple is wearing a short skirt and skimpy sweater set in gray-silver. This is a knockout with her fur color but the outfit does make her look about twelve years old, always a worry for a petite public relations woman who has to elbow her own way to the fore of a competitive profession.

Miss Temple tries to pull her skirt an inch or two below her kneecap, which I agree is an ugly human attribute and hairless to boot.

The ploy does not work, though I have to admit the legs below the kneecap are pretty elegant despite their unfurred condition.

"This damn Wong woman," she tells herself, the mirror, and me, "is supposed to be hell on Jimmy Choos."

I normally do not deign to answer the meaningless growlings of discontented humans, even my own.

Sherlock Holmes had the newspaper agony column. I have the remote and daytime TV. Thus I instantly recognize the Asian-American celebrities that Miss Temple refers to: Amelia Wong, the decor design queen of this feng shui mania, and the red-carpet footman to the stars, a spikemeister named Jimmy Choo. Except it turns out that the force behind Jimmy Choo is really an enterprising female named Tamara Mellon, who built the business under a male business name, like Laura Holt on TV's *Remington Steele*, which brought us Pierce Brosnan. (I have been told by female admirers that we have similar hair and sex appeal.)

Anyway, I must ponder what celebrity females adore more: the elusive Jimmy's costly and kicky footwear . . . or simply referring to their "Choo shoes," which sounds like something that used to chug into train stations.

My Miss Temple is no slug herself when it comes to slingbacks. She has a world-class high heel collection, including one covered with diamond-bright Austrian crystals. These updated Cinderella slippers bear my likeness in coal black crystal on the heels, so you could say they come with a Prince Charming attached. *You* could say it. I cannot, without sounding conceited. I guess the true Prince Charming in this case is Mr. Stuart Weitzman, who designed the fabled footwear.

But, hark, my Miss Temple addresses the mirror one last time.

"Well, I cannot dally." She spins from the mirror to snatch up a burgundy patent leather tote bag that matches her burgundy patent-leather Nine West clogs. (Now that Miss Temple has discovered platform clogs increase her height by two to three inches without the need for stiletto heels, she reserves her high-rise shoes for dress-up.)

Also, she can outrun crooks better in clogs, crooks being a little hobby of hers ever since I have known her.

The fact is that I am the pro PI in our ménage à deux here at the Circle Ritz. Still, Miss Temple is racking up quite a crime-busting résumé of her own . . . for a two-footed amateur sleuth.

Mind you, she is cute (which some benighted souls have erroneously said of me, to their regret) and smart. But I never like my mysteries dominated by little doll amateurs, even if those little dolls are my own personal property.

I hear Miss Temple scrape the car keys off the coffee table in the living room. A moment later the door plays patty cake with an open-and-shut case. I am alone in our digs at last.

I jump down from the zebra-pattern coverlet that is such an excellent backdrop for my midnight good looks and pad into the living room.

The Las Vegas papers, both morning and evening, are splayed open on the coffee table. Both feature ballyhoo about the imminent advent of the "dowager empress of enterprising interior designs, Amelia Wong." The accompanying photo pictures a domestic dominatrix of sleek but severe expression. I would not want to meet her in a dark disco.

Hmmm. I wonder briefly if I should tail my little doll to her meeting with this media Medusa. But, no. She is thirty now. It is time I let her face the big, bad world on her own occasionally. Since she is an ace PR freelancer with enough charm to sell Cheerios to Eskimos, I am sure she will handle the upcoming challenge with almost the same skill I would.

I settle into my favorite snoozing spot on the couch . . . dead center, stretched full out, so no one can sit there until I vacate the premises, and especially not if I garf up a hairball . . . and soon tiptoe through the catnip-dusted tulips of dreamland.

Look for

Spider Dance

By Carole Nelson Douglas

Available December 2004
From Tom Doherty Associates